CISI

FOR
ENT

CW00502068

Advar ...e

Advanced Global Securities Operations

Edition 4, July 2016

This learning manual relates to syllabus
version 4.1 and will cover the exams on
8 Dec 2016 and 29 June 2017

APPROVED WORKBOOK

Welcome to the Chartered Institute for Securities & Investment's Advanced Global Securities Operations study material.

This manual has been written to prepare you for the Chartered Institute for Securities & Investment's Advanced Global Securities Operations examination.

Published by:
Chartered Institute for Securities & Investment
© Chartered Institute for Securities & Investment 2016
20 Fenchurch Street
London
EC3M 3BY
Tel: +44 20 7645 0600
Fax: +44 20 7645 0601

Email: customersupport@cisi.org
www.cisi.org/qualifications

Author:
Anthony Meredith FCSI

Reviewers:
Matthew Westlake
Kevin Birch

The author and the CISI would like to thank the following firms for supplying market information which has been used as a source of reference throughout this publication:

Thomas Murray Ltd
RBC Investor & Treasury Services
International Securities Lending Association
HSBC Securities Services

A learning map, which contains the full syllabus, appears at the end of this manual. The syllabus can also be viewed on cisi.org and is also available by contacting the Customer Support Centre on +44 20 7645 0777. Please note that the examination is based upon the syllabus. Candidates are reminded to check the Candidate Update area details (cisi.org/candidateupdate) on a regular basis for updates as a result of industry change(s) that could affect their examination.

Learning manual version: 4.1 (July 2016)

Learning and Professional Development with the CISI

The Chartered Institute for Securities & Investment is the leading professional body for those who work in, or aspire to work in, the investment sector, and we are passionately committed to enhancing knowledge, skills and integrity – the three pillars of professionalism at the heart of our Chartered body.

CISI examinations are used extensively by firms to meet the requirements of government regulators. Besides the regulators in the UK, where the CISI head office is based, CISI examinations are recognised by a wide range of governments and their regulators, from Singapore to Dubai and the US. Around 50,000 examinations are taken each year, and it is compulsory for candidates to use CISI learning manuals to prepare for CISI examinations so that they have the best chance of success. Our learning manuals are normally revised every year by experts who themselves work in the industry and also by our Accredited Training Partners, who offer training and elearning to help prepare candidates for the examinations. Information for candidates is also posted on a special area of our website: cisi.org/candidateupdate.

This learning manual not only provides a thorough preparation for the examination it refers to, it is also a valuable desktop reference for practitioners, and studying from it counts towards your Continuing Professional Development (CPD). Mock examination papers, for most of our titles, will be made available on our website, as an additional revision tool.

CISI examination candidates are automatically registered, without additional charge, as student members for one year (should they not be members of the CISI already), and this enables you to use a vast range of online resources, including CISI TV, free of any additional charge. The CISI has more than 40,000 members, and nearly half of them have already completed relevant qualifications and transferred to a core membership grade.

Completing a higher level examination enables you to progress even more quickly towards personal Chartered status, the pinnacle of professionalism in the CISI. You will find more information about the next steps for this at the end of this manual.

With best wishes for your studies.

Lydia Romero, Global Director of Learning

Preface

In the spring of 2015, the CISI, together with leading figures in the securities industry, conducted a strategic review of the Advanced Global Securities Operations (AGSO) examination to ensure the relevance to the industry of the AGSO qualification. The review confirmed that the examination was still relevant because it helps to:

- enable firms to prepare their operations staff for more demanding roles which require a broader understanding of the technical environment in which they work
- equip operations staff in the financial services sector with a broader grasp of the business and regulatory issues faced by senior management and assist staff who wish to develop their professionalism, while further augmenting their technical and managerial skills.

The review also confirmed that the module is aimed at those who have a minimum of five years' experience in the operations sector of the investment industry. It is, by definition, an advanced paper, and it was therefore designed to test the candidate's knowledge beyond that which is necessary to achieve a successful mark in the Investment Operations Certificate (IOC).

The review panel also concluded that today's operations staff need to be more aware of how regulations now play an important part of their everyday working life. In order to comply with this view, the workbook now incorporates a more working day exploration of how regulations will affect the operation's day-to-day functions. This workbook attempts to link daily operations processes with the regulatory rules.

This module is primarily aimed at supervisors, team leaders, assistant managers, managers and senior technical specialists working in investment operations (custody, settlement, corporate actions, treasury operations/cash management, derivatives and reconciliations).

Candidates embarking on AGSO are expected to already possess the level of knowledge required to pass the IOC and are strongly advised to be familiar with the material in the Global Securities Operations (GSO) workbook. Candidates should also be aware that they should expect to be examined on relevant items that do not necessarily appear in either the GSO or AGSO workbooks.

The review concluded that, under the umbrella of investment operations, candidates are likely be working in firms, such as:

- private client firms
- custodians (including sub-custodians)
- asset managers
- brokers
- market makers
- fund administration
- support functionaries.

It was determined by the review group that for the purposes of the AGSO exam the following asset types constitute the term securities:

- mortgage-backed securities
- asset-backed securities
- government stocks, shares, bonds and depositary receipts
- cash
- derivatives (OTC and exchange-traded)
- market-traded funds and collective investment schemes (investment trusts, ETFs, REITs, OEICs, unit trusts and SICAVs).

Chapter One
Account Opening

1. Client Account Opening

Learning Objective

1.1 Explain the processes to be followed when opening an investment account with a UK-regulated entity

Before opening any client investment account within a UK-regulated entity, it is very important that the UK firm is fully aware of, and compliant with, the Client Asset (CASS) rules so as to know how that client account should be administered correctly. There will be decisions that need to be made at the outset of the relationship in relation to the CASS rules generally, but Section 3: Collateral, Section 5: Client Money: Insurance Mediation Activity, Section 6: Custody Rules and Section 7: Client Money Rules, in particular, must be adhered to.

As a business, the UK authorised firm needs to recognise that opening a client account could involve it in creating either a statutory trust, non-statutory trust or fiduciary trust situation. If a firm holds client money and assets, it has a legal duty to act solely in the client's interests. Trust law plays an important role in the relationship: if a firm holds client assets/money under either a statutory, non-statutory or fiduciary trust arrangement then, by law, the firm has a fiduciary duty to its clients.

Statutory trust is a client money account that a firm uses to segregate and safeguard client money, holding it on behalf of the client. Under English law, the mere segregation of money into separate bank accounts is not sufficient to establish a proprietary interest in those funds in anyone other than the account holder. A declaration of trust over the balances standing to the credit of the segregated accounts is needed to protect those funds in the event of the firm's insolvency. Segregation is a necessary part of the system but, on its own, it is not enough to provide that protection. When both elements (segregation and statutory trust) are present, they work together to give the complete protection against the risk of the firm's insolvency that the client requires.

Non-statutory trust is a client money account that expressively authorises a firm to make credits to clients and/or product providers before actually receiving the client money. (Client money can only be held on a non-statutory trust basis in relation to insurance mediation activities). Unlike statutory client money bank accounts, which happen automatically, non-statutory trust status has to be declared and a trust deed executed. The trust deed must make sure that the client money is held for the purpose and the terms of CASS 5.4 (insurance mediation), for the purpose and the terms of the applicable part of CASS 5.5 (segregation and the operation of client money accounts), for the purpose and the terms of the client money (insurance) mediation distribution rules, and, in the event that the firm fails, the process for redistribution of client money. Agreement from the client is required for their money to be held in this manner.

Fiduciary trust is where a firm or individual accepts the responsibility of the trust status that is created by the act of an entity (beneficiary) entrusting another with their assets, ie, using a nominee to hold stocks and shares and other assets. The beneficiary retains the absolute right to the capital and assets within the trust, as well as the income generated from these assets. Trust assets are generally held in the name of the trustee, who then takes on the responsibility of administering the trust assets in a prudent manner, so as to ensure maximum benefit for the beneficiaries.

Furthermore, the Conduct of Business Sourcebook (COBS) protocols published by the UK's Financial Conduct Authority (FCA), must be adhered to when dealing with the client's application to open any investment accounts.

Having given due regard to the above, there is a simple, fundamental principle that applies to accepting clients – know your customer (KYC). This principle applies to all of the countries of the world that accept the KYC principles.

Regulations exist worldwide to ensure that firms collect sufficient data to ensure that the KYC principles can be applied. In general terms, these will apply to:

- client classification
- client agreements
- client asset protection
- anti-money laundering (AML) laws.

In the UK, the account opening process falls under the FCA's COBS rules. Firms must ensure that they accurately correlate their client type with the services that they are providing to those clients, in order to ensure that they have correctly matched their client with the Markets in Financial Instruments Directive (MiFID) classifications. This must be done before client accounts can be activated. Also, client agreements must be in place prior to the commencement of business if an FCA-authorised firm carries on designated investment business, other than advising on investments, with or for a new retail client, on paper or other durable medium, with the management setting out the essential rights and obligations of the firm and the client, or otherwise exempted.

As part of the money laundering initiatives and laws, before opening any account and trading for a client, a firm must undertake due diligence to establish the legitimacy of the client and to check that the client is not suspected of being involved in money laundering or terrorist/criminal activity.

In regard to the AML regulations, in general terms, firms should have procedures and processes (due diligence) in place to ensure that the following areas are robustly covered:

1. customer identification
2. recognition and handling of suspicious transactions
3. appointment of a money laundering reporting officer
4. staff training
5. maintenance of records
6. audit of transactions.

Finally, an account cannot be opened for a customer if the firm's own credit department assesses that the client does not meet its required rating. Credit risk is a major risk for many firms and, therefore, credit controls should be rigorously invoked if credit is a concern for the firm.

Clients may also need to have supplementary documentation such as a risk warning depending on the type of client and product used.

1.1 Summary of Actions in Account Opening

Before a UK firm can operate an account for a customer, it needs to have gone through various steps:

1. The firm needs to verify the identity of the customer to comply with the AML regulations – the level of verification required depends on the nature of the customer. If the firm has suspicions, it must report them to the National Crime Agency (NCA). The firm cannot take any money from the customer unless and until cleared to do so by the NCA, which gives itself seven working days to give clearance. Care must be taken not to alert the suspected money launderer.

2. The firm has to classify and agree with the client whether they are a retail client, a professional client or an eligible counterparty (COB 3) – see Section 3.1. Specifically it must:
   a. notify a new client of its categorisation as a retail client, professional client, or eligible counterparty in accordance with the regulations; and
   b. prior to the provision of services, inform the client in a durable medium about: (a) any right that client has to request a different categorisation; and (b) any limitations to the level of client protection that such a different categorisation would entail

3. The firm needs to send out a client agreement if it is providing services that are categorised as conducting a designated investment business.

4. In the case of retail clients, the firm may need to send a risk warning which may, as in the case of a derivatives risk warning, have to be acknowledged by the client.

5. If the client is a retail client, and the service is discretionary or advisory, the firm will need to take personal information about the customer's circumstances and investment objectives to ensure suitability and as part of the KYC requirements.

6. If the firm is a broker, and if the agreement is not completed or undertaken face-to-face (ie, it is concluded at a distance), the client may be entitled to a 14-day cooling off period during which they can withdraw from the arrangements. This does not apply in some circumstances, such as the conclusion of a purchase before the 14-day period has elapsed.

2. Client Types

Learning Objective

1.2 Identify and distinguish between: retail clients; professional clients; eligible counterparties

2.1 Client Classification under the Markets in Financial Instruments Directive (MiFID)

This directive, which became law in November 2007, resulted in some changes in relation to opening client accounts and in particular the client types and classification. The importance of categorisation is also reinforced by the FCA's Conduct of Business rules under Section 3 of the COBS.

The introduction of the MiFID regulations also introduced to the UK market new terminology for client types. These are:

- retail client
- professional client
- eligible counterparty (ECP).

2.1.1   Retail Client

The point of the categorisation process is to determine the level of protection the firm needs to apply to the specific client. The MiFID retail client category is the classification that offers the most protection and imposes the most requirements in terms of communication, disclosure and transparency. By default, retail clients are all clients that do not belong to the professional or eligible counterparties categories.

2.1.2   Professional Client

Professional clients can include other entities, not classified as eligible counterparties, which are authorised or regulated to operate in the financial markets, such as credit institutions, investment firms, insurance companies and pension funds. This means that clients that could otherwise be classified as eligible counterparties are categorised as professional clients if the investment services they receive do not involve the reception and transmission or the execution of orders. Large undertakings can also qualify as professional clients if they meet at least two of the three large undertakings criteria:

1. a balance sheet total of at least €20 million
2. net turnover of at least €40 million
3. own capital of at least €2 million.

Under MiFID rules, professional clients need to provide less information to their financial institution than retail clients. In return, they receive a lower level of protection than retail clients. Professional clients get the benefit of best execution, however.

2.1.3   Eligible Counterparty

Each of the following is a *per se* eligible counterparty (ECP) (including an entity that is not from an European Economic Area (EEA) state that is equivalent to any of the following) unless and to the extent it is given a different categorisation:

1. an investment firm
2. a credit institution
3. an insurance company
4. a collective investment scheme (CIS) authorised under the UCITS Directive or its management company
5. a pension fund or its management company
6. another financial institution authorised or regulated under EU legislation or the national law of an EEA state
7. an undertaking exempted from the application of MiFID under either Article 2(1)(k) (certain own account dealers in commodities or commodity derivatives) or Article 2(1)(l) (locals) of that directive

8. a national government or its corresponding office, including a public body that deals with the public debt
9. a central bank
10. a supranational organisation.

An ECP is an entity that is authorised or regulated to operate in the financial markets that is not given investment advice and belongs to one of the following categories:

- If such clients are provided with investment advice, they will be treated as professional clients instead.
- ECPs receive the lowest level of protection under MiFID.

ECPs are clients but can opt out of best execution and other protections but, as clients, they still get benefit of rules on client assets and conflicts of interest.

Notification of Client Classification

Firms must be aware of what they need to do when they categorise a client and the following applies:

- Notification of classification to the client is mandatory.
- Consent to the classification must be expressed.
- Client classifications must be kept under review and firms are under a duty to act on information received to review a classification which appears inappropriate.

2.2 Definitions of Client Types

The MiFID classifications discussed in Section 2.1 are actually groupings which determine the level of protection (LOP) that a firm must offer to its client. They do not identify what client type the client actually is, eg, a private investor, a charity, a pension fund, a wholesale client or CIS. Client types, in global operations terms, are critical for the administrative purposes of KYC requirements and to determine the correct impacts of global taxation on the assets held by these client types. The client types can actually fit under different levels of protection groupings, owing to the fact that clients in certain circumstances have the right to determine what level of protection they wish to be afforded.

It is, therefore, very important that a firm clearly identifies not only the level of protection that should be offered, but also the type of the client they are servicing. This will have ramifications for the tax status that is applied to the client and the eventual domestic and international taxes that their investments attract.

Client types are defined by the market terminology and by regulation, and so we talk about private customers and institutional investors, for example. Below are some general definitions of types of clients:

- **Private investor** – investors who are either individuals or small entities, as distinct from institutional customers, who are larger corporate or financial entities.
- **Charity** – a registered organisation that invests the donations it receives and uses the proceeds on behalf of the charitable objectives of the organisation. It is often given tax-exempt status.
- **Pension fund** – a fund established by an employer to facilitate and organise the investment of employees' retirement funds contributed by the employer and employees. The pension fund is a

common asset pool meant to generate stable growth over the long term, and provide pensions for employees when they reach the end of their working years and commence retirement.

- **Wholesale client** – a client that is another financial institution rather than a retail-type client, hence the term wholesale banking when a bank deals with other banks in services.
- **Collective investment scheme (CIS)** – an investment scheme, such as a unit trust, investment trust, mutual fund or open-ended investment company, where investor's subscriptions are pooled together and invested by a fund manager.

3. Account Opening and Renewal Timescales

Learning Objective

1.3 Identify the timescales for market approval upon receipt of account opening applications

1.4 Understand the circumstances under which a client classification should be reviewed

3.1 UK Timescales

In the previous sections, we reviewed what needs to be accomplished in the UK when opening a client account. The timescales involved with this process depend largely on the efficiency of the firms and clients involved. When you consider the data that needs to be collected, especially the AML requirements that need personal identification and photo IDs, together with proof of residence of the applicants, it can be seen that the process can take days, weeks or even months to be brought to a satisfactory conclusion.

3.2 Global Timescales

When opening accounts in other countries, it is important to understand the nature of the requirements of the country involved. Generally, an investor might be able to invest globally using the good offices of an institution like a global custodian or an investment manager. However, in many countries, it is often the case that the underlying client details will need to be supplied, especially when there are investment restrictions on the level of shareholdings.

In some circumstances, rather than being able to have the assets held in the name of the institution applying for the account to be opened (in an omnibus fashion), the account may need to be opened in the name of the beneficial owner, in a segregated fashion. This means that the underlying client will actually need to complete the account opening documentation. This relates to both securities and cash. In some countries the beneficiary must also apply for a local tax identification number.

Depending on the client type, this could lead to delays, especially if the client is a corporate entity.

These local requirements could lead to the client having to provide tax certification from their own tax authorities, together with data such as certificates of incorporation and the Memorandum and Articles of Association. Some countries will require applications to be made to the country's authorities.

In some countries, regulatory approval to make investments is required before the client can buy assets. If this approval is required, no trading in assets can take place until the local authorities have given their approval. The procedures and the approval timelines differ from country to country and are subject to frequent change.

In terms of global operations, these countries are commonly known as the foreign institutional investor (FII) countries.

The following list identifies those countries where the details of the beneficiary are required. In these countries, the accounts may need to be held in the name of the beneficial owner, or they may have to be held in a sub-account in the name of their fund adviser. In many cases, the beneficiary's details will need to be held in the records of both the local custodian and the local depository. In some cases, the details of the beneficiary will only be required to be held either at the custodian level or the depository level.

Bahrain	Egypt	Oman	Sri Lanka
Bangladesh	Greece	Pakistan	Taiwan
Bosnia and Herzegovina	Hungary	Peru	Turkey
Brazil	India	Poland	UAE – Abu Dhabi
Bulgaria	Israel	Qatar	UAE – Dubai
Chile	Jordan	Romania	Ukraine
China – Shanghai	Kazakhstan	Saudi Arabia	Venezuela
China – Shenzhen	Kuwait	Serbia	Vietnam
Colombia	Lebanon	Slovak Republic	
Cyprus	Mauritius	South Korea	

There are different processes involved in the opening of accounts for trading in the markets around the world and, as a result, the time needed to open an account varies.

In many markets, the time needed to open an account for the trading of derivatives, where the likes of the sending and return of risk warnings and other documentation can be time-consuming, may be significantly longer than that for securities.

3.3   Renewal Timescales

Generally, all client classifications must be regularly reviewed by the authorised firms to ensure that clients can continue being categorised without any amendment to their categorisation. However, there is no prescribed review period under the MiFID regulations. Any changes in circumstances that the firms become aware of must be the trigger point for a full revision of the categorisation. The categorisation renewal will take into account, amongst other things, any changes in the client's financial (or other) circumstances and the level of financial knowledge that the client has. Furthermore, a client may request at any time for their categorised status to be changed. This should lead the firm to conduct a review of the status quo.

This also incorporates the FCA's KYC requirements, again making sure that the authorised firms correctly categorise their clients and also make enquiries of the client regarding their circumstances with regard to their investments, so that any advice that may be given to them is suitable for that client.

4.   Penalties

Learning Objective

1.5   Describe the potential penalties that are in place for non-compliance when opening investment accounts and outline the impact of penalties on clients and the firm

In today's world, the opening of client investment accounts is inextricably linked to the global AML procedures and client money segregation rules. So too are the sanctions for non-compliance. Each country that supports the global AML initiative will have appointed a body whose responsibility it is to ensure that their own rules are adhered to.

Globally, the breaching of any of the local regulatory investment account opening rules by firms failing to comply correctly is likely to result in enforcement action. Depending upon the local rules, this enforcement action will range from the firm being ordered to take remedial action, a monetary fine being imposed and/or public censures.

For the firm concerned, any imposition of such sanctions could lead to a loss of reputation, which in turn may open the firm up to the risk of a financial loss caused by the loss of revenue due to a client exodus. Also, it should be remembered that any serious disputes with a client caused by account opening and agreement issues could lead to legal action being taken by the client.

For example, in the UK the FCA has imposed monetary fines on firms that have breached the AML and segregation procedures. The level of these fines can be found on the FCA website (www.fca.org.uk). In Argentina, rules have been put in place that require the local agents to investigate and report any suspicious transaction based on the AML measures, within one month. Otherwise, the relevant entities will be penalised with a fine with a value between two and 20 times the value of the related assets.

5.   Client Assets

5.1   Fiduciary Principles

Learning Objective

1.6   Outline the fiduciary principles that apply to the holding of client assets

In the UK, when a firm operates for a client, they do so on the understanding that they will respect the obligation to protect the client's assets and to act in the best interest of the client at all times.

This fiduciary responsibility applies across all the activities and situations that a firm might find itself in during a relationship. For example, a firm must always, unless otherwise agreed under a permitted regulatory situation, segregate the client's assets from the firm's own assets and have those assets segregated in such a way that they are protected even if the firm were to fail. Another example is that firms cannot use a client's assets unless they have permission to do so.

The following is an extract from the FCA's COBS handbook, which identifies these fiduciary principles for businesses. Many other countries follow these principles closely.

1. Integrity	A firm must conduct its business with integrity
2. Skill, care and diligence	A firm must conduct its business with due skill, care and diligence
3. Management and control	A firm must take reasonable care to organise and control its affairs responsibly and effectively, with adequate risk management systems
4. Financial prudence	A firm must maintain adequate financial resources
5. Market conduct	A firm must observe proper standards of market conduct
6. Customers' interests	A firm must pay due regard to the interests of its customers and treat them fairly
7. Communications with clients	A firm must pay due regard to the information needs of its clients and communicate information to them in a way which is clear, fair and not misleading
8. Conflicts of interest	A firm must manage conflicts of interest fairly, both between itself and its customers and between a customer and another client
9. Customers: relationships of trust	A firm must take reasonable care to ensure the suitability of its advice and discretionary decisions for any customer who is entitled to rely upon its judgment
10. Clients' assets	A firm must arrange adequate protection for client's assets when it is responsible for them
11. Relations with regulators	A firm must deal with its regulators in an open and co-operative way, and must disclose to the FCA appropriately anything relating to the firm of which the FCA would reasonably expect notice

5.2 Segregated Accounts

Learning Objective

1.7 Understand the various reasons when and why segregated accounts will be required, when investing in global markets

1.8 Understand the importance of gathering the correct data to determine the client type for the purpose of correctly apportioning the clients' tax status globally

The key drivers that force the need for account segregation are primarily the regulatory organisations in the various global markets, but these regulatory drivers can be for differing reasons. This regulatory-driven requirement can be illustrated by referencing the FCA's COBS and CASS 5, 6 and 7. These business standards and principles determine that, in certain circumstances, for the protection of the client, client assets will be subject to segregation requirements.

In the UK, firms must, when holding client custody assets (including cash), make adequate arrangements to safeguard clients' ownership rights, especially in the event of the firm's insolvency, and to prevent the use of assets by the firm for its own use, except with the client's express consent.

Therefore, firms must introduce and maintain adequate organisational arrangements to minimise the risk of loss or diminution of clients' safe custody assets, or the rights in connection with those assets, as a result of their misuse, fraud, poor administration, inadequate record-keeping or negligence.

Also, other regulators around the world, such as the Securities and Exchange Commission (SEC) in the US, may dictate the conditions under which a custodian in another country may hold assets for a US entity. These are embodied in the US Employment Retirement Income Security Act (ERISA) regulation 17f-5 and the subsequent amendment in 17f-7.

Other global regulatory bodies in other countries have adopted very similar positions to that of the US.

An important element of the segregation required is that the firm's assets must be held separately from the client's assets. This, in everyday terms, means that, in the case of stocks and shares, the names on register relating to the assets held for the clients should be distinguishable from the assets held for the firm. The same applies to cash.

However, once this important primary principle of segregation between the client's assets and the firm's own assets has been applied, the segregation of assets for different clients might only be at the account level within the custodial organisation's books of record (system). This is evidenced by the fact that some custodial firms prefer to run omnibus nominee accounts, whereas others prefer to run segregated nominee accounts.

5.2.1 Omnibus Nominee Accounts

An omnibus nominee account is when a firm, as a business principle, decides that all assets in a particular asset type, that are beneficially owned by their clients, will be registered into a single nominee name, eg, Everyman Nominees Ltd, that belongs to that firm. Therefore, by way of example, if a firm's client base all hold shares in The ABC Tool Company, these shares will be registered into the firm's common nominee name. This will require that firm to regularly reconcile any holdings of a common asset held by their nominee name, to all their clients who they (the firm), record as holding that asset. This is known as a one-to-many reconciliation exercise.

5.2.2   Segregated Nominee Accounts

A segregated nominee account is when a firm, as a business principle, decides that it will allocate a unique designation to every client who beneficially owns assets that are registered into the firm's nominee name. By way of example, if client A beneficially owns 10,000 shares of The ABC Tool Company, these shares will be registered into the firms' nominee name, but will have a unique designation attached to the nominee name, eg, Everyman Nominees ltd 123 Account. This gives each client a distinct and recognisable holding. These will still have to be subject to a reconciliation on a regular basis, but this will be performed on a one-to-one basis.

This principle is also employed when opening accounts with third parties, such as sub-custodians. The firm may elect to have an omnibus account opened in its name in the books of the third party or sub-custodian or it may choose to have a separate designated account opened in its name with the third party or sub-custodian that represents the client in the firms' books.

There are pros and cons to each method used and each firm will have their own business reasons for choosing the method they employ.

The second regulatory driver is where the rules of the country in which an investor wishes to invest insist that the investor must hold the assets in their own name. This has the potential to lead to both cash and securities being held in the name of the beneficial owner of the assets.

The categorisation of clients, eg, retail client, professional client, eligible counterparty was discussed in Section 2. As stated, these categorisations are so that the firm can apply the correct level of protection in terms of safeguarding the client's best interests. As important as applying the correct categorisation is identifying the type of client that a firm is taking on. By this we mean: is the client a private individual, a charitable organisation, a pension fund or a CIS, for example?

This client type and supporting data is very important because it will affect, in particular, the correct levels of tax that will be paid by that client on their investments around the globe. The taxes that are levied by the global governments on a client's investment can be varied. The tax may pertain to capital gains, or on income via dividends or interest, or it might be the amount of stamp duty that they have to pay.

For example, in the UK, a charitable organisation may be exempt from paying stamp duty reserve tax (SDRT) and/or stamp duty on the purchases of shares. This charitable status could also have the same effect with regard to stamp duty and income tax in other countries of the world.

Globally, a pension fund will often be allowed to benefit from a reduction in the amount of income tax that it pays on income from dividends or interest paid on its global investments. This will likely be applied as either a reduction at source or by way of a reclaim of the tax paid.

The support data will include the proof required to corroborate the client as being a registered charity, a recognised pension fund or a CIS. This proof will include certification from well-known entities, such as the Charity Commission, The Pensions Regulator and/or HMRC or Companies House.

6.   Regulatory Impacts on Account Opening

Learning Objective

1.9   Understand how the global regulatory environment impacts the opening of client investment accounts in the UK

Recent global regulatory changes made as result of the fall-out from the financial crisis of 2008, have meant that the regulatory impact on the opening of client investment accounts in the UK has been profound. The main thrust of the global regulatory regimes is to try to create transparency and the protection of clients' assets and interests.

The regulatory environment in the UK, for the process of taking on a client and opening investment accounts, is currently under what has become known as a twin peaks regime.

In 2013, the UK's Financial Services Authority (FSA) ceased to operate as a sole regulator and was replaced by two regulators: a prudential regulator (the Prudential Regulation Authority (PRA)) and a separate conduct regulator (the Financial Conduct Authority (FCA)). The UK is not the first jurisdiction to separate regulation into these two strands, known as twin peaks regulation. Australia moved to a twin-peaks model in 1996 and the Netherlands in 2002.

One of the main reasons given for the UK adopting a twin peaks regulatory model was to create two centres of expertise: one which would focus on conduct regulation and the other on prudential regulation and supervision.

The FCA has been given four conduct objectives – a strategic objective, to ensure that 'the relevant markets function well', and three operational objectives: consumer protection, market integrity and competition.

The PRA was created as a part of the Bank of England (BoE) by the Financial Services Act (2012) and is responsible for the prudential regulation and supervision of around 1,700 banks, building societies, credit unions, insurers and major investment firms.

The PRA's objectives are set out in the Financial Services and Markets Act 2000 (FSMA). The PRA has three statutory objectives:

1.   A general objective to promote the safety and soundness of the firms it regulates.
2.   An objective specific to insurance firms, to contribute to the securing of an appropriate degree of protection for those who are or may become insurance policyholders.
3.   A secondary objective to facilitate effective competition (see Section 6.4 for more details on the PRA).

The PRA advances its objectives using two key tools. First, through regulation, it sets standards or policies that it expects firms to meet. Second, through supervision, it assesses the risks that firms pose to the PRA's objectives and, where necessary, takes action to reduce them.

The regulatory conduct of business guidelines and requirements are clearly outlined in the following;

1. Principles for Businesses (PRIN)
2. Statements of Principle and Code of Practice for Approved Persons (APER)
3. Senior Management Arrangements Systems and Controls (SYSC)
4. The Conduct of Business (COBS)
5. The Insurance Conduct of Business Sourcebook (ICOBS).

6.1   UK Regulation: FCA – CASS

When a firm opens investment accounts for a client, it must pay particular attention to the rules contained in the FCA's Client Asset sourcebook (CASS), which outlines how a firm must treat and conduct itself when administering the assets of a client.

Extracts from CASS are given below, but it is strongly advised that the reader should also access the FCA handbook at www.fca.org.uk for further details.

General Application

1. The approach in CASS is to ensure that the rules in a chapter are applied to firms in respect of particular regulated or unregulated activities.
2. The scope of the regulated activities to which CASS applies is determined by the description of the activity as it is set out in the Regulated Activities Order (RAO). Accordingly, a firm will not generally be subject to CASS in relation to any aspect of its business activities which fall within an exclusion found in the RAO. The definition of designated investment business includes, however, activities within the exclusion from dealing in investments as principal in Article 15 of the RAO (and absence of holding out, etc).
3. CASS 6 (Custody Rules), and CASS 3 (Collateral Rules) apply in relation to regulated activities, conducted by firms, which fall within the definition of designated investment business.
4. CASS 5 (Client Money: Insurance Mediation Activity) applies in relation to regulated activities, conducted by firms, which fall within the definition of insurance mediation activities.
5. CASS 5.5 (Client Money) applies in relation to regulated activities, conducted by firms, which fall within the definition of designated investment business.
6. CASS 7 (Client Money Rules): firms are reminded that the definition of inter-professional business does not include safekeeping and administration of assets or agreeing to carry on that activity: CASS will apply in this context (and will apply to the holding of money for clients in connection with inter-professional business).

Application for Retail Clients, Professional Clients and Eligible Counterparties

1. CASS applies directly in respect of activities conducted with, or for, eligible counterparties as well as with, or for, customers. The term client refers both to eligible counterparties and to both categories of clients.
2. In CASS 6 (Custody Rules), and CASS 3 (collateral rules), the term client refers to both retail and professional clients and to eligible counterparties. Where relevant, each of the provisions of CASS makes clear whether it applies to activities carried on with, or for, retail and professional clients, or both.

3. CASS 5 (Client Money: Insurance Mediation Activity) does not generally distinguish between different categories of client. However, the term retail customer is used for those to whom additional obligations are owed, rather than the term private customer. This is to be consistent with the client categories used in relation to the obligations in the insurance COBS rules in relation to insurance mediation activities.

6.2   UK Regulation: FCA – COBS

The stated aim of the FCA is to make sure that financial markets work well so that consumers get a fair deal. In order to facilitate this aim, the FCA has laid out guidelines for firms known as the Conduct of Business Sourcebook (COBS).

These rules are there to ensure that:

- the financial industry is run with integrity
- firms provide consumers with appropriate products and services
- consumers can trust that firms have their best interests at heart.

To oversee that its aims are being met, the FCA regulates the conduct of more than 70,000 businesses and, for many of these, the FCA will also consider whether they meet prudential standards that reduce the potential harm to the industry and consumers if they fail.

The FCA regulates firms and individuals that advise on, sell and arrange financial products and services. These include bank accounts, investment products, mortgages, insurance and some pension schemes.

The FCA provides firms and financial advisers with rules on how to do business, so that these firms are enabled to give consumers clear and accurate advice about financial products. The FCA also wants to make sure firms provide consumers with up-to-date and correct information about how financial products and services work.

There are specific COBS rules that apply to the opening of client investment accounts and these can be found under Section 3 of the COBS: Client Categorisation.

Section 2 of the COBS: The Principles (listed in Section 5.1) also apply to account opening.

6.3   UK Regulation: FCA Enforcement

In 2012, the Financial Services Act sought to reform financial regulation that failed to protect the UK's economy during the financial crisis. The FCA has a history of imposing censure and substantial fines on UK institutions when they contravene the rules, which the FCA has introduced.

The FCA is also proactively encouraging firms to bring themselves up to speed with what the new rules mean and what needs to be in place to ensure compliance. The FCA visits firms to show both senior management and staff what the UK regulations mean to them.

In simple terms, the regulations are there to:

- protect the client's assets from the liquidator in the event of a firm's insolvency
- ensure the firm's records of client assets are accurate and up to date

- prevent a firm misusing client assets
- encourage the firm to have appropriate governance and oversight at the highest level of management.

6.4   UK Regulation: PRA Rulebook

The PRA's purpose is to protect and improve the stability of the UK's financial system through regulation and supervision, working alongside the FCA.

The PRA is responsible for the prudential supervision and regulation of banks, building societies, credit unions, insurers and investment firms, and its three statutory objectives were covered in Section 6.

Some material that appears in this chapter may have been sourced from other areas, please refer to Appendix 4 for details of the relevant organisations.

End of Chapter Questions

1. List the internal procedures that may apply to a client account opening request.
    Answer reference: Section 1

2. What are fundamental KYC requirements?
    Answer reference: Section 1

3. What are the current client classification types as defined by the MiFID?
    Answer reference: Section 2.1

4. How, and under what circumstances, would segregation apply to a client account?
    Answer reference: Section 5.2

5. What does CASS refer to and how is it relevant to the client account?
    Answer reference: Section 6.1

6. What are the COBS rules?
    Answer reference: Section 6. 2

Chapter Two
Market and Stock Exchange Fees and Taxes

1. Market and Stock Exchange Fees and Taxes

Learning Objective

2.1 Identify sources of market and exchange fees and tax when trading securities for the following: retail clients; eligible counterparties; professional clients

It is important to recognise that for investors to transact securities in a structured and orderly fashion, there must be a structured and orderly marketplace; this, however, costs money. It is, therefore, necessary for these market places (stock exchanges) to charge both the companies (issuers) that wish to make their shares available to investors and those brokers, market makers and custodial banks whose business it is to participate in the marketplace. The charges levied on these market participants, as outlined in this chapter, are likely to be recovered from the investor either directly or indirectly.

In the course of carrying out transactions for its clients, therefore, firms will have charges levied against them and, in many cases, these fees and costs may need to be explained to clients.

Fees relating to unit trusts and open-ended investment companies (OEICs) are covered in Chapter 3, Section 8.2.

1.1 Stock Exchange Fees

Fees that are charged by the global stock exchanges which will form part of the income for that particular marketplace or exchange. This income enables the relevant organisation to, among other things:

*   maintain the exchange/market processes, including trading capability
*   cover the administrative costs of the exchange/market
*   develop new products
*   cover marketing expenses
*   provide market information.

As stated above, the fees charged will be levied on the issuers of securities and the firms that make up the market participants. The fees will be related to the following activities:

*   The listing of securities on the exchange.
*   The trading of securities on the exchange.
*   The clearing of transactions via a central counterparty/clearing house/central depository.
*   The settlement of transactions.
*   Quotation services (share prices).
*   Credit arrangements.
*   Fines for the contravention of standards regarding matching, settlement, buy-ins and sell-outs.

1.2   Regulatory Charges

In the UK, for example, there is a levy on certain transactions to help support the Panel on Takeovers and Mergers (the panel or PTM). The PTM is an independent body, established in 1968, whose main functions are to issue and administer the City Code on Takeovers and Mergers.

In certain circumstances, the panel also shares responsibility for the regulation of an offer with the takeover regulator in another EEA member state, eg, where the offeree company is registered in the UK and has its securities admitted to trading only on a regulated market in a member state other than the UK.

The PTM Levy is currently £1.00 and is levied on certain transactions in the UK that exceed the value of £10,000 or €15,000 (or, if any other currency, the equivalent value of £10,000).

A member firm should ensure the payment of the PTM levy by its customers in respect of any on-exchange transaction in securities of companies incorporated in the UK, the Channel Islands and the Isle of Man. The PTM levy should be charged at the rate notified from time to time. A member firm should account for the PTM levy charged in the manner directed by the exchange.

The PTM levy is not payable:

*   where the total consideration of the relevant transaction is less than £10,000, €15,000 or, if in any other currency, the equivalent of £10,000
*   where the security is held on a register outside the UK, the Channel Islands or the Isle of Man, or is an unregistered security
*   on covered warrants
*   on debentures and other debt securities
*   on preference shares
*   on permanent interest bearing securities (PIBS)
*   on contracts for differences (CFDs) and total return swaps
*   on spread bets
*   on option contracts
*   unless they are securities which are convertible into, or which will give the holder the right to subscribe for, equity share capital. However, the exercise of an option contract is a trade on which the PTM Levy is payable
*   on trades in securities of OEICs (as defined in Article 1(2) of the Directive on Takeover Bids (2004/25/ EC)), including exchange-traded funds (ETFs).

In the US, there is a fee that was created by the Securities Exchange Act of 1934 that has come to be an additional transaction cost attached to the selling of exchange-listed equities. This fee is usually listed as a separate SEC fee, independent of any associated brokerage commissions or fees. However, the SEC does not impose or set any of the brokerage fees that investors must pay. Instead, under Section 31 of the Securities Exchange Act of 1934, self-regulatory organisations (SROs) – such as the Financial Industry Regulatory Authority (FINRA) and all of the national securities exchanges (including the New York Stock Exchange (NYSE) – must pay transaction fees to the SEC based on the volume of securities that are sold on their markets. These fees recover the costs incurred by the government, including the SEC, for supervising and regulating the securities markets and securities professionals. Broker-dealers, in turn, pass the responsibility of paying the fees to their customers and there is a regulatory requirement on the SEC that these fees must be reviewed at least annually.

At the beginning of 2016, the SEC announced that, starting on 16 February 2016, the fee rates applicable to most securities transactions will be set at $21.80 per million dollars.

In Hong Kong, there is a Securities and Futures Commission (SFC) transaction levy of 0.0027% of trade value charged on each transaction. Both buyer and seller are also required to pay a stock exchange trading of 0.005% of trade value.

In South Africa, there is an investor protection levy, which finances the functions performed by market regulators other than the Johannesburg Stock Exchange (JSE). This levy is set at 0.0002% on all equity trades.

1.3   Government Taxes

Most of the governments of the world will, in some shape or form, generate revenue from the trading of assets, whatever those assets may be. These taxes take on various guises and can be called by many different names.

The following are some examples of how governments raise revenue based on the purchase and sale of securities.

1.3.1   Stamp Duties and Sales or Transfer Taxes

United Kingdom

The purchase of securities is subject to taxation. Included in this is stamp duty on the transfer of securities and SDRT on the transfer of uncertificated (or dematerialised) securities.

SDRT was first introduced in 1986. The main purpose of the tax was to cover paperless (dematerialised) share transactions on agreements to transfer chargeable securities for consideration in money or money's worth (Section 87 of the Finance Act 1986). The main provisions are in the Finance Act 1986 and the supporting regulations at SI 1986/1711. SDRT is collected primarily on share transactions that are not drawn up via a stock transfer form (dematerialised transactions) and thus do not fall within the chargeable realm of stamp duty. SDRT now accounts for the majority of taxation collected on share transactions effected through the UK's exchanges.

Stamp duty is paid on share transactions and the transfer of certificated issues at the same rate as SDRT. However, stamp duty on certificated trades is not charged on the trades where the value is less than £1000. The amount paid is also rounded up to the nearest £5.00.

In April 2014, the 0.5% stamp duty or SDRT was abolished on purchases of eligible shares traded on recognised growth markets.

A recognised growth market means a recognised stock exchange where the majority of the companies whose shares are traded on the exchange have a market capital less than £170 million. Recognised growth markets include the Alternative Investment Market (AIM) and the ICAP Securities & Derivatives Exchange (ISDX). Other markets may also be included on the list of recognised growth markets, which are available on HMRC's website (www.gov.uk/government/organisations/hm-revenue-customs).

Argentina

Through Law 23.966, the Argentine government created the tax on personal assets. This tax is assessed on specific assets belonging to individual persons, whether domestic- or overseas-domiciled, as of 31 December of each calendar year. The tax rate is 0.5% of the value of the assets exceeding US$102,300 and up to US$200,000. After this, the rate is 0.75%. Unless otherwise proved, all entities are considered as individuals. The issuer who has to pay the tax is entitled to recover the expense from the foreign investors (eg, withholding the tax from dividend distributions or claiming money back from the shareholder to reimburse the issuer for the tax burden suffered).

Brazil

According to Brazilian regulations, dividends relating to fiscal years prior to 1992 (inclusive) are subject to taxation of 25% for all investors, regardless of the country of domicile (tax haven or non-tax haven countries). Investors residing in countries that have a double tax treaty with Brazil, may have tax reductions; however as a general rule, the taxation is 25%.

Capital gains taxes and taxes on interest payments for fixed income instruments such as government bonds, corporate bonds and shares of investment funds vary according to the country of domicile and timeframe that the investor holds the instrument in its portfolio.

There is a governmental tax on the inflows of foreign exchange – the Imposto sobre Operações Financeiras (IOF). The rate of this tax has fluctuated over the last few years. Investors are currently subject to a zero rate IOF tax applicable to foreign exchange inflows related to equities and equity related derivatives and also to a zero rate IOF tax on fixed income instruments.

There is also an IOF on the redemption of fixed income. In order to encourage the longer-term holding of fixed income instruments, an IOF tax is imposed if a fixed income instrument is sold or redeemed within 30 days of purchase. The IOF tax is based on either 1% per day assessed on the total amount of the redemption amount or a sliding percentage (from 96% for one day to 0% for 30 days) of the capital gain based on the number of days between the investment date and the redemption date, whichever is lower.

China

There is a 0.1% stamp duty charge on the gross consideration which is payable by the seller only for A shares and B shares. Funds, warrants and bonds are exempted from stamp duty.

Egypt

There is fiscal stamp duty tax of 0.4% per annum on quarter-end overdraft balances which is collected by the tax authority. The quarterly rate applied is 0.05% going forward on all overdraft balances at the end of each quarter.

Hong Kong

There is an ad valorem stamp duty of 0.1% of trade value payable by both buyer and seller. Transactions with no change in beneficial ownership can be exempted by applying to the Inland Revenue. An embossed stamp duty of HK$5 per transfer deed, payable by the first seller, is levied on physical shares.

India

Stamp duty is payable on registration of physical securities. Stamp duty, at 0.25% of the consideration price or the market rate (whichever is higher), is payable by the buyer when physical shares are sent for registration. Stamp duty on debt instruments varies from state to state.

Indonesia

Stamp duty of IdR6,000 is paid on all cash statements and corporate action voting forms. There is also a sales tax of 0.1% applied on all sale transactions.

Malaysia

There is tax on any rights issue. An MYR10 charge is made for any rights subscription form or rights renunciation form for nil paid rights.

South Africa

Securities Transfer Tax (STT) has replaced stamp duty and the Uncertificated Securities Tax (UST) on securities (ie, single tax) in respect of any transfer of listed and unlisted securities. The STT Act ensures that the rules governing both listed and unlisted securities are aligned and came into effect on 1 July 2008. STT is calculated at the same rate of 0.25% based on the market value of listed and unlisted securities.

The foregoing are just a few examples of how governments raise revenue based on the purchase and sale of securities. The governments of many countries will allow certain categories of investors to benefit from being exempt from paying taxes such as stamp duty. By way of example, in the UK the following categories are exempt from SDRT: sales to intermediaries, transfers to charities, repos and stock lending.

1.3.2   Income and Capital Gains Tax (CGT)

In addition to market and exchange fees and stamp duty, tax may be payable on income generated from certain types of savings and investment, as well as from the profit generated from purchases and sales.

In the case of income tax on dividends, for instance, the tax may be deducted at source, ie, by the paying agent even if the investor is not a taxpayer, eg, a registered charity.

1.3.3   Value Added Tax (VAT)

A further tax that may be applicable when products and services are being provided is value added tax.

1.4   Other Fees and Charges

1.4.1   Third-Party Service Fees

There are service providers that are now considered an integral part of the global marketplace. These include the providers of services such as data provision and messaging services. In particular the Society for Worldwide Interbank Financial Telecommunications (SWIFT) is a major part of the global market infrastructure. Providers of data such as Bloomberg, Thomson Reuters and Telekurs are also considered as part of the global financial infrastructure. Some third party providers, such as ADP, supply proxy voting services, the costs of which could be passed on to the end investor.

1.4.2 Broker's Commission

Worldwide brokerage firms are also a major part of any securities market and, generally, these firms will earn part of their income by applying commission charges to each transaction that they execute. The commission rates are set by the brokerage firms but will be subject to competitive pressures within the marketplace.

2. Charges Applicable to Clients

Learning Objective

2.2   Identify the charges applicable for clients of: fund manager; custodian; advisor (eg, stockbroker, wealth manager, independent financial advisor)

In addition to the fees and tax that may be payable on trading of securities, clients of other parties may also face other potential fees, transaction commissions and charges.

2.1   Fees Payable by Clients to Fund Managers

Globally, fund managers can have various client types that they act for. They may also have different management mandates given to them by these clients.

For some clients they will have full discretionary powers which will allow them to act on behalf of their clients without reference to the client. Adopting a discretionary approach means that, having agreed the strategy the client wants to use, the client delegates the day-to-day investment decisions relating to their portfolio to the investment manager.

In some instances they will only have non-discretionary powers, which will mean they have to consult their clients prior to acting. By adopting a non-discretionary approach, the client becomes part of the investment management team. They have the final say in all decisions relating to their investments, but the fund manager works closely with the client to help formulate the ideal strategy and will advise on decisions and consult on any changes to the client's portfolio.

Fund managers will charge different rates for discretionary and non-discretionary management mandates.

2.2 Fund Managers' Proprietary Funds

Fund management companies often create their own proprietary funds. These funds will attract investment cash from investors from all walks of life and will have various charges that will apply to the purchaser (and sometimes seller) of units and shares in a fund.

The investor may pay an initial fee, which is usually quoted in the offering documents but which may be waived by the manager, a management fee, a performance fee, certainly in the case of a hedge fund and some other funds, and sometimes an exit fee.

In the case of umbrella funds, the investor may be entitled to move between funds in the umbrella without attracting additional initial fees.

The fund itself, and therefore the investors, will bear the costs and fees associated with the operation of the fund such as:

- custody fees
- auditors' fees
- administrators' fees
- trustee fees
- dealing and commission and fees associated with the portfolio.

Any costs and fees payable by the investor should be made clear to the investor in the Key Investor Information Document (KIID) associated with the fund.

The costs associated with the fund management company, such as salaries, will come out of the management fee.

2.3 Fees Payable by Clients of Custodians

A custodian charges its clients fees based on its core and added value services.

Core services, such as settlement, safekeeping and income collection, are often charged on a basis of a percentage fee of the value of the assets being held in custody. This is commonly known as an ad valorem fee and is likely to be charged on a sliding scale based on the value of the assets held.

Other services, such as those associated with proxy voting, tax reclamations, stock lending and borrowing and derivatives, may be charged on a usage basis.

Many custodians will normally have an ad valorem fee plus a transaction fee at the core of their fee structure. However, the basis of the custodial charges very much depends on the business model and pricing structure of the custodian. Custodians can show flexibility in their pricing structures.

Sliding scales based on activity, product, market and bespoke requirements may also apply.

2.4 Fees Payable by Clients of Brokers

Clients of brokers will generally pay a trading commission on the assets they trade, which can be charged in a variety of ways from a set rate to a percentage of the transaction value. Almost all brokers will have a range of services that they will offer to their clients. These services range from an execution-only service to a fully managed service which is, in fact, the same as offered by an investment management firm.

An execution-only stockbroker, as the name suggests, offers no advice and will deal only on a client's instruction. As no advice is offered or given, the fees are usually lower compared to those of an advisory broker.

Clients may hold their assets in their own name or they may request the broker to hold the assets in the name of the broker's nominee company.

The fees a client will pay will depend on the type of service they require. Commission and other fees like those mentioned in Section 1, eg, exchange fees, are often charged or shown on reports as a single amount.

Over-the-counter (OTC) transactions may well have no commission showing as the cost is included in the price (an all in price).

Again there may be a sliding scale of fees based on activity, product and market.

3. Regulatory Impacts on Market and Stock Exchange Fees Applicable to Clients

Learning Objective

2.3 Understand how the global regulatory environment impacts on market and stock exchange fees applicable to clients. In particular, how the UK regulatory environment dictates processes for a regulated UK firm when applying these fees and charges

3.1 Fee Transparency

Transparency of fees for the end investor has been gaining prominence with the global regulators over recent years.

The global regulators are active in their pursuit of any firm where they have had their suspicions aroused or have had investor complaints about fees and/or poor practice. They do investigate when they feel there is a necessity to do so.

In the US, for instance, one of the world's leading regulatory bodies, the SEC, has accused some of the world's biggest alternative asset managers of failing to fully inform investors about fee practices, which are said to eat away at the value of their holdings. Among those firms implicated were Blackstone and KKR who had large fines imposed on them.

In Canada, new transparency rules are coming into effect that will highlight to more Canadian investors how much of their dollars are going to paying investment fees rather than bolstering their retirement funds. As fees become more transparent, investors are going to get a clearer view of what they are paying, particularly if they are investing in mutual funds with high management expense ratio (MER) fees. As a result, investors may be drawn to lower-cost options, such as ETFs.

Also in Canada, the industry regulators have been pushing for greater transparency of fees for some time. As of July, 2016, when the second phase of the Client Relationship Model (known as CRM2) came into effect, it is mandatory for investment advisers to disclose all investment fees and investment performance directly to their clients.

In Australia and the UK, the regulators have implemented similar fee transparency models.

In Australia, there is a new regulatory mandate called the Future of Financial Advice (FOFA). The objectives of FOFA are to improve the trust and confidence of Australian retail investors in the financial services sector and ensure the availability, accessibility and affordability of high quality financial advice. Amongst other things it has highlighted investment advice fees and it is hoped will help investors to have a clearer view of the services provided and the costs incurred.

In 2012, the UK implemented the Retail Distribution Review (RDR), a regulatory change that affected how investors were paying for financial advice. The RDR is an initiative of the FCA. Its objective is to raise professional standards in the industry, introduce greater clarity between the different types of service available and make the charges associated with advice and services very clear.

The review covered the services offered by both financial advisers and investment firms. The rules which resulted from it required firms in the retail investment market to make significant changes.

As an example, the RDR introduced new rules from 6 April 2014 that related to retail investment products. This means many firms changed the way investors paid for administration services for certain investments. Much of this centred on applying these changes to funds only.

Fund managers charge investors an annual management charge (AMC). This is their fee for managing the fund and it is deducted directly from the fund rather than being charged to the investor or invoiced separately.

Previously, fund managers generally paid part of this AMC to brokers and intermediaries for providing services associated with distribution and administration of holdings in the funds. This part of the AMC is commonly referred to as a trail commission, trail fee or, sometimes, a fund manager rebate. This helped to pay for the services provide by the brokers and intermediaries including administration, custody, operating the website, processing dividends and corporate actions, providing fund factsheets and fund dealing services.

Instead of using trail commission payments, the regulator wants investment platforms, such as those firms that offer a range of funds, to charge clients explicitly for their services and therefore make charges clear and easy to understand.

End of Chapter Questions

1. What types of fees apply to share transactions?
   Answer reference: *Sections 1.1, 1.2*

2. What is the PTM levy?
   Answer reference: *Section 1.2*

3. Identify six exemptions to the PTM levy?
   Answer reference: *Section 1.2*

4. What are the main government taxes applied globally to share transactions?
   Answer reference: *Section 1.3*

5. What are the global regulators doing in relation to fees in the industry?
   Answer reference: *Section 3.1*

Chapter Three
Clearing and Settlement

For the purposes of this workbook, the definition of a security is deemed to be any of the following:

*   mortgage-backed securities (MESs)
*   asset-backed securities (ABSs)
*   stocks, shares, bonds, depositary receipts
*   cash
*   derivatives (OTC and exchange-traded)
*   market-traded funds.

It is hoped that the reader will appreciate that attempting to be generic when dealing with such a diverse set of asset types is extremely difficult. The reader will need to apply some leeway to terms like central securities depository (CSD) and central clearing counterparty (CCP) when trying to apply them to the different asset types. The reader must accept that each asset type in each of the global markets will have its own settlement regime. In attempting to be generic, a CSD is defined as being an automated mechanism of settling trades in assets, whatever that asset may be. A CCP is defined as an organisation/institution that interposes itself between the counterparties to trades, to ensure that both counterparties have matching obligations, acting as the buyer to every seller and the seller to every buyer thus taking on the financial risk attached to the trade.

It also has to be accepted that in some instances, especially when the asset is dealt OTC, the settlement may take place directly between the counterparties to the deal.

In this chapter we will be looking at various aspects of the lifecycle of the settlement process from the initial trade (purchase or sale) through to the settlement of that trade. This will include, where relevant, clearing, the role of the central clearing counterparty (CCP) and CSDs, issues such as settlement fails and the settlement procedures and practices in different locations.

1.   Transaction Lifecycle

Learning Objective

3.1   Describe the lifecycle of a transaction, ie, the purchase or sale of securities, through to the settlement in the UK and the other global markets, including the role of the broker in custody and settlement

1.1   The Core Processes

In any of the global markets that you may care to name, the processes associated with the lifecycle of the settlement of a transaction in assets are fundamentally the same. It is, of course, obvious that in order to settle a transaction, a transaction has to have taken place. The following is the generic list of events that have to take place. Later in the section, these events are examined in more detail. It is assumed that in this day and age most, if not all of these processes, are conducted by electronic means.

*   **Decision** – the first of the core processes is the decision to buy or sell an asset. This decision will be taken by the investor themselves or their appointed agent.

- **Order** – the investor or their agent will then place an order into the marketplace. This order will generally be given to a broker or a market maker, or an electronic trading system. This will be achieved via various mechanisms, such as internet, telephone, order routing systems, facsimile or any other market-acceptable method.
- **Execution** – the next stage is the execution of the order by the broker or the market maker. This entails finding a willing counterparty who wants to be a party to the trade, eg, a willing seller if you are a buyer.
- **Primary (transaction) matching** – the entities who are party to the market transaction have to ensure that they agree on the detail of the trade. This is done by comparing one side (buy-side) to the other (sell-side) to make sure that there is total agreement on all of the details by the trading parties. This is often referred to as clearing and may be undertaken by the local CCP.
- **Alleged trades** – having matched and confirmed that the trade details are correct, the details are sent to the local CSD by both parties and/or the local CCP and so the process of settlement begins.
- **Affirmation** – after the execution and primary matching of the transaction has been completed, then comes the affirmation to the investor or their agent by the broker or market maker that the order has been successfully executed in line with the instructions given.
- **Verification** – having received a confirmation from the broker that a transaction has taken place, the entity that has placed the order has to verify that the broker has executed its instructions correctly.
- **Issuance of primary settlement instructions** – having been advised that a transaction has been executed, the fund manager or the investor, having verified that the transaction was executed in line with their instructions, has to advise their custodial agent of the details of the trade. The broker to the trade will have been issued with standing settlement instructions as to who the custodial and settlement agent for their client is. They, in turn, will send a notification of the transaction to the custodial agent.
- **Trade capture** – it is very important that the custodial agent has a robust method to capture the settlement instructions that have been sent to them by the investor.
- **Secondary (settlement) matching** – having captured (received) an instruction to settle a transaction, the custodial agent has to ensure that the details of the trade they have been asked to settle correspond with those details they have received from the marketplace. This secondary matching takes place between the custodial agent and the entity (broker) who executed the trade.
- **Issuance of secondary settlement instructions** – the custodial agent then has to issue their own confirmation of settlement instruction to either the local CSD directly or to their settlement agent.
- **Tertiary pre-settlement matching** – the local CSD or custodial agent (sub-custodian) also conducts some pre-settlement matching. This is essentially the third time the same transaction has been matched.
- **Settlement** – having completed all of the stages noted above, the last thing to happen should be the settlement of the transaction. This means that the buyer of an asset receives what they bought and the seller receives the counter value to the asset they sold.

There are, of course, several further processes associated with the clearing and settlement of transaction of securities. Although there will be some variance depending on the particular market and products concerned, these processes will be generally the same and are discussed in the expanded detail of the core process.

1.1.1 Decision to Trade

The process of deciding what and when to trade is fundamental to the settlement process. Without a trade there is no settlement. The decisions to buy and sell assets are based on many factors, and some of these are captured below.

In today's world of high-speed communication of information, much of which could have a significant impact on the value of assets, some decision-makers have decided to write computer programmes that will automatically generate transaction orders if a given set of events come to fruition. For instance, the price of an asset may hit a certain price or an index may reach a certain level. Other decisions are driven by the make-up of a client's portfolio and the weightings assigned to each asset class within those portfolios; clients' portfolios may become underweight or overweight in any given asset class and remedial action must be taken. Some portfolios are linked to an index of securities and need to be adjusted to reflect the correlation between the index of securities and the client's portfolio. Some decisions are driven by fundamental economics such as the asset that is being held is not performing in line with expectations and so needs to be replaced or reduced. It may just be that a decision-maker has a gut feel about a certain asset and how they think it will perform.

1.1.2 Order

Having made the decision to do something specific with an asset, an order to transact the purchase and sale of the asset has to be placed into the marketplace. Depending upon what type of entity the decision-maker is – ie, a professional dealer, a fund manager, a private investor – the order to conduct an exchange of assets (a trade) will be channelled through either an electronic trading system linked directly to the marketplace or given to a broker by acceptable means to conduct the business.

The role of the broker in the execution of the trade is very important. The order itself can be very complex to handle. The way a transaction is handled depends very much on the marketplace and there are many marketplaces that will only transact business in securities in parcels that are known as board lots. These board lots are set down by the local authorities.

By way of example, let us say the investor has, over time, built up an odd holding of 1,023 shares of ABC Company. The board lot may only be 1,000 shares, so the order has to be split into a board lot parcel that is placed onto the regular market, with the odd lot having to be dealt with separately via an odd lot broker. As an aside, it is likely that the better custodial firms will deal with odd lots when they originate generally at the time of corporate events.

The order may have significant parameters or instructions associated with it such as a limit order or fill-or-kill instruction.

When the order is of a particularly large nature, the broker has to ensure, as best they can, that the way they deal with the order does not affect the price of the asset either upwards or downwards. Hence, to handle the complexity of orders, a significant investment by many firms has been made in what has become known as trade order management systems.

1.1.3 Execution

Giving due regard to the above paragraph, the execution of the order will have to take into account the type of market into which it is placed. This is because, generally, an asset will be tradeable in a marketplace that is either order-driven or quote-driven. It is also relevant whether the asset is exchange-traded or if there is an OTC element that needs to be taken into account.

MiFID classifies trading venues into three explicit categories:

1. **Regulated markets** – referring to regulated stock exchanges, such as NYSE Euronext, the London Stock Exchange (LSE) and the Frankfurt Stock Exchange.
2. **Multilateral trading facilities (MTFs)** – sometimes referred to as alternative trading systems, MTFs are registered non-exchange trading venues which bring together purchasers and sellers of securities. Subscribers can post orders into the system and these will be communicated (typically electronically via an electronic communication network (ECN)) for other subscribers to view. Matched orders will then proceed for execution. An example of an MTF is a dark pool, named as such due to lack of transparency and lack of accessibility to the general public. Dark pools facilitate trading of high value introduced predominantly by institutional investors. The idea is that willing buyers and sellers of those high value orders do not adversely affect the share price.
3. **Systematic internalisers** – an investment firm that, on an organised, frequent and systematic basis, deals on its own trading account by executing clients' orders outside a regulated market or an MTF. This practice is broadly synonymous with agency crossing, whereby a crossing network electronically matches orders for execution without routing these to an exchange or MTF.

Assuming that a broker is handling the order, a willing counterparty to the transaction has to be found. The mechanism for doing this is governed by the foregoing. The broker will find the willing counterparty by following the market convention and will execute the transaction as appropriate. The ability to execute a trade can be affected by various factors. For example, the liquidity of the marketplace, supply and demand of the shares in question and confidence in the general economy will all have an effect on the broker's ability to trade.

1.1.4 Transaction Matching

Following the execution of the transaction, the two transacting parties have to agree as to the details of the transaction they have entered into. This must include the pertinent details such as the date the transaction was entered into, the name of the asset including any security identifiers (ISIN, SEDOL etc), whether they have bought or sold that asset, the price at which the deal was struck, the consideration to be exchanged, the proposed settlement date of the transaction (the contracted settlement date) and whether there were any special conditions attributed to the transaction, ie, special ex or special cum dividend/event, plus or minus days of accrued interest. The consideration being exchanged will take into account any market fees, broker fees or taxes. This transaction matching can take place under the auspices of a clearing agent or CCP or be conducted between the two transacting parties. This matching generally has to take place within predetermined market timeframes following the execution of the transaction.

A well-known definition of a CCP is: '*an entity that interposes itself between the counterparties to trades, acting as the buyer to every seller and the seller to every buyer*'. By way of a mechanism known as novation, the CCP takes on the risk to both sides of the transaction.

1.1.5   Alleged Transactions

When dealing with on-exchange assets, the transacting parties, having agreed on the details of the trade, need to notify the local CSD. It is via the local CSD that the actual settlement, eg, the exchange of assets, will take place. This notification is commonly known as a trade allegation. This alerts the local CSD to the fact that member firms are party to a transaction that needs to be settled. This is a preliminary alert and is subject to change.

When dealing with off-exchange assets (OTC issues), the counterparties to the transaction will have to arrange settlement between themselves.

1.1.6   Affirmations

The broker who has conducted the transaction has to affirm to their client that they have executed a trade. They are required to give their client full details of the transaction including the time the trade was executed, the full amount of assets transacted, whether they have bought or sold the asset, the full name of the asset, the price at which the trade was executed, the brokerage charged to the client, any taxes to be paid, any exchange fees to be paid, any regulatory fees to be paid, and the full net cash amount (counter-value) they expect in exchange.

1.1.7   Verification

Having received an affirmation from the broker that a transaction has taken place, the entity that has placed the order has to verify that the broker has executed their instructions correctly.

Also at this stage, the party who has placed the order has to inform the broker if and how the trade has to be split between ordering parties' clients. When allocation has to be made amongst various clients, this is commonly known as having conducted a block trade. There will be market conventions of how and when this allocation has to be accomplished. Generally, this will start with agreeing the block amount of the asset traded, followed by the sibling amounts allocated and then a recapitulation of the whole. The broker will have to inform the local CSD that the trade that was preliminary sent to them has now been split into different shapes for settlement.

1.1.8   Issuance of Primary Settlement Instructions

Having been advised that a transaction has been executed, the fund manager or the investor, having verified that the transaction was executed in line with their instructions, has to advise their custodial agent of the details of the trade.

The broker to the trade will have been issued with standing settlement instructions as to who the custodial and settlement agent for their client is. They in turn will have to send a notification of the transaction to the custodial agent. This will need to be advised at allocation (sibling) level if the original trade was a block trade and will need to include the full details as itemised above, but split to each sibling trade.

The typical type of data to be sent as notification of a trade and to be matched, plus the type of data needed for settlement instructions, is as follows:

Trade Matching Data

- Trade level (block) mandatory fields: security identifier (International Securities Identification Number (ISIN)/Stock Exchange Daily Official List (SEDOL)); buy/sell indicator:
  - block quantity; executing broker; instructing party; trade date
  - deal price.

- Trade level (block) (alternative choice) fields for equity or debt: total trade amount:
  - settlement date; trade commissions
  - trade transaction indicator; charges or taxes
  - maturity date; date dated; coupon rate
  - number of days accrued; total accrued interest; net settlement amount; yield.

- Trade detail (allocations) (optional choice) fields for equity or debt: quantity allocated:
  - account Id (fund name); charges or taxes; commissions
  - accrued interest; net cash amount.

1.1.9 Trade Capture

It is very important that the custodial agent has a robust method to capture the settlement instructions that have been sent to them by the investor or fund manager. In this day and age of instantaneous communication, it is important that the capture of trade data is fully automated. It is highly unlikely that a business model that relies on manual processes in this area will prove to be cost-effective. Together with the type of data shown previously, it is important that the trade capture system can provide the users with additional aids. Whatever mechanism is used, whether manual or automated, anomalies must be spotted early and dealt with accordingly.

Ideally, today's trade capture systems will be programmed in such a way to flag to the user when things are not as expected. This enables the creation of exception processing queues so that the users may investigate. It would be useful if the system or the user would also flag when it would appear that a potential problem might occur, prior to the trade being released into the main database.

The typical things that the user or the system needs to take into consideration are as follows:

- Whenever a data field is not filled as expected, the trade will be placed into an exception queue for investigation.
- Things such as a potential duplicate trade being received will be identified.
- When assets are not available due to insufficient cash, shares on loan, unsettled transactions or assets not held.
- It will also be useful if the system or the user were able to identify when a timing convention was not as expected, eg, trade date vs settlement is not T+3.
- The notification of settlement was not received within the prescribed time deadlines as laid down in the firm's terms and conditions.

1.1.10 Secondary (Settlement) Matching

Having captured (received) an instruction to settle a transaction via their trade capture environment, the custodial agent has to ensure that the details of the trade they have been asked to settle correspond with those details they have received from the marketplace. This secondary settlement matching takes place between the custodial agent and the entity (broker) which executed the trade.

Again, this matching has become extremely sophisticated and probably mechanised to be able to cope with the very large volumes in the timeframes allowed by the marketplace. As the title of the process conveys, one set of data is matched against another set of data. However, in this process it is vital to have set and agreed tolerance levels to certain fields of the data. For instance, it might not be advisable to reject a transaction with a value of £1 million because the commission charged by the broker differs by a penny from that which the investor or fund manager has stated should have been charged, or that on the same transaction the overall settlement value differs by a few cents. On the other hand, there will be some data fields where the tolerance should be set to zero.

Some custodial agents do offer services whereby they check and monitor the levels of commission being charged to the investor or fund manager by the brokers.

Again, the use of exception queues will be employed in the process. This allows for the users to quickly identify, amend and agree the exceptions. This is a time critical process because, after matching has taken place, a confirmation message has to be sent back to the broker. This allows the broker to finalise the settlement within the local CSD.

1.1.11 Issuance of Secondary Settlement Instructions

After the completion of the matching, the custodial agent now has to issue their own settlement instruction to either the local CSD directly, or to their settlement agent. The data contained in this message is fundamentally the same as that which is sent to the custodian by the investor or fund manager; however, there will be some additional data, the adding of which is commonly known as enrichment.

Standard Settlement Instruction (SSI) Data

The easiest way to illustrate the additional data required to complete a settlement instruction is to show the data that is required to populate a typical SWIFT settlement instruction.

In order to populate the SWIFT header and certain data fields relating to the custodian and brokers, the following data elements will need to be populated. An important element is to ensure that the terms and conditions of the entity that the message is being sent to are adhered to. These terms and conditions will outline the timing parameters that the messages have to adhere to for each of the global markets.

Data Required	SWIFT Field and Sequence
Custodian business identifier code (BIC)	SWIFT header: no sequence applicable
Delivering or receiving agent's details	95P (BIC) 95R (local code) 95Q free format Securities E1 – settlement party: delivering or receiving agent
Buyer and seller details (broker)	95P (BIC) 95R (local code) 95Q free format Securities E1 – settlement party: buyer/seller
Safekeeping account of broker at settlement agent	97A: Sequence E1– settlement party: buyer/seller
Place of settlement	95P (BIC) 95Q (country code) Securities E1 – settlement party: place of settlement
Fund's account number at custodian	97A: Sequence C – financial instrument/account

1.1.12 Tertiary Pre-Settlement Matching

The local CSD or custodial agent (sub-custodian) also conducts some pre-settlement matching. This is essentially the third time the same transaction has been matched. This is, however, no less important, as it is at this stage that the fundamental indications of whether the settlement will actually come to fruition will actually occur. This matching stage is of paramount importance.

The local CSD or the agent should be advising as to the likelihood of the settlement taking place by giving feedback on the non-availability of the assets (cash or shares) to allow the settlement to proceed or whether the counterparty agrees to the terms of the transaction. In most countries, this notice of problems does give the parties to a transaction some time to resolve the differences prior to the settlement date.

1.1.13 Settlement

Having completed all of the stages noted above, the last thing to happen should be the settlement of the transaction. This means that the buyer of an asset receives what they bought and the seller receives the counter-value to the asset they sold on the date stipulated on the contract. Ultimately, the definition of settlement could be said to be the transfer of ownership of the assets that were traded.

The local CSD or the agent will be expected to issue a confirmation of settlement. This will hopefully be sent electronically to the custodian so that they may use it electronically to update their records by STP. Settlement of transactions in securities in the global markets should be achieved in a fashion known as delivery versus payment (DvP). This is the simultaneous irrevocable exchange of assets, such as shares and cash. DvP settlement eliminates the principal risk that occurs when there is a time gap between delivery and payment.

2. Fails Control: Repairs to Trades

2.1 Fails Control: Repairing a Trade Instruction

Learning Objective

3.7   Explain instances when a trade settlement instruction would need to be repaired

In many instances, a transaction fails to settle on the prescribed settlement date due to the instruction details being incorrectly transmitted. When reviewing the amount of data required in constructing a trade settlement instruction, it is not hard to imagine why sometimes the data needs to be repaired. Any one of the data elements could have a slight imperfection which will require it to be repaired.

The easiest way to demonstrate this is to look at the number of data elements contained within a typical trade settlement instruction as depicted by a typical SWIFT securities settlement message:

- Security identifier (eg, ISIN/SEDOL).
- Buy/sell.
- Quantity of asset.
- Executing broker.
- Instructing part.
- Trade date.
- Deal price.
- Deal time.
- Settlement date.
- Place of settlement.
- Safekeeping account number.
- Trade commissions.
- Charges or taxes.
- Government/regulatory charges.
- Maturity date.
- Date dated.
- Coupon rate.
- Number of days accrued (plus/minus).
- Withholding tax.
- Total accrued interest.
- Net settlement amount.
- Yield.
- Account Id (client name).
- Net cash amount.
- Foreign exchange instruction.
- Settlement agent.

As mentioned, a good trade capture system will be programmed to recognise what the settlement convention is in, say, the US, ie, T+3. So, if the system detected a trade with a place of settlement such as New York with a trade date of the 5th and a settlement date of the 6th, the system should place this trade into an exception queue because the trade date/settlement date relationship was contrary to the known convention. This is an example of where a settlement instruction was in need of repair. Likewise, the trade capture system should also be programmed to recognise when a sale of an asset was being apportioned to a client who had a zero holding in that particular asset. In that instance the trade would go to a repair queue for repair.

Even if there is no automated trade capture system, and the two examples are manually captured, they show when a trade settlement instruction is in need of repair. As described in the previous section, all transactions begin with a decision being made to execute a transaction. This decision is the asset management element of the process. This decision can be taken by an individual investor on their own behalf or by an institution such as a broker or investment management firm on behalf of their clients.

Learning objective 3.7, by definition, should convey to the reader that errors regarding trade instruction are possible. The process of repairing a trade (or rectifying the consequences) will have different degrees of difficulty depending upon when in the lifecycle this error is discovered and what the nature of the error is. The term 'repairing' really means to rectify the error as best you can.

2.2 Fails Control: Repairing a Trade Incorrectly Executed

Learning Objective

3.9 Explain the consequences when a trade is incorrectly executed and what would need to be done to repair the situation

An incorrectly executed trade order is, for most of those concerned, a very difficult situation to correct.

In the first instance it is possible to imagine a scenario where a market maker in a particular asset type might be asked to cancel an executed trade without consequences. This obviously depends on the sophistication of the market on which the asset has been traded. It is also possible to imagine that an off-market trade might be cancelled without consequence if discovered soon enough. It is also possible that in certain exceptional circumstances the regulatory authorities of a country might deem it appropriate to cancel executed trades.

However, an important general lesson in administration and audit is that you cannot change history.

First we need to look at what type of errors could be made to the instruction to trade that will require a repair to be made. Some of these are listed below:

- Incorrect order type (to buy/to sell).
- Incorrect asset traded (eg, wrong stock, currency, bond, derivative).
- Incorrect client account associated with trade.
- Incorrect order size (eg, 1,000 shares instead of 10,000 shares).
- Miscommunication or misunderstanding of decision (did not mean to trade at all).
- Incorrect pricing convention conveyed (at best, limit, no more than, no less than).

When it has been determined that an error has been made, it is important to discover quickly what stage in the trade lifecycle the trade is at. For instance, the order may have only just been placed by phone with a broker or the market maker and it may just be a case of countermanding or correcting the details of the order before it is executed. Alternatively, the trade may have been electronically executed, in which case the so-called repair becomes more difficult.

Assuming that the trade has been executed, the next stage is to determine what the error was and in which market it was, as each could have a different method employed to repair the effect.

The following two sections look in detail at two errors that could be made, giving a reasonably detailed explanation of how to rectify the situation. With regard to the other error types, there is a high level of correlation with the rectification process of the errors that are reviewed in detail.

2.3 Incorrect Order Type (To Buy/To Sell)

2.3.1 Asset Management Viewpoint

Transparency is a word that is often used these days. It is, of course, supposed to convey the fact that we have nothing to hide and should be unafraid to allow others to see how we conduct ourselves in business. This philosophy should be remembered when dealing with clients.

Imagine that an asset management firm has placed an order with a broker to buy 1,000 shares of the Acme Laundry Co, which has been executed, but the order should have been to sell 1,000 shares of the Acme Laundry Co.

When the error is discovered, the following action should be taken to repair the erroneous trade.

Once executed, the erroneous buy order has to be honoured and settled. As the firm has made the error, they should take the responsibility for settling the erroneous purchase. In theory this of course should mean that the firm should put up the money to pay for the shares and, in theory, have the shares delivered to an account that is in the name of the firm at the local CSD. At the same time, two sale orders need to be placed with the broker: the first sale order is to correct the original error and should be made on behalf of the firm and the second sale order should be on behalf of the client.

In practice, the course of action you take will likely depend on whether the transaction has been booked to the client's account prior to the discovery of the error.

What would almost certainly have happened is that the incorrect purchase order would have been booked to the client's account as it was a genuine error. An alternative to the pristine action detailed above is that all the transactions could take place over the client's account and this would afford the client total transparency. This is not something that a firm would necessarily want to do, as it exposes the error, but that is a consequence of being transparent.

In any case, what the firm must ensure is that the client's account is made whole should there be a cash difference on the client's account caused by the error.

2.3.2 Custodian's Viewpoint

If a custodian is used, the erroneous transaction will have been passed to the custodian in the normal way. The custodian will have accepted the trade at face value as being good, and will have processed the trade over the appropriate client account. This will have added the shares to the client's portfolio and debited the cash required to pay for the settlement to the client's account. Arrangements will have been made to issue a settlement instruction to either the local CSD or the custodian's sub-custodian. Cash will have been positioned as appropriate.

The asset manager should inform the custodian of the problem that needs to be rectified and then pass on to the custodian the trades that rectify the situation. These will be accepted and processed by the custodian in the normal way. The custodian will process both trades over the appropriate client account and pass on settlement instructions to their local CSD.

Importantly, the asset manager has to ensure that the client cash account at the custodian is made whole should there be any difference in cash terms on the client account.

2.3.3 Depository Viewpoint

From the depository point of view, there is no effect.

2.4 Incorrect Client Account Associated with the Trade

2.4.1 Asset Management Viewpoint

In general market terms, this is the least onerous error to deal with. This assertion is made because it is assumed that there is nothing wrong with the fundamentals of the trade itself, only the wrong client being associated with the trade.

It is, of course, important that the error be rectified as soon as possible. In the asset management area, attributing a trade to the wrong client can bring with it serious difficulties, such as temporary over/underweighting of the portfolio, incorrect net asset value (NAV) and valuations, possible performance measurement issues or value at risk (VAR) issues. The process outlined below makes the assumption that the error is spotted very quickly, say within hours of the trade being executed, but this may not necessarily be the case. It may be that the trade could have settled prior to the error being discovered, which brings a different layer of complexity.

This type of case does also bring to the fore some processing misnomers which we will explain. The unwinding process in this case is as follows.

Having discovered that the wrong client has been associated with a trade, the entity which ordered the trade to be executed must contact the broker/market maker or electronic market, by the prescribed methodology, to make the change. This should result in a new contract or trade confirmation (in the correct client name) being issued.

The asset management system that is used to record the client assets must of course be changed and so there will be an in-house methodology to do this. This is where there may be a processing misnomer employed. It is highly likely that this process will be called a trade cancellation. It is not actually a trade cancellation, but is more of a trade reversal. This is because, at the client account level, all cash and asset movements should be precisely reversed.

The trade reversal must be processed over the account of the client to whom the trade was originally erroneously allocated. At this stage it is important to remember that any custodian associated with the client must be informed of the change. Ideally, the reversal being posted to the asset management system will automatically generate a cancellation message to the custodian.

A trade must be posted to the account of the correct client using the original trade details, such as trade date, trade time, price and settlement date. Ideally, the trade being posted to the asset management system will automatically generate a trade settlement message to the custodian.

2.4.2   Custodian's Viewpoint

From the custodian's point of view there is a lot that needs to be done. Depending upon the design of the custodian's technical infrastructure, it is possible that their trade capture system will put the message into an exception queue to be dealt with. Alternatively, the system may be designed to allow a reversal to go straight through to the asset recording system.

Whatever happens, the custodian will be required to match both the reversal and the new settlement instruction to the broker or market messages.

Once matched, both the reversal message and the new settlement instruction will need to be processed in the custodian's asset recording system. This will have the effect of showing a reversal of the trade in the account of the wrongly allocated client and a transaction in the account of the correct client.

The custodian needs to be aware of the following:

* In which market of the world is the trade?
* Is the new client in a different tax category from the original client?

Both of these will have an effect on how the custodian reacts to the change of client allocation.

If the trade is in a country where the eventual beneficial owner is the name on the register, the custodian will have to amend the settlement instruction sent to their sub-custodian accordingly so as to adhere to local regulations.

If the trade is in a country where the custodian holds assets in a segregated fashion by way of choice (eg, in the UK in designated nominee accounts), then the custodian must inform the local CSD of the change of designation.

If the trade is in a country where it is possible to hold assets in an omnibus account, then, so long as the originally allocated client is in the same tax category as the newly allocated client (eg, 15% rate account or 30% rate account, etc), it will not be necessary to amend the original settlement instruction. If there is a difference, the custodian should inform their sub-custodian to make the switch. This can be instructed post-settlement.

3. Late Settlement: The Avoidance of a Failed Trade

Learning Objective

3.10 Describe the potential factors that can trigger late settlements and the controls for minimising late settlement

---

The primary causes or factors of late settlements around the world are mainly limited to four main areas:

1. **Shortage of assets** – in the world of stocks and shares, this is a very common reason given for a trade failing to settle on the contracted date. However, this is much less common in the area of cash transactions.

2. **Late or incorrectly matched transactions** – incorrect or the late matching of trades in any asset is on the list of reasons for late settlement of transactions. The potential for error is very high when considering the amount of data that has to be matched. However, given the number of worldwide transactions that take place every day, in percentage terms the number of transactions that fail to settle on time due to a mismatch is probably very low. There are three levels of matching that take place in the lifecycle of any transaction, and so even though the potential for mismatch is high, we should expect the incidence to be low.

3. **Incorrect settlement instructions being issued** – even in today's world of automated electronic processing, this is still a potential area of concern.

4. **Failure to manage processes correctly** – as we have seen, there are many checks and balances in the lifecycle of a transaction and, in theory, no trades should ever fail. However, the management of the processes is critical to this statement being true. The management of processes and knowing what to do in a particular situation is the backbone of our industry.

These then, are the areas which will be the most likely to cause a late settlement. It therefore follows that the controls to eradicate late settlement should be concentrated in these areas.

3.1 Shortage of Assets

Asset managers should be aware of the availability of assets prior to selling the said assets. They should comply with the terms and conditions that the custodians lay down in each marketplace with regard to the timing of their issuance of settlement instructions.

Custodians should have controls in place that alert them to any sales of assets that are not readily available. They should have programmes in place that will allow them to recall assets that are out on loan or that internally substitute one lender for another, making the assets technically available for delivery.

They should have mechanisms for alerting the asset managers when previously available assets become unavailable due to corporate events. In most countries, there are opportunities for investors to borrow securities to avoid fails. Custodians could invite their clients to sign agreements that will allow them to borrow securities to avoid fails. This will, of course, be subject to the client having the regulatory approval to do this. Custodians should have agreements with their sub-custodians with regard to this particular activity that allow the custodian to manage the process effectively.

Brokers/market makers should ensure that, if they have knowingly sold short, they have made arrangements to borrow the securities prior to the settlement date.

3.2   Late or Incorrectly Matched Transactions

Good management information is vital to process managers. When they are required to manage any process, information is the key. A process that is devoid of management information is a process that is not being managed. In many markets, there will be fines or remedial action, or both, for those that do not comply with the matching timeframes.

Asset managers should comply with the terms and conditions that the custodians lay down in each marketplace with regard to the timing of their issuance of settlement instructions. They should also give due regard to the rules in their local markets concerning the matching of transactions with the local brokers and market makers. The local rules will specify the deadlines for the matching of trades. There should be management information about any transactions that have been executed for which settlement instructions have not been issued.

With custodians in regard to this specific process, it is important that the process manager is aware of the number of transactions that remain unmatched at the end of any specific time period as dictated by the local rules.

It is recognised that some institutions will be conducting just a few transactions per day and that some will be conducting thousands of transactions per day. The level of automation the process manager will need will depend on these dynamics. It is also important that the department and the supporting infrastructure be structured in such a way so as to cater for these dynamics.

The important issue is to be able to manage at the 'exception' level, ie, any transactions that have not been matched. To be able to do this effectively (depending on the volumes) means that the 'exceptions' may have to be sorted into like categories. This could mean that the exception processing is managed at a country level, at the asset manager level or at broker level or whatever demographic works for the firm. By the end of any trading day, some action should be being taken in the event of unmatched transactions. Custodians should have agreements with their sub-custodians with regard to this particular activity that allows the custodian to manage the process effectively.

Brokers/market makers should have processes in place that ensure they have issued alleged trades to the local depository in line with the market rules.

3.3   Incorrect Settlement Instructions Being Issued

Asset managers should comply with the terms and conditions that the custodians lay down in each marketplace with regard to the timing of their issuance of settlement instructions. They should also ensure that their standard settlement instruction (SSI) database is kept up-to-date. In the event that a custodian informs them of a change to the SSIs, they must ensure that this notice is acted upon.

Custodians should regularly update their terms and conditions to take account of any changes in their sub-custodian infrastructure or any changes to market settlement conventions or timeframes. They should ensure that if a client account changes its taxable status, this is reflected in their own system, with regard to the SSIs, to their sub-custodian.

Brokers/market makers should comply with the terms and conditions that the regulatory authorities lay down in each marketplace in respect of the timing of their issuance of trade confirmations. They should also ensure that their SSI database is kept up-to-date. In the event that a custodian or sub-custodian informs them of a change to the SSIs, they must ensure that this notice is acted upon. They should have processes in place that ensure that they have issued alleged trades to the local depository in line with the market rules.

3.4   Failure to Manage Processes Correctly

Much of the above is designed to ensure that the processes are managed correctly. To help with this, a process that reports to senior management each month on how well or how badly the processes are working is a valuable management tool. This senior management oversight helps to concentrate the minds of those responsible for managing the process. It is also an excellent tool that can be given to internal auditors or regulators.

Senior management should be cognisant with the effects that a failed trade may have on the profitability of the firm:

- One failed settlement might prevent other trades from settling, either through lack of securities or insufficient cash.
- Funding costs and interest claims will occur.
- Resolving failure problems takes up valuable staff resources.
- When market failure costs are incurred, processes must be initiated to apportion the costs appropriately. This will add to the cost base of the firm.
- Organisations that repeatedly cause trades to fail will get a bad name in the market and counterparties may be less willing to undertake business with them.

4.   The Resolution of Failed Settlements

Learning Objective

3.11   Describe the process when a buy-in and sell-out occurs, the potential market and counterparty penalties for buy-ins and sell-outs and identify those markets in which buy-in and sell-out is automatic

The resolution of a failed settlement can only be achieved by providing the missing asset to the aggrieved party. This can often be achieved by rectifying incorrect settlement instructions which, as previously outlined, can be due to any number of data elements being incorrect.

The settlement failure may also be resolved by the borrowing of the missing asset.

However, in some instances the resolution of the failed settlement is taken out of the hands of the offending party by the authorities in the local marketplace. This occurs when the marketplace invokes their buy-in/sell-out procedures. The process for dealing with such an event will depend upon the local market jurisdiction. Each country will have a different methodology for the initial invocation and then the eventual processing of a buy-in or sell-out. Some countries do not have a buy-in or sell-out facility. Depending upon the country, the process may be invoked automatically on the day the transaction fails, after a prescribed period of time, or at the behest of the injured party.

There are three ways that the process may be invoked:

1. Automatically when the trade fails.
2. At a prescribed date after the fail.
3. At the behest of the injured party.

4.1 Close-Out Procedure

When a transaction is bought-in or sold-out against, the aim is to satisfy the injured party by supplying to them the assets they are entitled to under the original transaction. The buy-in/sell-out process is undertaken by an entity that is regulated to do so. In many instances this will be the local CSD. The aim can be achieved in various ways.

In the case of a buy-in, the CSD may attempt to borrow the securities, or the process may be to actually buy the securities from another party. In any event, the injured party will receive the assets they originally bought. In some instances when it is not possible to buy or borrow the securities, the CSD will make a payment of cash in lieu of the shares to the injured party. The formula for such payments will differ from country to country.

The offending party will have to pay all of the costs of this action and their original 'sale' is 'closed out'. There will likely be daily levies imposed on the offending party until the transaction is completed. Whether the resulting compensatory action is by purchase, borrowing, or cash in lieu, the offending party has to bear the final costs. The offending party, having paid all of the buy-in costs, will find themselves in a position where they retain the assets that they previously sold but failed to settle. Generally, in order to recoup their costs, they have to re-order the sale of the assets. When a sell-out occurs, it means a buyer is unable to receive the securities due to lack of cash. In this instance the seller has the right to close the trade by means of a sell-out. In this case the seller sells the securities to another counterparty (the out agent). The difference in transaction monies plus loss of interest on the sale proceeds is settled between the seller and buyer.

4.2 Global Buy-In/Sell-Out Rules

Many countries around the world apply rules that are designed to deter the failure of transactions to settle on time. Where rules are in place, the timing of the invocation of these rules varies. Some countries will invoke their rules immediately the transaction fails to settle; others will be more lenient and only invoke after a laid-down period of time. Some countries will leave the invocation of the rules to the parties involved in the trade. In some countries there is no mechanism to buy-in or sell-out.

A buy-in or sell-out is a mechanism that will ensure that the injured party receives the assets that they are entitled to. For instance, if a client has bought some shares and the seller fails to deliver these shares on the prescribed settlement date, the regulatory authorities will ensure that the buyer receives those shares at the expense of the seller.

Country	Buy-In/sell-out rules	When are they applied?
Argentina	Yes	Buy-in options exist; however they are only available for brokers trading at the Mervals floor. Applied after two days. There are no costs attached to the process.
Australia	Yes	The current fail fees applied to failed settlements are a rate of 0.10% of the value of the shortfall securities (based upon the previous day's closing price) with a minimum fee of AUD 100 and a maximum of AUD 5,000 per transaction per day. The ASX has implemented an automatic close out requirement whereby the delivering settlement participant is required to close out a client's delivery shortfall by purchasing or borrowing the shares to complete the settlement if the transaction has not settled by T+5. The requirement does not apply to participants who fail to deliver due to the failure of other participants to deliver to them and only applies to transactions which are matched in the CHESS system.
Brazil	Yes	T+3 If securities are not delivered by 10:00, CBLC stock lending programme will be triggered. If the securities are available for borrowing, then CBLC registers a borrowing transaction on behalf of the defaulting investor's clearing agent. If the securities are not available on the automatic stocks borrowing tool, the investors will be charged a penalty fee of 1% of transaction value. The penalty charge will be divided in two moments: i) 0.5% on T+3, which is not reversible, and ii) 0.5% on T+7 after the period in which the clearing agent can present a justification for the failure in order to avoid the additional 0.5% penalty fee. The applicable justification must indicate that the failure had a cause other than that the investor intentionally made a naked short sale (eg, operational error by the clearing agent). T+4 If securities are not available for borrowing by 10:00, CBLC keeps the delivery outstanding and charges a penalty fee of 10% of the value of the transaction to the defaulting clearing agent. The penalty charge will be divided in two moments: i) 0.5% on T+4, which is not reversible, and ii) 9.5% on T+7 in case the clearing agent does not present a justification for the failure in order to avoid the additional 9.5% penalty fee. The applicable justification must indicate that the failure had a cause other than that the investor intentionally made a naked short sale (eg, operational error by the clearing agent).

		If securities are delivered through the automatic stocks borrowing tool, the clearing agent will still be levied a 10% penalty fee of the value of the transaction and CBLC will issue the buy-in ticket in favour of the buying agent. All expenses resulting from the buy-in will be debited to the account of the seller's clearing agent for the defaulting counterparty. The buyer's broker can execute buy-in procedure between T+4 and T+6 and must confirm its execution to BM&FBOVESPA by T+7, otherwise the transaction will undergo reversal. T+6 If the buyer does not communicate the cancellation or execution of the repurchase to BM&FBOVESPA, such will be automatically reverted for settlement on T+6. The justifications for the failure must be executed in the system by 18:00 of T+6 of the trading date.
Canada	Yes	Initiated by the buying broker. The broker notifies the depository and the counterparty of the intent to buy-in. 48 hours after receipt the depository will submit the buy-in to the exchange for execution. The exchange will immediately then execute the trade and report back to the depository, which will in turn ensure that the buy-in is allocated properly, allowing for net settlement to take place. Any costs that arise as a result of the buy-in are attributed back to the seller.
Germany	Yes	Effective November 1, 2012, Eurex, the German Central Counterparty, implemented a new EU short-selling regulation. Article 15 of the regulation comprises the following two articles: 1. A central counterparty in a member state which provide clearing services for shares, must ensure that procedures are in place which comply with the following requirements: a. where a natural or legal person selling shares is not able to deliver the shares for settlement within four business days after the day on which settlement is due, procedures are automatically triggered for the buy-in of the shares to ensure delivery for settlement b. where the buy-in of the shares for delivery is not possible, an amount is paid to the buyer based on the value of the shares to be delivered at the delivery date, plus an amount of losses incurred by the buyer as a result of the settlement failure and

c. the natural or legal person who fails to settle reimburses all amounts paid pursuant to points (a) and (b).

2. A CCP in a member state that provides clearing services for shares must ensure that procedures are in place, which ensure that where a natural or legal person who sells shares fails to deliver the shares for settlement by the date on which settlement is due, such person must make daily payments for each day that the failure continues.

The new regulation includes ordinary and preferred shares, but does not include ETFs and bonds traded on the Frankfurt Stock Exchange. Xetra International Markets, the Irish Stock Exchange (Xetra Dublin) and Eurex exercises and assignments.

Should the clearing member not have fulfilled his delivery obligations by a certain date, only one buy-in attempt takes place on SD+4. In the event that this attempt is not successful, a cash settlement takes place on SD+8.

Other Securities:

Should the clearing member not have fulfilled his delivery obligations by a certain date, up to three buy-in attempts (SD+5, SD+10, SD+27) take place. In the event that these are not successful, a cash settlement attempt (SD+30-36) takes place. Should the cash settlement also not be successful, a further buy-in attempt (SD+37) is initiated and thereafter a second cash settlement attempt (SD+40-46) under the proviso that the fourth buy-in attempt has failed. The buy-in attempt and cash settlement are be repeated every 10 business days until (i) either a successful securities delivery or (ii) an effective cash settlement has taken place.

Penalties:

Penalties apply to (i) late deliveries on DAX stocks over the dividend record date and (ii) deliveries on CCP-eligible securities not delivered on the correct value date in connection with corporate actions with a cash value that can be determined immediately. The penalty is charged to the respective clearing member's account as of a counter-value of €5,000.

5. Risks and Risk Management in the Settlement Process

Learning Objective

3.2 Analyse the risks that arise at each stage of the settlement process post trade including the benefits and operational risks that can arise when using brokers and the additional actions that have to be taken when migrating customers

Finality of settlement is a key issue for market participants and it is important to understand why this is. In this section we explain and define what the risks are in the settlement process.

It is important to distinguish between cause and effect when talking about risks. It is also important that we begin to distinguish between the cause of risk and the risk itself. In the settlement process, and in most areas of securities processing, the ultimate risk is the crystallisation of a financial loss to either the client or the firm that you work for. Often it is the cause that is said to be the risk rather than the effect.

5.1 Causes that Might Crystallise the Definable Risk

There are multiple causes associated with the settlement process that could lead to the definable risk of financial loss; however, these causes are likely to be found under the following general headings:

- Default.
- Fraud.
- Process mismanagement errors.

5.1.1 Default

The default of a counterparty, whether that counterparty be a client or another market participant, is a traumatic event. It exposes all those associated with the counterparty to the prospect of crystallising a financial loss. This is because it could lead to many contracts having to be unwound or assets remaining uncollected.

It is for this reason that firms should employ regular credit checks on all their counterparties. The counterparties could include: brokers; sub-custodians; global custodians; clearing banks; clients; or even the companies that are employed to run the markets.

The introduction of CCPs in many of the global markets is an important initiative, as this removes the risk of default from the investor to the CCP.

In summary, whenever any type of asset transaction fails to settle, it is an important event. However, these events in and of themselves are not necessarily a risk or even the cause of risk. What they are is an exposure to an event that could come to pass, ie, a default. That is why it is important to ensure that any failed trade is investigated and settled as quickly as possible.

5.1.2 Fraud

Fraud can be a major contributor to the risk of a financial loss being crystallised. It is for this reason that, in the process of settlement, it is really important to get transactions settled as soon as possible so as to expose any fraud at the earliest opportunity. At the extreme, any failed trade has the potential for fraud as the cause of failure. In terms of settlement, fraud is more likely to be an issue in the OTC markets due to the fact that often in these markets settlement is a physical event, eg, delivery of transfer deeds and certificated securities.

However it is not unheard of for bearer bonds to be stolen and then sold on the open markets.

This underlines the importance of the (KYC) checks at the account opening stage and the ongoing regular checks when the circumstances surrounding a client change.

5.1.3 Process Mismanagement Errors

This is by far the most likely cause of exposure to the risk of a financial loss being crystallised.

Generally, a settlement failure is caused by a processing error or the mismanagement of the settlement process. The errors of mismanagement could have many labels, such as broker short of stock, cash not in account or shares not available for delivery. Whatever the cause, this could lead to the risk of a financial loss being crystallised.

These losses could be due to regulatory fines for shares being bought-in/sold-out together with the associated costs of such actions, or the failure could cause a cash overdraft to occur and so lead to a claim for interest.

5.2 Risks at Each Stage of the Settlement Process

The learning objective asks us to analyse the risks at each stage of the settlement process. If we review the settlement process as outlined in Section 1, it is difficult to imagine how it is possible for any settlement to fail due to the plethora of transaction-checking that takes place.

However, imagine the following if not processed correctly:

Step in the Process	What Could Go Wrong?	What is the Exposure?
Decision to trade	No decision made; decrease/increase decision wrong	Price of assets changes in the meantime; portfolio asset allocation incorrect; NAV value wrong; remedial action required
Order	Incorrect order size; incorrect price; wrong asset identified; unauthorised action	Price of assets changes in the meantime; portfolio asset allocation incorrect; NAV value wrong; remedial action required
Execution	Incorrect buy or sell sign applied; timing of execution incorrect; duplicated execution	Price of assets changes in the meantime; portfolio asset allocation incorrect; NAV value wrong; remedial action required

Transaction matching	Trade incorrectly accepted as correct; any element incorrectly matched; any element incorrectly declined	Price of assets changes in the meantime; portfolio is wrongly apportioned; NAV value exposed; remedial action required
Allegation	Not alleged in time; incorrect trade alleged	Value of assets changes in the meantime; portfolio is wrongly apportioned; NAV value exposed; remedial action required
Affirmation	Accepted as good trade when wrong	Value of assets changes in the meantime; trade is wrongly apportioned; NAV value exposed; remedial action required
Verification	Incorrect client allocation Incorrect client applied Duplicated transaction	Value of assets changes in the meantime; portfolio is wrongly apportioned; NAV value exposed; remedial action required
Primary settlement instructions	Late instructions; any element incorrect	Contractual settlement date may not be met; exposure to asset not being available on due date; remedial action required
Trade capture	Wrong data causes exception processing; exception queues not cleared quickly; duplicate trades not noticed	Contractual settlement date may not be met; exposure to asset not being available on due date; remedial action required
Secondary trade matching	Trade incorrectly accepted as correct; any element incorrectly matched	Contractual settlement date may not be met; exposure to asset not being available on due date; remedial action required
Secondary settlement instructions	Late instructions; any element incorrect	Contractual settlement date may not be met; exposure to asset not being available on due date; remedial action required
Tertiary trade matching	Late instructions; any element incorrect	Contractual settlement date may not be met; exposure to asset not being available on due date; remedial action required
Settlement	Settlement fails	Exposure to credit risk; exposure to potential fraud; exposure to buy-in/sell-out being invoked

5.3   Benefits of Using a Broker

Having explored what could be processed incorrectly and thereby lead to the risk of incurring a financial loss we have to review what the benefits are of using a broker.

Primarily the benefits are to do with the process of executing the trade instructions. We have already seen that, having made the decision to do something specific with an asset, an order to transact the purchase and sale of the asset has to be placed into the marketplace. Using a broker will ensure that the order will be channeled through the most appropriate mechanism either by using an electronic trading system linked directly to the marketplace or via a market maker.

The order itself can be a very complex thing to handle. The way a transaction is handled depends very much on the marketplace and there are many marketplaces that will only transact business in securities in parcels known as board lots. These board lot sizes are set by the local authorities. There may also be limited trading allowed to overseas investors, and the broker will be able to help keep the investor aligned to these policies.

The order may have significant parameters associated with it. These might be that:

- a **limit order** has been set on the price of the asset. This limit will constrain the broker to the price at which they can sell or buy the asset. There will likely be an agreed time constraint on this order limit – this being set to the day of issuance of the order – and, if the order is unfulfilled by the end of the business day, the order becomes null and void
- there could be an instruction something like **fill-or-kill**. This means that the transaction has to be completed in full on the day of issuance of the order otherwise the order is killed (cancelled) in its entirety
- there may be an instruction to deal **at best**, which means that the broker has to ensure that they are getting the best price they can for the client
- a limit is an order to buy or sell securities at a specified price. A limit order may also be placed **with discretion**, meaning the floor-broker executing the order may use their discretion to buy or sell at a set amount beyond the limit if they feel it is necessary to fill the order
- a **stop order** is an order either to buy a stock at the market price when the price rises to a certain level or to sell a stock at the market price when the price falls to a certain level
- a **stop limit order** is similar to a stop order, but it becomes a limit order, rather than a market order, when the security trades at the price specified on the stop
- a **day order** expires at the end of the day
- a **good-till-cancelled (GTC)** or **open order** remains in effect until it is either filled or cancelled.

Not all exchanges accept all these types of orders.

5.3.1 Four Types of Global Discretionary Order Execution Qualifiers

Typically, around the world, there are four discretionary order execution qualifiers that may be employed:

1. **All-or-none** orders are market or limit orders that must be executed in their entirety or not at all.
2. **Fill-or-kill** orders must be executed immediately and in their entirety or else the order is cancelled.
3. **Immediate-or-cancel (IOC)** orders are market or limit orders that are to be executed immediately in whole or in part and any portion that cannot be executed as soon as the order hits the trading floor is cancelled.
4. **Not-held (NH)** orders are market or limit orders in which the customer gives the trader or floor-broker time and price discretion; this qualifier, often invoked for trading in overseas markets when exchange hours are past your client's bedtime, does not hold the broker responsible for missing the best price.

When the order is of a particularly large nature, the broker has to ensure, as best they can, that the way they deal with the order does not affect the price of the asset either up or down. Hence, to handle the complexity of orders, a broker must have the appropriate expertise to be competent at trade order management.

5.4   Managing the Causes of Risk in the Settlement Process

The risk of crystallising a financial loss in the settlement process is addressed via several means at the market level. These are outlined in the following table.

Step in the Process	What Could Go Wrong?	What is the Management of the Exposure?
Decision to trade	No decision made; decrease/increase decision wrong	Management of the process to ensure that decisions taken are executed and signed off by management. Process needs to ensure that decisions are acted upon correctly
Order	Incorrect order size; incorrect price; wrong asset identified; unauthorised action	Order management and sign-off by managers of the process. Process needs to ensure that decisions are correctly authorised and acted upon correctly
Execution	Incorrect buy or sell sign applied; timing of execution incorrect; duplicated execution	Order management and sign-off by managers of the process. Process needs to ensure that decisions are acted upon correctly
Transaction matching	Trade incorrectly accepted as correct; any element incorrectly matched	Processes need to ensure that matching criteria are acted upon correctly Automated matching processes and exception queues are important components
Allegation	Not alleged in time; incorrect trade alleged	Process needs to ensure that trades are authenticated and are alleged within the market timeframes correctly
Affirmation	Accepted as good trade when wrong	Procedures need to ensure that only authenticated trades are confirmed
Verification	Incorrect client allocation; incorrect client applied; duplicated transaction	Procedures need to ensure that the management of the process is properly applied. Linkage of order process to verification process to alleviate errors is be desirable
Primary settlement instructions	Late instructions; any element incorrect	Process needs to ensure that SSIs are updated regularly and acted upon correctly
Trade capture	Wrong data causes exception processing; exception queues not cleared quickly; duplicate trades not noticed	Procedures need to ensure that exception processes are carried out in a timely manner
Secondary trade matching	Trade incorrectly accepted as correct; any element incorrectly matched	Processes need to ensure that matching criteria are acted upon correctly Automated matching processes and exception queues are important components

Secondary settlement instructions	Late instructions; any element incorrect	Process needs to ensure that SSIs are updated regularly and acted upon correctly
Tertiary trade matching	Late instructions; any element incorrect; unavailability of assets	Processes need to ensure that matching criteria are acted upon correctly. Asset shortages need to be reported. Automated matching processes and exception queues are important components
Settlement	Settlement fails	Reported with reason as soon as possible

In securities markets with high volumes, the turnover in a particular asset may exceed the total amount of the issue itself. This fact, allied to the issue being rather illiquid (investors retaining their holdings in custody and not actively trading the issue) may cause a blockage in the settlement chain.

It may be appropriate for the market to settle trades on a net basis rather than a gross (ie, trade-for-trade) basis. Depending on the volumes, the options are as follows:

- Trade-for-trade.
- Bilateral netting.
- Multilateral netting.
- Continuous net settlement (CNS).
- Real-time gross settlement (RTGS).

5.5   New Customers

Another risk mitigation process surrounds the introduction of new customers to the settlement process. New customers should have been subject to full credit/AMI reviews before being accepted and before accounts are opened. They will have returned any agreements/documentation where this is relevant.

In some cases they will have existing positions and assets at another counterparty that they may wish to be transferred to their new broker/custodian/agent.

Great care must be taken to ensure that any migration of a new customer's positions and assets is managed efficiently and accurately. There will need to be:

- a migration timetable
- an agreed list of positions with the customer and their current agent
- an agreed list of assets (including any cash and/or physical assets)
- an agreed list of outstanding benefits being accrued and that still need to be received
- an agreed level of exposure to risk and trading limits by the client
- collateral management during the process
- closures and re-opening of stock loans, overdrafts, etc, as appropriate
- agreement of final settlement payments for closing positions
- final reconciliation of incoming positions.

In addition, there will need to be an updating of static data, such as settlement instructions, commissions and contact details.

6. Central Securities Depositories (CSDs) and Central Clearing Counterparties (CCPs)

Learning Objective

3.12 Describe the functional features of a: central securities depository (CSD); international central securities depository (ICSD); central clearing counterparty (CCP)

6.1 Central Securities Depository (CSD)

A central securities depository (CSD) is an institution that is set up to do many things in relation to the trading and settlement in securities.

The principal function of a CSD is to centralise the immobilisation or dematerialisation of securities and to facilitate the settlement of transactions in securities in an electronic book entry form in a particular geographic market place. Securities depositories maintain the record of settlements and beneficial ownership and act as a conduit for the settlement of qualifying securities. CSDs often hold the legal record of shareholders. Globally, CSDs will likely have the capability to perform safe custody and post-settlement servicing of securities and information with regard to corporate events.

In this fashion they could be said to take on the role of a settlement agent. Globally, these settlement agents may take on other roles such as that of clearing and provide a central counterparty facility for trade clearance.

An international CSD (ICSD) such as Euroclear, Clearstream and the Depository Trust Co. is able to facilitate settlement across borders by maintaining links with local CSDs. They also perform the role of a CSD to their local markets, eg, Clearstream acts as a CSD for German and Luxembourg securities.

Euroclear and Clearstream are also the dominant settlement agents for eurobonds and international bond issues.

There are many services provided by CSDs, and this also extends into areas related to custody services, such as that of a clearing and central counterparty.

6.2   Central Clearing Counterparty (CCP)

The classic definition of a central clearing counterparty (also known as a clearing house) is an entity that interposes itself between the counterparties to a trade, acting as the buyer to every seller and the seller to every buyer.

For example in London, LCH.Clearnet and SIX x-clear both provide a central clearing service to the LSE and other major exchanges and the associated CSDs.

LCH.Clearnet is an independent clearing house, serving major international exchanges and platforms, as well as a range of OTC markets. It clears a broad range of asset classes including securities, exchange traded derivatives, commodities, energy, freight, interest rate swaps, credit default swaps and euro and sterling-denominated bonds and repos and works closely with market participants and exchanges to identify and develop clearing services for new asset classes.

By clearing through LCH.Clearnet, LSE clearing members benefit from counterparty risk management, settlement netting, straight-through processing (STP) and counterparty anonymity. LCH.Clearnet's direct connection to the CSD means the customer benefits from the lowest settlement costs and therefore the most efficient corporate event processing is offered.

Six x-clear Ltd is part of the SIX Group, the integrated Swiss financial market infrastructure provider. As CCP, SIX x-clear offers clearing and risk management services in the cash equity and bond markets.

The CCP sits in the middle of a trade, assuming the counterparty risk involved when two parties (or members) trade. When the trade is registered with the CCP, it becomes the legal counterparty to the trade, ensuring the financial performance; if one of the parties fails, LCH.Clearnet steps in. By assuming the counterparty risk, the CCP underpins many important financial markets, facilitating trading and increasing confidence within the market.

This principle and structure is replicated in most of the global markets.

The key functions and benefits of CCPs is that they offer a number of economic and risk-reducing benefits. A key benefit of central clearing is the multilateral netting of transactions between market participants, which simplifies outstanding exposures compared with a complex web of bilateral trades. Perhaps the most important benefit, however, is the role that a CCP plays in the event of one of its members defaulting: CCPs have a number of rules and resources in place to manage such a default in an orderly way.

Equity Settlement – Global Case Study

A clearing institution provides a centralised clearing service for securities traded on the local stock exchange system and as such becomes a central counterparty.

A central counterparty becomes the counterparty to the trade that has been made between two member firms on the dealing system or by market members and customers of a member firm who are not themselves members of the clearing house.

This process is known as novation and members may need to deposit margin until they honour the obligation of the delivery. The process also allows for netting.

The process can be illustrated by the following diagram:

Clearing Structure

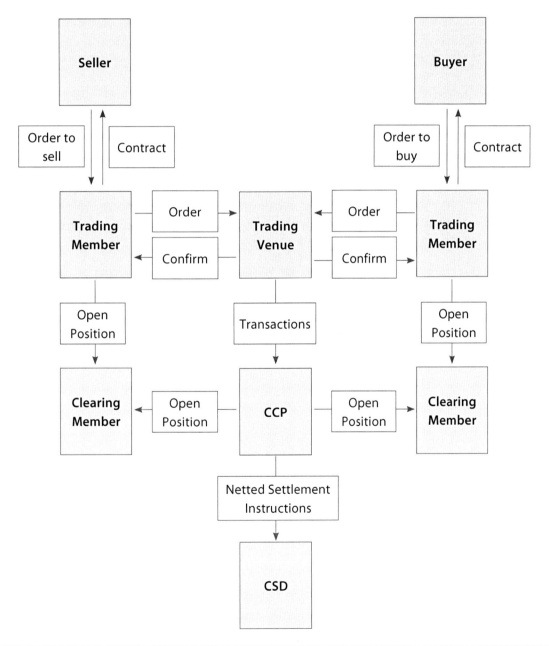

7. Registration

7.1 Options

Learning Objective

3.6 Describe the options for registration and the impact of options on the ability to receive benefits

7.1.1 Maintaining a Register

Registration is the process of registering the legal ownership of assets such as shares, units, stocks and bonds. Every company or entity that has unit holders, shareholders or bondholders has to maintain a register of the holders of their paper. This principle applies to all global issuers of shares and debt.

The issuer of shares or debt has the option to maintain the register of holders themselves or to employ an agent to do this for them. This agent is often called the company registrar or transfer agent. This is an organisation appointed by the company or the issuer of debt to record the names and addresses of the holders, together with the number of units, shares, stocks, or bonds they own. They are also obliged to make any changes to these holdings and record how and when those changes occurred.

They also provide many other services, including the distribution of benefits such as dividends and interest payments that become due to the registered holders.

They also act as the interface between the issuer and its holders of paper in terms of issuing information and paying benefits and entitlements.

An alternative to a separate company registrar is for the local CSD to act as the maintainer of the ownership details of the shares issued by a company. Essentially the same process happens, although other services, such as payment of benefits, may still be made by a separate agent acting on behalf of the company. If the register is maintained where both the record and payment of benefits can be handled, there will be less risk of delays and problems occurring in the receipt of those benefits by the right party.

Under the UK's FCA regulations, if a firm holds custody assets belonging to clients, it must make adequate arrangements to safeguard clients' ownership rights, especially in the event of the firm's insolvency and to prevent the use of custody assets belonging to a client on the firm's own account, except with the client's express consent. Firms must maintain appropriate and adequate organisational arrangements to minimise the risk of the loss or diminution of clients' safe custody assets, or the rights in connection with these, as a result of the misuse of the assets due to fraud, poor administration, inadequate record-keeping or negligence. Firms must effect appropriate registration or recording of legal title to a custody asset in the name of the client, unless the client has nominated a person to act on their behalf – in which case the assets may be registered in the name of that authorised person.

7.1.2   Book Entry or Physical

The options to effect a registration are either by book entry or by a physical means.

Most of the global markets now employ the book entry method as their main form of registration. This means that any change in the legal ownership of the underlying asset takes place electronically and on or near the actual settlement day. Simplistically, the seller of the asset has their account debited and the buyer of the asset has their account credited. However, the organisation that records the underlying legal ownership is required to have a technical infrastructure that can cope with the sophistication of recording the details of who the assets actually legally belong to and automated links to the local CSD, or an ICSD, or other such organisation.

The alternative method to electronic book entry is the maintaining of certificated records. The certificates bear the name of the legal owner and the number of shares that the certificate represents. These certificates will be uniquely numbered. The transfer of assets from one legal owner to another will be effected by some means that requires either the seller or the buyer or both to attest to the fact that they agree to the transfer by way of signing a deed of transfer. When a sale of the asset takes place, the certificate and, if required, a transfer form, are received by the registrar/transfer agent together with the details of the new owner. The old certificate is cancelled and a new one issued, with the register being simultaneously amended. If the seller has not sold all their holding, a certificate for the balance remaining in their name is issued to them.

This overall process is prone to time delays and these delays vary from country to country and can be anything from a few days to a few weeks depending upon the country.

For some assets, especially issues of debt, these certificates are better known as bonds and may not record the name of the legal owner. For this reason these bonds are referred to as bearer bonds which literally means that the bearer of the bond is the owner of the asset. However, it should be recognised that it is very common that the global markets will have both the book entry and physical registration methods operating at the same time.

There are certain terms that have become linked to the registration process, and it is important to understand what they mean. The terms we refer to are:

- dematerialised and
- immobilised.

These terms actually refer to the way that a particular country decides to deal with the problem of the existing certificates (and the production of new certificates) once that country has decided to use an electronic method for evidencing the legal ownership of an asset.

Dematerialised means that the local regime has taken the decision to cancel existing share certificates when the electronic record is created to evidence the legal ownership of the stocks and shares.

Immobilised means that the local regime will still issue certificates but that these certificates have to be held at a central location, eg, the Depository Trust Company (DTC) in the US.

Under either regime, it is still possible for some companies to issue physical share certificates to evidence legal ownership of the asset and also possible for a registered shareholder in a dematerialised regime to hold a share certificate. However, this does lead to complication when the holder wants to sell the asset.

Whatever regime or practice is adopted globally, it is essential that the changes in legal ownership are recorded as soon as is practicable. This is not only true because of today's regulatory regimes where firms are required to ensure the protection of client assets but also because of any subsequent benefits that might accrue to the legal owners.

7.2   Dematerialisation Drivers

Learning Objective

3.8   Identify key drivers behind changing from certificated settlement to a dematerialised status

Transactions in shares are processed in much the same way as with debt instruments, ie, trade confirmation is followed by instruction matching and then final settlement.

Across the global markets, shares are increasingly becoming immobilised or dematerialised. This enables shares to be delivered by book entry, rather than by physical transfer. This does lead to more efficient settlement and was one of the main recommendations put forward by the Group of 30, and subsequently advocated by the International Securities Services Association (ISSA) (see Appendix 1). The ISSA Recommendations 2000, which can be viewed in full at www.issanet.org/pdf/RecsStatus2001.pdf, contained Recommendation 5 which is shown below:

---

5. Reduction of Settlement Risk

The major risks in securities systems should be mitigated by five key measures, namely;

- *the implementation of real delivery versus payment*
- *the adoption of a trade date plus one settlement cycle in a form that does not increase operational risk*
- *the minimisation of funding and liquidity constraints by enabling stock lending and borrowing, broad based cross collateralisation, the use of repos and netting as appropriate*
- *the enforcement of scripless settlement*
- *the establishment of mandatory trade matching and settlement performance measures.*

Source: ISSA

The removal of certificated settlement is a key operational risk mitigation method. Not only is the speed of settlement improved but the risk of a fraud being perpetrated due to lost or missing certificates is reduced. The inconvenience of applying for indemnities and duplicate certificates is also removed.

In addition, paperless settlement creates greater capacity in the markets themselves, as clearly the delay in settlement, sometimes of many weeks, does little to attract issuers or, indeed, investors.

The benefits of paperless settlement can be seen in the settlement rates (as provided by benchmarking organisations, such as GSCS Benchmarks, which show settlement rates on due date in the upper nineties in percentage terms.

8. Fund Settlement

8.1 Trading and Settlement of Funds

Learning Objective

3.3 Understand how to trade, clear and settle UCITS and other types of funds

In this section of the workbook we will be reviewing and discussing the world of trading and settlement of funds and how that differs from the trading and settlement of stocks and shares. The term 'funds' has become well-known within our industry. What is not so well known is what the typical life cycle of trading and settlement of funds is.

Firstly we should understand what, in the modern day, a fund is. In Europe, a collective term that is used to describe what a fund is, and which has become accepted as a definitive description of a fund, is Undertakings for Collective Investments in Transferable Securities (UCITS). This has a regulatory background in as much as such fund vehicles may be marketed across Europe.

But what actually is a UCIT or fund?

A UCIT or an investment fund is a vehicle created to allow a number of separate and unrelated investors, such as a group of individuals or companies, to make investments together. By pooling their capital into an investment fund, investors are able to share costs and benefit from the advantages of investing larger amounts, including the possibility of achieving a broader range of different assets and as such spread their risks. There are many possible ways in which an investment fund can be set up and operated. They are often designed to appeal to specific investor needs.

The number of investors in a fund is not fixed. Investment funds can be designed in different forms; for example they might globally be called an investment company, or a unit trust, an OEIC, a SICAV, a mutual fund or an ETF. They all have slightly different characteristics. Funds can be initially set up with an indefinite lifespan or for a fixed period. They can hold traditional financial assets such as shares and bonds, or investments as exotic as vintage wines, paintings and copyright rights. They can generate income for investors or seek to maximise the capital value of their investments. They can be open for sale to any individual investor or be restricted to sophisticated investors such as financial institutions.

Before we move onto the actual lifecycle of trading and settlement, it is appropriate that the reader should be aware of the number of industry participants involved in the lifecycle. Below is a schematic that attempts to depict the industry participants that will be involved in the fund's lifecycle and which will be referred to in this chapter. It is into this world that the investor enters when making an investment into a UCIT.

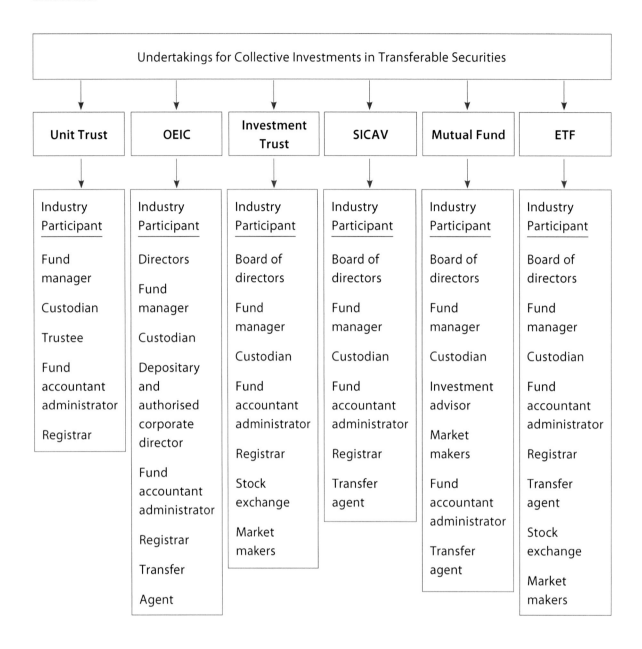

8.1.1 The Lifecycle

The term UCIT could be said to be the collective noun for that which we would probably know better as investment funds. Because most funds are issued by financial institutions, such as insurance companies, wealth management companies and banks, they have also come to be known as proprietary funds.

The lifecycle of a trade in a UCIT or investment funds depends on two main factors, these being the type of:

1. fund being traded (eg, unit trust, OEIC, SICAV, mutual, ETF)
2. investor making the trade (eg, institution, private investor).

8.1.2 Type of Fund (Unit Trust)

The lifecycle and settlement of funds depends on the type of fund being traded and the type of investor conducting the trade. Although all of the above-mentioned examples are typical types of investment funds, there could be a different trading and settlement convention aligned to each type of fund. To understand this better, we have chosen to use a unit trust as an example. The following will help to understand better the type of fund concerned.

A unit trust is a legal entity set up under the UK trust laws. The trust is one that allows investors to pool their money. The sponsor of a fund is typically an institution such as a fund management company, a bank or an insurance company. The sponsor of the fund, better known as the manager of the fund, has to appoint an independent trustee (typically banks or insurance companies) who is responsible for the safe-keeping of the pooled assets, ensuring that a register of holders is maintained and that the fund adheres to its investment policies and aims. The trustee must be an entity that is independent from the fund sponsor. Typically the fund will be allowed to invest in a varied range of companies and regions of the world, in line with the objectives set out in the trust deed.

It has to be said that unit trusts have a fairly complicated structure. They are effectively a large pot of money split up into different units, which investors buy from and sell to the managers of the fund. These managers are effectively the market maker. Because they are open-ended, there is no limit on the amount of money the fund can accept, so the number of units in existence will constantly vary in response to investor demand. The manager of the fund is allowed to cancel units or create units whenever they need to but only with the authority of the trustee. This is an important difference to note between buying and selling shares where there might several market makers in the same share, as opposed to only one market maker for proprietary funds.

Pricing of Units

The pricing of the units is based on the NAV of the fund at a given point in time. The price is typically determined by the manager of the fund on a daily basis, which might be 12 noon each business day. There is what is called the bid-offer spread. When you buy units in a unit trust, you'll pay the offer price, whereas if you choose to sell your units, you'll sell at the bid price. This is known as dual pricing. There are also pricing conventions known as historic pricing and forward pricing, and the manager of the fund can choose either method on which to base the unit price. This choice obviously has to be made clear to the investor at the time the fund is launched and before any subsequent transactions take place. Once the choice is made, the method is not normally changed.

Historic pricing – this means that the unit price used to determine the price at which units will be bought or sold will be based on the NAV of the fund, calculated at the last valuation point.

- The advantage is that buyers know exactly how many units they are going to get for their investment and sellers know exactly how much money they will get for their units.
- Managers are open to the risk that the trust's assets may increase in value between the valuation and dealing points, in which case the units will be priced at a value less than they are worth in NAV terms.

Forward pricing – this is the normal practice and entails basing prices on a NAV calculated at the next valuation point. So someone buying units at 4.00pm in a trust which uses a 12.00pm valuation point will buy on the basis of a price calculated on the next day's 12.00pm valuation.

- The disadvantage is that buyers do not know how many units they will get for their money and sellers do not know how much money they will get for their units until after the next valuation point. To an extent they are buying and selling blind.
- The managers like it, of course, because there is no risk of mispricing.

This is of course completely different from buying stock and shares, where the dealing price is known before the deal is struck.

8.1.3   Unit Trust Lifecycle (Private Investor)

The trade-to-settlement lifecycle of a unit trust has a fundamental similarity to the trade-to- settlement lifecycle of stocks and shares. This similarity is the decision to trade. After that the lifecycle is quite different. What comes after the decision to trade and the following trade-to-settlement lifecycle, depends upon the type of investor making that decision and the type of fund that the investor is dealing in. It should also be noted that a major difference between unit trusts and normal stocks and shares is that although there are many daily priced unit trust funds, some funds will only deal on a monthly, quarterly, or twice yearly basis. This might be the case if they invest in assets such as property, which can take a longer time to sell. Having said that, in the UK there are FCA regulations that govern when any particular type of fund should perform valuation points and that these valuation points should be clearly defined in the prospectus of the fund.

Units in unit trust funds are not listed or dealt in on any investment exchange. A private investor who makes the decision to trade in a particular unit trust will have the option to contact either their stockbroker or financial adviser to place the trade, or alternatively they contact the manager of the fund themselves. This decision of which route to take now has its own colloquialisms these being:

- **Consumer to Business (C2B)** – ie, the private investor trades directly with the fund provider.
- **Consumer to Business to Business (C2B2B)** – ie, the private investor contacts an intermediary who in turn trades with the fund provider.

The method of how to place the order with the manager of the unit trust will normally be set out in the prospectus of the unit trust.

Typically, the investor has to contact the dealing office of the manager during normal office hours (eg, 9.00am until 5.30pm) on any business day during which the manager receives requests for the buying and selling of units. The time and price at which a deal takes place depends on the manager of the fund. But this method must meet the local regulator's requirements affecting the pricing of units.

Unit Trust Lifecycle (Private Investor: C2B)

Buying Units – it is important to remember that when buying units in a unit trust the investor is effectively buying the units from the manager of the fund. The manager is therefore acting as the market maker of their fund. They are also the counterparty for the investor and in effect also the clearing house for the fund. Units might typically be purchased by sending a completed application form to the manager of the fund, by telephoning the manager's dealing desk, or by an online application. Any telephone calls are likely to be recorded. There will almost certainly be a minimum investment level attached to the buying of units.

When buying into a fund for the first time, whether using the postal application form, phone call to the dealing desk, or the manager's online application facility, the investor will be asked to instruct the manager to invest a lump sum of money into the fund, eg, not state a specific number of units to be acquired, but to buy the maximum amount of units that a given sum of money will buy. This is due to the fact that the manager is not likely to know what the unit price is until they have processed the application. They will also be asked to complete an extensive fact finding application form. This process is for either a private investor or a corporate/institutional investor.

The manager will not accept an application for units to the value of less than the minimum subscription amount as defined in the fund's prospectus. If for any reason a holding falls below the minimum allowed, the manager is likely to reserve the right to redeem the units on behalf of the unitholder. The manager will probably also reserve the right to reduce or waive the minimum investment levels to give the themselves maximum scope for decision making.

The manager will normally also reserve the right to reject, on reasonable grounds, any application for units in whole or in part. The manager will return any money sent, or the balance, for the purchase of units, at the risk of the applicant.

Application Details – the personal details that the investor has to provide to the manager are quite extensive. This is due mainly to the money laundering regulations but there are also some important tax implications that need to be satisfied. In order to explain the complexity of the details required, we have reproduced the type of data that might be asked for in a varied range of fund types, eg, unit trust, OEIC, SICAV, investment trust, with variable investment aims, eg, income funds, property funds, tracker funds.

Typical data required will include the following:

Shareholder Details
Title (Mr. Mrs. Miss. Ms. Other)
First names in full
Surname/organisation name
Permanent address
Postcode
Date of birth
Ditto above for other associated shareholders
Home phone number
Mobile phone number
Email address
If investment on behalf of a minor (under 18) full name of minor
Confirmation of beneficial ownership required
Direct Debit Instruction
Name of bank or building society
Address of bank or building society
Postcode
Name(s) of account holder(s)
Bank or building society account number
Branch sort code
Date of instruction
Investment details
Fund name
Lump sum invested £ (minimum level will be stated on form)
Unit type required (accumulation, income, etc)
Eligibility Declarations
Some funds will need the investor to be sure that they are eligible to invest in the fund
Declare whether individual or body corporate
Signature and date of all applicants

Corporate Declarations and Undertakings and Indemnities
If investing in UK property funds, corporate investors will be asked to complete certain undertakings regarding the level of investment versus the size of the overall fund.

Gross payment Declarations
Certain unit holders may be able to benefit from receiving income gross. They will be asked to confirm that they are: • a company resident in the UK • a UK registered pension scheme • UK charities • an account provider of child trust funds (CTFs) • an account manager of individual savings accounts (ISAs) • other qualifying investor.
Declaration, undertaking and indemnity from nominees: • Units registered are held as nominee for a beneficial owner(s). • Beneficial owner is one of the above types. • Nominee has taken sufficient steps to ensure eligibility for gross payment. • Undertakings obtained to immediately inform the manager of any changes to status.

Tax Regulations
Tax regulations require the manager of the fund to collect information about an investor's tax residency. The manager will therefore ask the investor to complete details relating to their status as an individual or corporate investor.
The term 'tax regulations' refers to regulations created to enable automatic exchange of information and will include the Foreign Account Tax Compliance Act (FATCA) and other agreements entered into between the UK and its Crown Protectorates, its overseas territories and the Organisation for Economic Co-operation and Development (OECD).

Individual Self-Certification:
• Individual(s) will be asked to inform the manager of all the countries where they are regarded as resident for tax purposes. • They will be asked to provide the associated tax reference number(s). • If they are resident in the US for tax purposes they will be asked to provide their US Tax ID number. • If they are not resident in any country for tax purposes they will be asked to signify this (tick box).

Declaration:
The investor will be asked to sign a declaration that the information provided, that the information is accurate and complete. They will need to provide: • name • permanent residence address • place of birth • National Insurance number (UK residents only) • signature • date signed.

> **Entity Self-Certification:**
>
> **Tax Residency**
>
> - The entity(s) will be asked to inform the manager of all the countries where they are regarded as resident for tax purposes.
> - They will be asked to provide the associated tax reference number(s).
> - If they are resident in the US for tax purposes they will be asked to provide their US Tax ID number.
>
> **Organisation's FATCA Classification**
>
> The entity will be asked to identify themselves from the following:
>
> - Exempt beneficial owner.
> - Participating foreign financial institution.
> - Non-participating foreign financial institution.
> - UK financial institution or partner jurisdiction financial institution.
> - Financial institution resident in the US or in a US Territory.
> - Deemed compliant foreign financial institution (besides those listed above).
> - Active non-financial foreign entity.
> - Passive non-financial foreign entity.
> - Excepted non-financial foreign entity.
> - US non-financial entity.
>
> **Organisation's classification under other applicable tax regulations**
>
> Similar with the US FATCA rules, the entity will be asked to identify themselves under other applicable tax regulations.
>
> **Declaration:**
>
> The entity will be asked to sign and date that all the data supplied is accurate and complete. The person signing the declaration will be asked to identify the capacity under which they sign.

Confirmations – a contract or confirmation note giving details of the units purchased and the price used to purchase the units will be issued to the investor no later than the next business day after the dealing day on which an application to purchase units is processed by the manager.

Cash Settlement – orders to purchase units will not normally be processed until cleared funds are received by the manager. This means that if a cheque is sent to the manager, the order may not be processed until the cheque clears. If the orders are made by phone or online, the manager will ask for the investor's bank details, so that the cash funds required to pay for the order will generally be available to the manager before the end of that business day, essentially meaning the earliest possible dealing day will be achieved by the investor. The settlement timeframes depend on the type of fund being purchased, but generally the timeframe for settlement will be T+1 to T+4.

Registration – the trustee of the find has the legal responsibility to maintain a register of holders. The trustee may however, delegate this task to a third party but they cannot delegate the legal responsibility for the quality and integrity of the register. Details of the purchaser, such as names and addresses, units held, date purchased and date sold, will be placed on a register maintained by the manager. All unit trust managers must ensure that a register of all unit holders is maintained. Globally, registration services have moved forward very dramatically in the funds world. There are now many third-party providers of these services. This advance has brought with it many technological advances as well and many of these providers will have the ability to hold electronic records of unit trust unit holders. They could also have direct links to an automated order routing/settlement platform for funds.

Selling Units: C2B – when an investor wishes to sell (redeem) their units, they first have to contact the manager of the fund. Each manager will have their own terms and conditions that regulate the selling process. Generally, however, the investor can instruct the manager of the fund or their financial adviser of their wish to sell units/shares. This would normally be done in writing or by telephone. These instructions will require the unit holder to send to the manager a signed renunciation form. In some instances it may be that an original certificate needs to be renounced and sent to the manager.

Depending upon the terms and conditions of the fund the manager will cancel (redeem) the holdings on the day of receipt of the instructions, providing that these instructions are received before the fund's next valuation point.

The dealing price the unit trust investor receives will be the bid price as determined by the manager of the fund under the terms and conditions of the unit trust.

Cash Settlement – generally the manager of the fund will either send a cheque or provide for electronic transfer for the value of the proceeds to the investor by the close of business four working days later, providing that they have received the investor's signed confirmation. If (after the investor has sold units) the investor has less than the minimum investment allowed by the terms and conditions, the manager may cancel (redeem) the investor's remaining units on their behalf.

Unit Trust Lifecycle (Private Investor: C2B2B)

Buying Units – in this instance the private investor contacts a stockbroker or financial intermediary with their order to buy units. In order to be able to trade via the intermediary the investor will have to open an account or already have an account opened with the intermediary. At this stage the regulatory parameters will have to be adhered to by both the investor and the intermediary with regards to account opening. This of course means that they will follow the rules as set out in this workbook.

In this day and age it is highly likely that the intermediary will have some form of automation and electronic links that will allow the investor to make the required investment decision and place an order with the intermediary. If there is no automation available then a paper based application will have to be made.

At this point it is the intermediary who will place the order with the manager of the fund on behalf of the investor. On the other side of the intermediary's proprietary system, it is highly likely that they will have automated links or interfaces with the manager of the fund's systems. In this way, STP for the order can be achieved.

Application Details – the application details required by the manager of the fund will still have to be adhered to. All the facts that are shown in the typical application form above will be relevant. These will have to be passed on by the intermediary to the fund manager of the fund in some shape or form. Depending upon the technical abilities of the infrastructure of both intermediary and the fund manager, this could be achieved automatically, semi-automatically or manually.

Confirmations – confirmation will be sent by the intermediary that the deal has been placed. In turn the intermediary will receive an agreed type of confirmation from the fund manager.

Cash Settlement – the investor will have had to fund their cash account with the intermediary at the time of placing the order. This is likely to be achieved by using a debit card that is linked to the investor's external bank account or by direct debit mechanisms. Cheques may still be acceptable; this depends on the intermediary. In the case of a cheque being used by the investor, this will have an impact on the dealing date and eventual settlement date due to the normal cheque clearance requirements.

Registration – globally registration services have moved forward very dramatically in the funds world. There are now many third-party providers of these services. This has brought with it many technological advances as well and many of these providers will have the ability to hold electronic records of unit trust unit holders. They could also have direct links to an automated settlement platform for funds.

Having said this, the investor still has a decision to make prior to using an intermediary. This decision relates to the name on register that is to be used. The investor may decide to have the units registered in their own name or they may elect to use the nominee name of the intermediary. If they use their own name they will receive a statement and any subsequent corporate events notices directly from the manager of the fund. If they use the intermediary's nominee name they will receive these details from the intermediary. In the UK many fund distributors and fund sponsors now have direct links to such third-party providers for both registration and settlement.

Selling Units: C2B2B – when an investor wishes to sell (redeem) their units, they first have to contact the intermediary, using the mechanisms available. In turn the intermediary has to inform the manager of the fund. Each manager will have their own terms and conditions that regulate the selling process. If the investor had decided to have the units registered in their own name, the unit holder will be required to give the intermediary a signed renunciation form. In some instances it may be that an original certificate needs to be renounced and sent to the intermediary. If the investor had decided to use the nominee name of the intermediary, the intermediary will have to complete the necessary renunciation.

Depending upon the terms and conditions of the fund, the manager will cancel (redeem) the investor's holdings on the day of receipt of their instructions, providing that they are received before the fund's next valuation point. The dealing price the unit trust investor receives will be the bid price as determined by the manager of the fund under the terms and conditions of the unit trust.

Cash Settlement – generally, the manager of the fund will either send a cheque or provide for electronic transfer for the value of the proceeds to the investor by the close of business four working days later, providing that they have received the investor's signed confirmation. If (after the investor has sold units) the investor has less than the minimum investment allowed by the terms and conditions, the manager may cancel (redeem) the investor's remaining units on their behalf.

8.1.4   Lifecycle of a Unit Trust (Corporate/Institutional Investor)

As units in unit trust funds are not listed or dealt in on any investment exchange, any corporate or institutional investor still has a decision to make about how they will route the trade to the manager of the fund. They can also choose whether to use an intermediary or, alternatively, they can contact the manager of the fund themselves.

Again, the decision of which route to take also has its own colloquialisms these being;

- **Business to Business (B2B)** – the corporate or institutional investor trades directly with the fund provider.
- **Business to Business to Business (B2B2B)** – the corporate or institutional investor contacts an intermediary who in turn trades with the fund provider.

Trade and Settlement Lifecycle

Almost all of which has already been written about the lifecycle for a private investor who wishes to invest in a unit trust will apply to the corporate/institutional investor. It is for this reason that we will not reiterate each process here. Having said this it is important to mention that there is evidence to suggest that much of the professional corporate investor activity has moved away from unit trust and OEICs and has moved towards ETFs which we explore in Section 8.1.5 of this chapter.

The B2B area of the funds marketplace is highly automated. Proprietary systems to fully automate the processes we have outlined are now in place. In the UK, Europe, the US and the rest of the developed funds markets, sponsors or distributors of funds will contract with various third party service providers to provide a fund supermarket for the institutional investors. So through the lifecycle of decision, execution, settlement and registration there is automation.

It is important to state that we have attempted to describe the fundamental processes involved in the lifecycle so that practitioners in the world of global securities operations understand the underlying processes that occur, because with the advent of almost total automation in the funds world, much of this understanding will be lost, due to the automation. Automation, of course, is not a bad thing, but the loss of the understanding of what is fundamentally going on in the background could be.

8.1.5   Other Fund Types

Open-Ended Investment Company (OEIC)

Three main factors influenced the introduction of the OEICs in the UK. Firstly, the British investment management skills were seen as a potentially valuable producer of revenue to the UK retail market from Europe. Secondly, European Union (EU) legislature had introduced the machinery for the cross-border marketing of investment funds within the EU, through the UCITS passport. Thirdly, there was considerable incomprehension in Europe of the concept of a trust, on which the unit trust is based. For there to be a British retail investment export, it could not take the same trust form as a unit trust.

To overcome this, the British Treasury consulted the investment industry widely on the introduction of an investment vehicle in corporate form and OEICs were born.

An OEIC is an investment company with variable capital (ICVC). Although OEICs and unit trusts operate in a similar way, there are three distinct differences between them. Firstly a unit trust is governed by trust law, whereas an OEIC is governed by company law. Secondly a unit trust issues units whereas an OEIC (because of its company status) issues shares.

The third difference is that OEICs will almost certainly be set up so as to enable the manager to quote a single price at which an investor will buy and sell shares, as opposed to the dual pricing convention of bid and offer (buy and sell) prices that a unit trust will quote.

The management structure of an OEIC is similar but different to that of a unit trust. For instance an OEIC has an authorised corporate director (ACD) which has similar responsibilities to that of a unit trust Manager. It also has a depositary. The depositary has the same duties and legal responsibility as a trustee of a unit trust has. The regulations say that the ACD and depositary must be independent of each other.

From a trade to settlement lifecycle point of view, the buying and selling of shares in an OEIC takes much the same form as that of buying and selling of units in a unit trust. Because of this we do not need to repeat the processes again.

Société d'Investissement À Capital Variable (SICAV)

A SICAV is an open-ended collective investment scheme common in Western Europe, especially Luxemburg, Switzerland, Italy, Spain, Belgium, Malta, France and the Czech Republic. Société d'investissement à capital variable can be translated as an 'investment company with variable capital'. These funds are regulated under the UCITS directives from the EU but each country will have its own regulatory authority to oversee the conduct of the funds.

These funds are essentially the same as a UK OEIC, although there are some structural differences. However, from an operations point of view, the processes involved in the trading to settlement lifecycle are the same as with their UK counterparts. SICAVs are increasingly being cross-border marketed in the EU under the UCITS directive.

Mutual Funds

A mutual fund is the equivalent North American version of the European UCITS schemes. Mutual funds in the US are issued in accordance with the US Securities Act of 1933. This act was passed to ensure that all new securities offered to the public are described in adequate detail in the registration statement and prospectus. The SEC is the federal regulatory agency responsible for enforcing the act.

These funds are very active and popular in both the US and Canada among other countries. All other countries will have their own regulatory agencies that oversee the issue and running of the funds.

Mutual funds are investment schemes, similar to an OEIC. Though there are three different types of mutual funds, ie, open-ended, unit investment trust, and closed-ended, the most common is the open-ended fund. They work on the same principle as an OEIC in as much as they are an investment company that issues redeemable shares. From an operations processing point of view, the processes involved in the trading to settlement lifecycle are the same as with their UK counterparts.

Investment Trusts

Investment trusts are set up as companies and traded on a stock exchange. As with any company quoted on the stock market, investment trusts have to publish an annual report and audited accounts. They also have a board of directors to which the manager of the trust is accountable. When you invest in an investment trust, you become a shareholder in that company.

Investment trusts have been around since the 1860s and they have often been more popular with some investors than ICVC funds, because they have traditionally had lower ongoing charges than unit trusts, OEICs, SICAVs and other types of UCITS and therefore the potential for producing higher returns.

There are important structural differences between OEICs, SICAVs unit trusts and investment trusts. Investment trusts are closed-ended investments, meaning they issue a fixed number of shares when they are set up, which investors can then buy and sell on the stock market.

Like other UCITS the fundamental value of an investment trust is its NAV which is the total sum of the investment trust's holdings, minus any liabilities. However, there are other elements involved. Because shares in an investment trust are traded on the stock market, the price of its shares is based on what investors think the investment trust is worth, rather than the strict value of the assets it holds. There is also the normal market supply and demand issue that comes into play. If a market maker is being hit with lots of sales, they will lower the price to try and attract some buyers. The converse is also true. As with any shares listed on a stock market investor sentiment has an effect. If investors are generally in a bullish or bearish frame of mind it will impact the share price of an investment trust. So the trust can be undervalued or overvalued compared to its NAV.

Because investment trusts are companies that are traded on a stock market, the normal trade-to-settlement lifecycle is that which applies to the local market place.

Exchange-Traded Funds (ETFs)

Exchange-traded funds (ETFs) aim to reflect the performance of a particular market or index, such as the FTSE 100 or the S&P 500 and, like a traditional tracker, their value is determined by whether or not the index rises or falls.

ETFs differ in that they are traded like individual stocks, on an exchange, such as the LSE or Euronext, and can be bought and sold through brokers in the same way as any other listed stock. An investor can also reach international markets that are sometimes out of reach of the ordinary investor.

Although some ETFs are active, they are predominantly passive investments in that they are not actively managed by a fund manager who chooses which assets to buy and sell. An ETF has holdings in every company on the index and only buys and sells holdings to reflect movements in the market.

One of the main attractions of ETFs over traditional trackers or active funds is that they are priced intra-day, whereas conventional funds are priced just once a day or worse. With ETFs, as with investment trusts or other shares, you know what the price will be before you buy or sell.

ETFs are therefore ideal for investors who want to profit from short-term market movements. You can buy ETFs that track exotic markets such as Brazil, Eastern Europe, Taiwan, and even Korea – areas that historically have been difficult for small investors to gain access to.

As ETFs are companies that are traded on a stock market, the normal trade-to-settlement lifecycle is that which applies to the local market place.

8.2   Unit Trust and OEIC Settlement – Additional Costs

Learning Objective

3.4   Identify the additional costs arising from the settlement of unit trusts and OEICs

The purchase and sale of securities globally involves certain costs, such as dealing costs/commissions, exchange fees, depository fees, custody fees, stamp duty (when applicable) and local regulatory fees such as the PTM levy (see Chapter 2, Section 1.2). These costs are either directly or indirectly borne by the funds and are reflected in the unit price of the unit trusts and OEICs.

In addition to these costs there may be significant other costs when buying and selling unit trusts or OEICs. In the settlement of funds such as OEICs and unit trusts, the fees and charges that apply can include the following:

- Depository fees.
- Custody fees.
- Stamp duty (where applicable).
- Initial fees (purchase).
- Management fees.
- Exit fees (sales).
- Dilution levy.

8.3   Automating Fund Settlement

Learning Objective

3.5   Describe the potential to fully automate the settlement of unit trusts and OEICs and analyse its benefits, drawbacks and implementation considerations

To develop a seamless STP environment in fund dealing and settlement has been a long-standing goal for many firms in the industry. In North America, the problems highlighted earlier appear to have been largely overcome, and settlement of most of the collective investment-type funds have become automated. Many other countries have also been able to automate the settlement of such funds.

In October 2009, the ISSA Fund Working Group issued its *Investment Funds Processing in Europe* report. This was aimed at identifying and documenting the core investment fund processing models and patterns in Europe and highlighting local best practices which could – or should – be extended on a pan-European level, with the intention of making cross-border fund processing more consistent and more efficient. A number of practical recommendations are documented in the ISSA report; however, in addition to these, the group issued ten more high-level guiding principles to serve as a reference in streamlining cross-border investment fund processing in Europe.

These ten principles are:

1. Paperless processes, STP based on International Organization for Standardization (ISO) standards.
2. Mitigation of operational risk.
3. Clarity of account structures.
4. Key identifiers.
5. Commission reporting.
6. Fund processing passport.
7. Completeness of data throughout the intermediary chain.
8. Acknowledgement of order receipt and confirmation of order execution.
9. Flexibility of position reporting systems.
10. Transfers of holdings.

Considerable developments have been made in this field over recent years, with the launching of the FundSettle and Vestima services in Europe. Euroclear provide FundSettle and EMX and Clearstream provide Vestima. Fund/SERV is available in both the US and Canada. Calastone is yet another proprietary system that can be used by the funds community to enhance the investor's experience with regards to order routing and eventual settlement. To enable automation and standardisation in the fund market, FundSettle, for instance, offers fund distributors and transfer agents access to its services via SWIFT.

In order to achieve this automation there are certain difficulties that have to be overcome. These difficulties relate to:

• settlement
• reconciliation
• registration.

Settlement

In the equity and treasury markets today, both parties to a transaction have some degree of certainty regarding the timing and finality of settlement. The only regulated standard for the settlement of units, or shares, in a fund, however, is between the trustee and the fund manager, where transactions settle on a T+4 basis. Although the majority of providers aim to settle on a T+4 basis, the product provider is under no obligation to settle with any other counterparty within a given timeframe.

Often the product provider's counterparty only knows when a transaction has settled when it receives either a cash payment (for a redemption) or a statement of holdings (for a purchase).

This lack of certainty and the manual processes that inevitably surround it are labour-intensive and, as a result, expensive. In addition, the low quality of settlement finality, primarily attributable to the lack of simultaneous DvP, gives rise to a number of risks during the settlement process, especially with respect to the disposal of funds. The precise procedures adopted for the disposal of shares or units in funds vary from one fund manager to another but, in essence, involve the holder (or someone acting on his behalf) arranging the disposal with the fund manager.

Settlement is defined as the transfer of the ownership of a security, often against a simultaneous cash payment. The securities are not normally delivered against simultaneous payment of the redemption proceeds which results in:

- the holder having control of neither the securities nor the proceeds for a period of time
- a credit risk arising against either the manager of the OEIC or the trustees of the unit trust (the holder will not necessarily know which one).

While a financial exposure to any counterparty is undesirable if it can be avoided, it is the exposure to the manager that causes particular concern. Were the manager to become insolvent during the period after delivery or cancellation of the securities, but before payment, the delivering holder would have to seek payment of the proceeds, either by proving themselves in the insolvency as an unsecured creditor, or by pursuing some other remedy, such as tracing of the proceeds. The holder could not be assured of receiving the full amount due and the amounts recovered are likely to be paid only after significant delay (and, possibly, expense).

In relation to exposures to the manager of the OEIC or the trustees of the unit trust, the expectation is that the OEIC or trust will have the appropriate assets to back any claim, as indicated by the relevant valuation, although there can be no certainty of this. Of course, before pursuing any claim the (former) holder will need to identify whether the manager or the fund is his debtor (ie, whether the manager had dealt as principal or agent). This will be highlighted on any redemptions notice/contract note from the manager. The current practice, which can see cancellation of the securities prior to settlement of the trade, also gives rise to some concerns. It removes the holder's title to the securities, often in advance of the point at which the holder considers himself to be delivering the securities and can result in the credit exposures (referred to above) arising. The practice also admits the possibility (technically, at least) that the holder may fail to settle the trade and, instead, (purport to) transfer the securities, which he may be unaware have been cancelled, elsewhere. We understand that these weaknesses relating to DvP are a deterrent to some overseas investors holding UK funds.

Reconciliation

The other major problem faced by investment managers is that reconciliation (which is a regulatory requirement for every market participant holding assets on behalf of an underlying investor) is complex and expensive.

With a CSD, firms tend to reconcile daily as it is a simple and efficient process that can be automated easily. Reconciliation of funds, however, could be an entirely manual process with the fund manager's counterparty (and/or the share or unit holder) left to reconcile against data that is not available in a standard electronic format, thus complicating the process. The greater degree of manual intervention required is both expensive and also prone to a greater degree of error. Some investment firms have had such problems in receiving both timely and quality reconciliation data that they have successfully sought temporary regulatory dispensation from the task.

Re-registration

An additional obstacle to efficient reconciliation is the absence of common standards for registration.

In the equity market, when a registrar updates a register of holdings it does so by using information delivered electronically to a single data-processing standard. The information delivered by a CSD to the registrar is exactly the same as that input by the relevant system member; this ensures that any entry on the register can always reconcile with the member's records.

In the funds industry, investment firms have found that they have been unable to reconcile even this static data, as the information used by the product provider to identify clients on the register is not the same as that used by the intermediary. Therefore, reconciliation breaks down because the means of identifying a client is not consistent across market participants and across securities. The absence of standardisation, the low quality of settlement finality and the inefficiency of reconciliation for funds increases operational risk and have held back development of the market.

8.3.1 Current Fund Lifecycle Automation

FundSettle

Euroclear launched FundSettle to enable the automation (through a single access point) of the dealing and settlement of funds. This service links together transfer agents, fund distributors and fund management companies in both domestic and offshore markets. It also enhances the move towards STP in this environment.

The FundSettle concept is illustrated in the following diagram.

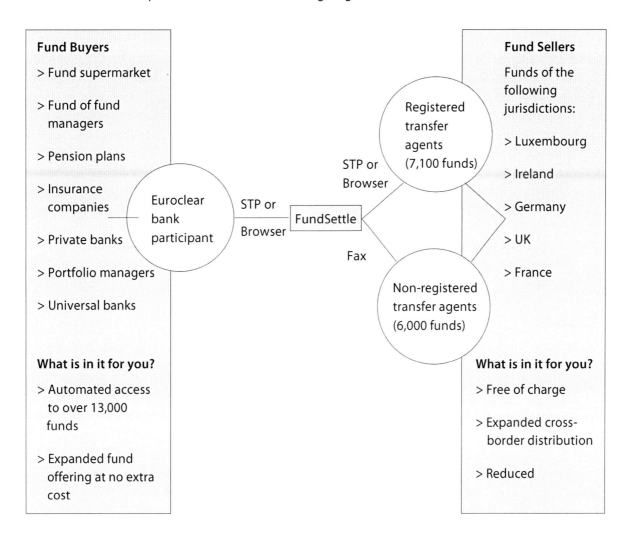

FundSettle also offers the following benefits to custodians:

- A single gateway to the largest European and offshore investment fund markets.
- The ability to include investment fund order processing in the services offered.
- Integration of settlement and custody activity into a single standard settlement process.
- Centralised and efficient cash management.

Euroclear UK/CREST

The settlement of fund transactions in the UK has begun to change. Recently, Euroclear UK the UK's CSD, using their CREST system and EMXCo, a message protocol company, have put in place an infrastructure to enable UK fund distributors and hundreds of fund promoters, representing a substantial number of funds worldwide, to access each other electronically, without any changes in operational procedures or new technology investments.

In October 2010, the EMX message system became able to route orders from UK fund distributors to Euroclear bank's FundSettle platform, providing seamless access to the most active fund promoters worldwide. As a result, UK fund distributors are able to provide many new investment opportunities for their clients while continuing to use the existing EMX order-routing service. International fund promoters, in turn, have an easy and automated channel to reach fund investors in the UK. This new development eases the often complex and costly challenge to processing cross-border fund transactions.

Distributors have the choice to route their orders through the new service and to direct their cross-border fund transaction orders to Euroclear bank's FundSettle platform and domestic UK fund transaction orders to the ICSD for settlement. Via a single connection, UK fund distributors and cross-border promoters can drastically increase their back-office efficiency, reach and flexibility, with no technology investment required. The EMX/FundSettle link is FIX and ISO message-type neutral, as both are compatible.

Many of the commentators on the fund processing scene believe this to be very good news for both the distributors of funds and the underlying investors. It is said to be beneficial to the industry because it delivers a single automated processing platform that purges the fund industry of unnecessary costs and inefficiencies associated with disjointed, manual transaction processing. It is expected that this will it automate the entire lifecycle of a fund transaction, irrespective of jurisdiction, network provider and technology.

Vestima

Vestima+ is the automated order-routing service used for fund order processing by Clearstream. It is aimed at reducing the costs and difficulties of order processing within the investment fund industry. It provides order issuers with a single entry point for funds, allowing them to route their orders to transfer agents (TAs) using electronic media like an internet-based workstation or SWIFT messages, both in ISO 15022 or the new XML 20022 format.

Vestima+ can be used for third-party as well as internal order flows. It is the only available system offering free choice of settlement and custody routes. Over 34,000 investment funds are now available on Clearstream's Vestima+.

According to Clearstream, Vestima provides the user with a single, fully automated point of entry for routing orders to fund agents. This allows the user to use the same standardised process at all times, independent of the variety of markets and investment funds dealt with.

Vestima is integrated into the Clearstream settlement and custody platform, enabling the user to benefit from an end-to-end STP process, from order issuance to final settlement.

As a result, the user can streamline their fund processing by applying the same operational procedures to their investment fund activity as to other instruments.

Calastone

Calastone enables the buyers and sellers of mutual funds to communicate orders electronically by providing a universal message communication and translation service. Calastone provides access to the whole of the global funds market through a single connection. The distributors of funds send orders from around the world into the Calastone transaction network and Calastone routes them on to the appropriate destination in the format of the fund manager (or transfer agent's) choice.

This is achieved by Calastone enabling the users to send a buy or sell message in any format (SWIFT, FIX, XML, .CSV, .XLS, etc) to the fund provider. At the core of the Calastone Transaction Network is the ISO 20022 message format into which all messages are translated. By means of configurable adaptors, Calastone can translate any message format into any other message format.

Fund/SERV

In the US, they have, for many years, had an STP capability. Fund/SERV, developed in 1986 by the National Securities Clearing Corporation (NSCC), offers a platform for the processing and settling of investment funds, including both the 1940 Act and other pooled investment products for investment companies, money managers and financial intermediaries. The service provides standardised formats and centralised processing of purchase, redemption and exchange orders and account registrations, and provides participants with a single daily net settlement.

Fund/SERV offers different processing cycles over 22 hours, giving trading partners access to a single automated trading platform. Fund/SERV significantly reduces the time and cost of processing transactions.

Fund/SERV is accessible via CPU-to-CPU links, PCWeb direct (a web interface that allows NSCC participants direct access to NSCC services over the internet) and with Fund/SPEEd (NSCC's XML interface).

Any qualified and interested NSCC members can participate in Fund/SERV. Special mutual fund-only memberships are available.

Benefits

It enhances operations by providing:

- automated and standardised procedures which make processing more efficient and cost-effective
- a 22-hour operating day with 29 processing cycles offering flexible order entry

- standard formats which reduce errors associated with manual order entry
- volume growth accommodation
- open formats that implement easily into various processing systems.

It reduces risk by providing:

- standardised orders which are captured in an automated processing environment that reduces operations and compliance risk
- daily net settlement of total mutual fund activity that allows one payment that eliminates the risks associated with multiple settlement venues.

It supports multiple product types by supporting:

- 1940 Act funds: loads, no-loads, open- and closed-end funds, money market funds
- other pooled investment products: offshore funds
  - stable value funds
  - guaranteed investment contracts (GICs)
  - separate accounts – bank collective investment trusts; bank investment contracts (BICs)
  - unit investment trusts (UITs)
  - section 529 qualified state tuition programmes.

How the Service Works
- Fund order types:
  - regular orders; as-of orders; exchange orders; as-of exchanges
  - fund-originated orders
  - fund-originated as-of orders.
- **Fund order processing** – order processing occurs in one of 29 scheduled processing cycles. Cycles run from 2:00am Eastern time until midnight, Monday to Friday.
- **Fund account registration** – firms may transmit registration files any time during the order processing period. Funds can opt to warehouse the files at the NSCC until settlement. Money market fund registrations must be submitted with orders.
- **Order confirmation** – funds may confirm orders and firms may retrieve confirmations from 2:00am Eastern time until midnight. Money market orders may be confirmed after settlement.
- **Settlement** – flexible settlement features support various investment product requirements, such as same day, next day and T+3 settlement cycles. All obligations are settled in Federal Reserve funds at the NSCC.
- **Alternate settlement** – allows firms to establish a settlement date for particular orders, to settle between one and seven days from the day the order is placed. Benefits 401(k) transactions or WRAP programs that may require a different settlement date from traditional retail orders. Funds have the same capability if they originate the order. In addition, Fund/SPEEd transmissions through Fund/SERV can be designated as settling outside the NSCC's Fund/SERV system.
- **Exception processing** – allows for pre-settlement and post-settlement corrections, as well as firm exits, firm deletes and cash adjustments.
- **Cash adjustment** – allows funds and firms to make claims for dividends, commission billing and commission adjustment. Funds may also update contingent-deferred sales charges and long- and short-term capital gains using this feature.
- **ACATS – Fund/SERV interface** – Automated Customer Account Transfer Service (ACATS) links to Fund/SERV and allows mutual funds to electronically update account registrations when a customer account is transferred from one broker to another.

- **Underwritings and tender offers** – investment companies can take advantage of this centralised automated environment to process fund offers. The NSCC's underwriting service supports initial public offerings (IPOs), while tender offers support the redemption of mutual fund shares. In Canada, the market is serviced by their own Fund/SERV system that performs similar activities as those found in the US version.

9. Regulatory Impact on Clearing and Settlement

Learning Objective

3.13 Understand how the global regulatory environment impacts on clearing and settlement and in particular how the UK regulatory environment dictates processes for a regulated UK firm

9.1 Settlement Timeframes

Following the financial crisis in 2008, many regulatory organisations felt that there was a need to reduce the settlement timeframes, this being the elapse time from trade to settlement. This elapse time is normally expressed as T+ something.

By way of example after the 2008 financial crisis, the European Commission (EC) decided that national CSDs, in their position as key institutions performing the vital post-trade process of securities settlement, as well as maintaining records of securities accounts and transactions, needed to harmonise their practices and improve the safety and efficiency of transaction settlement.

At that time, in the vast majority of European markets, the settlement period for securities was T+3. In 2009, the European Commission set up the Harmonisation of Settlement Cycles Working Group. The group recommended a shorter settlement cycle of T+2. This would also harmonise with the foreign exchange settlement periods. It was also recognised that the move to a shorter settlement cycle would mitigate counterparty risk for all industry participants.

On the 6 October 2014, 29 markets moved to T+2. These were Austria, Belgium, Croatia, Cyprus, the Czech Republic, Denmark, Estonia, Finland, France, Greece, Hungary, Iceland, Italy, Ireland, the Netherlands, Latvia, Lichtenstein, Lithuania, Luxembourg, Malta, Norway, Poland, Portugal, Romania, Slovakia, Spain (for bonds), Sweden, Switzerland, and the UK.

Bulgaria, Germany and Slovenia were already settling on a T+2 basis.

Currently, the US settlement has a three-day settlement cycle (T+3). The Depository Trust & Clearing Corporation (DTCC), along with other industry organisations, believes that shortening the settlement cycle to T+2 will substantially reduce operational and systemic risk across the industry and for investors, lower liquidity needs and limit pro-cyclicality. The shortened settlement cycle will also align the US settlement cycle with other markets across the globe.

9.1.1   Impacts of Reduced Timeframes

- **Systems** – these regulatory driven changes to the settlement timeframes have of course meant that firms have had to amend their internal administrative processes and the system processes and data libraries that handle settlement.
- **Lifecycle** – the lifecycle of trades was of course affected by the regulatory change as, in most cases, a day was shaved from the processes that need to be accomplished prior to settlement.

9.2   Central Securities Depositories Regulation (CSDR)

As mentioned in Section 9.1, the EC decided that the CSDs should be required to play a significant role in the EC's ambitions for better settlement procedures. In order to bring this about the CSDR was brought into effect.

The aim of CSDR is to harmonise certain aspects of the settlement cycle and settlement discipline and to provide a set of common requirements for CSDs operating securities settlement systems across the EU. CSDR plays a pivotal role for post-trade harmonisation efforts in Europe, as it enhances the legal and operational conditions for cross-border settlement in the EU.

9.2.1   Key Elements of CSDR

The main objective of CSDR is to increase the safety and efficiency of securities settlement and settlement infrastructures in the EU by providing the following:

- shorter settlement periods
- settlement discipline measures (mandatory cash penalties and buy-ins for settlement fails)
- an obligation regarding dematerialisation for most securities
- strict prudential and conduct of business rules for CSDs
- strict access rights to CSD services
- increased prudential and supervisory requirements for CSDs and other institutions providing banking services ancillary to securities settlement.

9.2.2   UK Regulated Firms

In the UK, regulated firms have to ensure that all their processes and procedures regarding client assets, adhere to the rules laid down by the FCA. These rules are laid out in the FCA's CASS Sourcebook.

Many of these rules have a direct impact on the firm's ability to be efficient in the settlement and clearing of trades. The specific rules in the Sourcebook that have relevance are found under:

- 6.2: Holding of clients assets.
- 6.3: Depositing assets and arranging for assets to be deposited with third parties.
- 6.6.54: Treatment of shortfalls.

These rules are expansive and therefore it is not felt appropriate to elaborate much further here but it is recommended that UK candidates make themselves aware of these rules and the FCA CASS Sourcebook as a whole. Under these rules the FCA requires firms to pay particular attention to the correct manner of safeguarding a client's assets and accuracy of the records kept of the client's assets. Therefore, firms must introduce and have/maintain adequate organisational arrangements to minimise the risk of loss or diminution of clients' safe custody assets or the rights in connection with those assets, as a result of their misuse, fraud, poor administration, inadequate record-keeping or negligence.

Other regulators in other countries will have similar publications. Although we attempt to be as global as possible, candidates will understand the enormity of the task to try and present these global rules here. So we do not attempt to do that. However, at a minimum it is recommended that students are familiar with their own country's financial authority's rules.

3

End of Chapter Questions

1. Why may a trade need repair?
   Answer reference: *Section 2*

2. What are the primary causes of late settlement and what methods can be employed to control them?
   Answer reference: *Section 3*

3. What do you see as the operational risks arising from settlement?
   Answer reference: *Section 5*

4. What is LCH.Clearnet?
   Answer reference: *Section 6.2*

5. What are the drivers behind dematerialisation?
   Answer reference: *Section 7.2*

6. What is Fund/SERV?
   Answer reference: *Section 8.3.1*

Chapter Four
Custodians

1. Background to the Evolution of Custody Services

The origins of custody reach far back into the annals of time. Indeed, whoever the first person on earth was who asked a neighbour or a friend to look after, keep from harm or keep safe from others one of their treasured possessions had sown the seeds of our industry. For custody in its simplest form is just that: it is an act of trust.

Custody as we know it today almost certainly started with the early farmers and traders. The first depositories were established in the third millennium bc. Deposits initially consisted of grain and later other goods, including cattle, agricultural implements and, eventually, precious metals, such as gold in the form of easy-to-carry compressed plates. It is known that the Greek and Roman empires as far back as the 2nd century ad had a flourishing banking industry.

Coming much more up to date, by the end of the 17th century the world banking system as we know it today was becoming very well-established. As debt became securitised, the issuers of the debt would issue certificates detailing the nature of the debt owed by the issuer to the lender, eg, share certificates, certificates of deposit (CDs), bearer bonds, mortgage deeds, etc. The holders of these valuable certificates had an obvious need to keep them safe and secure, as they were the only legal proof of the debt. The natural place to turn to for this service was the local bank, which had vaults or a strong-room especially designed for the job of keeping safe items of value such as gold and cash. They could also provide record-keeping services of those items deposited in their vaults by way of what were known as 'passbooks'.

Following on from these safekeeping duties, as their clients would buy and sell their assets in the developing markets, the banks began to get into other services such as settlement of the asset transactions and the collection of the issuers' obligation of interest or dividend payments.

More recently, for close on 50 years now, banks, brokers and investment managers in Europe have maintained a sophisticated network of correspondent banks that were used to help them trade in international securities. This obviously included the now so-called value-added services, such as dealing with the vagaries of withholding tax and the collection of foreign dividends in foreign currencies, facilitating corporate events and voting at meetings and, not least, the settlement of transactions in securities (which include cash).

The term 'global custody' is a fairly recent innovation which is said to have been coined by a manager at the US bank, Chase Manhattan, in around 1974. The US interest in investing in foreign markets probably started at around the same time and would have been because at this time there was a lot of debate in the US on the whole subject of pensions. The debate also started to look at returns and it was felt that to generate better returns there was a need to diversify away from the domestic market.

In September 1974, the Employee Retirement Income Security Act (ERISA) became law in the US. ERISA was enacted to protect the interests of employee benefit plan participants and their beneficiaries by requiring the disclosure to them of financial and other information concerning the plan and establishing standards of conduct for the fiduciaries associated with the plan.

When the US banks were looking for greater exposure to the rest of the world (something that had been happening in Europe for many years previously), they found a ready-made infrastructure in Europe. It is certainly true that the ERISA regulations and the influence of the US have had a major impact on custody and have driven the development of the comprehensive ranges of products that are on offer today.

Europe is also a very large geographic customer base for the global custody industry. These customers (that require custody services), eg, pension funds, UCITS and high net worth individuals, have the greatest choice when choosing a custodian. They can choose to use US-based, European-based or niche global custodians. The larger global custodians are all competing heavily in the European markets. In the US markets, the US-based global custodians are dominant.

The important worldwide trends relating to the provision of global custody services are at their most striking in Europe, ie:

- the rise of the pensions market
- the growth of cross-border investment
- the emergence of the super wealthy.

In recent times in Germany, there has been an initiative to introduce private pensions, which is expected to generate much extra revenue for the financial services sector and for global custodians.

Another reason for the global custodians to be attracted to the European client base is the increasing importance of corporate governance across the continent. Many global custodians play an important role in helping pension funds and others to fulfil their duties as shareholders by providing proxy voting services.

Many of the already sophisticated global markets as well as the developing markets are also encouraging their people to save and invest for their retirement and so these savers are looking for custody outlets as well. The large domestic custody banks in these countries are therefore linking in some way with the already established global custodians to supply services to their home market place.

The global marketplaces and the custodians within those marketplaces have, over the years, become more sophisticated. Initiatives aimed at reducing costs and removing risks have led to the markets becoming either dematerialised or immobilised, meaning that the holding of physical certificates that represent the legal ownership of debt is becoming a secondary service, being replaced by what are known as value added services such as the servicing of the debt.

2. Selecting a Custodian

Learning Objective

4.1 Describe the due diligence process for the selection of custodians/sub-custodians, including requests for information (RFIs)/requests for proposals (RFPs)

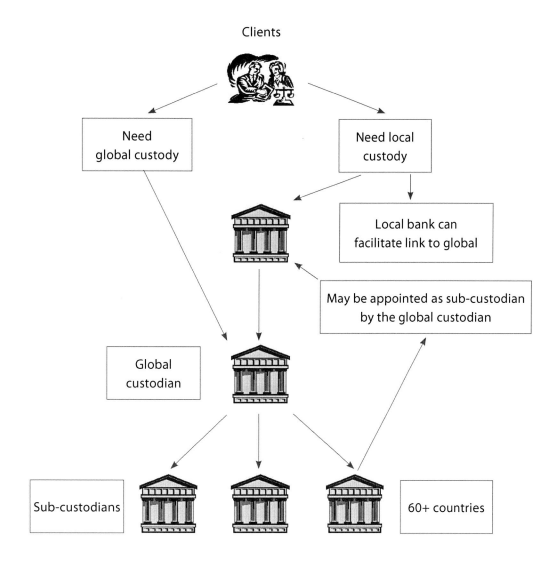

Before embarking on describing the process for selecting a custodian or sub-custodian it should be remembered that some clients may have a predetermined list of preferences as to which type of custodial bank they will or will not appoint. Such a list could include the credit rating or cost of the service and may also include whether the global custodian bank uses their own branches as their sub-custodians in the markets where that is possible. This is not to say that one model is better than the other, as there as pros and cons for each scenario, but just that the client preference will be part of the selection process.

A very significant relationship of trust exists between a custodian and a client and it is, therefore, very important to assess whether a prospective counterparty is worthy of that extended trust. This means that a thorough vetting process needs to take place. This is generally known as due diligence.

Recently, there has been significant debate within Europe with regard to the question of trust, especially in relation to the liability to the unit holders of a fund by a depository of a UCITS fund. This debate was started by the Madoff scandal of 2008 and centres on the responsibilities and functions of a depository bank. In essence, there is a school of thought that suggests that the depository could be liable to the unit holders of a fund for any losses created by any misappropriation of the assets of the fund, by any entity within the infrastructure that supports the fund, due to a lack of due diligence by the depository bank.

This debate has led to a new UCITS directive (UCITS V) being prepared by the European authorities. At present, the debate is limited to the assets held by the eurocentric UCITS funds and does not include assets held by private pension funds, charities, sovereign funds or high net worth individuals.

However, in the UCITS parlance, a depository bank is a custodian of the assets. The outcome of this debate and eventual legislation could therefore have significant implications for those institutions who supply custodial services and the selection of a sub-custodian and the due diligence performed, although always critical, is suddenly of particular importance.

This due diligence process should start with a set of selection criteria being established by the client or custodian bank that is looking for a custodian or sub-custodian. This set will outline the things that the supplier of service must provide and includes:

- cost
- good credit worthiness
- services available
- reliability and performance
- responses to requests for additional information
- in-person presentations
- references.

The initial approach to the custodian or sub-custodian will be by the means of a request for information (RFI) based on their selection criteria. The client or bank will invite the custodian or sub-custodian to provide them with the vital information needed for due diligence before deciding on progressing to a full shortlist of candidates.

These RFIs are reviewed by the client or the custodian to whittle down the respondents to a shortlist of likely suppliers. Once this shortlist has been agreed by those who are in charge of the selection process, a request for proposal (RFP) will be sent to each of the names on the shortlist.

2.1   Request For Proposal (RFP)

A generic RFP is detailed below:

Request for Proposal on Custodial Services
Example Table of Contents
Background information
General overview of our custodial clients
Our requirements
Timetable
General provisions
Selection criteria
Interpretation of RFP document
Contract
Demonstrations
Proposal preparation costs
News release
Authorising officer
Proposal validity
Proposal format
Proposal submission
Subjects Requiring Detailed Response
General information
Client services
Accounting
Reporting
Online communications
Computer/system facilities
Audit control
Governance
Global custodial services
Safekeeping
Cash management
Securities lending
Fees
Derivatives
References
Other services

2.1.1 Table of Contents Breakdown

Background Information

This section of the RFP will detail the relevant information about the organisation that is making the request and will describe the background to the company and the type(s) of business that it is involved in. There will also be details of the structure of the company, including main and subsidiary offices, numbers employed, who it is regulated by and what markets and related institutions it may be a member of.

General Overview of the Fund(s) for which Custody/Sub-custody is Sought

This section will provide the prospective custodian or sub-custodian with details about the fund or funds for which the services are sought. This will include whether they are retail or institutional, closed or open-ended, income or growth or both, how they are marketed, who oversees the investments and who manages the investments, ie, who the fund managers are (internal or external).

Example

The Breakdown of Assets

(This will change depending on whether the target is a custodian or sub-custodian.)

The portfolio is overseen by an investment committee comprised of several members of the board of directors and external representatives. There are currently five external fund managers consisting of two UK equity managers, one US equity manager, one fixed income manager and one Asia-Pacific equity manager.

The asset mix policy includes 25% fixed income and equities 70% of the portfolio, with plus or minus 15% tactical allocation. the fund will undertake, on average, approximately 55 acquisitions and 48 disposal transactions per month, including a number of short-term transactions. The average value of acquisitions monthly is £50 million, with average disposal of £32 million. For the 12 months ended 31 December 2015, the total sterling value of acquisitions, at cost, was £415 million, with disposals of £348 million. Performance is measured with quarterly performance summary reports.

The Client's Requirements

It will then be important to provide the custodian or sub-custodian with the information about the reasons for seeking an RFP.

Example

Although services such as actuarial, auditing, banking, custodial, administration, accounting, legal and performance measurement are not required to be outsourced, the board of the fund management company has decided to call for proposals for such services on a rotating basis. The proposal with the lowest price will not necessarily be awarded the contract, as other qualitative factors will often have a significant impact on a supplier's fit with the overall requirements of the company and funds. Generally, RFPs for such services will be called for at least every five years the company is looking for a custodian/sub-custodian that provides excellent customer service, whilst consistently delivering accurate, reliable, and timely financial reports at a competitive price.

The successful custodian/sub-custodian will be expected to provide online access to individual security data to enable the company to monitor the investment funds on a daily basis. Technology will, therefore, be a significant element of the selection criteria. However, the accuracy and reliability of the data provided is also of paramount importance. The successful custodian will be expected to demonstrate its ability to ensure the correctness of the data they provide through rigorous quality control measures and other methods including, but not limited to, extensive training of their staff and continuing professional development. Fee quotations must be provided for a five-year period.

Timetable

The custodian must know the proposal timetable they are working to.

Example

RFP issued: 10 January

Vendor question deadline: 23 January

Closing date for proposals: 9 February

Responses mailed must be postmarked no later than: 6 February

Evaluation period: 10 February–7 March

General Provisions

Any general provisions will need to be outlined; below is an example of what this section might contain.

Example

To facilitate the information-gathering and evaluation process, this RFP includes a series of questions to be answered by respondents. Questions must be answered completely, with responses carrying the same identification number as listed in this document. An evaluation process will be conducted to determine which proposal best meets the overall requirements of the company. Acceptance of a proposal will be based on a number of criteria, therefore the company reserves the right not to accept the lowest proposal or any proposal submitted. Also, the company has the right, at any time, to waive any of the requirements of the RFP.

All bidders must agree, in writing, in a letter accompanying the proposal, that they will be bound by what is stated in their proposal. The bidder whose proposal best meets the requirements of this RFP, will be designated as the preferred bidder. No obligation arises, however, until a mutually acceptable contract, based on the proposal, is negotiated and executed. This RFP will be part of the contract. All proposals become the property of the company on the closing date and will not be returned.

Any presentations that are required in support of a bidder's proposal will be arranged at a mutually satisfactory time by the company during the evaluation period. There should be no costs to the company for the preparation of responses or subsequent presentations and/or meetings.

Should the company deem it necessary to augment, modify or clarify this RFP, all bidders will be notified and will receive a written addendum. Receipt of such revisions must be acknowledged in writing. If revisions are necessary after the closing date, vendors will then have an opportunity to respond specifically to the revised section(s) of the RFP. Also, the company reserves the right to discuss any and all proposals and to request additional information from the respondents.

Responses to this RFP and all supporting documentation submitted by bidders will become the property of the company and will not be returned. Such information will be used only in conjunction with the bidder selection process.

The company will only evaluate proposals addressing all aspects of the requirements.

Products and services may come from one source, or may be joint proposals. Joint proposals must specify the involvement of, and be signed by, all parties. Prices must be valid for a period of 120 days from the closing date.

Selection Criteria

The prospective custodians/sub-custodians should be given the criteria for selecting the successful organisation, as the example below shows.

Example

In selecting the preferred vendor, the company will not use any single criterion. The company is not obligated to select the lowest or any proposal received in response to the RFP.

Any proposals not containing sufficient information to permit a thorough analysis may be rejected. The company reserves the right to verify the validity of the information supplied and to reject any proposal where the contents appear to be incorrect, misleading, or otherwise inaccurate in the company's estimation. Criteria to be considered include:

1. cost
2. good creditworthiness
3. services available
4. reliability and performance
5. responses to requests for additional information
6. oral presentations
7. references.

Interpretation of the RFP Document

The prospective custodians/sub-custodians may also need to have clarification of certain points included in the RFP. This can be covered by wording similar to that shown below.

Example

At all times, the service provider has the responsibility to notify the company, in writing, of any ambiguity, divergence, error, omission, oversight or contradiction contained in the RFP as it is discovered and to request any instructions, decisions or descriptions which may be required to prepare a proposal.

All questions concerning the RFP itself, or issues that may change the requirements of this RFP, must be received in writing no later than 4:00pm GMT on 23 January xxxx at the following address for the attention of the project manager, custody selection. Any technical questions can be addressed to the same person.

Should it become necessary for the company to revise any part of this RFP, the revisions will be provided to all vendors who have received the RFP.

Contract

Selection of the preferred bidder does not oblige the company to negotiate or execute a contract with that bidder. The company reserves the right to negotiate details of the agreement and to make the necessary enhancements, modifications or changes as may be required. The company reserves the right to terminate the agreement, without cause, at any time. If any change requested by the company causes an increase or decrease in the cost elements of the vendor's proposal, a request for an adjustment must be made within 30 days after receipt by the vendor of notification of the change by the company.

Breach of any condition of the agreement may be treated by the company as grounds for rejecting the services and terminating the agreement.

The selected service provider shall not assign or transfer the agreement with the company to any third party without the company's prior written consent. The company may withhold such consent and may choose to terminate the agreement, depending on whether the assignment is in the best interests of the company.

The successful service provider must agree to sign a contract for performance of work, generally covering conditions as outlined herein prior to commencement of work. The contract will stipulate termination by the company upon 48 hours' written notice to the consultant, with full reimbursement to the consultant for time and costs incurred up to the date of written notice.

Demonstrations

The company reserves the right to have a demonstration of the products and services offered prior to the awarding of the agreement. The company also reserves the right to shortlist the proposals prior to undertaking formal demonstrations. Presentations or demonstrations will be made at a mutually acceptable time.

Proposal Preparation Costs

The company will not be responsible for any costs incurred by a bidder in preparing and submitting a proposal. The company accepts no liability of any kind to a bidder unless and until its proposal is accepted by the company and there is a signed agreement between the company and the service provider with respect to the services outlined in this RFP.

News Release

The service provider shall not issue any publicity or news release pertaining to this RFP, or contract, without the prior written consent of the company.

Authorising Officer

The proposal must designate the individual who is authorised to negotiate and sign on behalf of the service provider. The proposal must also express the vendor's resolution to abide by the rules set out in this RFP. A copy of the bid form is contained in the appendix of the RFP.

Proposal Validity

Proposals, including pricing, must be valid for a period of at least 120 days following the closing date.

Proposal Format

Service providers should submit their proposals in the following format to facilitate evaluation of the questions/issues outlined above:

1. General information.
2. Client services.
3. Accounting.
4. Reporting.
5. Online communications.
6. Computer facilities/systems.
7. Audit control.
8. Governance.
9. Global custodial services.
10. Safekeeping.
11. Cash management.
12. Securities lending.
13. Fees.
14. Derivatives.
15. References.
16. Other services.

Proposal Submission

Bidders are responsible for the proper delivery of their proposals to the company.

Requests for extensions of time will not be granted. Any proposals, or modifications and additions to proposals received by the company after the closing date and time may, at the company's discretion, not be considered.

The original and three complete unbound copies (that are easily photocopied) of the proposal, including all attachments, must be received by the company no later than 2:00pm GMT on 9 February xxxx (or postmarked no later than 6 February xxxx) at the address previously given above for the attention of the purchasing manager.

2.1.2   Examples of Information Required

General Information

1. What is the name of your company?
2. What is the address of your head office?
3. What is the address and telephone number of the office where this account will be administered? Who interfaces with the client? How often?
4. For non-domestic custodial services, show the process of growth in your organisation and identify any recent technological installations and/or strategic alliances.
5. Provide a list of all custodial clients lost since 31 December xxxx, showing the sterling value size, the year lost and the reason why.
6. Please provide a brief historical summary of your company's operation, including date of incorporation, ownership, subsidiaries (with percent ownership) and all affiliated and associated companies.

7. Describe how the custody accounts are allocated within your structure. How many accounts does your typical account representative manage?

8. Describe the key features of your client service programme. Please describe your company's commitment to service quality and customer service.

9. Please provide an organisational chart of your company showing the major operating divisions and functions, indicating where the custodial services fit in relation to the whole.

10. Provide a brief description of the history and development of your custodian/trustee services, including the dates of both implementation of key elements and enhancements to the system(s) and service. Please list which portions have been made on a global basis and which are specific to certain markets.

11. Please summarise the long-term strategy for business development in the area of trustee/custody services (ie, significant investments, planned technological installations, strategic alliances). This should include whether you are able to provide a guarantee of continuing participation in providing custody services for at least the next five years. What is your commitment to custodial services? Summarise your corporate goals and business plan for custodial services for the next three years. What support does senior management provide in the search for improvement in the custodial area?

12. Please explain briefly why the company should select your firm to provide the required services.

13. Provide details of all insurance policies that you have in place that are relevant to the department handling the custody functions and services.

14. Identify and describe any litigation or investigation by a regulatory authority or contingent liabilities your firm, its officers or principles have been involved in within the last five years relative to your custody services.

15. Provide an overview of your compliance and risk management policy and evidence of its implementation.

16. Illustrate the financial stability of your firm.

17. In the event of termination, what notice will be required? What termination charges, if any, will be levied?

18. How do you determine and prioritise the allocation of research and development (R&D) funds in your organisation?

19. Briefly describe your custody capabilities and competitive advantages that set you apart from your competitors.

20. Please provide your most recent audited financial statements and most recent quarterly financial statements (if available).

21. Please provide your current credit rating as measured by an independent credit rating agency.

22. How do you monitor legislative and/or regulatory changes affecting custodial service administration? How are these communicated to clients?

23. Describe any ongoing educational sessions, user conferences, publications or other means that you have for keeping clients fully educated and for providing a forum for new ideas and needs.

Client Services

1. Please describe the key feature of your client service programme. Do you have a standards programme?

2. Identify all key personnel involved in the delivering of your custodial services, including the following information: name, function, work experience, education, training and CVs.

3. Identify the specific personnel who will be involved in the administration of this account, their specific functions, length of time in that function, the number of other accounts they currently handle and their back-up support.

4. Provide information on the personnel turnover (including personnel that have moved to other areas of your firm) in the format listed below:
   a. Senior.
   b. Personnel.
   c. Joined/left.
   d. Total.
   e. Support.
   f. Personnel.
   g. Joined/left.
   h. Total.
   i. 2014.
   j. 2013.
   k. 2012.
   l. 2011.
   m. 2010.
5. Describe your ongoing and new employee training programmes.
6. In what ways do you distinguish yourself from other custodians in the area of client service and relations?
7. Do you have dedicated trustee/custodial legal staff and, if so, how many?
8. Describe any ongoing educational sessions or services for keeping the client fully educated.
9. Describe how you measure the success of your client service.
10. Is there staff specialisation by client type?

Accounting

(The accounting requirements will change depending on whether the target is a custodian or sub-custodian.)

1. Provide a complete description of your accounting system, including, but not limited to, the following:
   a. processing cycles (eg, cut-offs)
   b. reconciliation reports and processes
   c. interfaces with securities movement and performance measurement systems
   d. accounting for receipts, disbursements, gains, losses, forward contracts and income accruals.
2. Describe the procedures you have taken to provide an audit for your custodial services and systems. How often is it conducted?
3. Trade settlement – is it an in-house function? To what extent is it fully automated?
4. Do your asset valuations include accrued income, domestic and foreign?
5. What is the time lag between trade execution, availability of online transaction data to the client, and the posting of the transaction to your accounting system?
6. Describe your income collection procedures for both marketable and non-marketable securities.
7. Describe your compliance procedures with respect to investment legislation.
8. Identify and list all internal audit reports and management reports performed in the past three years specifically related to your custodial services.
9. How do you ensure complete payment of interest and dividend income?
10. Describe how your accounting system deals with unitised accounts? (ie, is it integrated or stand-alone?)
11. Describe your process for amortising bond premiums and discounts. Do you have a process to calculate the moving average market (MAM) adjustment?

12. What currency exchange rates does your organisation use?
13. How does your system account for non-standard investment vehicles such as:
    a. pooled funds of your own company
    b. pooled funds of other investment managers
    c. real estate
    d. venture capital
    e. private equity
    f. hedge funds
    g. options and futures
    h. corporate actions
    i. securities lending.
14. Describe the pricing sources used to obtain market values for each type of security in your system, specifically for the following asset classes:
    a. Canadian equities
    b. US equities
    c. non-North American equities
    d. Canadian bonds
    e. US bonds
    f. non-North American bonds
    g. real return bonds
    h. real estate
    i. mortgage-backed securities
    j. mortgages
    k. index-linked mortgages
    l. asset-backed securities
    m. short-term securities
    n. infrequently priced securities
    o. futures
    p. options
    q. private placements
    r. forwards and swaps.

Given the information in 14 above, what controls are used to guard against pricing errors and how frequently are the securities priced?

Reporting

(The reporting requirements will change depending on whether the target is a custodian or sub-custodian.)

1. Describe your current standard reporting package. Provide a complete description of all reports available, their timeliness of delivery and sample copies. Indicate how many business days after month-end the report will be available to the company.
2. Which of the standard reports are available online? How soon are they available after month-end?
3. Are you willing and able to prepare special ad hoc or customised reports? Is there an additional charge for this service?
4. Describe, and provide examples of, any performance measurement reporting facilities that are available to clients.
5. Describe any other analytical reports that are available to clients.
6. Detail the frequency and the timeliness of all these reports separately.

7. What optional reports are available? Which of these are available online? How soon are they available?

8. Is it possible for selected reports to be generated automatically every day, ie, a summary of the previous day's posted transactions?

9. Describe any unique features of your standard and customised reporting package.

10. Describe the procedures you have in place for retaining historical data.

11. What steps are taken to ensure the accuracy of your reports? Are the reports audited before they are sent to clients? If so, by whom?

12. Do you have the capability to capture and report brokerage companies generated by an account or investment manager?

13. Describe the daily, weekly, monthly, quarterly and annual reporting timetables to which your organisation will commit.

14. Are monthly custodial statements reconciled with managers' statements? If so, how (electronically or by mail)? Is this completed before or after the monthly custodial statements are issued?

15. How and when do you record and report (within your system to clients, to investment managers, etc) corporate actions (stock splits, dividends, name changes, tender offers, called bonds, etc)?

Online Communications

1. Please describe your online system available to clients and their investment managers. Describe what information is available, ie, pending trades, accounting information, asset lists by account including market value, transaction history, summary of account market values for the portfolio and securities on loan.

2. What operating systems can your online service support?

3. How long have you offered online services? Provide a description of remote site hardware and software required by clients and investment managers.

4. Is a help desk available? If yes, how many hours per day is it available?

5. Describe in detail all reports available online (ie, standard, non-standard, customised).

6. How current is online information and how many hours per day is it available?

7. Can clients retrieve online information in a customised reporting format? If so, describe your customised reporting flexibility and limitations. Is the data compatible with Microsoft Excel or other Windows-based software?

8. What provisions are made for the training of current personnel in the use of your system?

9. What terminal emulator is needed to communicate with your system? What modem types and speeds are supported by your system? Do you have an email/internet connection for client communication?

10. How many times has the system been either changed or updated since inception? Are there any plans to make changes or modifications in the next couple of years?

11. What information, current and historical, is provided and available online in raw data elements? Indicate when and how this information is available/accessible.

12. Describe your security procedures for online retrieval and processing.

Computer Facilities/Systems

1. Describe your computer facilities, highlighting the hardware used, the operating systems and the database(s). How long has the current hardware been in place?

2. When was the software developed? Was it developed internally or externally? What enhancements are planned now and over the next three years? How many persons actually support your system?

3. If you have acquired other related business over the past three years, please describe the conversion practices. How many accounts are still not converted, and what is the plan for these?

4. Describe your security procedures for online retrieval and processing. What back-up and recovery capabilities are in place? Where is the back-up system located?
5. Detail the number of staff dedicated to your custodial systems development on a year-to-year basis for the past five years.
6. Describe the physical security systems of your value and custody areas.
7. Are you planning any modifications/enhancements or redesign to the system(s)? If so, what are they? What is the time frame? What disruption, if any, is anticipated?
8. What investments in technology have been made in the last two years? What percentage of the budget is typically allocated to technology expenditures? How much does this amount to?
9. What is anticipated in expenditure for the next three years in hardware, software and support?
10. Do you provide online, real-time data access to your customers?

Audit Control

1. Do you provide your clients with an external audit report on your internal controls?
2. Describe the procedures you have taken to audit your custodial services and systems. How often is auditing and compliance monitoring conducted?
3. What levels of management review are made of audit reports and who or what level is required to implement changes to correct audit deficiencies noted?
4. Do you have an internal audit department? If so, provide details as to its structure and responsibilities.
5. Do you have a catastrophic and/or operational failure plan that is in place? If so, has it been tested recently?

Governance

1. How can your company assist the investment committee in fiduciary governance?
2. What types of monitoring, auditing or reporting systems are available to ensure that the fund is complying with investment guidelines such as, but not limited to:
   a. percentage held in a security, industry or country
   b. cash constraints.
3. Please provide, in detail, the processes and reports available with respect to proxy voting:
   a. when voted by the custodian
   b. when voted by the investment manager or client.

Global Custodial Services

1. Do you provide global custodial services? When did you first offer this capability? Is it an internal system or are you affiliated with another company in offering global custody services?
2. If you do not use an internal system for this service, list all of the affiliations you have had since inception of the service and include the date and reason(s) why you moved from, and moved to, certain organisations.
3. Briefly describe your global custody capabilities, including those items that currently set you apart from your competition.
4. What proportion of your total assets in custody is global?
5. Do you use sub-custodians and/or central depository facilities? If so, list all and provide your selection criteria for them. Also, describe your sub-custodian arrangements.
6. How are settlements communicated?
7. Describe your ability to handle foreign exchange transactions.
8. How do you handle foreign tax reclaim processing?
9. Do you offer proxy voting services?
10. Do you supply availability reporting?

Safekeeping

1. Describe your system for registration and custody of pension fund assets, including the name of the depository services used.
2. Are you currently accepting trade and cash information from investment managers and dealers electronically? If so, what means are you using?
3. Where and how are settlements transacted physically?
4. What sort of tracking system do you have to monitor the accuracy of the performance of your custodial and clearance area activities?
5. Describe how you monitor and distribute proxy information.

Cash Management

1. What is your policy towards crediting dividends and interest on the appropriate dates?
2. What interest is paid on positive cash balances, both within an investment manager's portfolio and on a separate cash account? What interest is charged for negative cash balances? How is it calculated and on what frequency is it calculated and paid/charged?
3. Describe your system for monitoring and projecting cash balances. How do you interface with the client and investment managers?
4. Do you sweep cash automatically? If so, how often, to what balance and in what vehicle(s) is it invested?
5. What procedures do you use to notify the investment managers of the day's available cash?
6. What short-term investment vehicles do you make available to clients? Is there a minimum cash requirement?
7. Do you automatically invest cash balances (not yet distributed to fund managers) at the end of each day?
8. Do you provide cash projections on request or automatically, including pending transactions, income and maturities?
9. When is the account credited with the proceeds of sale and when are the funds available for reinvestment – trade date, scheduled settlement date or actual settlement date?
10. What do you do to actively pursue timely settlement?

Securities Lending

1. Provide a complete overview of your securities lending operation, including the processes and systems. How long have you been engaged in securities lending?
2. In what year did you first offer securities lending?
3. What is the dollar size of your domestic and global (separately) securities lending pools?
4. How many of your clients currently participate in your securities lending programme?
5. Describe your policy for screening borrowers.
6. With how many and with which borrowers do you have a business relationship (provide list)? how are they selected? May the client override any of the brokers on your list?
   a. Which are your primary borrowers?
   b. How often is the creditworthiness reviewed?
   c. Can the client select or eliminate a given borrower for their account?
   d. Can the client establish a limit for loans to a given borrower?
   e. Has a borrower ever defaulted? If yes, please describe.
7. How many are actually used (eg, 80% of the business to eight borrowers)?
8. What is the maximum loan made to single borrowers?
9. What percentage of collateral do you require? Do you require collateral to cover both market and accrued income?

10. What forms of collateral are accepted?
11. Describe the procedures and the frequency of marking-to-market.
12. What procedures do you have in place to ensure that securities on loan are returned on a timely basis to meet trade settlement requirements?
13. Describe the allocation system used in determining which clients' securities are lent.
14. Do you operate international lending? If yes, in which countries?
15. How is the income generated from securities split between the client and your company?
16. Provide your revenue split percentage and estimated annual revenue to be earned from securities lending.
17. What protection is available for risk of loss? How is client indemnification offered?
18. Can the income be forgone in return for a lower custodial/trustee fee structure?

Fees

1. Describe, in detail, your standard fee schedule for the basic custodial/trustee services: indicate what assets it is based upon (ie, book value or market value), the frequency of billing, the date of the last fee increase and the guarantee period available.
2. Describe all other fees associated with the custodial services, such as:
   a. basic reporting for segregated and pooled fund accounts
   b. international transaction fees
   c. additional global custody fees (note whether based on book or market value)
   d. wire transfer
   e. derivative services
   f. brokerage report
   g. external audit
   h. mortgage administration
   i. address change
   j. set-up
   k. online inquiry
   l. tax returns
   m. performance measurement
   n. sweeping of cash and investment vehicle.
3. Please indicate any differences between fees for electronic settlements and any requiring manual intervention. Please indicate the expected frequency or types of manual intervention required in your systems which could trigger different fee schedules.
4. How do your fee structures differ when accounting for pooled funds compared with segregated portfolios of stocks, bonds, etc?
5. Describe any additional fees charged for online access to custodial data.
6. Provide a detailed estimate of custody and trustee costs (including legal, if any) given the expected asset size and transaction activity described earlier.
7. Variance fees for multiple investment managers, global investments and any initial asset transfer in kind compared to cash.
8. What commitment is available regarding future cost increases? A five-year fee quote must be provided.
9. Are there any fees associated with additional reports over a specific base number? If yes, what is the base number and what is the fee per report?
10. Please provide a sample custodial/trust agreement.

Derivatives

1. Please provide us with a list of the asset types that you consider to be derivative products in your marketplace.
2. Do you offer any kind of service for derivatives?
3. Are you a member of any derivative clearing house?
4. Do you offer any OTC derivative clearing services?
5. Describe how and when you conduct mark-to-market valuations for the purpose of calculating collateral margin movements.
6. What mechanisms do you use to make margin payments?
7. Describe how and when you would inform us of such movement requirements.
8. What would your policy be in the event of a non-receipt of instructions from us for a collateral movement?
9. Do you create a separate cash account for margin payments or are the margin movements conducted over our normal trading cash account?
10. Do you provide us with a service that informs us of upcoming expiry dates of any derivatives?
11. If 'yes', at what time periods do these take place?

References

1. Provide a list of five custodial clients, including names and telephone numbers, that can be called as references. The clients should have funds of similar size and structure to this fund.
2. Provide a list of clients that have recently appointed your organisation as their custodian.
3. Provide a list of the top ten money managers who have the most accounts under your custody.
4. Provide a list of clients that have recently departed your organisation, complete with reasons why.
5. Provide a list of all current custody clients similar to ourselves.
6. Provide a list of all current custody clients with global services.

Other Services

1. Please describe your approach to the conversion process to your system, including resources, controls, timing, etc.
2. Describe any other services you offer to custodial/trustee clients.

3. Custody Fees

Learning Objective

4.2   Describe the factors that influence the rates of custodian charging and which are considered in the construction of the fee tariff

The factors that influence the rates a custodian charges for their services are the same as for any other business which is trying to make a profit. The business must produce more in revenue than they pay in costs. Therefore they must have an understanding of what their cost base is.

With regard to a custodian, their cost base is likely to be made up of the following main components:

- The cost of their agent network (sub-custodian costs).
- Staffing costs.

- The cost of maintaining their place of business and the property overheads.
- The cost of external suppliers of technology, data and services.

Under these four headings there will be a myriad of incidental costs that must be taken into consideration.

Another factor that comes into consideration when a custodian is designing their fee tariff is whether the client is willing to allow the custodian to retain the client's cash balances and allow the custodian to execute the necessary foreign exchange transactions, or at least to be amongst the banks that are able give a price quote for this business. The reason for this is simple – it gives the custodian the opportunity to make (but not the certainty of making) additional revenue.

Lastly, what is the package of services that the client wants? The answer to this question will have an impact on the fees charged. Most custodians will not want to lose out on product, so most will try to satisfy the client's requirements as best they can. However, the willingness to do this has to be weighed against the cost of providing the service required.

The factors that are considered in the construction of the fee tariff are all of the above. However, as with any business, a custodian will be looking to reduce their cost base but improve their product line whenever and wherever they can.

3.1 Standard Practice for the Construction of a Fee Tariff

Standard practice is to charge a fee for principal transactions (trade instruction and/or settlement) and a composite fee for safekeeping plus the range of asset servicing activities. The ad valorem charge is also likely to be tiered on a sliding scale to reflect the more you have the cheaper it gets principle. A number of small additional fees may also apply for any value added services or bespoke reporting.

3.1.1 Safekeeping and Asset Servicing

Ad-valorem

The composite fee for safekeeping and servicing portfolios is usually computed as a basis point charge on the market value, with the rate varying according to the market (reflecting the efficiency and costs in the respective market). Alternatives include a flat rate for a market or a fixed fee per line of stock; where this is adopted it is more often applied to the domestic market only.

3.1.2 Unbundling

In some cases, fees are unbundled, with perhaps a lower flat rate or rate per line of stock applying for safekeeping, plus individual charges for each of the services provided.

3.1.3 Principal Transaction Charge

The principal transaction charge might be levied on settlement of all trades or perhaps for physical certificates only. There may be a supplementary charge for trade instructions requiring repair or manual input, by the service provider.

3.1.4 Additional Fees

Additional fees might apply for:

- the inward or outward transition of portfolios
- each tax reclaim
- each proxy voted (or proxies reported)
- cash movements
- third-party foreign exchange transactions
- derivatives processing
- account maintenance
- additional or tailored reports
- telecommunications fees for a direct link
- provision of a workstation, training services and other costs.

3.1.5 Securities Lending Programmes

With securities lending programmes, it is standard practice for service providers to bear the cost of the programme and to share in the lending fee income. Out-of-pocket expenses (including stamp duty/securities transfer taxes, certificate fees, charges levied by central depositories on the deposit or withdrawal of securities and registration fees) are generally passed on.

3.2 Trends in Fee Structure

Most often, it is the principal transaction fee, plus basis point charge, which is levied, and there has been a trend away from the practice of applying a wide range of additional fees, making it simpler for clients to track and control costs.

3.3 Cash Management and Foreign Exchange

A client may bear a significant hidden cost if its service provider offers uncompetitive rates and it does not have easy access to alternative providers and the tools to make a quick comparison across providers. So quoting competitive rates consistently across all major, emerging and exotic markets may well warrant a higher fee than another provider that offers poor rates.

In cash management, credit and debit interest rates should follow an appropriate, published interbank lending rate for the currency concerned, plus a competitive spread. The custodian may choose to pay credit interest on a tiered balance basis or have a minimum balance policy. Netting of debit and credit balances, with interest applied to the net balance, is an advantage.

3.4 Value Added Tax (VAT)

Depending upon the domicile of the service provider, the provider's services may be partly or wholly subject to value added tax (VAT), goods and services tax (GST), or other taxes. The treatment may vary from one provider to another.

4. Custodian Third-Party Relationships

Learning Objective

4.3 Identify the types of third-party service supplier custodians appoint and explain the governance considerations that arise from their appointment

In the provision of their custody services, the custodian firm is likely to have several third-party relationships.

These relationships are similar in nature to the relationship between a global custodian and the sub-custody network, ie, the quality of the provider is of paramount importance as a client will not accept third-party suppliers' fault as any kind of excuse for delivery of poor service to them.

Types of third-party relationships might be:

- price source
- corporate actions data
- stock-borrowing counterparty
- systems suppliers (asset management, etc)
- sub-agents (for example, for foreign exchange, tax, transfer agency or derivatives services)
- sub-custodian network (agent banks)
- brokers
- messaging networks (eg, SWIFT).

There are clearly issues here about the service provision through a number of different areas:

1. Reliability.
2. Timely provision.
3. Continuity and disaster recovery.
4. Credit.
5. Regulatory implication of outsourcing.
6. Legal.
7. Liability for errors, costs and losses.

Global custodians utilising sub-custodians are aware of the client's requirement for guarantee of sub-custody performance but the same requirement inevitably applies in all cases of third-party relationship.

As a result, the outsource – supplier relationship must be managed actively through a structured process, comprising:

1. effective service level agreements (SLAs)
2. effective management information
3. effective performance measurement procedures
4. problem resolution via relationship managers
5. contingency plans to switch counterpart/supplier
6. effective communication channels.

Third-party relationships must be closely and constantly monitored and managed to prevent not only reputational damage (and loss of clients) but financial loss (through claims) and regulatory risk (breaches of regulation).

5. Monitoring Custodian Services

Learning Objective

4.4   Explain how custodian performance, compliance and regulation can be monitored

Whenever a service (which has to be monitored) is provided, it is important that a service level agreement (SLA) is established.

Essentially, the performance of a custodian service is measured in two ways:

1.   The service received on the basis of the client's own assessment.
2.   The performance of the custodian relevant to a benchmark.

5.1   Client Assessment

The most usual source of assessment by the client is from their own internal management information and problem logs.

These will be maintained with reference to internal benchmarks known as key performance indicators (KPIs), such as response to queries and custodian-sourced errors, as well as to the SLA and issues that have arisen in that context.

A problem is, of course, that the custodian will not necessarily agree with the assessment, as there are numerous cases where the blame may be in doubt.

Assessment of the custodian's performance must be carried out on the basis of current performance and trends. All firms have periods of change where performance may fluctuate temporarily. The assessment must also be against realistic KPIs, for example error-free may be desirable but is it actually realistic? However, the number of acceptable errors in a period, and even the type of error given a particular aspect of the service, are reasonable benchmarks to set.

5.2   Custodian Benchmarks

Various benchmarks are available, either in the public domain or by the payment of a fee to commission an organisation, to carry out the survey.

Surveys are published periodically by organisations such as Global Custody, Euromoney and GSCS benchmarks. Examples can be found on the relevant company's website.

What can be important is the methodology used. For example, these firms carry out periodic surveys of sub-custodians and global custody providers. The role of the sub-custodian is important in the overall securities processing environment and the performance of these sub-custodians is, therefore, of great interest and importance in terms of selection.

Methodology

There can be several ways in which a survey can be carried out. A common way is to poll a selection of organisations using the sub-custody networks or global custodians.

An issue is obviously the number of participants in the poll, the breadth of geographical spread and the type of organisation (if it is a global survey).

Typically, the poll will take the form of a questionnaire on experiences, services offered, problems encountered, etc. and then probably a request to rank the sub-custodians in terms of satisfaction.

This type of survey enables a broad picture to be created covering:

*   which custodians offer the defined services
*   the ranking of custodians in different locations
*   the types and extent of problems experienced by clients
*   satisfaction levels.

A scoring system can be used that awards points for placing generated by assessment of answers based on a four- or five-point rating, ie, excellent, good, fair, below average, poor, etc. It is also likely that a weighting system will be applied that is based on assets under management and may even be further weighted according to location.

Questionnaire

The questions asked will relate to the activity of the custodian, so there could be questions relating to core custody services such as settlement, safekeeping, corporate actions, information supply; then questions about added-value services, like cash management and securities lending; and finally questions about how the custodian applies itself to client services, communication, managing operational risk, etc.

5.3   Summary

Surveys, polls and benchmarks are all vital in the overall context of measuring service levels, costs and competitive advantage. All organisations are subject to change, and custodians are no different.

Performance, therefore, is likely to fluctuate and, certainly in emerging markets, the impact of increasing numbers of clients and higher workloads can materially affect the performance of a domestic custodian and also, therefore, the global custodian.

Surveys, polls and benchmarking enable monitoring of this impact on service levels and are important for both the custodians themselves and their customers.

6. Sub-Custodians

Learning Objective

4.5   Describe the significance of the role of the sub-custodian

When selecting a global custodian it is important for a customer to understand the structure beneath the global custodian that allows them to provide the services they offer. In some jurisdictions, it is a legal requirement to use a local custodian.

Equally, if a firm is looking to establish custody arrangements, they may choose to appoint custodians across a range of markets or geographical locations.

Either way there will be an organisation performing a crucial role in this process – the sub-custodian.

A sub-custodian maintains links with the local CSDs and clearing houses and the local regulatory bodies such as the tax authorities. The sub-custodian provides settlement and other services associated with the custody services that it offers to the clients. Those clients can be local institutions, internationally based clients or firms offering global custody facilities in the international markets.

As such, sub-custodians perform the functions of custody that are pre-eminent in the mind of the global custodian's client. Therefore, when perception is said to be the truth, the global custodian is only as good as its sub-custodian. So, when viewed in this light, their significance is of paramount importance to the global custodian. The client appoints the global custodian, not their agents.

There are several options for the structure as shown below:

Clients

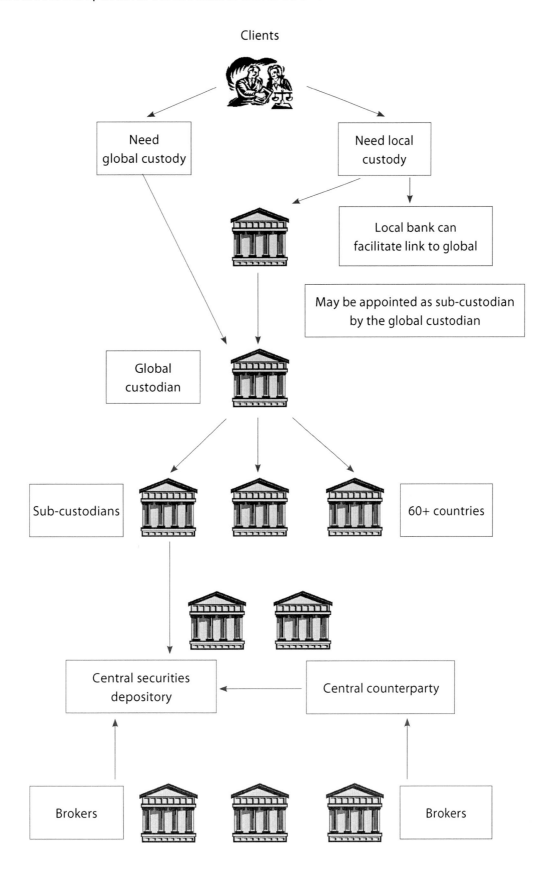

Need global custody

Need local custody

Local bank can facilitate link to global

May be appointed as sub-custodian by the global custodian

Global custodian

Sub-custodians

60+ countries

Central securities depository

Central counterparty

Brokers

Brokers

6.1   Selecting A Sub-Custodian

Key questions about the proposed firm will include how they deliver services related to:

- cash management
- risk management
- pricing
- CSD/clearing house access (membership)
- corporate actions
- access
- reporting capability.

In addition, there will be business issues such as:

- credit rating
- management
- audit and controls
- technology capability
- planned developments (technology, growth)
- capacity
- global custody client services.

This list is not exhaustive and specific requirements may well be appropriate for particular relationships. Section 2 in which RFIs and RFPs are discussed gives the reader a much more exhaustive list of questions to be asked.

For a global custodian, the sub-custody service may be provided by a subsidiary or branch of the firm. In general, this will have the advantage of maintaining corporate standards, technology capability, risk policies, support, etc.

6.2   Regulatory Issues

Before appointing a sub-custodian, a firm must make certain that there are no impediments to the selection of a particular sub-custodian. For example, there may be restrictions on appointing sub-custody firms with less than a set minimum capital base. This could be a particular problem in emerging markets and will restrict the choice for the customer. The US ERISA regulations, mentioned in Section 1 of this chapter, are very keen on capital adequacy, as are many other governmental regulatory organisations around the world.

If a global custodian or an institution cannot find a suitable sub-custodian, it may have little choice but to establish a presence and capability itself. However, they can always choose not to do the business in that country.

6.3 Sub-Custodian Performance

Learning Objective

4.6   Describe the monitoring and operational controls which should be used with local sub-custodians

As with any relationship it is important to:

- establish the terms of the relationship
- encompass those terms in a binding legal agreement that is enforceable
- establish a service level agreement with agreed KPIs
- monitor performance by producing relevant management information
- meet periodically in person, by video link or by phone to discuss the current performance and future service requirements and developments and other issues going forward.

Surveys (see Section 5.2) are carried out on sub-custodians just as they are on global custodians – they can provide important information in terms of assessing the sub-custody relationship wanted.

6.3.1 Operational Controls

At an agreed period of time, the custodian should expect to receive a report from the sub-custodians on their auditor's opinion of their internal controls. This should give an unbiased report on the management controls within the sub-custodian.

Also, when a sub-custodian is used, it will be necessary to have a robust reconciliation procedure to ensure that all the tasks, actions and instructions have been received and dealt with correctly. These are likely to be performed on a daily basis. Communication between the client and the sub-custodian is vitally important, particularly in markets outside the client's time zone.

Escalation procedures must be in place, understood by staff and activated as necessary if and when problems, decisions and issues arise.

The client should expect to receive adequate management information to be able to assess the performance of the sub-custodian. A relationship manager needs to be in place and able to deal quickly and effectively with issues that arise.

For a global custodian it is important to remember that their service is only as good as its sub-custodian service.

7. Client Reporting and Valuation

Learning Objective

4.7   Describe the information custodians are expected to pass on to their clients

In this learning objective the term 'custodian' refers to any organisation that holds a record of assets on behalf of another party, which can either be an electronic record or a physical item. This, therefore, refers to CSDs, ICSDs, sub-custodians and global custodians. However, not all of the information described will be reported by all of the organisations named.

As part of the comprehensive reporting services provided by the custodians, in general there should be reports covering all the custody operations events. The reports can be categorised as follows:

Preliminary Advice/Information Reports

- Floating rate note (FRN) coupon fixing.
- Interest rate changes.
- Forthcoming redemptions.
- Forthcoming coupon payments.
- Conversion opportunity timings.
- Exercise opportunity timings.
- Dividend rates/income/payment date.
- Corporate action events.
- Corporate governance (proxy voting) events.

Portfolio Position Reports

- Unmatched trades.
- Non-availability of assets (cash and other assets).
- Unsettled trades.
- Buy-in/sell-out notices.
- Securities lent/borrowed.
- List of securities held (cash and other assets).
- Collateral held/deposited.
- Valuation of portfolio in currency of security/base currency of investor.

Corporate Actions Reports

It is the global custodian's duty to provide as much information as possible to enable the client to make the necessary decisions to ensure that the information is accurate and to allow enough time for the client's instructions, where appropriate, to be relayed back to the company.

As there is a variety of information types, it has not been easy for global custodians to translate this into electronic message formats for the client. Instead, information on corporate actions has, in the past, tended to be sent by telex and mail. However, this situation is quickly changing as the quality and the delivery mechanism of information from overseas markets improves.

Under this heading, a global custodian may be expected to report back to the client on any AGMs or EGMs that the client had requested to be represented at by way of proxy voting.

Investment accounting is the provision of a full range of reports which may include fully accrued, multi-currency valuations, performance measurement and investment analysis, at both detailed and summary levels.

Not all of the custodians referred to in this section will be expected to produce this type of reporting. This is more likely to be the domain of the global custodians. Reports may apply to a single portfolio or to a consolidation of a number of portfolios.

Pricing and Valuation Reporting

Prices of individual securities are obtained from a variety of external price feeds, such as companies, stock exchanges, Extel and Thomson Reuters and allow the calculation of market value. From this the investors' portfolios can be valued, both in the currency of the security and in the base currency of the investor.

It is important that the re-pricing of securities is carried out accurately and at timely intervals so funds' NAV calculations can be performed. An incorrectly priced security will lead to an erroneous NAV, with the consequence that compensation may have to be paid to unit holders of the funds.

Investment Analysis

Using pricing information, the investments can be analysed in a variety of ways:

- instrument type – equities (ordinary/common shares, preference shares, etc), bonds (eurobonds, government bonds, convertible bonds, etc) and cash and cash equivalents.
- industrial sector.
- geographical location.
- percentage of the portfolio that each security or its type, industrial sector and geographical location represents.
- what-if analysis – examining how changes in securities or country allocations affect the return on the portfolio.

Investment Performance Evaluation

The information provided allows the investor to evaluate the marketability of the securities by stock selection, markets and currencies.

There are a number of external performance measurement companies who collect relevant data from investors and global custodians in order to determine how investor types compare with each other or against industry-recognised indices. This is relevant, for example, for marketing purposes when fund managers, hoping to win new business, state that they have outperformed the relevant index by, say, 2% when the average has been 1%.

Investment Income Tracking

The investment performance of a security includes the income received and income due. This is especially important for debt securities for which income (interest) accrues on a daily basis until the payment is made (usually annually or bi-annually, depending on the security type and domicile).

Foreign Exchange Reporting

Foreign exchange transactions should be related back to the underlying securities trades or income receipts. Historical exchange rates and interest rates should be reported to allow the investor to check the actual rates obtained against the market closing rates.

Consolidated Reporting

Investors may use two or more fund managers because each has a particular specialist investment skill. If the fund managers use their own global custodian, the investors have the problem of consolidating a range of reports from the fund managers and their global custodians into one combined set of reports.

To save the investor's time and effort in making the consolidation, one global custodian acts as recipient for the reports generated by the other global custodians and prepares a consolidated set of reports.

Distribution

Depending on the nature of the reports, the custodians will communicate by one of the following methods: mail, proprietary system or SWIFT messaging.

8. Managing Transitions Among Custodians

8.1 The Role of Client Transition Teams

Learning Objective

4.8 Describe the role of the client transition teams and the reasons for their introduction

Institutional investors (eg, pension funds, charities) and other investors will occasionally decide to make strategic changes in asset portfolios such as:

- changing asset allocation
- changing their investment manager(s)
- changing their investment style (eg, active to passive or growth to value).

They may also, from time to time, decide to change their custodian. Custodians themselves may decide to leave an existing sub-custodian and appoint a different sub-custodian within their agent network.

Another trigger for change is when mergers, acquisitions or liquidations of funds occur.

Any of these reasons can result in the movement of large amounts of assets. These movements have to be orchestrated and controlled in a very strict way. In the early days of global custody, when the value of the assets and the actual number of lines of assets held were not of the magnitude they are today, these movements would have probably been orchestrated by the settlement teams. However, as the values increased, so did the lines of assets and the number of clients coming to the marketplace. It became clear that an area of expertise within the custodians was needed to control these events and so transition teams were born.

Similarly, in the area of fund management, because of the large movements of capital and assets, it was felt that clients could be well served by a third party not necessarily previously associated with the client to manage the strategic change in the portfolio structure. This became known as a business called transition management.

Traditionally, when making a strategic change to the portfolio, the institutional investor would sell the affected portfolio for cash and arrange for the investment manager to reinvest the proceeds into appropriate investments. This strategy, really little more than a trading exercise, held a number of risks for the institutional investor such as:

- **Time** – it could take some time to find the right price at which to trade.
- **Opportunity risk** – the portfolio would be cash-based for a period of time until fully invested. During this time, opportunities to benefit from hoped-for investments would be lost.
- **Market impact** – liquidating large portfolios in short periods of time will have a negative impact on the market. Similarly, the reinvestment of large amounts of cash will also impact the market. However, if liquidation and reinvestment are undertaken over a longer period of time, while there will be a reduced market impact, the opportunity risk issues become prominent.

As an alternative, an institutional investor will appoint a transition manager to provide a more measured approach. Transition managers, typically banks with index management capabilities, investment banks and global custodian banks, will take overall responsibility for the transition programme. In recent years, appointing a transition manager has become common practice in many, if not all, of the global markets.

The responsibilities of transition managers include:

- helping clients to control risk and protect investment returns during the transition period
- providing oversight throughout the transition process, from pre-trade planning to post-trade analysis.

Transition managers have expertise in the following areas:

- project management
- trading
- custody
- trade settlement and asset distribution
- portfolio management
- cost measurement and reporting.

Similarly, when a custodian has to make a change to its sub-custodian network, it has to be accomplished by a seamless process that has little or no impact on their underlying client base or the associated brokers and fund managers.

Transition teams within the custodian have expertise in the following areas:

- project management
- planning
- market timeframes for movement of assets
- availability of assets
- ongoing communication of progress.

8.2   The Process of Transition

The process of a typical transition includes the following main stages:

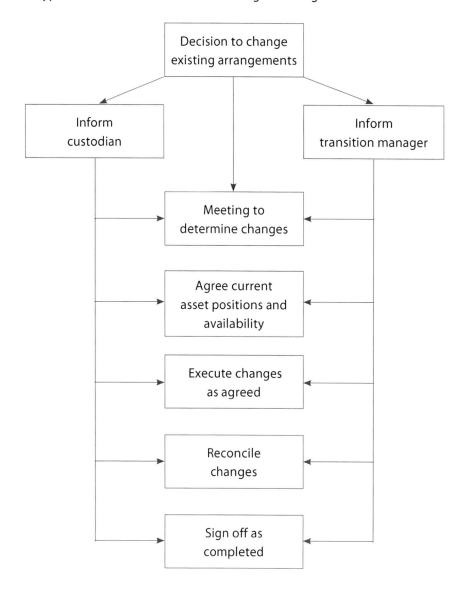

For a more detailed transition plan, see Section 8.4.

8.3   Transition Management Tasks

Transaction Objectives within Transition Management

The first step is to identify the client's needs and goals regarding timing, risk-tolerance and benchmarks. This includes a consideration of the trade-off between market impact and opportunity costs. Finally, those assets that can be transferred from the old portfolio to the target portfolio will be identified.

These are known as in-kind assets.

Pre-trade Analysis

A pre-trade analysis is performed on the remainder of the portfolio. The pre-trade analysis allows the transition manager to develop a trade programme that will meet the client's goals for the transition. The various sources of liquidity for the transition are identified at this point.

Trading

The trading programme includes a combination of internal and external crossing and open-market trading. The objective of the trading programme is to minimise the total cost of the transition for the client while considering the particular constraints as to timing, benchmarks and risk. This could require the use of derivatives for hedging purposes.

Operations (Settlements and Safekeeping)

The in-kind assets, previously identified during the transition objectives stage, are transferred to a holding account for the duration of the transition project, where they are monitored for corporate actions and dividends. Transactions that originate out of internal/external crossing and open-market trading are processed according to normal market practices. These include DvP transactions, margin payments on derivatives, re-registration of securities (where appropriate), income collection, corporate actions and reconciliation.

In addition to the normal day-to-day client reporting, progress reports are prepared showing values of executed trades, remaining assets in the portfolio and the relative performance of the pre-trade, actual and benchmark portfolios.

Post-trade Analysis

Trade executions are reviewed against the benchmarks previously agreed upon and a final analysis report prepared for the client. This final analysis will include details of the transition trading strategy used, the costs incurred (actual versus expected) and trade execution reports. Where the transition objective was to be a change of fund manager, the portfolio assets can then be transitioned to the new manager(s).

Custodians' Objectives

These will be to ensure that the transition management programme can be facilitated and so they have to be an integral part of planning and effecting the transition.

8.4   Transition Plans

Learning Objective

4.9   Describe the milestones of a typical transition plan developed by a client transition team

Stage	Action
Meeting with customer	Agreement on the targets for the transition Confirmation of parties currently holding assets Confirm current positions Give expected duration of transition
Planning	Development of transition plan Identification of resources needed, ie, tax advice Creation of new accounts Instructions required Project checklist
Reconciliation	Continuous reconciliation of assets at counterparties
Valuations	Maintenance of valuation process
Oversight	Continuous monitoring of trades Monitoring positions Managing risks
Migration	Movement of stock positions Movement of cash positions Agree accrued positions
Reconciliation	Reconciliation of new positions Reconciliation of location of assets Reconciliation of portfolio composition Confirm all outstanding assets
Completion	Agreement with counterparties of asset positions Agree portfolio balances Transition completion reports (audit trail) Sign off by customer
Post-completion	Review by transition team of the project Analysis of customer comments (if any) Lessons learned

Note: depending on the transition, there will almost certainly be other action points that will be needed. Managing operational risk during the transition period is a key function of the transition team and the actions should incorporate this.

In more recent times, some firms now actually buy, sell and 'fine tune' any assets that are to be transferred between fund managers, before the particular asset is passed to the new fund manager. An example of such a firm is State Street Global Advisors.

Some material that appears in this chapter may have been sourced from other areas – see Appendix 4 for details of the relevant organisations.

9.   Regulatory Impacts on Custodians

Learning Objective

4.10   Understand how the global Regulatory environment impacts on custodians and in particular how the UK regulatory environment dictates processes for a regulated UK firm

In this section of the chapter a custodian is defined as being any organisation that purports to be safekeeping assets on behalf of a client, whether that client is a retail, institutional or corporate investor or entity.

Many of the world's leading regulators, such as the Securities and Exchange Commission (SEC) in the US, the Office of the Superintendent of Financial Institutions (OSFI) and the Investment Industry Regulatory Organisation of Canada (IIROC) in Canada, the FCA in the UK and the European Banking Authority (EBA) in Europe, to name just a few, are actively bringing forward rules and regulations backed up by legislation, that are placing much more control and oversight requirements on the custodial community. This legislation has a two-pronged focus, these prongs being the actual viability of the custodial organisation in terms of capital adequacy and the introduction of transparency on the beneficial ownership of the assets they have under custody. This is forcing changes in the process and procedures that both custodians and the financial advisory community employ, meaning that they have to have much more account segregation to ensure the integrity of the assets and the recognition of the beneficial owners of the assets under their control.

Most of the regulatory changes were of course prompted by the financial crisis in 2008 and some high profile fraud cases, especially the Madoff and Lehman Bros scandals both in 2008.

A good example of this regulatory reaction is the Dodd-Frank Wall Street Reform and Consumer Protection Act in the US. Under this SEC regulatory framework is something that has become known as the custody rule. The custody rule is intended to provide protection for client's assets such as cash and securities. This regulation essentially forces both financial advisors and the custodians into changes. In brief, it forces the financial advisor to use a qualified custodian and custodians have to recognise the beneficial ownership of the assets by segregation into an account under the name of the client, or by creating an omnibus account that only holds client assets of a particular financial advisor. It also forces certain reporting of the assets held on behalf of the beneficial owner, directly to the beneficial owner of the assets.

In Europe there has been significant progress made to ensure that the custodial banks are much more able to withstand financial shocks to the system. The European Banking Authority (EBA) has introduced the Capital Requirements Directive (CRD) which, in essence, rules on capital requirements for credit institutions and investment firms. These firms must aim to put in place a comprehensive and risk-sensitive framework and to foster enhanced risk management amongst financial institutions. Briefly the main areas focused on under this regulation are as follows:

- **Corporate Governance Systems and Controls** – the management body of the firm is responsible for the firm's overall risk strategy and for the adequacy of the firm's risk management system and must devote sufficient time to risk issues.
- **Recovery and resolution planning** – from a real or potential financial collapse requires the generation of recovery and resolution plans. Recovery plans fall to the firm: resolution plans to the competent authorities.
- **Disclosure** – seeks to improve the transparency of firm activities by requiring annual disclosure of profits, taxes and subsidies in different jurisdictions from 1 January 2015. It also requires disclosure of return on assets in the annual report.
- **Remuneration** – requires firms to have in place remuneration policies and practices that do not encourage or reward excessive risk taking and to make disclosures about the approach adopted in relation to certain prescribed employees and disclosure of remuneration and policies on bonus payments.
- **Reliance on external credit ratings** – the avoidance of too much reliance on the standardised credit rating agency approach, to use internal models, rather than where they have a material number of credit risk exposures or a significant number of counterparties in a particular portfolio.
- **Credit risk adjustments** – defines credit risk adjustments as '*the amount of specific and general loan loss provision for credit risks recognised in the financial statements of the institution in accordance with the applicable accounting framework*'. The definition was introduced in order to broadly replace the term 'value adjustment' that was used in the CRD.
- **Supervisory reporting requirements** – the CRR introduced common reporting standards for firms in relation to capital (COREP) and financial reporting (FINREP) from 1 January 2014. COREP reporting obligations apply to all firms. FINREP reporting obligations apply to those firms which provide consolidated accounts. EU member states may retain some local reporting requirements.
- **Sanctions under CRD IV and the CRR** – the EC has, through the current rules, introduced certain minimum requirements regarding administrative sanctions. The requirements do not extend to cover criminal sanctions. This, in essence, is trying to standardise the penalties imposed on firms.

The impact on firms to incorporate these directives into their process and procedures has been and still is significant. Many processes have had to change and new procedures be introduced.

Candidates should be aware that the above is heavily abridged from the original directives. It only attempts to give them a flavour of what the European Central Bank (ECB) is doing and should in no way be interpreted as being an authoritative version.

In the UK the FCA has introduced the CASS rules that are designed to ensure that UK firms control the safety of their clients' assets. The FCA's CASS protection regime has had a big impact on banks, brokers and asset managers. The new rules affect how businesses handle client money and assets – through customer relationships, outsourcing arrangements, operations, IT systems and the policies and procedures they have in place.

In particular, under section CASS 6.3 Depositing assets and arranging for assets to be deposited with third parties, there are strict rules and guidelines on how firms must conduct themselves. These rules and guidelines relate to many of the learning objectives that this chapter of the workbook refers to.

End of Chapter Questions

1. Explain the purpose of an RFP.
    Answer reference: *Section 2*

2. List six major questions to be contained within an RFP.
    Answer reference: *Section 2.1*

3. What are the charges a custodian might make for their services?
    Answer reference: *Section 3*

4. What issues arise for custodians using third-party services?
    Answer reference: *Section 4*

5. How can a custodian's service be measured?
    Answer reference: *Section 5*

6. What is a sub-custodian?
    Answer reference: *Section 6*

7. What reporting services will a client require?
    Answer reference: *Section 7*

Chapter Five
Securities Lending and Securities Borrowing

5

1.   Introduction

Securities lending is now a worldwide business stream and is practised in many countries. However, there are some countries that do not allow the practice. Securities lending is the lending of equities and bonds by, or on behalf of, an investor to counterparties who are authorised to borrow securities in return for a fee. It should also be recognised that all loans are collateralised.

1.1   International Securities Lending Association (ISLA)

The ISLA is an independent trade association based in the UK and established in 1989 to represent the interests of the securities-lending industry. The primary goal of the ISLA is to assist in the orderly, efficient and competitive development of the international securities lending markets.

The ISLA works closely with international regulators of securities markets. Most of the ISLA members are based in the UK or elsewhere in Europe but there is growing membership from industry participants in the US and the Far East.

There are risks associated with securities lending, one of which is the legal risk. This can be reduced or avoided if there is up-to-date legal documentation in place between the borrower and the lender. The vast majority of today's market participants use a standard agreement drawn up by the ISLA.

ISLA's principal agreement document is the Global Master Securities Lending Agreement (GMSLA), which has superseded earlier forms of agreement. The GMSLA is primarily designed for the strategic international lenders, whereas many of the local market participants, including both the local Japanese and German markets, have chosen to use their own documentation. This is effectively a customised contract under which to conduct business. The customised agreement must be approved before trading can begin and this process adds to the time between the initial contact and the commencement of business. There should be no trading before there is valid documentation in place.

1.2   Global Systems

Many countries now have fully functional securities and lending systems and facilities in place and this lending is primarily to satisfy the local market settlement fails. Securities for these purposes are also offered via the pools operated by Clearstream and Euroclear bank. The table overleaf gives some examples of the global structures where securities lending takes place in order to alleviate settlement fails.

There will also be differing tax implications for those who choose to lend or borrow securities but, because of the global nature of securities lending, it is not possible to document those implications within this workbook.

Country	Securities-lending Arrangements
Argentina	Lending via CSD only for local brokers to cover fails.
Australia	Lending very active. ASX provides a programme for brokers to cover short positions in CHESS-eligible securities.
Austria	Available on a single-trade basis.
China (Shenzhen and Shanghai)	Lending by foreigners not permitted.
Denmark	Lending is permitted but volume is low.
Finland	Commercial banks offer programmes settled through Euroclear Finland.
Hong Kong	Lending allowed.
India	Permitted by National Stock Exchange via the NSCC. Very structured programme.

1.3 Legal And Beneficial Ownership

Legal ownership or legal title to the securities passes from the lender to the borrower, but the benefits of ownership are retained by the lender. This means that the lender maintains beneficial ownership and continues to receive income and benefit from corporate actions and retains the right to sell the securities in the stock market.

Income will not be paid directly to the lender, as their name will have been removed from the company's register. Instead, the income is paid by the borrower to the lender. This process is known as the 'manufactured income process'. The lender, however, loses the right to vote, although shares can be recalled if the lender wishes to vote at a meeting.

2. Lending And Borrowing Securities

Learning Objective

5.1 Describe benefits and risks to organisations that borrow/lend securities: the mechanics of the process; the methods of selection of the lender/ borrower; understand the implications of perfected collateral

2.1 Benefits of Securities Lending and Borrowing

The Group of 30 (G30) recognised the importance of securities lending in Recommendation 8, which states that:

> 'Securities lending and borrowing should be encouraged as a method of expediting the settlement of securities transactions. Existing regulatory and taxation barriers that inhibit the practice of lending and borrowing securities should be removed.'

The principal benefit that securities lending provides to the organisations that borrow stock is essentially to provide liquidity in that particular asset. It does this by tapping into securities that otherwise would be sidelined by being held in safekeeping.

The G30's view of the benefits, ie, *'expediting the settlement of securities transactions'*, is not the only reason why the borrowing of securities takes place in today's market place (see below). Furthermore, not every market has yet implemented appropriate measures to encourage the practice.

Market participants borrow securities for a variety of reasons, including to:

- cover short positions (where participants sell securities which they do not hold)
- support derivatives activities (where participants may be subjected to an options exercise)
- cover settlement fails (where participants do not have sufficient securities to settle a delivery). This is the reason that the G30 cited.

The benefit that the lending of securities provides to the organisations that lend stock is primarily financial. The benefit is twofold:

1. Fee income enhances the investment performance of the securities portfolio.
2. As securities lending decreases the size of the portfolio, there may be a corresponding reduction in safekeeping charges depending on whether the custodian agrees to this.

Because there is no change in beneficial ownership, the beneficial owner (ie, the lender) still enjoys the benefits of receiving income and other benefits.

The international global custodians that provide their clients with the opportunity of securities lending and borrowing, by providing the infrastructure which allows them to act as an intermediary or a conduit in the process, can also benefit. Depending upon the business model the global custodian operates, they may benefit by:

- retaining a share of the fee income whilst running a discretionary lending programme for their client
- charging a transaction fee for every movement across their client's securities account where the custodian is unaware of the reasons for the securities movements.

As a global custodian holds sizeable quantities of any particular issue, it is able to play an important role by providing liquidity to the market. Furthermore, lenders and borrowers benefit from increased operational reliability and reduced risk by using the global custodian's services, such as:

- clearance
- payment
- settlement
- pledging of collateral and valuation (mark-to-market)
- collateral recall
- automatic loan substitution.

2.2   Securities Lending Risks

The lender is primarily concerned with the safe return of his securities by the borrower and that there are adequate means of recompense in the event that the securities are not returned.

There are four situations, each of which could place the lender at a disadvantage:

1. The most serious situation is where a borrower defaults with no chance of the lender retrieving the securities.
2. Timing differences between delivery of the loaned securities and the corresponding receipt of sufficient collateral, although many agents will require receipt of collateral prior to delivering the loaned securities.
3. The late/delayed return of securities due to settlement and securities liquidity problems experienced by the borrower.
4. Settlement inefficiencies or a systemic collapse within the local market itself.

Various countermeasures are taken in order to reduce the risks associated with each of the above situations and these are explained below. However, the primary control is the management oversight of the processes involved and swift action to negate the impacts.

2.2.1   Borrower Default

Loans of securities are delivered by the lender to the borrower on a free of payment basis. For his part, the borrower covers the loan by delivering collateral to the lender.

It is of utmost importance that the collateral should be of such quality and quantity that it may be readily exchangeable into cash in the event that the borrower defaults. In this case, the lender is able to replace the missing securities. Some lenders will place a significant constraint on the type of collateral to be used such as: must be sovereign debt; must be AAA quality paper and so on (see Section 2.5).

To satisfy the quantity requirement, the borrower must deliver collateral with a market value that exceeds the market value of the loaned securities (the outstanding loans) by a predetermined margin, typically between 5% and 15%.

This margin allows for any variation in the value of the outstanding loans. The values can be affected by both the price movement of the securities and the change in the foreign exchange rates. The securities out on loan are marked-to-market (priced at the current market value) at least daily using the previous business day's closing prices and compared to the value of the collateral. Any resulting shortfall in the amount of collateral is made good by the borrower. Conversely, any excess collateral is returned to the borrower.

2.2.2   Daylight Exposure

Although most loans are protected by the pre-delivery of the collateral prior to release of the loaned securities, if for any reason this does not occur, there is the risk of daylight exposure. This is the intra-day settlement risk that loan securities may be delivered before the collateral is received. If the borrower should then default during the intervening period, the lender would be unsecured. The reverse is also true for a loan return.

Example _____

A lender who delivers securities to the borrower at 10:00am, but does not receive the collateral until 3:00pm, has a daylight exposure of five hours. There is a particular problem when the parties to a loan transaction and the domicile of the securities are all in different time zones.

- Lender in London.
- Borrower in New York Securities in Tokyo.
- The loan transaction is for value Wednesday: securities delivered on Wednesday (Tokyo time zone).
- The collateral is due for delivery value Wednesday: collateral delivered Wednesday (New York time zone).
- In the lender's time zone, there is an exposure of at least 14 hours, ie, from the time the securities are delivered (before close of business in Tokyo), to the receipt of collateral (after start of business in New York).

The Bank of England's Securities Lending and Repo Committee issued a code of guidance on the management of this issue in December 2004. This guidance is as follows:

'All participants should be alert to possible settlement risks and take steps to ensure that daylight exposure is recognised and properly controlled; this should include controls on the replacement or renewal of collateral. Where securities and collateral do not move within the same settlement system or country, particular care should be exercised to ensure that value for security is provided in a timely fashion to minimise daylight exposure and settlement/counterparty risk. This may include requirements for the pre-delivery of collateral in appropriate cases.'

2.2.3   Settlement Delays

Delays can be caused by the usual settlement failure types:

- Insufficient securities to satisfy the total delivery.
- The lender or borrower gives late or incorrect delivery/receipt instructions.

For a market maker with a net short trading position, these delays will have an impact on the settlement process.

2.2.4   Market Inefficiencies

Investors will always want to invest in countries where there are opportunities for capital gain and income growth and may pay scant attention to the efficient operation of the settlement systems.

Effective securities lending does, however, depend on the ability to deliver securities without delays and complications. For this reason, securities lending is only undertaken in the established markets with reliable and robust settlement.

2.3 The Mechanics of the Process

The mechanics of lending securities has to start with the investor who holds a portfolio of assets. The investor must want to enhance their income by lending their inactive securities. However, they need to ask themselves some questions before proceeding. An industry checklist has been produced to help with this, and an abridged version is reproduced below (the full version can be reviewed at www. bankofengland.co.uk):

Approval to lend	Do you have the necessary powers to enter into a lending programme, eg, board resolutions?
Risks	Have you researched and understood the various risks?
Agreements	Have you sought legal advice and what tax advice have you taken? Is an indemnity being offered?
Ongoing lending reporting and reviews	How often do you plan to review your lending activity?
Segregated vs pooled	Do you understand the difference between lending from pools and a segregated portfolio?
Lending counterparties	What counterparties will be lent to? Will you limit what is lent to each counterparty? What proportion of your portfolio will you lend? have you established credit limits?
Collateral	What is acceptable collateral? What happens in the case of default? Is the collateral segregated or pooled?
Corporate governance and voting	Will you wish to vote at meetings? Do you understand the recall policies?
Corporate Actions	How will you be alerted to corporate actions?
Fees	Do you understand the level of fees you can expect to earn?
Training	Which of the previous questions flag the need for further research?

2.3.1 Selecting the Business Model

Having satisfied themselves on all of the categories above, the investor then has another decision to make. This decision is how they intend to participate in this business sector. There are fundamentally three different routes or business models the investor can follow:

1. A direct lending programme.
2. A non-discretionary programme.
3. A discretionary (or managed) programme.

Within these business models, the investor also has the scope to determine whether they would want to run an exclusive model or to auction the portfolio or to use a hybrid of these approaches.

When the investor has determined which of the options above suits them best, they need to enter into the appropriate types of legal agreements that cover the business model chosen.

Agreements should have been put in place that detail:

- acceptable collateral, margin levels and the collateral method to be used
- collateralisation following dividends and other corporate events
- an approach to daylight and settlement exposures and pre-delivery of collateral
- business day conventions
- notice periods for voting, elections, recalls and substitutions
- where the lender is acting as agent, the information to be provided about the underlying principals and the allocation of stock lent/collateral between them
- pricing sources for marking to market and currency conversions
- settlement arrangements
- designated offices
- the parties' tax status and manufactured dividend entitlements.

2.3.2   Broadcasting Asset Positions

The investor's asset portfolio that is available to the market needs to be broadcast to the borrowing community so that the counterparties are aware of the assets available. The way this is achieved will depend upon the business model chosen.

2.3.3   Transaction

The borrowing counterparty will make contact with the investor or the investor's agent by the available mechanism, which will depend on the market and participant infrastructure available.

When the trade is made, participants will need to agree:

- the essential economic terms of the transaction, in particular the securities to be lent, rate and term
- any of the matters set out above to the extent that they have not previously been dealt with, for example, acceptable collateral and margin percentages and any non-standard features of the particular transaction.

2.3.4   Confirmations

Confirmations may be unnecessary if participants use electronic trading platforms, but any loan confirmations will normally contain the following information:

- Contract date.
- Loaned securities (type, ISIN or other identifying number and quantity).
- Lender (underlying principal unless otherwise agreed).
- Borrower (as for lender).
- Delivery date.
- Acceptable collateral and margin percentages (if not specified in the legal agreement).
- Term (termination date for term transactions or terminable on demand).
- Rates applicable to loaned securities.
- Rates applicable to cash collateral.
- Lender's settlement system and account.
- Borrower's settlement system and account.
- Lender's bank account details.
- Borrower's bank account details.

2.3.5 Delivery

Delivery of the collateral being supplied should, wherever possible, take place before the release of the loaned securities or, at a minimum, at the same time.

2.4 Selection of Lender/Borrower

The investor does have some choices over who they choose as lender of their securities. As stated in Section 2.3.1, there are three business models that can be followed. However, if either the non-discretionary or managed models is selected, the investor still has to choose their preferred organisation to perform the lending.

Generally, the investor will select their own custodian to be their preferred lender but it is possible that they could choose to have their assets lent out by a local CSD such as the DTCC in the US or the NSCC in India. There are several worldwide CSDs that offer to lend an investor's assets. In some countries this is the only method to be employed.

The investor should also have a view on the type of borrower that they are prepared to lend their securities to. Generally, the credit rating of the counterparty will be the significant factor but other factors could be taken into account, such as the type of business the counterparty is conducting and the residency of the borrower, which may have a detrimental effect on dividend income that the investor can expect to receive by way of manufactured dividends.

2.5 Perfected Collateral

The term 'perfected collateral' referred to in the learning objective normally means, in layman's terms, taking possession of something that the lender has an unencumbered and absolute right to negotiate (turn into cash) in order to protect their loan in the event of failure to return or default of the loan.

The laws on how to accomplish this perfection of collateral in the various countries around the world will vary from country to country. Whether it is ever possible to achieve perfection has to be open to question.

It is therefore of the utmost importance that at the very minimum there are agreements in place between the parties involved in the loans that give the lender an unencumbered lien over the collateral. This should be supported by the actual movement of the collateral by physical means or by book-entry means to an account under the control of the lender or the lender's agent. Daily reports itemising the collateral pledged and the value of that collateral must be continuously produced. Continuous collateral management must be employed by both parties to the loans. This management and reporting has to ensure that the collateral pledged is:

- the agreed quality and type
- maintained within the agreed margins
- being serviced correctly (protecting the borrower's/lender's interests).

2.5.1 Collateral Management

To satisfy the quality requirement referred to previously, the following types of collateral are generally acceptable:

Cash

The lender places the cash out into the money markets and agrees to pay interest (a rebate) to the borrower at a rate lower than the market rate. The difference in rates reflects the lending fee payable to the lender.

The advantages of accepting cash as collateral include the following:

- Acceptance of cash collateral allows the securities to move on a DvP basis and so eliminates the risk that the securities delivery and collateral receipt do not occur simultaneously.
- Cash is regarded as the safest form of collateral in domestic markets, including the US dollar, euro and pound sterling, where it is used in the majority of cases.

The disadvantages of accepting cash as collateral include the following:

- Many institutional lenders are not prepared or are not able to undertake the extra administrative burden of reinvesting the cash (ie, operational issues).
- The tax and regulatory situations in such countries as the UK and Germany make the use of cash impractical.
- There are the added problems of foreign currencies which require one or two days' notice prior to placing funds.
- There is an exposure to adverse exchange rates when using foreign currencies.
- In most cases, there will be no indemnity offered to the lenders when cash is used.

Organisation for Economic Development (OECD) Collateral

By far the most common security type used as collateral is OECD collateral. This is sovereign debt such as government bonds (UK gilts, US treasury bonds, German bunds and French OATs) which also benefit from high credit ratings and ease of sale issued by the governments of the member countries of the OECD. The OECD consists of 30 countries which includes the G10 (Group of Ten) countries. The G10 is actually made up of 11 industrial countries which consult and co-operate on economic, monetary and financial matters.

The countries are: Belgium; Canada; France; Germany; Italy; Japan; the Netherlands; Sweden; Switzerland; the United Kingdom; and the United States.

Certificates of Deposit (CDs)

A certificate of deposit (CD) is still acceptable collateral. CDs give ownership of a deposit at a bank and for which there is an established market.

The advantages of using CDs as collateral include the following:

- CDs are considered to be of high quality and near-cash; they are guaranteed by the banks on which they are drawn. The lender is able to specify the creditworthiness of the banks by only accepting paper with a specified credit rating, eg, AA.

- CDs are in bearer form and therefore straightforward to sell should the need arise. Movements of CDs in the UK take place almost exclusively by book entry within the Central Money Markets Office operated by the bank of England through CREST.

The disadvantages of CDs as collateral include the following:

- The nominal amount of CDs tends to be in shapes of £1,000,000 or $1,000,000 and this makes it difficult to ensure that the margined collateral value matches the value of outstanding loans.
- CDs have a limited lifespan and borrowers must ensure that new CDs are substituted as old CDs mature.

Corporate Debt

Corporate debt (bonds) and equities can be used but the perception that issuer creditworthiness and the security type are of a higher-risk nature are not conducive to making the collateral type generally acceptable to some lenders. In addition, long settlement periods can delay the time from borrower default to receipt of the collateral sale proceeds.

Irrevocable Letters of Credit (L/Cs)

Another acceptable method of providing collateral cover, L/Cs are, nevertheless, under threat as the cost of an L/C is making borrowing against them unprofitable.

The advantages of taking L/Cs as collateral include the following:

- The lender does not need to reinvest or revalue the L/C.
- Daylight exposure (see Section 2.2.2) is eliminated if receipt of an L/C is pre-advised to the lender before the securities are released to the borrower.
- The face amount of an L/C is more than adequate to cover the margined value of the outstanding loans and this results in less collateral movement to maintain the margin levels.

The disadvantages of taking L/Cs as collateral include the following:

- The credit risk of the bank that issued the L/C.
- The high cost of obtaining an L/C from the bank (for the borrower).

Summary

It would be preferable that the system used to monitor the collateral was equipped to define the creditworthiness of the collateral being recorded. It is important to do this because, when the credit rating of the collateral changes to an inferior class, it should be replaced by collateral with the agreed credit rating. This places a burden of management on those who are charged with the responsibility of managing the collateral.

2.5.2 Margin

To satisfy the requirement to maintain the correct level of margin, in the first instance within the legal agreement that binds the lender and borrower, it should be stated what the minimum margin is. To satisfy this requirement there has to be a daily mark-to-market of the value of the collateral. There should be a process in place that conducts this daily valuation and alerts management to any changes.

This change should then initiate the required movement of collateral (in and out) each day. These movements have to be monitored to ensure that they take place in the correct manner. When the additional margin is satisfied by a different type of collateral, then that new collateral has to go through the same vetting and servicing processes.

2.5.3 Servicing of Collateral

Whenever the collateral that is received is of a type that has the potential to effect a change in the terms of the collateral by the issuer, or the benefits of the collateral by the issuer, or to bear interest from the issuer, there is a responsibility to both the lender and borrower that these changes or payments of interest are effectively collected and recorded. There needs to be a section within the agreement stating to whom these benefits will accrue or be paid. The servicing of the collateral has to correctly monitor the collateral for these events, report these events to the lender or borrower, protect the interests of the entitled party and distribute the benefits appropriately. If the investor uses the services of a custodian to safeguard their assets, the custodian will ensure that the investor receives their full entitlement.

2.6   Securities Lending Agreements

In order to protect the interests of the lending parties, the borrowing parties and the intermediaries, agreement forms are drawn up to clearly define the rights, duties and liabilities of those concerned. An agreement will contain references to, inter alia, the following topics:

Agreement Topic	Comments
Interpretation	Definitions of the terms used in the agreement.
Rights and title	Includes reference to the protection of lender's entitlements.
Collateral	Loans should be secured with collateral. Agreement on the forms of collateral.
Equivalent securities	Securities and collateral should be returned in an equivalent form to the original deliveries.
Lender's/borrower's warranties	Statement that both parties are permitted to undertake the lending/borrowing activities.
Default	Remedies available in the event that one or other party defaults on its obligations.
Arbitration and jurisdiction	How and where disputes will be submitted for resolution and under which governing law.
Terms of lending	Basis of how fees will be calculated. How a client's assets will be allocated for loan on a fair and equitable basis with other clients in the lending pool. Is the lending third party or primary? Recall limitations.
Conditions of lending	What happens if F/M sells assets that are on loan? Dividend and withholding tax issues.

3. Third-Party Securities Lending

Learning Objective

5.2 Describe the operational impact of third-party securities lending

Third-party securities lending is different from the normal bilateral lending/borrowing process whereby the two parties to the loan exchange the lent security and receive the non-cash collateral.

With a third-party securities loan, the process takes place through an independent third party such as a custodian bank, which typically will not be the investor's incumbent custodial bank. The securities borrowed and the collateral to be used to secure the borrowing are transferred to the third-party custodian bank, which then manages the operational issues of the loan for its duration. The lender is afforded the same protection as they would have in a bilateral arrangement.

In this process there can be operational impacts on both parties to the loan:

- In the event of a sale of the on loan securities, instructions for the recall must be sent to the third party rather than directly to the borrower. This may add a time delay to the repatriation of the lent securities, which may cause a settlement delay.
- Collateral has to be moved to and from the third party in line with the mark-to-market calculations.
- Manufactured dividends and income have to be paid by the borrower to the lender via the third party. This could cause delay to the income being processed to the beneficiary.
- Corporate benefits and the relative instructions will have to be passed through the third party. This adds another level of complexity to the already complex situation.
- In the movements of assets there is another leg in the chain, which in all other areas of operation would be considered as introducing additional unnecessary risk to the process.

Generally, because of this, when a third party is involved it will have an impact on the terms and conditions applied to the settlement instruction deadlines.

Depending upon the accuracy of the required audit trail of the lender, there may be a need to record both the name of the third party and the name of the borrower in the lender's database.

4. The Role of the Global Custodian

4.1 Options for Lending Assets

Lenders of securities do, however, have the following options and mechanisms for lending their assets:

- **Direct** lending programme.
- **Non-discretionary** programme.
- **Discretionary** (or **managed**) programme.

4.1.1 Direct Lending by Investor

Direct lending will suit bigger investors who are able to offer portfolios with large and varied holdings. They are therefore able to enhance their returns by going directly to the market owing to the fact that they do not have to share the revenue.

The key points are:

- the investor negotiates loan agreements and recalls/returns with the intermediaries or borrowers
- the investor controls the movement of collateral and ensures that margins are maintained
- the investor assumes the counterparty risk of the intermediary
- the global custodian delivers and receives securities on a 'free of payment' basis on instructions taken from the investor.

The investor assumes all risks associated with stock lending, including the following:

- **Intra-day exposure** – the investor must ensure that securities are not released until adequate margined securities are under their control (directly in-house or indirectly through a global custodian or settlement agent).
- **Settlement risk** – the investor must ensure that deliveries of securities for loans are made on time. Deliveries of securities free of payment demand a higher level of authorisation and control than deliveries made on a DvP basis. The investor must be able to identify sufficient situations where securities on loan are required to settle a sale transaction and to initiate timely recalls.
- **Market risk** – collateral should be revalued more frequently in volatile markets.
- **Counterparty risk** – the investor must ensure that the creditworthiness checks and management of the counterparties they use are constantly updated.
- **Operational risk** – the investor has to take full responsibility for ensuring that all processes are carried out efficiently and on time.
- **Legal risk** – the investor is responsible for arranging and monitoring the legal stock-lending agreements.

The reward is:

- **Fee income** – the investor receives the full amount of the fees.

4.1.2 Non-Discretionary Programme

Non-discretionary lending differs from direct lending in so far as the global custodian takes a more involved role in the process.

The key points are:

- the custodian seeks approval from the client for each loan request
- the custodian receives collateral from the borrowers and ensures that the margins are adequate
- a fee is charged by the custodian for this service
- the client assumes the risk of the borrowers.

The extra advantages for the client are:

- the custodian ensures that the collateral is matched to the movement of securities
- the custodian is better placed to initiate timely loan recalls to cover the client's sales.

The disadvantage is:

- the client's relationship with the intermediaries might suffer now that they approach the custodian and not the client for loan requests and returns.

4.1.3 Discretionary (or Managed) Programme

Discretionary programmes (commonly known as agent lending) tend to suit a client who wants an entirely managed programme and attracts many types of lenders.

The stock lending is delegated entirely to the custodian in the following key ways:

- The custodian actively seeks to place securities out on loan with the intermediaries.
- The custodian takes collateral and monitors the margins.
- A portion of the risk of the borrower is transferred from the client to the custodian.
- Depending on the level of risk assumed by the custodian, anything from 15–20% of the fee income is retained by the custodian.

The advantages for the investor are:

- the service is totally linked into the custodian's settlement systems, thus ensuring that the risk of settlement failure through late recalls is almost eliminated
- the investor benefits from being a part of substantially larger holdings which may be more attractive to potential borrowers
- no underlying investment in infrastructure is required
- it gives the investor a wider scope and choice in the lending market.

The disadvantages for the investor are:

- depending on the method of loan allocation adopted by the custodian (see Section 4.2), the investor's assets may not be fully utilised
- the investor receives only a portion of the fee income. However, this will be offset by reductions in transaction charges and safekeeping fees.

4.2   Loan Apportionment

Learning Objective

5.3   Describe how lenders/custodians apportion loans

Any custodian that operates a securities lending programme and that wishes to lend out some of the securities belonging to one or many of its clients must have their permission to do so in the first instance. The stock must then be lent out fairly and in an equitable manner.

For example, a custodian may actually hold a stock on behalf of, say, five different clients, all of whom have agreed to lend out their stock. The custodian then has to be careful when deciding which of the clients' stock is lent out and which clients do not have their stock lent out. Undue favouritism must not be shown to any one client or clients. The global custodian must ensure therefore that loans and fee income are allocated fairly. To cope with this, global custodians use sophisticated algorithms to allocate loans and fee accruals fairly.

4.3   Benefits and Entitlements

As stated in Section 1.3, the lender loses legal ownership and voting rights of the securities but retains the benefits of ownership.

It is important to appreciate that the lender is treated as if he had not lent the securities; any shortfalls are made good by the borrower who, as temporary legal owner of the securities, will receive the benefits in the first instance. It is the responsibility of the intermediary or global custodian to ensure that the lender is not disadvantaged through securities lending activities.

This part focuses on the expectations of the securities lender and the actions which the borrower or intermediary/custodian must take in order to satisfy the lender's requirements.

4.3.1   Types of Corporate Action

Companies become involved for a variety of reasons, such as:

Rights issues	Raise cash in order to: • finance acquisitions • expand business • reduce borrowings • stay afloat
Convertibles	Lower interest payments
Warrants	Future cash inflow at no cost
Capitalisation issues	Convert reserves into share capital Increase marketability by reducing price
Repayment of share capital	Return surplus cash to shareholders

The main types of corporate action fall into two key categories: those which are voluntary or optional in nature; and those which are mandatory.

4.3.2 Lenders' Rights

Lenders retain the right to participate in all dividends, interest payments and other benefits on securities that are on loan. The one exception is that lenders lose the right to vote. It is therefore essential that lenders are able to focus on two areas by having:

- certainty in the knowledge that incoming corporate action information is sufficient to ensure that they can make an informed decision
- assurances that all decisions are dealt with in accordance with their instructions.

4.3.3 Manufactured Income

If securities are on loan over the record date, the issuing company will pay the dividend or interest to the party at the end of the borrowing chain, ie, the legal owner. The lender, the beneficial owner, must therefore be paid an amount of cash in lieu of the actual dividend. In other words, the borrower manufactures a dividend by making a payment of the value of the dividend that the lender has forgone in order to make the lender whole.

The amount generated reflects the amount of the net dividend the lender would have actually received after any withholding tax that would have been deducted from the payment. It is this cash amount that will be made in lieu of the dividend.

The Role of the Intermediary

The lending intermediary's prime role is to ensure that the lender is made whole. This can be achieved in the following ways:

- Gathering information from numerous sources.
- Comparing information from one source with another to ensure consistency.
- Rearranging the information (including any translations) into a form from which the lender can make a decision.
- Ensuring that all expected instructions are received from the lenders.
- Giving accurate and timely instructions to the correct destination.
- Informing the lender of the corporate action results.

The need for the intermediaries to receive the lender's instructions in advance of the issuing company's own deadlines can cause problems with the lender. The lender may wish to delay a decision until the last possible moment, sometimes past the intermediary's deadline. Nevertheless, the intermediary should, in this situation, attempt to comply with the instructions on a best efforts basis.

Importance of Accuracy and Timeliness

Information on impending events is obtained from a variety of sources, for example:

- the issuing companies
- CSDs

- sub-custodians
- stock exchanges
- the financial press
- information vendors.

The way in which the investor receives information depends very much on the nature of the event itself and the manner in which the investor chooses to hold the securities in safekeeping.

All corporate actions have deadlines, especially those which require a decision (the optional events). Unfortunately, differing worldwide standards do not make the task of monitoring corporate actions any easier. For this reason, it is important for the intermediaries and/or their agents to ensure that:

- the information received is accurate
- any instructions are given in the form, and within the deadlines, specified by the company.

Failure to settle situations such as market purchases and sales on time will result in delays and inconvenience. There may be occasions when penalty interest is payable and both counterparties will be exposed to an element of risk while the trade remains unsettled.

However, the obligation to settle the trades remains until such time as the delivery of securities (together with the underlying cash payment) takes place.

With an optional corporate action, however, failure to give and act upon accurate and timely instructions will usually result in a loss of entitlement to the benefit. The defaulting party will have to purchase securities (if securities were to be the benefit) in the market and pay the extra costs.

4.3.4   Actions Required

Voting Rights

Lenders who wish to exercise their right to vote must arrange for the loans to be recalled in sufficient time to comply with local voting rules. These rules may call for the re-registration of the securities into the lender's (or their appointed nominee's) name or may necessitate the blocking of the shares until the annual (or extraordinary) general meeting has taken place. Sufficient time should be allowed for this to happen.

Corporate Actions

It is the responsibility of the agent/lender to work with the borrower to ensure that the lender is made whole with respect to corporate actions. The borrower can either unwind the loan, returning the securities to the lender or can take up any entitlements on behalf of the lender, making any extra cash payments as and when required.

Implications for Collateral

There are two points to note with respect to collateral:

- The amount of collateral pledged may have to increase or decrease in order to maintain the required (margined) levels of cover. This applies equally to collateral that is taken in the form of cash or other securities (whether in the same currency or different currencies).

- If other securities are used, there will come a time when corporate actions will affect the collateral itself. In this case, the collateral can either be substituted or treated in much the same way as the loaned securities. In many cases, the collateral will be substituted prior to the corporate event as a means to mitigate the risk.

5.   Securities Lending, Repos, Reverse Repos and Buy-Sell-Back

Learning Objective

5.4   Distinguish between securities lending, repo, reverse repo and buy-sell-back

A repo, or a repurchase agreement to give it its full name, is, by its nature, considered a loan. As the agreement usually has its focus on a security, it falls into the securities lending arena.

It is a transaction where one party lends cash and another party borrows that cash. But, sometimes confusingly, each side of the same transaction carries different market terminology and descriptive nouns. If you are the borrower of the cash you have conducted a repo but if you are the lender of that cash you have conducted a reverse repo.

However, unlike securities lending, where a fee is received for the loan of a stock, a repo is a sale of securities with an agreement to repurchase the security at a point in the future. Typically, a repo enables a holder of securities to obtain funding (raise cash) against the securities as collateral and for a lender of cash to obtain high-quality collateral against a loan. This puts vital liquidity into the markets.

A repo also has a different legal agreement structure such as the Global Master Repo Agreement (GMRA) as designed by the International Security Management Association (ISMA).

Most or the collateral management is conducted under a tri-party arrangement such as the services provided by Euroclear bank and Clearstream.

A repo transaction can be illustrated by the following diagram:

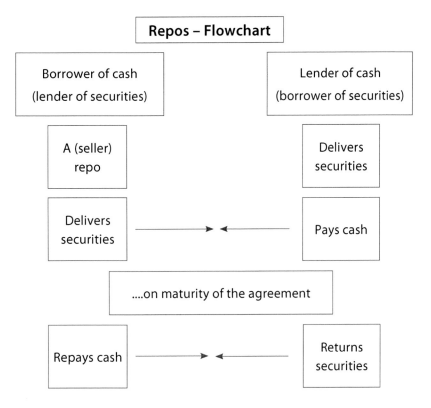

Source: The Derivatives and Securities Consultancy ltd

To follow the flow of a repo more closely, we can see the process from beginning to end as shown below:

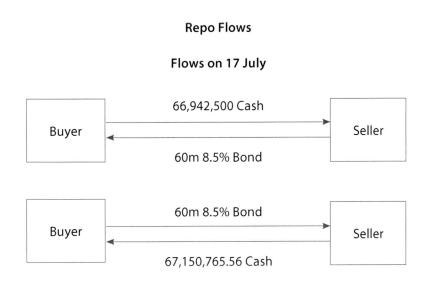

Source: The Derivatives and Securities Consultancy ltd

Buy/sell back transaction differ from repos in as much as they are transactions that have a different structure. They are still loans of cash but the borrower and lender of the cash enter into an agreement whereby a transaction is conducted based on a price differential between a spot price versus a forward price for the collateral being used. So the seller (the borrower of cash) sells the collateral today at, say, £10,000 but agrees to buy the same collateral back at a contracted date in the future for, say, £11,000. This means that instead of the transaction being based on an interest rate (the repo rate) it is based on an agreed value (spot and forward) for the collateral. The party providing the loan of cash obviously benefits by the price differential.

Buy/sell back transactions are identical to repo transactions in terms of the collateral movements and cash flows.

The following table illustrates the differences between stock lending, repos and buy-sell-back.

	Classic Repo	Buy-Sell-Back	Securities Lending
Basis of transaction	Cash vs securities	Cash vs securities	Securities vs other securities, cash or any other acceptable collateral
Documentation	Single agreement, full rights of offset in case of default	Two separate transactions with often no right of offset in case of default	Single lending agreement with full rights of offset in the case of default
Coupon payment	Returned to seller	No obligation to return to income as factored into price. Kept by buyer	Returned to lender; other rights can be subject to the agreement
Fee/cost	Quoted as repo rate, paid as interest on cash amount	Quoted as repo rate, paid through price differential between purchase and forward repurchase price	Quoted as a fee as a % per annum on cash value. If cash is used as collateral, rebate is offset against interest paid on cash
Margin rights	Initial margin (IM) and variation margin (VM) both possible; IM usually in favour of the borrower	IM possible, usually in favour of borrower. VM possible only by close out and repricing	IM and VM both possible; IM in favour of lender
Substitution	Lender can substitute collateral	Possible only through close-out and repricing	Borrower can substitute collateral
Maturity	Fixed-term or open	Fixed-term only	Fixed-term or open

6.   Reports Related to Securities Lending

Learning Objective

5.5   Illustrate the types of reporting required to support a securities lending programme

- Direct lending programme.
- Non-discretionary programme.
- Discretionary (or managed) programme.
- Third party lending.

When thinking about the reporting that needs to be provided, the type of lending arrangement noted above needs to be taken into account.

There also needs to be a distinction made between whether the programme the investor has entered is a strategic programme designed to be part of their portfolio management structure and aimed at all borrowers or as part of some of the global lending programmes that are offered via CSDs, ICSDs and clearing corporations. These are effectively large pools of assets and are akin to the third-party arrangements described previously, but which are primarily aimed at eradicating fails in the local marketplace.

6.1   Intermediary And Third-Party Lending

The reports and information that will be provided by the lending party include the following:

1. List of securities available to the pool (for lenders).
2. List of securities available from the pool (for borrowers).
3. List of securities/type of borrower designated as not available for loan by the client.
4. Lending and borrowing rates.
5. Specific securities needed (this is for highly illiquid/scarce securities, ie, non-registered/unlisted).
6. List of securities currently borrowed.
7. List of securities currently loaned.
8. Periodically: statement of lending/borrowing and fees credited/debited to the client's account including any administration fee charged by the third party.
9. List of benefits and entitlements occurring on loaned/borrowed stock.
10. Record of the receipts/payments and postings to the client account related to corporate actions and fees.

There needs to be a flexible approach taken to reporting which allows the investor to mix and match from a menu of reports. Other reports and topics are becoming increasingly important, eg, benchmarking and risk reporting such as VAR.

There are some important issues here, however, and none more so than point 3 above.

Today, many funds are investing with mandate requirements relating to ethical and responsible investing. This means that certain securities cannot be included in portfolios but, equally, it also relates more and more to the lending of securities to certain types of organisation. For example, some funds are not permitted to engage in loaning securities to hedge funds to cover short selling. This is not particularly easy to manage, as the ultimate borrower may not be easily identified. Nevertheless, the lending agent must not engage the client's securities in the lending pool if they have been designated. The client must review and update this list as required.

Also, some funds pledge their support to some of the management of the companies they have in the portfolio, often in a period of restructuring or if a takeover is in the offing. Again, to prevent the use of those shares by a short seller in the market (like a hedge fund), where such use could suppress the share price, the securities are made unavailable to be lent.

6.2   Direct Lending

Direct lending is much the same as other lending programmes but the types of reports that are required do have some significant differences.

6.2.1   List of Borrowers

A key report will be the list of borrowers who need to be advised of securities that can be borrowed from the direct lending programme. This list may be periodically added to or reduced, depending on risk and credit issues.

6.2.2   Collateral Reports

Another major report in direct lending is one showing the collateral held against loans or provided against borrowings. Collateral is essential to manage the credit risk in lending and the direct lending relationship requires the borrower to make collateral available. This must:

1. be acceptable to the lender
2. be recorded
3. be re-valued by mark-to-market daily and compared to the re-valued loaned security
4. be re-valued intra-day in volatile markets
5. show such movements in and out of collateral
6. show the impact of any corporate action and the relevant postings/credits/debits/claims, etc.

In addition, the direct lending process requires a report on the exposure being created with counterparties for business management reasons and monitoring of compliance with ethical investment policies. While this is reported to the credit and risk management teams as part of the control process, the exposure should, of course, be more than offset by the collateral held.

Reports will also be needed to provide summary information of the lending fees obtained and any expenses incurred so that the fund administrator and portfolio accounting teams can make certain that the fund reflects the income obtained.

6.2.3 Mandated Funds

Internally there will be a report showing which funds are mandated to allow securities lending. Periodic checks will be made and this report updated accordingly to reflect additions and deletions of funds mandated and/or the restrictions to be applied.

6.2.4 Reconciliation

Must continually take place against this report to ensure that no breaches occur.

6.2.5 Fee Schedules

A report showing the various fees charged/obtainable from different sources may also be required for actively managed, direct-lending programmes.

Some material that appears in this chapter may have been sourced from other areas – see Appendix 4 for details of the relevant organisations.

7. Regulatory Impacts on Securities Lending and Borrowing

Learning Objective

5.6 Understand how the global regulatory environment impacts on securities lending and borrowing and in particular how the UK regulatory environment dictates processes for a regulated UK firm

As mentioned in the previous chapters, the financial crisis in 2008 that followed the various financial scandals like Lehman Bros., Madoff and MF Global, has forced the regulatory bodies to act in light of the frauds and the misappropriation of clients assets found to being perpetrated against investors.

In the US there has been the introduction of the Dodd–Frank Wall Street Reform and Consumer Protection Act. In Europe there have been several initiatives, such as the CSDR as well as the Short Selling Regulation (SSR) brought in by the EC; and the FCA has issued rules and guidelines on the effects in the UK.

There is also the ongoing saga of something that is known as shadow banking. The definition of shadow banking is the *'non-bank credit intermediation, involving activities outside of the normal banking system'*. Under this definition, certain activities of securities lending like indemnified lending and the collateral activities in repurchase agreements are brought into focus by the various global regulatory bodies and the global financial watchdogs, such as the Financial Stability Board (FSB) and the US Financial Stability Oversight Council (FSOC).

Because of the default indemnification that is said to be happening when these shadow banking activities are undertaken, there are some pieces of legislation that shadow banking may be deemed to fall under such as the Basel III Capital Rules and Dodd-Frank Single Counterparty limits. At the time of writing, this is something that is still not clear.

All of this regulatory activity has, to a greater or lesser degree, had an effect on the processes and procedures associated with securities lending and borrowing. Especially in Europe, legislation has not yet been fully implemented, and so the full effects are not yet known. Candidates should keep a watching brief on developments.

UK Regulation

In the UK, the FCA CASS sourcebook has general rules and guidelines for UK regulated firms in connection with client assets and their protection. Under CASS 3 they have specific rules and guidelines regarding the level of protection afforded to collateral which is an important factor in the lending and Borrowing of securities. There is another important and relevant section to lending and borrowing which is CASS 8 Mandates.

The FCA also produces a sourcebook regarding the rules and guidelines governing collective investment schemes (COLL). Within this sourcebook, under Section 5 (5.5), there are specific guidelines and rules as to the lending and borrowing of securities and of the associated collateral.

End of Chapter Questions

1. What are the main benefits of stock lending/borrowing?
   Answer reference: *Section 2.1*

2. What are the risks of stock lending?
   Answer reference: *Section 2.2*

3. What key clauses will there be in a stock lending agreement?
   Answer reference: *Section 2.6*

4. What is third-party securities lending?
   Answer reference: *Section 3*

5. Describe the stock-lending process through a custodian.
   Answer reference: *Section 4.1*

6. How do corporate actions affect stock loans?
   Answer reference: *Section 4.3.1*

7. What is a repo?
   Answer reference: *Section 5*

8. How is a repo different from stock lending?
   Answer reference: *Section 5*

9. List six elements that would form part of the report provided by a lending intermediary to its client, and state which is the most important and why.
   Answer reference: *Section 6*

Chapter Six
Cash Management

6

1. Managing Surplus Cash

Learning Objective

6.1   Describe the methods used to manage surplus cash balances

1.1   The Importance of Cash Management

In any global organisation the efficient use of money is of paramount importance. Every extra basis point that is earned on money can, over a financial period, add significantly to the return and performance of the trading entity or fund.

Identifying surplus cash is, therefore, important. It is achieved through a process called positioning. Positioning is the analysis of the current balances held in accounts and the expected inflow and outflow of funds.

The movement of securities and, in particular, the settlement of securities trades, is linked to the movement of the corresponding counter-value of cash. Cash must be found to cover purchases; proceeds of sales and income payments must be reinvested in some way or another.

The prediction of cash requirements (funding requirements) and the movement of cash itself is known as cash management.

The performance of an investor's portfolio is made up of:

- profit (or loss), either notional or realised, on their trading activity
- yield of the portfolio through receipt of income.

If little attention is paid to cash management to produce additional income then, together with poor capital growth performance, the overall performance of the securities portfolio will be affected.

Investors therefore need to be using their idle cash balances to increase their income.

There are several ways that this can be achieved but each method fundamentally entails lending their cash to a counterparty which will pay them interest on their loan. (It is, however, recognised that for some clients who operate under the principles of Sharia'a law, the specified ways of earning interest on their surplus cash may not be appropriate.)

1.2   Types of Account

It is assumed that the client has deposited their cash with a bank or a custodian. The client has the option of carrying out self-directed lending of their surplus cash but many clients will prefer their bank or custodian to perform these duties.

There are two main ways that the client can hold their cash with the bank or the custodian – these are known as single-currency accounts or multi-currency accounts.

1.2.1 Single-Currency Accounts

Clients whose business generates cash in (mainly) one currency and who wish to enter into cross-border trading may prefer to operate with cash accounts in a single currency.

They will arrange for all purchase costs, sale proceeds and income receipts to be exchanged (a foreign exchange (FX) trade) into their base currency as and when the need arises.

For the investor, the advantages of single-currency accounts include the following:

- The exposure to adverse foreign exchange rate movements is removed once the FX trade has been executed.
- With only one currency, the funding requirement calculations are simplified.
- The investor is free to obtain the most advantageous exchange rates from the FX marketplace.
- Cash reconciliation and control processes are more straightforward.

The disadvantages of single-currency accounts include the following:

- There will be extra FX trading charges to consider over and above the securities trading commissions.
- In most but not necessarily all cases the securities trade settlements will no longer be on a DvP basis, as the currency movements will take place independently from the securities movements. The risk of non-performance of the trade as a whole is greater than it would be for a DvP settlement.
- For FX trades dealt with counterparties other than the global custodian, the investor must give settlement instructions for the cash side in addition to instructions for the securities.

The implications for the global custodian of single-currency accounts include the following:

- The relationship is not one of global custodianship as defined by ISSA.
- All income receipts are exchanged into the base currency.
- The global custodian will not necessarily be responsible for exchanging the purchase and sale amounts as the investor will look around the FX market for the best FX rates.
- The global custodian will continue to settle trades in the relevant currency on a DvP basis (where applicable).
- The global custodian is under no obligation to offer contractual settlement date accounting (CSDA), as the transfer of securities occurs independently from the movement of clients' cash.

1.2.2 Multi-Currency Accounts

Multi-currency banking will suit those investors whose ordinary business activities generate cash flows in foreign currencies and/or who prefer to settle the securities trades on a DvP basis in the foreign currency. The cash funding requirements will be undertaken as a separate process.

For the investor, the advantages are the following:

- The securities trades benefit from DvP settlement.
- The investor is able to take advantage of the global custodian's CSDA service.
- There are more options available in terms of the subsequent use of the foreign currency balances.

160

The disadvantages is that:

- there is an increased control and administrative burden as a result of operating many different currency accounts.

For the global custodian, the implications are the following:

- A more rounded custody and banking service can be provided to the client.
- The need to exchange all income into the base currency is removed, thus reducing the number of relatively small-value FX trades that must be executed.

1.3   Income on Cash Surpluses

Having determined the account structure that they wish to employ, the investor will probably find that the bank or custodian will offer the following methods to generate additional income on their cash balances.

1.3.1   Interest-Bearing Accounts

Although banks and custodians are likely to be prepared to pay interest on a client's cash account, they will only be able to do so in times when idle balances attract a positive interest rate. In recent times when interest rates have been very low or, in some cases, negative, it requires a more pro-active and a more structured approach with regard to the use of idle balances. Most idle balances will attract the lowest levels of income because they are held in what are known as call accounts. This means that the client is not obliged to give a prescribed time of notice to the bank or custodian when the cash is required for other purposes. They may also be attracting interest on a tiered or minimum balance basis.

Investors who want to actively manage their cash balances to obtain better levels of income need to transfer their cash balances to time-specified deposit accounts or other financial products.

Although this achieves the objective, it increases the administrative burden and becomes expensive to operate. However, banks and custodians now provide mechanisms to move surplus cash to various products, thus helping to cut the number of cash movements across the accounts.

1.3.2   Sweeping and Repo

The bank or custodian may offer to transfer automatically (or sweep) surplus and uncommitted balances overnight from non- or low-interest-bearing accounts into interest-bearing deposit accounts or into short-term investment funds (STIFs), by buying time-specified CDs. The repo market can also be tapped. This ensures that cash balances are being used in a more efficient manner.

1.3.3   Pooling

Banks or custodians hold: (a) accounts in the same currency; and/or (b) multi-currency accounts for their clients. Some currencies will of course attract better rates of interest and so some banks and custodians will offer to pool the client's low interest balances into a currency that attracts a higher interest rate or to move balances from one currency to another to reduce the effect of some accounts being overdrawn.

1.4   The Risk Element of Cash Management

Where cash is concerned, the risk of a counterparty failing is always there.

It has recently been established that the ways in which clients' non-cash assets are held by custodians have been sufficient for the liquidator to separately identify those assets which are beneficially owned by the clients from those which belong to the global custodian. Globally the position for cash assets, however, is not so secure; the banks (or deposit takers) with whom a client's cash is placed become the owners of the cash (under the deposit-taking rules). The clients who deposit the money are considered by the liquidator to be unsecured creditors in the accounts of the bank/custodian (see the deposit-taking rules). The problems that will be created should a bank/custodian fall into receivership should be considered. This issue is further discussed in Section 5 of this chapter.

It is, therefore, wise to deposit cash only with those organisations which are well placed to honour debts and repay loans as and when they fall due. An indication of this ability is provided by credit rating companies, such as Moody's and Standard & Poor's. These organisations constantly monitor the banks and will upgrade or downgrade the rating to reflect the changed situation. A bank with a rating of AAA is considered more able to honour all debts, while a bank with a rating of B is considered to be much more risky.

Investors can reduce this risk by:

*   implementing in-house rules that might allow exposure limits of, say, $10 million with a AAA-rated bank, down to $5 million with an A-rated bank and no exposure to banks with a B rating or lower
*   making sure that the cash assets are placed with a number of highly rated banks.

While this will help to reduce the levels of risk, there is a price to be paid in terms of requiring more sophisticated cash monitoring systems and the extra expense associated with transferring cash around the banking system. The banks and custodians are aware of the problems involved and are constantly seeking new ways to keep clients' cash-related business in-house.

1.5   Banking Services

Banks and custodians are able to offer a wide range of banking services, including the following:

Funds Transmission Systems

These enable the client to transfer funds electronically, covering clean payments (ie, those not directly connected to a securities trade).

Treasury Services

Provide dealing facilities to purchase and sell foreign currency, place funds on deposit and draw down funds on loan.

Screen-Based Dealing Systems

Some banks and custodians have now made available screen-based facilities which allow clients to execute their smaller FX deals without reference to a bank dealer. Clients are able to accept or reject the rates offered on the screen; should the rate be acceptable, the transaction is immediately confirmed.

1.6   Worldwide Cash Management in General

Globally, there are differing views on what cash management actually is. In the US banking, cash management or treasury management is a marketing term for certain services offered, in the main, to larger business customers. It may be used to describe all bank accounts provided to businesses of a certain size but it is more often used to describe specific services such as cash concentration, zero balance accounting and automated clearing house facilities. Sometimes private bank customers are offered cash management services.

Many aspects of cash management and banking in Germany are becoming increasingly standardised and harmonised with other countries in Europe. However, the German cash management and banking sector is quite distinctive with over 2,000 banks, most of which are publicly owned savings banks or private co-operative banking institutions. The German market for payments and cash management is therefore highly competitive. Payment systems and payment instruments in Germany generally operate at a high level of reliability and efficiency.

Cash management techniques in India are evolving, with many institutions dispensing with time-consuming paper-based systems, including the writing out of many cheques and replacing these with more efficient and faster electronic methods of payment. There are nine separate clearing systems in operation across 1,040 decentralised clearing zones and the different clearing systems relate to the size of the payment being made.

In Japan, the management of cash is highly developed, with many international institutions offering a range of ever-increasing services to customers, including real-time account and market information. Some developments in Japan relating to cash management include the introduction of the Zengin System (a domestic fund transfer system) and also the ANSER network. The Zengin system is the main domestic Japanese yen payment network in Japan. The ANSER system is a speech recognition system in Japan that offers telephone banking to millions of Japanese customers.

In countries where the Islamic beliefs are fundamental to people's way of life, Sharia'a law must be taken into account. Under Islamic principles, Sharia'a law (prescribed in the Koran) defines the framework within which Muslims should conduct their lives. The overarching principle of Islamic finance and banking products is that all forms of interest are forbidden. The Islamic financial model works on the basis of risk-sharing. The customer and the bank share the risk of any investment on agreed terms and divide any profits or losses between them. In addition, investments should only support practices that are not forbidden – trades in alcohol, betting and pornography are not allowed. Moreover, an Islamic banking institution is not permitted to lend to other banks at interest.

2. Unauthorised Overdrafts

Learning Objective

6.2 Describe how unauthorised overdrafts can arise on client accounts

When considering this learning objective it has to be recognised that, in some countries, having an overdraft, whether authorised or unauthorised, is not allowed. This means that the banks or custodians in those countries will not honour an instruction to move cash if there are insufficient funds in the client account to honour the full payment.

In those countries where having an unauthorised overdraft is a possibility, it occurs when the client uses cash that it does not own and has not been given the permission by the bank or custodian to have access to funds that it does not own. This is likely to occur for a variety of reasons, including:

- late receipt of incoming funds to the account with an outflow taking place
- a contingent liability occurring that exceeds the available balance on the account
- uncleared funds are included in the balance which is subsequently fully utilised
- payment taken from an account by mistake/fraudulently.

The danger is that, firstly, a bank may be breaching regulations and/or internal controls if it lends money to a client.

Secondly, if an overdraft facility is available, a bank may refuse to accept values for payment above this figure, causing settlement fails.

Thirdly, any amount by which a client exceeds the agreed limit may be charged at very high rates.

In addition, any bank providing an overdraft on a securities account may need to provide cover from its own sources to comply with the client money rules.

In the worst case scenario, an unauthorised overdraft may be a precursor to a default.

Example

A client has purchased some S&P futures contracts on the Chicago Mercantile Exchange (CME) in the US. They deposit $10,000 to cover the variation margin (daily movement in value) and initial margin (security deposit) which initially is calculated at, say, $6,000. Unfortunately, there is a very sharp movement in US equities against the client and the margin requirement jumps to $15,000.

The clearing broker must settle with the clearing house and, in turn, the investor must settle with the broker. However, owing to an error on a payment instruction to the custodian, the investor fails to settle the additional amount T+1 and, as a result, they have an overdrawn position on the account.

They have no borrowing arrangement with the broker and, under the terms of the broker agreement, the broker could probably close the positions out to avoid either a regulatory breach or a potential default.

3. Foreign Exchange (FX) Transactions

Learning Objective

6.3 Explain when and why foreign exchange transactions need to be executed to align with and in relation to a settlement of a transaction in the stock markets

Settlement of securities and derivatives transactions may involve the need for an FX transaction. This need occurs when a client buys an asset for which they do not currently have sufficient amounts of the settlement currency to satisfy the purchase. The timing of the FX trade is important if unnecessary funding costs are to be avoided.

Example

A simplistic example might be that of a European investor who has their base currency accounts maintained in euros who carries out the following trades:

Purchase of 100,000 ABC Inc. shares on the NYSE @ US$1.50. = US$150,000 gross.
Settles T+3 (15th of month)

Sale of 10,000 XYZ AG shares on the Deutsche Bourse @ €20.00 = €200,000 gross.
Settles T+2 (14th of month)

A spot FX trade needs to be executed in time to convert the €200,000 settling 14th into US$150,000 and deposit the resulting US$ with the client's New York agent in order to settle the securities transaction settling 15th.

The convention for settlement of a spot FX trade is T+2. So if the FX trade (€/US$) is executed on the settlement date of the securities sale (ie, 14th) the US$ will not be delivered in New York until the 16th thus one day after they are needed. This will almost certainly result in funding costs at best but at worst it will result in a failed settlement of the securities trade plus funding costs.

The client's euro account will receive the proceeds from the securities sale on the 14th but the € will not be taken from the client's euro account to settle the FX trade until the 16th which essentially means they have had surplus euro currency, doing nothing and probably earning nothing for two days.

This example hopefully shows the student the importance of understanding the linkages between two different disciplines, these being money market disciplines and securities market disciplines. So the timing of the FX trade is vital to ensure efficacy for the client. In the above example, for the best result to be achieved for the client, the FX trade should have been placed on the 13th of the month.

This would have resulted in reducing the elapse time the client had surplus €s and would have meant the US$ would be in New York on time, alleviating potential funding costs and a failed settlement: a win/win situation.

The risk in FX transactions is greatly reduced for members of CLS Bank (see Appendix 2 for more information on CLS Bank).

CISI
CHARTERED INSTITUTE FOR
SECURITIES & INVESTMENT

4. Asset-Backed and Mortgage-Backed Securities

4.1 Features of Asset-Backed and Mortgage-Backed Securities

Learning Objective

6.4 Distinguish the key differences between the features of asset-backed and mortgage-backed securities and other fixed interest products

---

Asset-backed securities (ABSs) are securities that are created by the securitisation of other assets that are owned by an entity. Like bonds, they pay periodic interest until maturity, when the principal is paid back. The income from the ABS is derived from pools of loans and or other receivables that are owned by the entity and have been securitised into the ABS. Certainty of receipt of both income and the redemption value of bonds is vitally important. Credit risk is, therefore, paramount in the decision to invest in a debt instrument.

In order to make an issue attractive to the investor from a credit point of view, the sponsor of the ABS will engage with another corporate entity which will create a trust known as a special purpose vehicle (SPV) and will sell the principle and income derived from the assets to the SPV. The SPV then becomes the issuer of the ABS that is offered to investors. By doing so, the issuer removes any credit concerns about the sponsor that may exist.

Example

ABC plc is keen to acquire a portfolio of office properties worth around £50 million, which will generates good levels of rentals. To finance the acquisition, ABC needs to raise £30 million in the markets. It has the following choices:

- a rights issue of new shares
- a loan
- issue corporate debt (bond issue).

Given the market conditions, which we will assume are not easy, ie, investors are reluctant to buy straight debt issues, ABC will need to pay a very attractive interest rate if it issued a fixed-rate bond based on its own credit.

Alternatively, ABC could raise the money by using other assets that they have on their balance sheet, for example outstanding business loans, rental income or car loans.

It is likely they will do this via the creation of an SPV that will issue an ABS. The investors know that the security's interest payments are secured by the SPV trust and that the rental income and the repayment against the value of the properties is paid through the SPV trust rather than against the cash position of ABC.

The principal difference for the investor between ABSs and other debt issued by the company is the transference of the risk from the credit risk associated with that of the company, whose debt is backed by assets that belong to that company, to the credit risk associated with that of an SPV trust. For the sponsor, the difference is the ability to raise and the cost of raising the finance. The sponsor is able to reduce their balance sheet size by removing the assets that have been securitised.

Mortgage-backed securities (MBSs) are very similar in principle to ABSs. With an MBS the backing of the security is potentially much more attractive to the investor and so the interest rate they will accept may well be lower than that which an issuer would otherwise need to offer.

In the US there are many private institutions (brokerage firms, financial institutions, and even construction companies) that create and sell MBSs. However, the US government via the Federal National Mortgage Association (Fannie Mae) and the Federal Home Loan Mortgage Corporation (Freddie Mac) also purchase a very large portion of US mortgages. Freddie Mac and Fannie Mae (both government- sponsored entities) guarantee timely payment of interest and principal on the MBSs they issue, that is, if the borrowers do not make their mortgage payments on time, Freddie Mac and Fannie Mae will still make their payments to their MBS investors. It is important to note that the US government does not guarantee Freddie Mac or Fannie Mae. That is, if these entities cannot fulfil their obligations to their MBS investors, the federal government has no responsibility to rescue them. However, both entities have lines of credit with the government and investors generally believe that the government would not actually let them default on any of their securities.

Example

MBSs in the US

When the assets used to create a security are residential properties, the investor will receive title to a portion of the underlying pool of mortgages, in exchange for the cash they paid to the issuer. The investor is relying on the performance of the mortgage payments and property values. In this case they would be called MBSs.

Gold participation certificate (PC) securities are the cornerstone of Freddie Mac's MBS programme, offering investors a pass-through security, representing an undivided interest in a pool of residential mortgages.

Freddie Mac offers traditional 30-year fixed-rate gold PCs, as well as 15-year gold PCs, which offer flexibility for those investors searching for a security with a shorter held-to-maturity date.

Gold PCs generally provide a higher yield on a held-to-maturity basis than other comparable mortgage products.

Freddie Mac guarantees the full and timely payment of principal and interest on all Gold PCs.

Gold PCs feature a payment delay of only 45 days from the time interest begins to accrue to when the investor receives a payment.

Gold PCs are also known as pass-through or pool certificates.

4.2   Mortgage-Backed Securities: The Pool Factor

Learning Objective

6.5   Explain the role of the pool factor and how it is determined

6.6   Calculate and comment on old and new positions based on a changing pool factor

The definition of a mortgage pool is a group of related financial instruments, such as mortgages, combined for resale to investors on a secondary market.

Holders of MBS issues are, in effect therefore, owners of an instrument secured against a pool of assets. As these mortgages could be repaid early, the effect on the ability of the remaining pool of assets to cover the redemption and interest of the MBSs may become unbalanced. For this reason, an MBS may partially redeem at fixed or floating times.

The value or share of the amended pool that an investor has is calculable.

The definition of the pool factor can be given as: outstanding mortgage pool principal, divided by the original principal balance, and expressed as a decimal between 0 and 1.

Example

Original pool principal value: 30,000,000

Outstanding pool principal value: 20,000,000

Pool factor = 20,000,000/30,000,000 = 0.66

5.   The Regulatory Impact on Cash Management

Learning Objective

6.7   Understand how the global regulatory environment impacts on cash management and in particular how the UK regulatory environment dictates processes for a regulated UK firm

As with many other areas of operations within this workbook, since the financial crash of 2008 the impact of the global regulation on cash management has been very significant. It is often said that the area of MBSs was the epicentre of the financial crisis, leading to the collapse of credit globally. During this crisis, many governments, using taxpayers' money, were forced to bail out many of the failing leading global institutions. Institutions that were once thought of as being too big to fail were shown to be vulnerable. It is important to remember that it was not the institutions *per se* that were at fault in creating this crisis. Rather, it was the senior management and the culture that they permeated within the institutions that was really to blame.

In the US, the crisis brought about the Dodd-Frank Consumer Protection Act and, in relation to banking, the Volcker Rule. In the UK, the crisis brought about the formation of the two-pronged regulatory structure of the FCA and the PRA with new rules and guidance, such as the FCA's COBS, and the authority given by parliament to the PRA of the Financial Services (Banking Reform) Act 2013. In Europe, a raft of new regulation has been introduced to deal with both the market structure and the banking structure. This includes Basel III and the CRD regarding capital and the European Market Infrastructure Regulation (EMIR) and MiFID regarding market structure.

It should be noted that many of the other developed markets have had their own new regulations to deal with and that the above is just an example and indication of what has been happening globally.

Consequently since the 2008 financial crisis, all financial institutions globally have had a massive amount of regulation to deal with in order to ensure that their processes and procedures adhere to the regulation.

5.1   UK Specific Regulation

Within the UK regulation there are specific rules that pertain to a client's cash and the management of that cash. The FCA, in the CASS sourcebook, has published its rules and guidance with regards to client money (CASS 7 Client Money).

It should be remembered that the objective of cash management is to earn additional income from the cash pool that a client maintains, whether this be daily idle cash balances or more specific larger cash balances held for investment purposes as cash as an asset class. In order to generate income from either type of cash pool the money has to be put to work. This at the end of the day in real terms means that it has to be lent to a third party, for them to do what they will with it. The ways in which this money can be lent was discussed in Section 4.

As we saw in Chapter 1, in the UK, when a client entrusts another with their assets, this is entered into under some kind of trust arrangement. This is fine whilst that cash element is dormant with the trustee. However, if the client wants their cash assets to earn additional income, this trust arrangement is no longer sufficient as the cash has to be passed into the world of deposit takers (banks, credit unions etc) so that the cash can be put to work to earn the required interest.

At the outset of the client/firm relationship, the firm is obliged to categorise their client as either a retail, professional or eligible counterparty category. This is so that the firm can apportion the correct level of protection for the client's assets and ascertain which elements of legislation will apply (large parts of the FCA rules are not applicable to eligible counterparties). This categorisation and the agreement by the client to the categorisation, is particularly important when dealing with cash and the management of that cash.

The best way to describe how this level of protection works in a cash scenario is to create an example for each category.

5.1.1   Protection for a Retail Client (Including Corporate Companies)

Let us say that a retail client is an individual with a nest egg of £50,000. This individual wants to invest in stocks and shares but also wants to retain, say, £10,000 in cash as a rainy day contingency. They contact a solicitor or a stockbroker to put these plans into action. Once all of the requisite checks are done by the regulated firm they are categorised as a retail client and agree to this categorisation. Investments up to £40,000 are made into stocks and shares and £10,000 remains in cash. So what happens now?

The firm will open in their books (computer system) both portfolio (share) accounts and cash accounts in the name of the client, which record the assets that the client beneficially owns. Both the portfolio accounts and the cash accounts will be ring fenced from the firm's own assets by means of segregation. The stocks and shares will likely be in a nominee name used by the firm but they will not be mingled with the firm's assets.

The cash portion of the client's assets will almost certainly be placed with a UK bank. However the firm has to make sure that the bank is aware that the cash deposited with them is client money. The bank has a duty to ensure that they recognise this as client money in their records. The bank is not obliged to run an account for every individual client of the firm but they must at least run an omnibus client money account for each firm that banks with them for client money purposes. However, the bank as a deposit taker is allowed to use this money as they wish.

So Where is the Protection?

In the event that the firm goes bust, because the retail client can easily prove to the liquidators of the firm the assets they beneficially own, in terms of both cash and stocks and shares, the creditors of the firm will not have a claim on the assets of the retail client. Therefore, because the bank used for the cash will have an account in the name of the firm, that is designated as client money, the bank is obliged on request to honour any validated claim on the cash.

In the event that the bank the firm has used for the cash goes bust, because in the banks' books it is designated as client money these accounts go higher up the list of creditors who get paid first. So any money recouped by the liquidators will be offset against the client money accounts. This does not necessarily mean that the client will get their full beneficial value back from this process.

There is however the Financial Services Compensation Scheme (FSCS) which offers compensation to eligible customers up to a maximum of £75,000. This scheme is only open to clients of FCA and PRA regulated firms. The deposit protection rules are in the PRA rule book.

5.1.2   Professional/Eligible Counterparty

Professional clients and clients categorised as eligible counterparties are afforded a different and lower level of protection than that which a retail client enjoys. But in actual fact this lower level of protection in real terms only relates to the cash portion of their portfolio.

As with the retail client, the firm entrusted with looking after the client's assets will open in their books (computer system) both portfolio (share) accounts and cash accounts in the name of the client, which record the assets that the client beneficially owns. Both the portfolio accounts and the cash accounts will be ring fenced from the firm's own assets by means of segregation. The stocks and shares are likely to be in a nominee name used by the firm but they will not be mingled with the firm's own assets. In some instances, the professional client/eligible counterparty may knowingly waive their rights to this protection under the title transfer, eg, a prime brokerage agreement.

The cash portion of the client's assets will almost certainly be placed with a bank (or deposit taker). However in this instance the firm does not have to designate the cash deposited with the bank as client money. The bank has a duty to ensure that they recognise this as an omnibus account in the name of the firm and that they owe the firm that money but their obligation ceases there. In this instance the bank or deposit taker is accepting the cash under the banking exemption and not as client money and will explain this to their clients in their terms of business.

So Where is the Protection?

In the event that the firm goes bust, because the professional/eligible counterparty client can easily prove to the liquidators of the firm the identity of the assets they beneficially own, in terms of stocks and shares, the creditors of the firm will not have a claim on the assets of the professional/eligible counterparty client.

However, where cash accounts with the bank are in the name of the firm that deposited the cash with the bank, the bank will be obliged to recognise the appointed liquidator of the firm as the beneficial owner. The professional/eligible counterparties become unsecured creditors.

In the event that the bank the firm has used for the cash goes bust, because in the banks' books the cash is held in the name of the firm, the firm becomes an unsecured creditor of the bank.

The FSCS offers compensation to eligible depositors (namely retail clients, small and medium entities and corporate companies, eg, Rolls Royce Plc) of regulated banks in the UK up to a maximum of £75,000. No protection is offered to non-eligible depositors such as other regulated firms (investment banks, insurance companies, UCITS and pension funds/schemes).

Other countries around the world have similar deposit protection schemes. Which type of client they cover may differ as does the amount of deposit they protect. The insurance schemes generally do not cover all the monies that have been deposited in the bank, but rather a limited amount, eg, $250,000 in the US by the Federal Deposit Insurance Corporation (FDIC) and in Europe an amount of €100,000 by the local country deposit scheme.

Many of the UK's custodial firms (global custodians) will make use of the banking exemption that was authorised by the FCA in March 2007 because they hold a UK banking licence. Therefore, they can treat all client monies received by them as a deposit taker, rather than as a trustee. As a consequence of this approach, their clients do not benefit from the protection afforded under CASS 7 client money rules and are reliant on compensation payable under the FSCS.

These risks have to be clearly set out in the client agreements between the custodians and their clients.

However, the custodians will still apply many of the procedures (such as reconciliations) set out in CASS 7 as this will support the firm's required systems and control environment.

Custodians and firms operating under the banking exemption are required to comply with CASS 7.10.21R which ensures funds are identified and credited to clients account within ten business days of receipt.

5.1.3   FCA Client Money Rules

Candidates are advised to become familiar with the CASS regulations via the FCA CASS Sourcebook. There is also an excellent publication by the CISI called the Client Money and Assets workbook which gives details of the CASS rules.

The following is taken from that publication and gives a flavour of some of the important rules.

Money Due to a Client from a Firm

If a firm is liable to pay money to a client, it must, as soon as possible and no later than one business day after the money is due and payable:

- pay it into a client bank account, in accordance with CASS 5.5.5 R
- pay it to, or to the order of, the client.

Segregation

Except to the extent permitted by CASS 5.5, a firm must hold client money separate from the firm's money.

A firm must segregate client money by either:

- paying it as soon as is practicable into a client bank account
- paying it out in accordance with CASS 5.5.80 R.

The FCA expects that, in most circumstances, it will be practicable for a firm to pay client money into a client bank account by not later than the next business day after receipt. A firm may segregate client money in a different currency from that of receipt. If it does so, the firm must ensure that the amount held is adjusted at intervals of not more than 25 business days to an amount at least equal to the original currency amount (or the currency in which the firm has its liability to its clients, if different), translated at the previous day's closing spot exchange rate.

A firm must not hold money, other than client money, in a client bank account, unless it is:

- a minimum sum required to open the account, or to keep it open
- money temporarily in the account in accordance with CASS 5.5.16 R (withdrawal of commission and mixed remittance)
- interest credited to the account which exceeds the amount due to clients as interest and has not yet been withdrawn by the firm.

A firm can allow for any charges related to the bank account in respect of the client account. If it is prudent to do so to ensure that client money is protected (and provided that doing so would otherwise be in accordance with CASS 5.5.63 R (1)(b)(ii)1), a firm may pay into, or maintain in, a client bank account money of its own. That money will then become client money for the purposes of CASS 5 and the client money (insurance) distribution rules.

A firm, when acting in accordance with CASS 5.3 (statutory trust) must ensure that the total amount of client money held for each client in any of the firm's client money bank accounts is positive and that no payment is made from any such account for the benefit of a client, unless the client has provided the firm with cleared funds to enable the payment to be made.

Note that when a firm acts in accordance with CASS 5.3 (statutory trust) it should not make a payment from the client bank account unless it is satisfied, on reasonable grounds, that the client has provided it with cleared funds. Accordingly, a firm should normally allow a reasonable period of time for cheques to clear. If a withdrawal is made, and the client's cheque is subsequently dishonoured, it will be the firm's responsibility to make good the shortfall in the account as quickly as possible (and without delay whilst a cheque is re-presented).

If client money is received by the firm in the form of an automated transfer, the firm must take reasonable steps to ensure that:

- the money is received directly into a client bank account
- if money is received directly into the firm's own account, the money is transferred into a client bank account no later than the next business day after receipt.

A firm can hold client money in either a general client bank account (CASS 5.5.38 R) or a designated client bank account (CASS 5.5.39 R). A firm holds all client money in general client bank accounts for its clients, as part of a common pool of money, so those particular clients do not have a claim against a specific sum in a specific account: they only have a claim to the client money in general. A firm holds client money in designated client bank accounts for those clients who requested that their client money be part of a specific pool of money, so those particular clients do have a claim against a specific sum in a specific account: they do not have a claim to the client money in general unless a primary pooling event occurs. If the firm becomes insolvent and there is (for whatever reason) a shortfall in money held for a client compared with that client's entitlements, the available funds will be distributed in accordance with the client money (insurance) distribution rules.

Some material that appears in this chapter may have been sourced from other areas – see Appendix 4 for details of the relevant organisations.

End of Chapter Questions

1. Describe what sweeping is.
   Answer reference: *Section 1.3.2*

2. Describe why a client overdrawn position might occur?
   Answer reference: *Section 2*

3. Why is the timing of an FX settlement important in relation to a share and or derivative trade?
   Answer reference: *Section 3*

4. What is an MBS?
   Answer reference: *Section 4.1*

5. What is an ABS?
   Answer reference: *Section 4.1*

6. How does an ABS differ from a straight corporate bond?
   Answer reference: *Section 4.1*

7. What is a pool factor?
   Answer reference: *Section 4.2*

8. What is CLS bank?
   Answer reference: *Section 3 and Appendix 2*

Chapter Seven
Corporate Entitlements

1. Rationale for a Corporate Action

Learning Objective

7.1 Explain the reasons for a corporation initiating a particular corporate action: rights issue; bonus issue; dividend stock option

When any worldwide publicly traded company issues a corporate action, it is initiating a process that will bring actual change to its issued shares. By understanding the different types of processes and their effects, an investor can have a clearer picture of what a corporate action indicates about a company's financial affairs and how that action will influence the company's share price and performance.

Corporate actions are typically agreed upon by a company's board of directors and authorised by the shareholders. Some examples are stock splits, dividends, takeovers and mergers, rights issues and bonus issues.

1.1 Rights Issues

A rights issue is an invitation to existing shareholders to purchase additional new shares in the company. More specifically, this type of issue gives existing shareholders' securities called rights, giving the shareholders the right to purchase new shares at a discount to the market price on a stated future date. The company is giving shareholders a chance to increase their exposure to the stock at a discounted price.

The reasons why a company may have a rights issue can be varied but the main purpose is to raise finance. It is possible that a troubled company might use rights issues to reduce debt, especially when they are unable to borrow more money. However, not all companies that pursue rights offerings are having problems with financing. Some use rights issues to raise capital to fund acquisitions and to implement growth strategies.

1.2 Bonus Issues

A bonus issue is the issue of free shares to current/existing shareholders in a company, based upon the number of shares that the shareholder already owns at the record date. While the issue of bonus shares increases the total number of shares issued and owned, it does not increase the value of the company, as the market price is adjusted to take account of the bonus issue.

The bonus shares are issued against the cash reserves held by the company that have been generated by past profits. When a company has accumulated large reserves, the directors may decide to distribute some of them among the shareholders in the form of bonus shares.

Among other reasons, companies will do this to:

* bring cash reserves into the working capital of the company
* create confidence for the investors/shareholders in the company
* improve market reputation
* increase the liquidity of shares by reducing the share price without reducing the overall value of the company.

1.3   Dividend Stock Option

A dividend stock option is actually the declaration of a cash dividend with an option given to the shareholders by the directors of the company to take the equivalent of the cash dividend in shares of the company.

For the company this is a very cheap way of raising capital, as the effects are essentially to take money from the reserves and put that money into the working capital.

The amount of shares that a shareholder will be allocated in lieu of their cash dividend will be calculated by the company's dividing the shareholder's cash dividend entitlement by the share price at a given date.

Depending on the jurisdiction of the issued company or the residence of the shareholder, there could be differing tax implications on the whole process. In some countries this may have the effect of making the whole exercise unattractive to either the company or the shareholder.

2.   Ratios

Learning Objective

7.2   Demonstrate knowledge of the differing ratio terminology (calculations) between North America and globally

It is important to understand the terminology used with regards to the ratios and issues in the US compared with other parts of the world.

2.1   Stock Split

In the US a popular corporate action is a stock split. A stock split is usually undertaken by companies that have seen their share price increase to levels that are either too high or are beyond the price levels of similar companies in their sector. The primary motive is to make shares seem more affordable to small investors, even though the underlying value of the company has not changed.

So if a company announces a 2-for-1 (2:1) stock split, the effect will be that the company will distribute one additional share for every one share currently in issue and so the total shares now in issue will double. For example, if the investor in the company has 100 shares in their portfolio, they will hold 200 shares after the stock split. At the same time the price per share will drop by half, ie, if the pre-split price was $80 per share, the new price will be $40 per share.

The significant difference in the terminology of the ratio is that in the US the multiplier to signify the resulting number of shares which the shareholder will hold after the event is quoted first and the divisor to be used in conjunction with the shares which the shareholder held before the event is quoted last.

In the UK and other countries there is a significant difference in what the ratio conveys. In these markets the ratio conveys the number of additional new shares to be given to a shareholder, which is quoted first, and the number of shares the shareholder held before the event, and on which the ratio is based, is quoted last.

So, in the US, if a ratio is quoted as 2-for-1 it means that the shareholder will end up with 200 shares when they previously held 100. The calculation to determine the holding after the event is:

Current holding = 100 divided by 1 = 100 multiplied by 2 = 200

In the UK or other countries, if a ratio is quoted as 2-for-1 it means that the shareholder will end up with 300 shares, because they will be given 200 shares to add to their previously held 100 shares. The calculation to determine the holding after the event is:

Current holding = 100 divided by 1 = 100 multiplied by 2 = 200 + 100 = 300

This ratio terminology is also present in other corporate event types, such as a rights issue.

The significant difference in the issue type is that it is often thought that a US stock split is the same as a bonus issue or capitalisation issue. However, in reality, the only thing they have in common is that the shareholder does not have to pay for the shares. A bonus or capitalisation issue has the effect of moving cash at the balance sheet level of a company, whereas a stock split has nothing to do with cash. A US stock split is more akin to a subdivision in the rest of the world.

3. Apportionment and Trading Rights

Learning Objective

7.3   Demonstrate the difference between the UK's and major European markets' approaches to apportionment and trading of rights issues

Rights issues in the UK and Europe are generally based on the issue of new shares under the concept of pre-emption (the existing, and only the existing, registered holders). This is necessary to give the existing shareholders the potential to maintain the overall percentage of shares held, ie, not to dilute their overall holding.

However, not all countries require a new issue of shares to be made exclusively under a pre-emptive rights basis. In Germany, for instance, a fund-raising process may involve a mix of pre-emptive rights and offering, ie, existing shareholders have the right to a certain number of shares but other shares are offered to investors, whether existing shareholders or not.

In the US, rights issues are not very common but the notion of pre-emption seems to be no longer relevant.

3.1   UK Rights Issues

In the UK, at the outset of the rights issue, a company will allocate and issue to its existing shareholders what are known as new nil paid shares and these new shares will be separately listed on the stock exchange. The number of new shares allocated to the shareholders will be determined by a prescribed ratio. For instance, the ratio agreed by the board of directors might be 1-for-2. This means that the shareholder will receive one new nil paid share for every two existing shares that they currently hold. The allocation of these shares will be based on the shareholder's holding at a prescribed record date.

Fractions of a shareholding are not taken into account when determining the number of new shares to be allocated. So, under the 1-for-2 example, if a shareholder has 333 existing shares they will be allocated 166 shares not 166.5. There is also an ex-rights date set by the stock exchange on the existing shares, on or after which date transactions in the existing shares do not carry the entitlement to receive new nil paid shares.

Once issued, the shareholder commonly has up to 21 days to make up their mind as to whether they want to subscribe to (buy) the new shares. The new nil paid rights that have been issued are usually freely tradeable.

The investor has several options. They can:

- sell the new nil paid shares
- take up the new nil paid shares
- buy additional new nil paid shares
- allow the new nil paid shares to lapse
- sell enough new nil paid shares to fund the take up of any remaining new nil paid shares.

Eventually the shareholder, having determined their course of action, will either subscribe to (buy) the new shares or they will not. In the event that the shareholder lapses their entitlement (neither buys nor sells) they may, under the terms of the rights issue, be entitled to receive an amount of money known as lapsed share proceeds – this being cash raised by the company via the sale of the lapsed shares in the open market.

In the UK, once subscribed to, the new nil paid shares go to another stage where they become new fully paid shares until they eventually rank pari passu with the existing shares.

3.2   Rights Issues in Europe

In Europe, at the outset of the rights issue, a company will allocate and issue to its existing shareholders what are known as subscription rights. These subscription rights will be separately listed on the stock exchange. The number of subscription rights allocated to the shareholders will be the same number as their existing shareholding. The allocation of subscription rights will take place on a date usually known as the record or reconciliation date.

The number of new shares that the shareholder may apply for is determined by using a prescribed ratio of new share to subscription rights. For instance, if the ratio agreed by the board of directors is 1-for-2, this means that the shareholder will receive the right to subscribe for one new share for every two subscription rights that they have been allocated.

There is a subscription period usually set at 14 days. Shareholders are also allowed to apply to receive additional shares in excess of their prescribed allotment and the subscription rights are freely tradeable.

The investor has several options. They can:

- sell the subscription rights
- use the subscription rights to apply for new shares at the prescribed ratio
- buy additional subscription rights
- allow the subscription rights to lapse
- sell enough subscription rights to fund the application for the remaining new share entitlement
- apply for additional shares.

Eventually the shareholder, having determined their course of action, will either subscribe to (buy) the new shares or they will not. In the event that the shareholder lapses their entitlement (neither buys nor sells), generally, under the terms of the rights issue, they will not be entitled to receive an amount of money for shares they have lapsed. These shares will be used by the company to satisfy any oversubscription requests or be taken up by the underwriters.

4. The Role of Underwriters

Learning Objective

7.4   Describe the underwriting procedures within initial public offerings (IPOs), rights issues and placing

---

4.1   Underwriting

Underwriters play an important role in the issue of securities via initial public offerings (IPOs), rights issues and the placing of shares. Among other things they advise the issuing firms, estimate their values, determine the optimum offering prices (price discovery) and distribute new issues. These processes, however, are primarily about the corporate finance world.

4.1.1   Why Is the Underwriting Process Important?

The fundamental reason for issuers to have their new issue underwritten is so that they can be sure that the capital sum that they want to raise is actually achieved. Consider the case where shares are to be issued by inviting the public and financial institutions to subscribe. There is a possibility that there will be insufficient demand for all the shares to be sold. This is an important consideration when the price of the new shares is set in advance of the issue date, taking into account stock market volatility.

In such cases, there is a danger that stock market movements will make an offer unattractive at the time of its public announcement, even though it may have appeared attractive whilst it was being arranged. Failure to sell all of the shares offered may undermine a company's investment plans (or the other reasons it is raising money). Hence, underwriting is a form of insurance which ensures that all shares are sold and the firm can be certain of obtaining the funds required.

4.1.2   The Cost of Underwriting

The main disadvantage of underwriting is its cost. The cost depends upon the characteristics of the company issuing the shares and the state of the market. The cost is payable even if the underwriter is not called upon to take up any remaining shares. For taking the risk of being left with shares that others do not want, the underwriters will expect to be paid. The way this is achieved is discussed in Section 6.2.

4.2   Mechanisms for Price Discovery

The investment bank that is leading the issue or placement of shares will also be expected to ensure that it secures the funding required by its client. Globally, there are different mechanisms for ensuring the issuer will receive the full capital sum that they desire.

'Price discovery' of what the market will pay the issuer for the new shares, and therefore what the new shares should be priced at, is a very important aspect of ensuring that the issuer receives full value. Globally there are five main mechanisms for achieving this aim:

1. Book building.
2. Dutch auction.
3. Tender.
4. Fixed price.
5. Placement.

4.2.1   Book Building

According to the book building method, the IPO issuing company does not fix the price in advance; rather, it gives a price band to the investors within which they are entitled to bid.

The investors, in turn, bid for the same by stating the quantity as well as the price of the IPO shares at which they are interested in purchasing. The IPO's final price is then determined on the basis of all the bid prices.

Investors place their preferences (that is, quantity and price of IPO shares) through a broker. The brokers place these bids/orders on behalf of their clients through the electronic media into an electronic book where they are stored. These stored bids are henceforth evaluated by the investment banker along with the IPO issuing company on the basis of certain criteria, such as earliness of bid, aggression of price and quality of investor. A cut-off price is then decided by accepting the lowest price at which all the IPO securities can be disposed of.

IPOs are then allotted to those investors whose bid prices are above the cut-off mark until the IPO shares are exhausted.

4.2.2   Dutch Auction

In a Dutch auction the process is somewhat different. The issuing company typically reveals the maximum amount of shares to be sold, together with a potential price range. Investors then enter a conditional order for the quantity of shares they wish to buy and the highest price they are willing to pay. This leads to the discovery of what could be called the equilibrium clearing price. Investors who bid at least that price are allocated shares in the offering. If more shares are bid for than shares are available then allocation allotments are awarded on a pro-rata basis.

This is in sharp contrast to the traditional book-building price-setting process, whereby prices are set by underwriters using a negotiated book building pricing process. The auction process is designed to maximise the amount of money raised by the company issuing the shares, leaving less room for the IPO investors to profit in the secondary market. It is often argued that the Dutch auction process is more beneficial to the company going public.

This type of auction is extensively used by many global governments to sell their treasury debt issues.

4.2.3   Tender

A tender offer is another form of auction where investors are invited to tender a bid to secure the shares that they wish to purchase. Each investor submits a single, sealed bid for a block of shares at a specified price at, or above, a minimum tender price. Once all bids are submitted, the issuing firm allocates shares at a single strike price under advice from its investment bank.

If the IPO is oversubscribed, the strike price will be set somewhere above the minimum price but below the market-clearing price and shares are allocated pro rata to investors; if undersubscribed, the offer price will be fixed at the minimum tender price and the underwriting investment bank has to purchase any untendered shares at this minimum price.

4.2.4   Fixed Price

The fixed price IPO, rights issue or placing is another traditional method of a company selling its shares to the general public. The investment bank(s) used by the issuer determine(s) what the fixed price should be based on many economic factors, not least of which is consultation as to what the market is willing to pay under the prevailing market conditions at the time of the issue

Investors are invited to send in an application form stating how many shares they would wish to purchase. There are generally rules associated with the parcels of shares that an investor may apply for and the number of applications a single investor is allowed to make.

Generally the application form (bid) will need to be accompanied by the cash payment for the full amount required to satisfy the application (bid). The method of payment will vary from country to country but will either be by a cheque or an electronic payment of some description.

4.2.5   Placement

A placing is when an existing publicly-owned company wishes to raise additional capital but does not want to go to the mass of their existing shareholder base via the pre-emptive rights issue route.

The issuer will use its broker or an investment bank to secure the sale of the new shares either to existing shareholders or to a mix of new institutional investors and existing shareholders. The issuer and the investment bank or broker will determine the number of new shares that need to be offered and the price that the new shares will be offered at in order to raise the capital required.

The broker or investment bank, together with the issuer, will determine who they wish to invite to buy the new shares.

Having received enough indications of intent (enough interest in the issue) to secure the capital requirement, the issuer and their advisers will proceed with the issue.

It is not a general principle that a placing needs to be underwritten and, by definition, generally it does not need to be underwritten. However, this is a decision that is left to the investment bank or broker.

For more on placing, see Section 5.

4.3   Fixed Price Stand-By Commitment

Generally, in the UK and Europe, IPOs, rights issues and placings are issued under the fixed-price method. This means that the lead underwriter and their sub-underwriters will undertake to purchase at the fixed issue price any shares not taken up by the public or the shareholders in exchange for a fixed fee. In terms of global securities operations, it is this area that becomes the primary focus.

The investment bank will, therefore, take on the role known as the lead underwriter. In this role it is generally required to find other institutions who will act as the sub-underwriters. It is this collection of institutions that will collectively insure the company against any shortfall of funds in the financing exercise.

The lead underwriter will already have a number of institutions on its books that it uses as sub-underwriters which, collectively, may be referred to as an underwriting syndicate. It will contact these sub-underwriters and offer them a chance to join in the underwriting of shares in the issue. This will generally be done by telephone in the first instance and then be followed up by a formal offer letter and documentation that will contain a précis of the issuer and the reasons for the new issue of shares.

The documentation will contain an underwriting commitment form that the sub-underwriter will be expected to complete, sign and return by a given date. The body of this document will outline the maximum number of shares that the sub-underwriter agrees to accept. The action of signing and returning the document irrevocably commits the sub-underwriter to the underwriting obligation. Many of these sub-underwriting firms will have clients that are prepared to accept a higher degree of risk than others. These clients will have already agreed to participate in the underwriting of new issues and will have accepted the risk profile required.

The sub-underwriting institution has the opportunity to sub-contract to these clients a proportion of the risk that they have just accepted and will, in their books, allocate a number of shares to the clients in a discretionary fashion but in line with the risk profile of their client. This then becomes an obligation on the client.

This obligation has to be formally recognised within the sub-underwriter's books and the accounts of their client. This should indicate the monetary level of commitment (shares x price) and also the fee that is payable for accepting this commitment. How this is done is up to the firm themselves but it should be recognised that this is a legal obligation on the client and so the process should be both legally binding and auditable.

Having accepted the obligation, the sub-underwriters should diarise when the obligation becomes due. This will be a date close to, but after, the closing date of the new issue.

The lead underwriter has the duty of informing all of those firms in the underwriting syndicate of the result of the new issue and the effect on their underwriting commitments.

In the event of a successful issue, the large bulk of the shares will have been taken up by the general public or the existing shareholders and the underwriting syndicate will have no shares to pay for. In these circumstances the lead underwriter should contact the sub-underwriters and inform them by letter that their underwriting commitment has lapsed. This is formally known as being relieved of the commitment. At this time the lead underwriter should also send out the payments for the underwriting commission that the sub-underwriters have earned.

In turn, the sub-underwriter should make a note in their own books and in the accounts of their clients of the obligation lapsing and credit their clients' cash accounts with the fee income. How this is achieved is a matter for the firms themselves as there is an element of fund accounting that may need to be considered.

What happens in the event that the new issue is not so successful and the lead underwriter has to invoke the obligations is dealt with in Section 6.2.

5.   Placing and Underwriting

Learning Objective

7.5   Explain placing/underwriting in the issue of new shares

A placing is when an existing publicly owned company wishes to raise additional capital for specific reasons but does not want to go to the mass of their existing shareholder base via the pre-emptive rights issue route.

In the UK, under Sections 89 to 96 of the Companies Act 1985, it is required that where a public company is intending to issue new shares for cash, it must offer those shares first to existing shareholders unless they have previously received agreement from the existing shareholders not to do so. Listing rules also require listed companies to comply with these requirements. Similarly, in Europe, under the 2nd Company Law Directive there has to be special consideration given to the existing shareholders, although in some countries within Europe there is an allowed mixture of pre-emption and public offer.

Having complied with and received the above pre-emption waiver from its shareholders, the issuer will use its broker or an investment bank to secure the sale of the new shares to either existing shareholders or a mix of new institutional investors and existing shareholders. The issuer and the investment bank or broker will determine the number of new shares that need to be offered and the price that the new shares will be offered at to raise the capital required.

The broker or investment bank, together with the issuer, will determine who they wish to invite to buy the new shares. Having determined who their preferred invitees are, they will make a formal offer to the investors to commit to buying the new shares on the condition that, inter alia, the new shares will be admitted to the local stock exchange for dealing purposes. Generally the new shares will also rank pari passu with the existing shares.

Having received enough indications of intent (enough interest in the issue) to secure the capital requirement, the issuer and their advisers will proceed with the issue.

It is not a general principle that a placing needs to be underwritten and, by definition, generally it does not need to be underwritten. However, this is a decision that is left to the investment bank or broker.

6.   Settlement in Underwriting

Learning Objective

7.6   Understand the processes of settlement within an IPO, underwriting and placing

We have previously discussed both rights issues (in Section 3) and placing (in Section 5), but not an IPO. An IPO happens when a privately owned company issues shares or stock that it wishes to be sold to the general public. This means the company will no longer be privately owned but will instead be owned by a variety of investors, most of which are not involved with the day-to-day operations of the company. These investors simply own some of the company's shares, which they purchased on the open market.

Although IPOs can vary greatly from one company to another and they require a long, expensive and complicated process, the IPO is basically a way for the existing owners of the company to raise capital based on expectations of future success and profit.

As described in Section 4.3, globally, IPOs will be offered (sold) to the public by various mechanisms. These mechanisms can be known by various names, such as book building, Dutch auction, tender or fixed price. Whatever mechanism of price discovery is used, it must entail the public completing an application form of some description. Whatever the mechanism, there will always be a last date for application and this will probably have a time attached to it. It will be by this time and date that the application forms have to be lodged with the investment bank that the issuer has appointed.

6.1   Initial Public Offering (IPO) Settlement

Settlement in regard to an IPO means the following need to happen:

1. The investment bank being used by the issuer will determine which applications (bids) have been successful.
2. The investment bank and the issuer will determine the basis on which shares will be allocated.
3. All successful applicants (bidders) will be informed if they are successful, either in full or in part, by the investment bank.

4. New shares will be issued either in book entry form at the local CSD or in certificated form in non-dematerialised markets.

5. Any unsuccessful applicants (bidders) or any applicants who have had their applications (bids) scaled down due to over subscription will receive their application monies back from the investment bank. Generally, if the investor is asked to attach a cheque to the application (bid), the investment bank will reserve the right to clear all cheques. In practice, however, only those cheques over a certain monetary threshold will be cleared. This means in many instances that cheques will not be cleared and the unsuccessful investors will receive their cheques back.

6.2 Settlement and Underwriting Commitments

Underwriting commitments only become active when the IPO, rights issue or placing have not been entirely successful. Settlement in regard to underwriting commitments means the following need to happen:

1. The investment bank (lead underwriter) determines how many shares have not been subscribed for and will allocate these shares to those institutions (sub-underwriters) who have committed to buy the shares on a pro rata basis.

2. The lead underwriter will formally contact the sub-underwriters and inform them of the number of shares that they are required to accept and the cash counter-value that they need to make available.

3. The lead underwriters will ask the sub-underwriters into which shareholder names the residue shares are to be registered and will ask the sub-underwriters to pay the cash counter-value to a bank account by electronic means by a certain date.

4. The sub-underwriters have to respond to both these requests by the given date.

5. The lead underwriter, having received both the cash and the shareholder names, will release the details of the shareholders to the issuer's registrar via the local CSD or by another electronic mechanism.

6. The lead underwriter will confirm to the sub-underwriters that the shareholdings have been allocated.

7. The lead underwriter will also release the underwriting fee to the sub-underwriter.

8. The sub-underwriters who have sub-contracted the underwriting obligation to their clients now have to inform those clients of their obligation.

9. This has to be a formal contracted process as this is essentially a market transaction that has implications for NAV and capital gains tax purposes.

10. The client's portfolio has to be increased via a holding of shares and decreased by a reduction in their cash balance of the monetary counter-value of the shareholding.

11. The sub-underwriter will release the underwriting fee to the client account where this is appropriate.

6.3 Placing Settlement

Settlement in regard to a placing means the following need to happen:

1. The investment bank or broker to the issue will receive commitment letters to participate in the placing from their preferred investors (placees).

2. An application will be made to the local stock exchange for the new shares to be admitted to the stock exchange.

3. Assuming that this application is successful, the investment bank or broker will inform the placees as to how many shares they have been placed with and instruct them how they should pay the monetary counter-value.

4. The investment bank or broker will ask the placees as to which name they would like the new shares to be registered in and to be placed on the register of shareholders.

5. This placing process has to be a formal contracted process as this is essentially a market transaction that has implications for NAV and capital gains tax purposes.

7. Risks in Underwriting

Learning Objective

7.7 Analyse the risks and benefits associated with underwriting

7.1 Risks

The major risk in underwriting is that something will happen that will affect the attractiveness of the issue to the public or existing shareholders. This event could happen to either the issuer or the marketplace in general. It could have the effect of making the issue a total or partial failure and the underwriter and sub-underwriters having to fulfil their commitment to buy the shares.

The risk, therefore, is that the underwriters create a situation for themselves where they are holding shares that are valued at less than they paid for them. This in itself might only be a temporary situation, as there is always a chance for the share price to recover. The greater risk is if the company that they have invested in is not a sound proposition for recovery. This may cause the underwriters to consider crystallising the loss.

7.2 Benefits

The benefit of underwriting is the fact that the underwriters will earn fees or commission for the risk they are taking (see Section 8). Perversely it could be argued that another benefit is that there is the potential for the underwriters to buy into a company that they really like, at a price that they really like, and that in the long term they do not see having an investment as a risk.

8. Underwriting Commission

Learning Objective

7.8   Demonstrate the calculation of underwriting commission

When considering how to demonstrate the calculation of underwriting commission, it is important to recognise the different mechanisms that are used worldwide by the investment banks to underwrite an issue of shares. The mechanisms used for price discovery (book building, Dutch auction, tender or fixed price) were discussed in Section 4.2. In conjunction with this we now have to discuss how the investment banks earn their commissions or fees.

8.1   US Procedures

8.1.1   Firm Commitment

In the US the investment bank may make what is known as a firm commitment to the company issuing the shares. This mechanism is where the investment bank will buy the new securities for an agreed price and resell the securities to the public at a mark-up – essentially becoming a market maker. However, the investment bank will bear all of the expenses associated with the sale out of the profit they make.

8.1.2   Standby Commitment

This is where the investment bank agrees to only buy any shares not taken up by the public or existing shareholders; it will then sell these shares to the general public as a broker/dealer.

The fundamental principal is that the underwriters make their money by realising a profit from the onward sale of shares.

8.2   UK and Europe

In the UK and the European markets, underwriting is much more like the US standby commitment. However, the difference is that the investment bank and the associated sub-underwriters will be paid a commission. The sub-underwriters are of course free to sell the shares if they so wish but they may not be a broker/dealer-type institution.

The research that has been carried out into the commissions charged or revenue generated in the underwriting arena has outlined a big difference between the European and US markets. Typically, in Europe, the rates paid by the issuers are said to be 3% to 4.5% whereas in the US they are said to be 6% to 7.5%. In the US the underwriter also has the duty of price discovery.

It should be remembered that the risk/reward profiles are different, which is likely to account for the difference in rates.

So, in Europe, where the business model allows for a specific fee to be charged to the issuer, this will be in the 3% to 4.5% range but could be higher. This is charged as a percentage of the overall value of the issue. The actual fee charged will depend on the degree of difficulty the underwriter perceives there to be in arranging a successful issue. For instance, in a difficult, perhaps volatile market, the chances of the underwriter being left with some or even all of the issue is much greater than in a market where investors are looking for opportunities.

This fee is likely to be distributed by the investment bank as follows:

- 25% retained for expenses
- 12.5% paid to the brokers to the issue
- 62.5% paid as underwriting commission to the underwriters.

The commissions paid to the sub-underwriters are likely to be in the range of 1% to 3% depending upon the difficulty of securing investor interest in the issue. The following is an example of how the calculation works for the sub-underwriters' commission:

Example

Commitment = 250,000 shares priced @ £1.00 = £250,000.00.

Commission @ 1.75% on £250,000.00 = £4,375.00.

VAT may be applicable depending on the jurisdiction and VAT rules.

9.   Corporate Actions Checklist

Learning Objective

7.9   Analyse a typical corporate action describing the management of the process and the timetable applicable at each stage

As each corporate event occurs, it is important that the management of the process becomes active. It is important that at each critical stage of the process there is a management review and authorisation of the action taken and the accuracy of that action. Whether the process is a manual or an automated one, there needs to be continuous sign-off by senior personnel at critical times.

The following is an example of the issues related to a corporate action that need to be considered.

Corporate Actions Checklist	
Procedure/Task/Job	✓ or N/A
Preliminary announcement; create numbered event/task file (automated or manual)	
Scrub data; verify details with another source	
Identify event type, eg, rights, merger, bonus, dividend, etc	
Automated/create printout of holders to operations	
Sign off to authorise release to inform existing holders of prelim announcement	
Diarise review of event (awaiting event to materialise)	
Update to event	
Scrub data; verify details with another source	
Identify if voluntary, mandatory or mandatory with options	
Create updated event/task file with holders as of ex-date	
Create event timetable, eg, closing date for offer, last dates for instructions (internal and external), payment dates taking into consideration global timeframes and ensuring diary reminders are updated	
Request automated statement of entitlements	
Calculate entitlements if manual	
Reconcile automated/manual entitlement position	
Sign off to authorise release of data and instruction requests	
Notify asset managers/client of entitlement and timetable	
Create new temporary security in system, eg, XYZ new nil paid, subscription rights	
Add new entitlements to portfolios	
Identify claims to be made, eg, settlement fails, stock loans	
Identify claims to be received, eg, settlement fails	
Reconcile issuer documentation, eg, allotment letter, sub-custodian allocation	
Add regular and timely review dates to system or manual diary	
Send timely reminders to asset managers/clients	
Confirm all decisions received, eg, take up rights, are correctly authorised	
Sign off to confirm all instructions received and correct instructions being sent	
Send instructions to CSD, custodian, sub-custodian, issuer's agent by secure mechanism	
Confirm all instructions have been processed	
Confirm receipt of entitlement	
Release updated positions to portfolios	
Reconcile entitlements received	

Reconcile account updates – confirm result of corporate action booked to portfolios	
Chase/deal with claims	
Confirm corporate action to be successfully closed	
Sign off to close	
Regular checks need to be made to an outstanding preliminary events schedule to ensure nothing has been missed	

The major problem with corporate actions is the diversity of the events and the timetable of processes associated with each one. The above is a generic example of a procedure that any team dealing with corporate actions may find helpful in managing what can be a difficult process which, if done poorly, can cause both financial and reputation loss and is a category of operational risk.

Additional boxes will almost certainly need to be added to reflect internal systems and procedures. It is also desirable to have the verification box signed by a manager/supervisor and, where applicable, the trader, as a double check that nothing has been missed.

It is important that key management reports are created to allow the supervisors and managers to have an overview of both individual events and consolidated events for daily management (eg, diary of today's tasks to be completed) and for ongoing key performance indicators of the efficiency of the area.

10. Corporate Actions Road Map

Learning Objective

7.10 Apply the key deadlines and decision options applicable to the companies involved, fund managers, custodian, registrar, stock settlement teams, corporate actions teams and data vendors

10.1 Companies

10.1.1 Decision Options

The board of directors of any company will, from time to time, believe it to be in the best interests of the company and shareholders to invoke a particular corporate event such as a bonus issue, rights issue, sub-division or consolidation stock dividend. The primary decisions that companies have to make with regards to any corporate event are:

1. Should we do it?
2. If so, when do we do it?
3. What will it cost?

Of course, the event types will cause the company a differing level of complexity with the decision process. For instance, it is probably easier for a company to decide when it is time to make a bonus issue than it is to announce a rights issue.

Timing is often the most critical decision that has to be made. Picking the right time can often be the difference between failure and success of the issue. In this regard, before making any final decisions companies will almost certainly seek advice from their brokers and investment bankers and maybe from some influential existing shareholders. Especially in regard to new issues such as rights issues, they need to take into account the market place and to get their offer into the market queue. They also need to take into account the market regulators, the market CSDs and their registrars.

Once the decision has been made, the company will probably handle some things themselves but will delegate other things to their investment bankers and/or brokers.

The company itself will almost certainly handle the shareholder decisions needed to ratify the new issue or to allow it to go ahead, via an extraordinary general meeting (EGM) or annual general meeting (AGM). Depending on the jurisdiction of the company, there may government tax to be paid. If there is a registrar involved, this could be done in conjunction with them. This will also include when announcements are made in the financial press.

A company will probably delegate to its investment banker and/or broker, at least in part, the communication with the local stock exchanges to handle things like the admission to the exchange of the new shares created.

10.1.2 Key Deadlines

key deadlines will include the production of the documentation required to be presented to the regulators, shareholders and stock exchanges, outlining the reasons for the issue and requesting permissions to issue, list and proceed. Within these documents they will have to outline other key deadlines such as the:

- record date
- admission to stock exchange date
- documents posted date
- ex-date
- close of offer date
- publication of details date.

10.2   Fund Managers

10.2.1 Decision Options

For fund managers it might be thought that the decisions to be made will only be relevant when the corporate event is a voluntary corporate action such as a rights issue or offer for sale. This is not strictly the case, because fund managers may have another decision to make, irrespective of whether the issue is mandatory or voluntary, which is whether to support the board of directors by casting a vote at the EGM or AGM held to ratify the event.

In the case of a rights issue, the fund managers/shareholders essentially have a single decision to make when considering what to do in response to the rights issue: do they want additional exposure to this company at this price?

After making that decision, they can:

* subscribe to the rights issue in full (ie, take up the new shares in full) or
* ignore (lapse) the rights issue or
* sell the rights to the new shares or
* sell sufficient rights to take up the new shares for a zero cost.

10.2.2 Key Deadlines

The key deadlines for the fund managers are essentially:

* When do we need to vote by?
* When is the last date for selling our rights to the new shares?
* When do we need to accept the offer by?

10.3   Custodians

The key decisions and key deadlines for custodians are essentially those encompassed in the Corporate Actions Checklist (when completed) listed in Section 9.

10.4   Registrars

10.4.1 Decision Options

Several countries of the world still maintain share registrars. When a client of a registrar (a company) determines it is going to go ahead with a particular corporate event the registrar will be contacted.

Obviously the event will determine what the registrar is required to do. For instance if it is a regular occurrence like a dividend, the registrar will already have processes in place for ensuring that dividend warrants are produced and sent out. If the event is something out of the ordinary for that particular company, but not unusual in general, they will have their response templates in place that prescribes what needs to happen.

The questions that the registrar is likely to have to consider are:

1. What will be the cost?
2. How long will it take to prepare?
3. How long is the elapse time of the event?

The data that the registrar will need to make its decisions are likely to be as follows:

1. What is the event (bonus, rights, open offer, sub-division, takeover/merger, scheme of arrangement, etc)?
2. What is the client's requirement of us? (Prepare EGM/AGM documentation, prepare voting cards, handle proxy voting, prepare share documentation, send out documents, engage with shareholders regarding the issue, receiving agent to the event.)
3. How many shareholders are there?
4. How will shareholders registered abroad be dealt with?
5. What is the record date for the event?

Depending upon the answer to these questions, the registrar will be able to make an informed decision and estimates of the cost and duration of the effort required.

10.4.2 Key Deadlines

The key deadlines will be determined by how the country involved deals with certain issues. Several countries still maintain the practice of issuing renounceable documents. This being the case, the deadlines could include:

- documents posting date
- return of proxy cards date
- EGM/AGM date
- informing board of result of vote
- posting of renounceable documents (where applicable)
- closing date for certain actions (splitting)
- informing board of ongoing data regarding acceptance levels (eg, by 2:00pm)
- informing investment banker of ongoing data regarding acceptance levels (eg, by 2:00pm)
- offer closing date
- results of offer
- posting of resulting documentation.

10.5   Stock Settlement Teams

In countries where physical delivery of documents associated with new issues is still operating settlement teams will have to make the following decisions:

1. Is the document correctly renounced, assigned to the new buyer?
2. Has the closing date for the issue passed?
3. Is the delivery 'good delivery'?

10.6 Corporate Action Teams

The key decisions and key deadlines for the corporate actions team will be those encompassed in the Corporate Actions Checklist (when completed) listed in Section 9.

10.7 Data Vendors

10.7.1 Decision Options

The decisions for data vendors with regard to corporate events will typically revolve around the following:

- Where do they get their data from?
- How can they be assured that the data is correct?
- At what times will they receive their data?
- What are the costs associated with collecting the data?

To make them competitive they have to able to answer a client's questions and compete in areas that relate to:

- worldwide market coverage
- events coverage
- client support for their product
- web-based product that can be used
- service costs.

The data that needs to be included in the corporate action feed needs to include high-level data such as the following:

- Event type.
- Currency.
- Creation date.
- ISIN.
- US code.
- Local code.
- Change date.
- Primary exchange.
- Issuer name.
- Exchange and country.
- Country of incorporation.
- Country of registration.
- Instrument type.
- Listing status.
- Security description.
- Listing date.
- Par value.
- Ex-date.
- Pay date.
- Record date.
- Market deadlines for the event.

10.7.2 Key Deadlines

By way of example of the low-level data and key deadlines that need to be included in the data feed, the following event types are depicted:

- **Bonus/Capitalisation** – record date; ex-date; pay date; previous and new ratio; fractions; offered security type; resultant security type; resultant ISIN, SEDOL; lapsed premium; record date Id and notes; registration date; priority; notes.
- **Consolidation/Reverse Stock Split** – record date; ex-date; pay date; currency; previous and new par value; previous and new ratio; fractions; new code (ISIN, US); new code effective date; record date Id and notes; registration date; priority; notes.
- **Rights** – record date; ex-date; pay date; previous and new ratio; fractions; currency; issue price; subscription starting and ending date; split date; trade starting and ending date; offered security type; resultant security type; resultant ISIN, SEDOL; trading security type; trading security ISIN; lapsed premium; over subscription; record date Id and notes; registration date; priority; notes.

11. The Impact of Corporate Actions

Learning Objective

7.11   Calculate the old and new positions pre- and post-capital events

It is vitally important that the impact of the corporate action is reflected in the records of the client and firm. For instance, if an investor has a holding in ABC plc where the company decides to have a bonus issue, the outcome will be as shown below.

Example

ABC plc 2-for-3 Bonus Issue

ABC has a share price of £15 and decides to make a 2-for-3 bonus issue. A shareholder has 3,000 shares so their position will be:

Before bonus issue	3,000 shares @ £15	£45,000
Bonus shares allocated	2,000 shares	–
After bonus issue	5,000 shares	£45,000

The effective share price is now £9 (£45,000/5,000 – called the ex-bonus price) which equates to cum bonus value of the client's holding.

The key points to note are:

- the entitlement must be calculated at ex-date
- the new shares received must be reconciled to the expected entitlement
- the portfolio position must be updated at ex-date.

If any of this process is not done correctly major problems may occur, for example the position may not have changed so it shows as 3,000 shares and when valued at the ex-bonus price of £9 results in a significant valuation error.

12. Timeframes

Learning Objective

7.12 Define the standard trading timeframes that apply during capital events

Globally, timeframes for corporate actions such as rights and bonus issues are based on market practice. Bonus issues are mandatory and the investor is given details of when the change to the shares will take place. The only date that will affect the trading patterns is the ex-date.

Rights issues, however, need the investor to make a decision on whether to take up the rights or to activate the other options available. Therefore, a timetable exists; a generic example for a rights issue might be as follows:

1. The issuer announces the rights issue at the stock exchange.
2. If they are tradeable, a new entitlement security (nil paid rights, nil paid new shares, rights subscription shares, subscription rights) is listed.
3. A notification or allotment letter is sent to each investor on the company register detailing the entitlement. (Note: this is only the case if the rights issue is not processed via a CSD.)
4. The date that trading in the new entitlement security can begin is announced.
5. The latest time and date for the subscription and payment in full for the new shares is given.
6. The date for expected credit to the CSD stock accounts is given (as well as expected despatch of definitive certificates if appropriate).
7. The date the new shares become ordinary shares is announced.

Globally, the timeframes for trading in the entitlement securities will differ because of the differing infrastructures. However, it is possible to give a generalisation of the subscription timeframes and, therefore, the trading timeframes. This will equate to a trading period of two to 16 days. By way of example, the subscription period in Singapore is approximately eight days, in Korea approximately 14 days, in Europe approximately 14 days and in the UK approximately 21 days.

13. Double Taxation Agreements

Learning Objective

7.13 Explain the impact of double taxation agreements on clients

Double taxation treaties are agreements between sovereign states which are designed to:

- .protect the beneficial owner against the risk of paying too much tax where the same income is taxable in two countries
- allow for the beneficial owner's status (pension fund, charity, sovereign) to be taken into account and benefit from reduced or zero taxation
- provide certainty of treatment for cross-border trade
- prevent tax discrimination against a nation's business interests abroad.

Double taxation treaties are also drawn up to protect the government's taxing rights and protect against attempts to avoid or evade a tax liability. They also contain provisions for the exchange of information between the taxation authorities of different countries. There are more than 1,300 double taxation treaties worldwide. For example, the UK has in excess of 100 double taxation agreements (DTAs), Canada in excess of 90 DTAs and the US in excess of 60 DTAs in existence.

The word double in the title is often mistakenly taken as meaning that the client avoids paying tax twice. This is not the case because, in actual fact, the client will often actually pay tax twice, eg, once in the country of origin of the income and once in their country of residence. These payments are of course to two different taxation authorities. Double in the title should actually be taken to mean designed for two as in double room rather than double the amount as in twice as much.

The agreements generally cover income tax, corporation tax and capital gains tax (direct taxes).

13.1 Benefits to a Client

A client may invest overseas and, as a result, income and/or capital gain may be taxed in the country of the origin of the income. If the client is a taxpayer in their own country, they will also be taxed in that country on the income or gain – in other words, taxed twice.

Tax treaties will often enable the client to recoup some of the tax applied by either, a reduction at source or by enabling a reclaim from the overseas tax authorities. The process of reclaiming withheld tax (called withholding tax) is often carried out by the custodian used to hold the overseas asset(s).

Some material that appears in this chapter may have been sourced from other areas – see Appendix 4 for details of the relevant organisations.

14. Regulatory Impacts on Corporate Actions

Learning Objective

7.14 Understand how the global Regulatory environment impacts on the processing of corporate actions and in particular how the UK regulatory environment dictates processes for a regulated UK firm

In this section it is important to try and clarify the parameters of the learning objective.

We are not attempting to stray into the regulations and rules that surround corporate finance issues or company law that govern how issues are structured and comply with how the new issue is brought to the market. Our focus is on what regulations are in place to ensure that consumers are safeguarded from fraud, counterparty risk or mismanagement of processing whilst their assets are being safeguarded.

14.1 Global View

The securities industry and corporate actions in particular are governed and regulated by several different national and international bodies and regulations. Corporate actions as such are not dealt with as a topic on their own. Most of the global regulators will deal with corporate actions as part of a broader spectrum of issues of which a corporate action will be part. Below are some of the world's leading regulatory bodies.

Australia

The Australian Securities and Investment Commission (ASIC) is Australia's corporate, markets and financial services regulator. Its role is to ensure that Australia's financial markets are fair and transparent. It is an independent Commonwealth government body. It is set up under and administers the Australian Securities and Investments Commission Act 2001 (ASIC Act), and carries out most of its work under the Corporations Act 2001 (Corporations Act).

Europe

The European Securities and Markets Authority (ESMA) is an EU financial regulatory institution and is the European supervisory authority located in Paris. ESMA works in the field of securities legislation and regulation to improve the functioning of financial markets in Europe, strengthening investor protection and cooperation between national competent authorities. The idea behind ESMA is to establish an EU-wide financial markets watchdog. One of its main tasks is to regulate credit rating agencies.

Each member state of the EU will have its own regulatory authority. By way of example we have listed three.

France

Autorité des marchés financiers (AMF) is the stock market regulator in France. The AMF is an independent public body that is responsible for safeguarding investments in financial instruments and in all other savings and investment as well as maintaining orderly financial markets.

Its stated remit is to:

- safeguard investments in financial products
- ensure that investors receive material information
- maintain orderly financial markets.

Germany

The Federal Financial Supervisory Authority (BaFin) is responsible for the supervision of banks and financial services providers, insurance undertakings and securities trading. It is an autonomous public-law institution and is subject to the legal and technical oversight of the Federal Ministry of Finance. BaFin operates in the public interest. Its primary objective is to ensure the proper functioning, stability and integrity of the German financial system. BaFin states that *'bank customers, insurance policyholders and investors ought to be able to trust the financial system'*.

UK

The FCA aims to ensure that financial markets work well so that consumers get a fair deal. This means ensuring that:

- the financial industry is run with integrity
- firms provide consumers with appropriate products and services
- consumers can trust that firms have their best interests at heart.

To do this, the FCA regulates the conduct of businesses and, for many of these, it considers whether they meet prudential standards that reduce the potential harm to the industry and consumers if they fail.

India

The Securities and Exchange Board of India (SEBI) is the regulator for the securities market in India. It was established in 1988 and given statutory powers on 12 April 1992 through the SEBI Act 1992. The basic functions of the SEBI are to:

- protect the interests of investors in securities
- promote the development of the securities market
- regulate the securities market.

The SEBI says it has to be: *'responsive to the needs of three groups, which constitute the market'*:

1. The issuers of securities.
2. The investors.
3. The market intermediaries.

US

The SEC's mission is the protection of investors; the maintenance of fair, orderly, and efficient markets; and to facilitate capital formation. The SEC says that it: *'strives to promote a market environment that is worthy of the public's trust'*.

The SEC is an agency of the US federal government. It holds primary responsibility for enforcing the federal securities laws and proposing securities rules.

As can be seen, all of these regulatory bodies have very similar objectives based around fairness to and trust by the consumers. Other global regulators have similar ambitions.

14.2 Regulatory Actions

There are several instances where the regulators can be seen to be trying to fulfil their mission statements.

Europe

The European Securities and Markets Authority (ESMA) oversees the introduction of the MiFID regulations. This European law became effective on 1 November 2007 and provides a harmonised regulatory regime for investment services across the member states of the EEA. Although MiFID does not describe corporate actions as a topic in itself, corporate actions in Europe are subject to this directive. Further upgraded regulations were introduced in MiFID II which became effective in July 2014.

The FCA has also introduced rules and guidelines under the CASS rules. Although again there are no specific rules and guidelines for corporate actions per se, they do fall under these rules and guidelines.

US

The SEC has been implementing the Dodd-Frank Consumer Protection Act, a wide-ranging piece of legislation that deals with many aspects of operations, under which the administration of any corporate actions will fall.

The SEC refers to corporate actions within its rules and regulations but this is more in the context of how the actions are brought to the market, rather than how the resulting assets should be safeguarded for the beneficiaries once issued. This is dealt with by Dodd-Frank.

End of Chapter Questions

1. Why would a corporate announce a rights issue?
   Answer reference: *Section 1.1*

2. Why would a corporate announce a stock split?
   Answer reference: *Section 2.1*

3. Why would a 2-for-1 in the US be different from a 2-for-1 in the UK?
   Answer reference: *Section 2.1*

4. What is a pre-emptive right?
   Answer reference: *Section 3*

5. Are all rights issues pre-emptive in:
   a. the UK
   b. Germany?
   Answer reference: *Section 3*

6. What are the main mechanisms for price discovery?
   Answer reference: *Section 4.2*

7. What is a placement of shares?
   Answer reference: *Section 5*

8. What happens if a client account is not amended following a 2-for-3 bonus issue if the client holds 3,000 shares at a pre-share split price of £15?
   Answer reference: *Section 11*

9. What are double taxation treaties?
   Answer reference: *Section 13*

Chapter Eight
Straight-Through Processing

8

1. Straight-Through Processing (STP)

Learning Objective

8.1   Describe straight-through processing (STP)

1.1   What is STP?

Definition of STP

'The automated end-to-end processing of trades/payment transfers including the automated completion of confirmation, generation, clearing and settlement of instructions.'

Source: ECB Glossary

It is perfectly justifiable to say that STP is not a panacea for operational efficiency in the financial services industry. Many factors are required before it can be successfully deployed, including the availability of both internal and external capabilities.

Many organisations talk about STP capability when, in reality, they mean automated processes with operational areas, which do not have the end-to-end functionality mentioned in the definition.

There can be no doubt that the advent of electronic data processing has played a significant part in improved efficiency and, to some extent, has also led to increased competition, which itself has generated new products and services.

With both evolution and revolution evident in developments in technology, it is of little surprise that STP has gone (and is going) through significant evolution and change. Furthermore, it will continue to do so.

1.2   The Basic Objective of STP

The basic objective of STP in the global securities operations arena is to improve efficiency and control and reduce risks by automating linked manual activities. This is achieved by creating an environment that can use a single set of instructions to automatically conduct all the manual stages in a process such as input, verification, activation, confirmation and implementation in the operational area in which it is deployed.

Currently, STP is deployed mainly in the areas of settlement and custody, such as reconciliations, corporate actions and cash management. The goal is to employ this philosophy in as many processes as possible.

Many of the problems that occur in establishing an STP environment in global securities processing are based on the fact that banks, brokers and settlement agents often carry a high degree of legacy of systems, procedures and policies that do not lend themselves to linked automation.

We can prepare to analyse the potential benefits of STP by looking at the generic typical trading workflow.

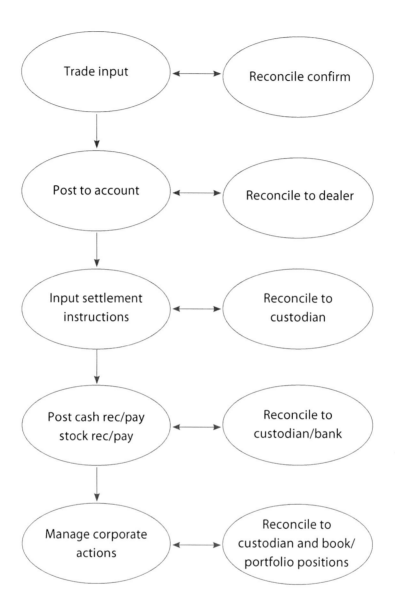

The schematic above illustrates the type of trading transaction workflow that might have existed, or may still exist, in many banks before implementing, in one form or another, an STP environment.

When we consider that this process is being applied for every single transaction during a working day, it is obvious that:

- the manual element is considerable
- it is an expensive process
- it introduces a significant potential for human error at every stage
- this could result in additional cost
- the time taken is longer than it should be.

This, in turn, can impact significantly on:

- profitability and viability of services
- capacity for growth of the business
- operational risk levels.

The streamlining of this series of processes to eliminate the manual intervention to a single point is the goal of STP.

There are, however, obstacles to the implementation of a total STP environment, including that of standing data. If there is incorrect, missing or unrecognised standing data relating to clients, markets, products and instructions, then STP processes are halted.

1.3   Enterprise-Wide STP and Market-Wide STP

In reality, there are two forms of STP. One is a structure established internally in an organisation and the other is one that extends beyond the boundary of the firm and reaches out to the market infrastructure and the client base.

Today, many exchanges, clearing houses and CSDs offer access to their systems and data, enabling inward and outward messaging, data transfer and instructions. Likewise, custodians provide clients with interface capabilities that will enable a real STP structure to be achieved and organisations like SWIFT provide the messaging facilities that can be incorporated into the STP structure.

2.   Enabling STP

Learning Objective

8.2   Explain the business reasons behind the development of STP

The financial services industry has become increasingly complex, with hundreds of trading participants. As a result, financial institutions seek ways to reduce the risks and costs associated with trade processing from order to settlement.

The creation of an STP environment enables organisations to gain certain potential benefits. These include:

- connecting electronically with trading partners
- transparently changing or adding trading partners and information sources
- quickly enabling expansion into new markets and lines of business
- increasing access to liquidity
- reducing cost per trade
- adhering to best and timely execution
- reducing operational risk
- reducing errors and processing delays

- improving customer satisfaction
- enabling quick growth to increase volume and revenue.

Markets around the world are embracing the concept of STP and this is reflected in the automation of processes and interfaces available from exchanges, clearing houses and CSDs.

3. Key Initiatives Behind STP

Learning Objective

8.3   Describe the key initiatives behind STP

Resources in the operational environment often work under a great deal of pressure and their performance can become dulled through the repetition associated with many of the processes in clearing and settlement, corporate actions, reconciliations and cash management. Managers in both operations and risk should be aware that in any heavily manual process the degree of control effectively exercised can fall short of prudent practice.

The diagram below concentrates on all aspects of operations and shows what an overall STP environment might look like.

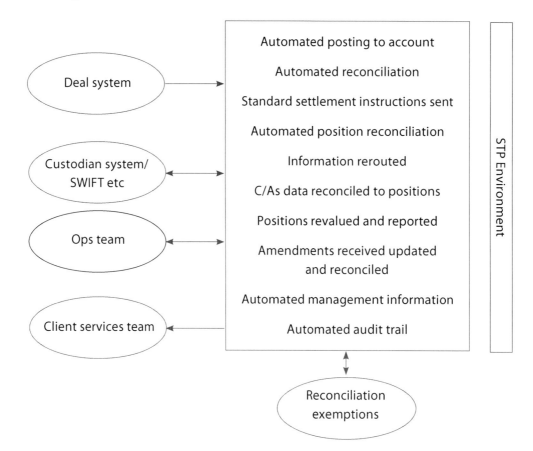

We can see that after the introduction of STP, the whole process has undergone a fairly radical change. We should note, in particular, the elimination of manual involvement throughout the process. The STP structure provides a completely automated process, after initial input, for the majority of settlements. We can also see that the need to match/confirm manually has been removed and, as a result, the risk of incorrect or premature payment has also been removed. The vital components in an STP structure include:

- automatic trade capture
- electronic confirmation
- rule-based transaction queuing
- automated confirmation matching
- automated position reconciliation
- exception reporting
- automated and up-to-date SSIs
- automated payment release
- interfaces to settlement parties (ie, clearing houses, CSDs, custodians)
- external netting
- internal netting.

The STP environment is likely to include specialist applications/systems, eg, electronic confirmation matching systems that are provided by external parties, which are integrated with the in-house systems and other external systems to achieve the goal of a wholly automated processing system. The STP system automates the process from front, to middle, to back office. It can also be taken a stage further to provide STP across geographical centres of business, as shown in the diagram below:

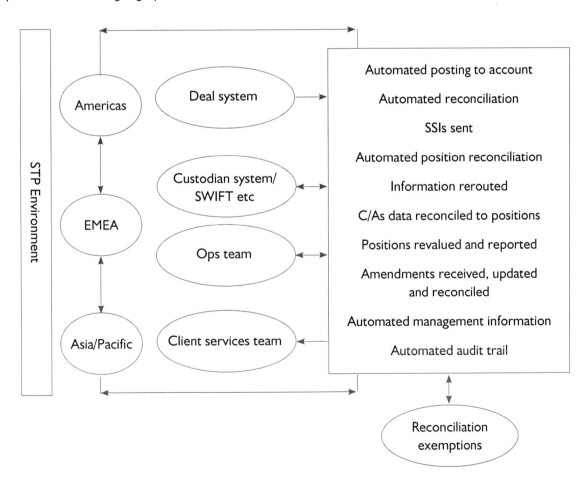

3.1 Global STP Initiatives

The ability of the external parties that a bank or broker deals with in order to provide automated and accessible processes is vital to the creation of a full or true STP process. A common requirement for STP is the standardisation of processes. We can see how two global organisations at the heart of the process have worked together with various market elements by looking at initiatives taken by them.

Securities Market Practices

Market practice rules for existing securities messaging standards have been historically defined after industry participants have implemented the standards. To further complicate industry information flows, each industry participant defined these rules separately and differently. This resulted in an inefficient exchange of information, whereby standards and their associated market practice rules were interpreted and implemented differently by every industry participant in each geographic market. This inefficient exchange of information within and across different markets limited STP in the securities industry.

Securities Market Practice Group (SMPG)

SMPG was created in July 1998 and since its inception has established a local presence in more than 30 countries through National Market Practice Groups (NMPGs). These groups are comprised of broker/dealers, investment managers, custodian banks, CSDSs and regulators. The SMPG has been extremely successful in creating globally agreed harmonised market practices which, integrated with ISO standards has brought the securities industry closer to achieving STP. The SMPG is focused on enhancing the current securities industry practices. It realises the benefit of industry utilities and other industry groups conforming to standards and market practices. As such, there is active dialogue between the SMPG and other industry groups/organisations (ie, Omgeo, the European Central Securities Depositories Association (ECSDA), the Americas Central Securities Depositories Association (ACSDA), the International Securities Association for Institutional Trade Communication (ISITC) and ISSA).

SMPG Process

The SMPG is open to all participants interested in creating globally agreed market practices for the securities industry. This objective includes the harmonisation of non-regulated geographic differences, as well as consistent implementation by securities industry participants for processing within and across all markets. Monthly meetings of the NMPGs and the two physical meetings per year of the SMPG, as well as periodic conference calls, cover issues ranging from standardised methods of informing custodians to transfer securities and the resolution of cross-matching at central securities depositories, to the creation of NMPGs in non-participating countries and the development of multi-year project plans.

The detailed process begins with the NMPGs' analysis and documentation of local practices. The SMPG then collates common elements, specifies additional country requirements and identifies further opportunities for harmonisation of non-regulated differences. After final review and refinement by the SMPG, the documents are published on their website.

To date, the SMPG has produced a significant number of market practice recommendations about trade initiation/confirmation, settlement, reconciliation and corporate actions. Additionally, the SMPG has since expanded to define market practices for the investment funds industry.

Sourced via the SMPG website

FIX Trading Community

FIX Trading Community™ is a non-profit, industry-driven standards body at the heart of global trading.

The organisation is independent and neutral and addresses business and regulatory issues impacting multi-asset trading in global markets through standardisation, delivering operational efficiency, increased transparency, and reduced costs and risks for all market participants. Central to FIX Trading Community's work is the continuous development and promotion of the FIX family of standards, including the core FIX protocol messaging language, which has revolutionised the trading environment and has become the way the world trades.

As an industry-driven organisation, all FIX Trading Community initiatives are pursued in response to market participant requests. This work is organised through a global network of committees and working groups.

FIX Trading Community was previously known as FIX Protocol ltd (and this remains its full legal entity name). Since its launch in 1998, the organisation has developed and encouraged adoption of the FIX messaging standard. The organisation also explores how other non-proprietary, free and open standards could effectively support evolving needs.

Sourced via FIX Trading Community website

Further information can be found on the relevant websites.

However, other initiatives are just as vital in creating the right environment for real STP to be achieved. For instance, harmonisation in payment systems and corporate actions is essential.

4. Advantages and Disadvantages of STP

Learning Objective

8.4 Explain the advantages and disadvantages that arise with STP

4.1 Disadvantages of STP

By implementing change on such a scale there are, of course, a number of disadvantages that need to be considered. Most are associated with the STP project itself.

An STP project uses considerable resources and, as a result, it can:

- be expensive in terms of management and project team costs
- divert resources from the crucially important day-to-day process
- create a significant re-training requirement
- require complete revision and documentation of procedures.

In addition, the STP project:

- can create an increased risk environment before delivering a reduced (in theory) risk environment post-implementation
- may, in the longer term, lead to a loss of skill sets by redeployment or redundancy, making a manual back-up capability unlikely
- may create a need for a major change to the business continuity and disaster recovery procedures
- can identify some residual trades/products that cannot be processed via an STP process.

We must also recognise that, in addition to the development cost, there is also the potentially high cost of maintenance. Indeed, if any component in the STP structure requires changing, then all of the related interfaces must potentially be redeveloped.

However, there are some possible solutions, including middleware. Middleware offers the capability to specify and write new interface programs in, according to providers, just four to six person-weeks, compared with the three to six person-months that might have previously been required. It also isolates the two main processing systems from one another. Thus any modification required for one component is confined to that element of the environment.

Given the above, and the obvious cost and risk implications, how does real STP justify itself as an investment? An analysis of the benefits of STP will go some way towards providing a general answer.

4.2   Advantages of STP

In some respects, the important benefits (ie, reduction in costs and increased capacity) are self-evident. People are expensive and have limitations in the workload they can manage efficiently.

As we would expect, there is initially a steep rise in costs as the systems required in support of STP processing are introduced. However, we can reasonably assume that, as around 50% of transactions become subject to the STP process, the investment should start to yield returns. The return may fall slightly as more activity is generated through the greater capacity but, nevertheless, the cost of the clearing and settlement process should be lower than in the pre-STP environment.

However, the benefits of STP are certainly not simply about cost reduction. Capacity and risk reduction are more important benefits.

Capacity will undoubtedly be greater and will enable not only growth in the organisation's own business but also, for certain types of organisations, create the basic infrastructure needed for considering in-sourcing work. STP also provides the base to develop a wide range of automated value-added services that can be offered to clients.

Operational risk issues, particularly those related to human error and performance (ie, efficiency), are significantly reduced and even eliminated, although there is naturally a technology risk associated with STP that must be recognised and addressed.

5. Regulatory Impacts on STP

Learning Objective

8.5 Understand how the global regulatory environment impacts on the processing in an STP environment and in particular how the UK regulatory environment dictates STP processes for a regulated UK firm

As with so much in the securities industry, following the financial crisis, markets globally have witnessed a massive increase in the level of new regulations.

The systems that help the industry, when operating in an increasingly global environment, need to be aligned with the new regulation so that they produce the required effect. This means that in order to do this, the industry practitioners need to understand the implications of emerging regulations in different regions so that they may be interpreted and incorporated into the technical (systems) infrastructure. These regulations are impacting various areas not only of the trade lifecycle, but also many other areas of the securities industry and often operates across multiple asset classes. It is really important that the industry interprets them correctly.

It is therefore unsurprising that meeting the new regulatory requirements is frequently cited as one of the top risks facing firms across the industry.

Some examples of the recent regulatory demands are shown below.

5.1 European Market Infrastructure Regulation (EMIR)

EMIR is an EU law that aims to reduce the risks posed to the financial system by derivatives transactions. It impacts European and non-European financial institutions and corporates. The regulation on derivatives, central counterparties and trade repositories has introduced new requirements to improve transparency and reduce the risks associated with the derivatives market.

EMIR also establishes common organisational, conduct of business and prudential standards for CCPs and trade repositories.

EMIR imposes requirements on all types and sizes of entities that enter into any form of derivative contract, including those not involved in financial services. It applies indirectly to non-EU firms trading with EU firms.

The new regulation came into force during 2013 and 2014. It requires entities that enter into any form of derivative contract, including interest rate, FX, equity, credit and commodity derivatives, to:

- report every derivative contract that they enter into to a trade repository
- implement new risk management standards, including operational processes and margining for all bilateral OTC derivatives, ie, trades that are not cleared by a CCP
- clear, via a CCP, those OTC derivatives subject to a mandatory clearing obligation.

Since 12 February 2014, all counterparties have been required to report details of any derivative contract (OTC or exchange traded) they have concluded or which they have modified or terminated, to a registered or recognised trade repository (TR) under the EMIR reporting requirements.

There are six trade repositories currently registered with and recognised by, ESMA:

- Chicago Mercantile Exchange (CME) Trade Repository ltd (CME TR), based in the UK.
- DTCC Derivatives Repository ltd (DDRL), based in the UK.
- ICE Trade Vault Europe ltd (ICE TVEL), based in the UK.
- Krajowy Depozyt Papierów Wartosciowych S.A. (KDPW), based in Poland.
- Regis-TR SA, based in Luxembourg.
- UnaVista ltd, based in the UK.

5.2 Automatic Exchange of Information (AEOI)

OECD, a non-regulatory organisation, in conjunction with the G20 countries and in close cooperation with the EU, has begun to introduce its common reporting standards (CRSs) for the automatic exchange of financial information. The aim of the AEOI is to reduce tax evasion through transparency. The standards build on the US FATCA to take another step towards a globally coordinated approach to the automatic exchange of financial account information of non-resident customers and investors.

This means that financial institutions around the globe are faced with significant additional identification and reporting responsibilities, which may vary in detail and timing by jurisdiction. Crucially, they need to be able to collect and track complex, varied customer information quickly and easily to report domestically in each jurisdiction where they operate. There are both reputational and financial risks to getting AEOI wrong.

FATCA is designed to prevent tax evasion by US citizens using offshore banking facilities. It requires foreign financial institutions (FFIs) outside of the US to provide information to the US tax authorities regarding financial accounts held by US nationals. If financial institutions do not agree to provide this information they will suffer a 30% withholding tax on payments of US source income. FATCA creates a new tax information, reporting and withholding regime, designed to enable the US IRS to gain information about US persons and US source income held outside the US. FATCA is not designed to raise revenue.

The definition of an FFI is very wide. It includes not only banks, insurance companies and broker-dealers but extends to clearing organisations, trust companies, hedge funds, private equity funds and pension funds. It also includes securitisation vehicles and other investment vehicles.

HMRC is not a regulatory body as such because there are issues regarding confidentiality and data protection. However, to allow UK FIs to comply with their FATCA obligations, the UK has entered into an intergovernmental agreement (IGA) with the US for the information required under FATCA from the UK FIs, to be provided to HMRC to forward onto the US. Many other countries have also entered into IGA arrangements with the US.

5.3   UK Regulation

The PRA in the UK is the regulator for the following institutions:

- Banks, building societies, and investment firms (CRD firms).
- Credit unions.
- Friendly societies.
- Insurance firms – Solvency II.
- Insurance firms – non-directive firms (NDFs).

All these firms are required to provide regulatory data that is relevant to their sectors. For example the firms that are subject to the CRD have to provide data that is pertinent to the following:

- Own funds and leverage.
- Large exposures.
- Net stable funding.
- Liquidity coverage ratio.
- Asset encumbrance.
- Financial reporting.

The FCA also require certain UK regulated firms to make periodic reports. These reports relate to the following:

- **Adviser reporting requirements** – for effective supervision reasons the FCA needs information to show that the firms are complying with the RDR rules.
- **Annual accounts and reports** – certain firms have to send their annual accounts and reports, in line with Section 262(1) of the Companies Act 1985 and section 471 of the Companies Act 2006, as laid out in the supervision processes of the FCA Handbook.
- **Annual controllers' reporting** – firms should report to the FCA once a year, within four months of their accounting reference date. This is in order to ensure that the FCA receives regular and comprehensive information about the identities of all of the controllers of the firm. The FCA has to check that certain threshold conditions can be met. This supports their functions under Part XII of the FSMA.
- **Clients asset reports** – all regulated investment firms (with limited exceptions set out in SUP 3.1) have to send the FCA an annual report. The report has to provide a reasonable assurance on the client money and/or custody assets held by the firm.
- **Client money and asset reporting** – CASS medium and large firms have to complete a client money and assets return (CMAR) each month through GABRIEL, the FCA's reporting system for collecting, validating and storing regulatory data.
- **Compliance reporting** – most reporting for banks, building societies and designated investment firms (who are all covered by the CRD) is made through the PRA. Firms are required to send the FCA their reports via GABRIEL.

5.4   Impact

As can be seen from the foregoing examples, there is a massive amount of differing data that needs to be identified, collected, stored, captured and downloaded into various formats in order to deal with today's regulatory requirements. This is probably only the tip of the iceberg. This is of course on top of the systems work that has to be done to allow the daily operations to continue to function.

The new breed of STP has to be accomplished if today's firms are to meet their regulatory requirements. It could be summed up as compliance and regulatory processing. To accomplish the correct data flows, firms will require the correct system architecture. This is of course dependent on what their current architecture is. It is also a matter of design. Some firms may prefer to build on the STP concept and have only the data required to satisfy the reports they are required to submit to the authorities in order to flow to pre-determined data storage banks from which future reports will be ordered, or they may prefer to interrogate the main database with programmes designed to find the data when required.

Some material that appears in this chapter may have been sourced from other areas – see Appendix 4 for details of the relevant organisations.

End of Chapter Questions

1. What are some of the benefits to financial institutions of an STP environment?
   Answer reference: *Section 2*

2. How is the enabling of STP occurring in non-UK/US markets?
   Answer reference: *Section 3.1*

3. What issues does STP bring for settlement teams?
   Answer reference: *Section 4.1*

4. What is the benefit of STP in the clearing and settlement process?
   Answer reference: *Section 4.2*

Chapter Nine
Outsourcing-Offshoring

9

1. Introduction

Learning Objective

9.1   Explain the definitions of outsourcing and offshoring and why they are different

There has been a major shift in the corporate thinking behind how firms need to structure themselves to compete in today's global marketplace. In the world of securities processing, the original stance was that all the processes needed to be done in-house in the jurisdiction in which the firm was based. This was of course understandable in the days when most things were done manually.

With the advent of much better and faster communication methods the world has relatively suddenly became much smaller. This has led to firms questioning whether they have to do everything in-house and presented new opportunities to look at their business architecture of firms.

Over the last few years, new terminology has entered the vocabulary of business architecture. These terms are outsourcing and offshoring.

1.1   Outsourcing

Generally the definition of outsourcing is said to be an arrangement in which one company provides services for another company, where those services could be provided or usually have been provided in-house. Previously, those services would have been considered an intrinsic part of managing a business.

1.2   Offshoring

Offshoring is often used in the same breath as outsourcing, meaning that they are the same. In fact, this is wrong, and the two terms mean different things. The definition of offshoring is where a company moves certain services or functions to either a third party provider or to a branch of their company in a country, other than the one in which the company moving the function is based. The company will do this primarily to take advantage of lower labour costs. In other words it could be said to be offshore outsourcing.

2.   Why Outsource or Offshore?

Learning Objective

9.2   Discuss why a firm might want to outsource or offshore some processing functions

Outsourcing and offshoring are trends that are becoming more common. However, it is important to remember that our industry has a history of outsourcing. Many years ago, most fund managers and brokers would have had their own network of overseas sub-custodian banks in which they would have held their clients' overseas assets. This started to change in the 1970s when the fund management community and the regulators decided that it was better to concentrate on that which they did best, ie, picking the investments. Stockbrokers also followed this trend. The functions that were primarily targeted were in the custody, fund accounting, systems and information technology areas. In later years in the securities processing arena, trade matching engines and proxy services are examples of functions subject to outsourcing. Today, whole departments, such as trade capture, settlement and corporate actions, are being outsourced or put offshore.

There are various reasons why a firm may want to do this including:

*   lower costs (due to economies of scale or lower labour rates)
*   variable capacity
*   the ability to focus on core competencies by removing peripheral ones
*   lack of in-house resources
*   increased efficiency
*   access to specific IT skills
*   increased flexibility to meet changing business and commercial conditions
*   tighter control of budget through predictable costs
*   lower ongoing investment in internal infrastructure
*   access to innovation and thought leadership.

3. What are the Advantages and Disadvantages?

Learning Objective

9.3   Explain what the advantages and disadvantages of outsourcing or offshoring are

3.1   The Advantages of Outsourcing and Offshoring

*   **Swiftness and Expertise** – most of the time functions or tasks are outsourced or placed offshore to suppliers of services who specialise in that function. The supplier could also have specific equipment and technical expertise that could be considered as superior to that of the outsourcing organisation. Effectively the tasks can be completed faster and with better quality output.
*   **Concentrating on the core processes** – rather than doing the functions that could be considered as supporting the core, outsourcing or offshoring the supporting processes gives the organisation more time to strengthen their core business process.
*   **Risk-sharing** – the reduction of risk in the business could be considered as a good reason to outsource. Outsourcing certain components of the business process helps the organisation to shift certain responsibilities to the service supplier.
*   **Economies of scale** – potential for the outsourcing firm to realise the economic goal of the firm's cost of production rising at a slower rate that the firms' output (productivity).
*   **Reduced operational and recruitment costs** – outsourcing does away with the need to hire individuals in-house; recruitment and operational costs can be minimized to a great extent. This is seen as one of the prime advantages of offshore outsourcing

3.2   The Disadvantages of Outsourcing and Offshoring

*   **Risk of exposing confidential data** – when an organisation outsources or offshores HR, payroll and recruitment services, it involves a risk of exposing confidential company information to a third party. When using an offshore branch, that branch becomes exposed to additional risks.
*   **Synchronising the deliverables** – at times it becomes evident that it is easier to manage the processes that have been outsourced rather than managing an outsourced or offshore partner. When the firm does not choose a suitable partner for outsourcing, some of the common problem areas include stretched delivery time frames, sub-standard quality output and inappropriate categorisation of responsibilities.
*   **Hidden costs** – although outsourcing and offshoring are usually cost-effective, at times the hidden costs involved in signing a contract across international boundaries may pose a serious threat. There is also the cost of the maintenance of SLAs and KPI tracking.
*   **Lack of customer focus** – an outsourced vendor may be catering to the expertise-needs of multiple organisations at a time. In such situations vendors may lack complete focus on your organisation's tasks
*   **Deskilling the business** – many of the skills of the workforce that have been built up over time could be lost. If things do turn out badly, getting those skills re-hired may cost more.
*   **Cost of downsizing** – there is likely to be a cost to the firm in terms of redundancy payments to those people who have lost their jobs.
*   **Dependency** – becoming too dependent on the outsource provider who actually is delivering the service to the firm's customer base.

4. How to Measure Success

Learning Objective

9.4   Discuss how a firm might monitor the success of any outsourcing/offshoring project.

4.1   Predicted Outcomes

When undertaking a major project such as outsourcing or offshoring either to an external supplier or an inter-company supplier, initially the firm should have conducted a major cost/benefit analysis and due diligence process. The point of this analysis is to give the firm a clear understanding of what they can expect to pay out over a period of time and how they can expect to benefit. Unless there is a catastrophic event in the early stages, this cost/benefit and due diligence analysis will have to be judged over a number of years.

*   One way of judging whether the project is a success is to track the predicted financial costs and benefits against that cost/benefit analysis by an ongoing due diligence process of the overall plan.
*   Another way is to ensure that the services being outsourced are being provided in a way that the supplier has promised. Regular review meetings with the supplier could be used to measure the success of the outsourced/offshored services or functions.
*   A third critical measure will be the reaction of the firms' clients to the outsource arrangement. A review of those customers affected by the new arrangements should be conducted to ensure that no ill effects are being felt by the customer base. These results should be fed into the due diligence analysis referred to above.

Even though the outsourcing/offshoring will have started as a project, it is important for firms to keep in mind that, as time goes by, it is still relevant to keep benchmarking the ongoing results against the anticipated benefits.

4.2   Service Level Agreements (SLAs)

Learning Objective

9.5   Explain where service level agreements (SLAs) are used in the industry and the parties who would typically be involved

9.6   Outline the principles underpinning service level agreements and the range and typical content of SLAs

SLAs are an essential part of the relationship process between organisations in the financial markets.

SLAs are used to monitor the performance of the service provider and to provide clear guidelines to both the customer and the provider of the services that are expected to be delivered.

Typically, they will be used between the provider of the service, who is seeking to clarify what they are contracted to supply, and the user of the service, who is seeking to clarify the level of service they expect to receive.

Without SLAs there is the potential for constant argument and disagreement about the quality, timeliness and content of services provided.

Written SLAs need to be in place, alongside any necessary legal contracts, in order to clarify each party's obligations, irrespective of where they are based throughout the world and in which parties they operate. The developed markets already operate a sophisticated range of SLAs but SLAs in the rapidly growing emerging markets are evolving in terms of their suitability.

In recent years, SLAs have become a very important feature in many global jurisdictions. They are used to measure the delivery of service in the areas of:

- custody
- fund administration
- computer systems
- other outsourced functions.

Outsourcing of any function presents an operational risk. In the light of the recent focus on capital requirements of the Basel II directive and the EU Solvency II Directive, it is important to recognise that SLAs are an integral part of managing the operational risk associated with outsourcing.

They are, therefore, typically used by global custodians, sub-custodians, fund managers, brokers, registrars, transfer agents, data vendors, software providers and the customers that use these service providers.

The principles that should underpin the creation of an SLA can be summed up as follows:

1. The measurements that are chosen should motivate the correct behaviour from the provider of the service. To motivate the correct behaviour, each side should understand the others' expectations and goals.
2. The factors measured should be within the control of the service provider. The SLA should also be two-sided in as much as, if the factor to be measured has a dependence on the customer, the customer is linked to the measurement.
3. Factors should be chosen where the measurement data can be easily collected. This is in the interests of all the parties of the SLA.
4. There should not be too many factors chosen to be measured. Having too many factors to be measured will detract from the SLA because both sides will be likely to become bored with the endless process of discussing meaningless measurement.
5. A proper baseline to the SLA should be set. To be meaningful, the measurements must be of reasonable and attainable performance levels.

The following is an example of the content of an SLA and will give a good idea of the kind of areas covered by these agreements.

Example

This SLA is made the xx day of 20xx. between:

1. ABC ltd (the licensor) and
2. XYZ ltd (the licensee).

Recitals:

A. The licensor has developed and owns certain computer software programs and applications as specified in the licence agreement.
B. The licensor has agreed to grant to the licensee a non-exclusive licence to use such programs and applications (under the terms of the licence agreement).
C. this SLA is a schedule to the licence agreement and all words and expressions in this agreement shall have the same meanings as set out in that document.

1. Support and Maintenance Services

1.1 For the duration of the licence agreement, the licensor shall provide the licensee with all or any of the support services as set out in clause 2 below.
1.2 The licensee shall supply in writing to the licensor a detailed description of any fault requiring the support services in clause 2 and the circumstances in which it arose, and shall submit sufficient material and information to enable the licensor's support staff to duplicate the problem.
1.3 When appropriate, the licensor will endeavour to give an estimate of how long a problem may take to resolve. The licensor will keep the licensee informed of the progress of problem resolution. The licensor's support staff will attempt to solve a problem immediately or as soon thereafter as possible, and the response times shall be in accordance with the service parameters set out in clause 3.
1.4 For the duration of the licence agreement the licensor shall provide the licensee with maintenance services set out below in order to keep the licensed program materials up to date and compliant with all relevant business requirements specified in the licence agreement.

2. Support Services

2.1 Hotline support: For an urgent problem, the licensee can telephone the licensor's hotline which is available during the normal support hours. An urgent problem is degradation or failure of the system, defective software distribution media or software performance inconsistent with documentation. Problems which do not delay or inhibit system operation will be handled by written reports.
2.2 On-site support will be provided by the licensor, where appropriate, in the event that telephone support does not resolve a software problem.
2.3 Modem support: the licensor shall, where necessary, supply on loan a modem for online problem resolution.
2.4 Out-of-hours support shall, where appropriate, be provided by the licensor.
2.5 Correction of critical errors or assistance to overcome specific software problems. the licensor may, in its sole discretion, correct errors by patch or by new version.
2.6 Information on availability of new versions of software.
2.7 Consultancy advice on software development, enhancements and modifications, together with estimates for the same.

3. Response Times

3.1 Standard service: between Monday to Friday from 09:00 to 17:30 (excluding national holidays) the licensor shall use its reasonable endeavours to respond within eight hours of receipt of a request.

3.2 Priority service: between Monday to Saturday from 08:00 to 19:30 (excluding national holidays) the licensor shall use its reasonable endeavours to respond within three hours of receipt of a request.

4. Error Correction

4.1 If a licensee discovers that a current release fails to perform in accordance with the documentation, then the licensee shall, within 14 days after such discovery, notify the licensor in writing of the defect or error in question and provide the licensor (so far as the licensee is able) with a documented example of such defect or error.

4.2 The licensor shall thereupon use its reasonable endeavours to correct promptly such defect or error. Forthwith upon such correction being completed, the licensor shall deliver to the licensee the corrected version of the object code of the current release in machine-readable form, together with the appropriate amendments (if any) to the documentation, specifying the nature of the correction and providing instructions for the proper use of the corrected version of the current release. The licensor shall provide the licensee with all assistance reasonably required by the licensee to enable the licensee to implement the use of the corrected version of the current release.

4.3 The foregoing error correction service shall not include service in respect of:

  a. defects or errors resulting from any modifications of the current release made by any person other than the licensor

  b. any version of the licensed programs other than the current release or the immediate current release

  c. incorrect use of the current release or operator error

  d. any fault in the equipment or in any programs used in conjunction with the current release

  e. defects or errors caused by the use of the current release on or with equipment or programs not supplied by or approved in writing by the licensor, provided that for this purpose any programs designated for use with the current release in the specification shall be deemed to have the written approval of the licensor.

5. Software Releases

5.1 The licensor shall promptly notify the licensee of any improved version of the licensed programs that the licensor shall from time to time make.

5.2 Upon receipt of such notification, the licensor shall deliver to the licensee as soon as reasonably practicable (having regard to the number of other users requiring the new release) the object code of the new release in machine-readable form together with the documentation.

5.3 If required by the licensee, the licensor shall provide training for the licensee's staff in the use of the new release at the licensor's standard scale of charges for the time being in force as soon as reasonably practicable after the delivery of any new release.

5.4 The new release shall thereby become the current release and the provisions of this licence shall apply accordingly.

6. Technical Advice

6.1 The licensor will provide the licensee with such technical advice by telephone or mail (including email) as shall be necessary to resolve the licensee's difficulties and queries in using the current release.

7. Changes in Law

7.1 The licensor will from time to time make such modifications to the current release as shall ensure that the current release conforms to any change of legislation or new legal requirements which affect the application of any function or facility described in the documentation. The licensor shall promptly notify the licensee in writing of all such changes and new requirements and shall implement the modifications to the current release (and all consequential amendments to the documentation which may be necessary to enable proper use of such modifications) as soon as reasonably practicable thereafter.

4.3 Key Performance Indicators (KPIs)

Learning Objective

9.7 Explain the mechanisms that can be employed for monitoring and managing the relationship including the typical key performance indicators (KPIs) used

It is hugely important to understand what it is that is being monitored and why.

An SLA will set out the details of services to be provided, including timings, quantities and deadlines. It is reasonably easy to manage this process from standard management information drawn from automated logs or reports that contain the data required.

SLAs are a performance indicator but too rigid an application can be massively counterproductive to the relationship and, in fact, can lead to a poorer performance being delivered. There needs to be a sensible process invoked otherwise two things can easily happen:

1. The focus of the administrators becomes box-ticking rather than developing the service.
2. The time involved in dealing with issues can become significant for both parties.

Adherence to the terms of the SLA must, therefore, be meaningful but workable. However, issues do, and will, arise. A case study showing an example of one such issue is shown next.

Case Study

Service delivery elapsed time example

Member's expectations – time elapsed

A = Date notice given by employee.
B = Date administrator notified of member leaving.
C = Date leaver options issued to member.
D = Date member advises selected option.
E = Date claim settled.

The example illustrated in the diagram above highlights some of the difficulties. The member resigns at date A, but does not receive their final claim settlement (which could be a refund or deferred benefit statement) until date E. Their experience of the service delivery is the elapsed time between A and E. the fact that the administrator delivered their work between dates B–C and D–E within their SLA is not relevant to the member.

Clients have an important role to play in the successful completion of this process too. If their HR and payroll processes are inefficient, then the time elapsed between point A and point B becomes extended. Work cannot commence until the client notifies the administrator of the action so, no matter how efficient the administrator may be, their procedures are only part of a chain of events that affects the outcome.

Both member and client have an active part to play in the process. From the member's point of view, they need to understand their options and what they are being asked to do. Their ability to understand directly relates to the effectiveness of the communication material and the clarity of the option details they receive from the administrator. If there is a lack of clarity or a poor understanding then all parties have to spend more time resolving issues. This does not improve the member's experience and causes frustration and delay for all parties involved.

KPIs must be reflective of the arrangement that is to be employed by the parties to the SLA.

If a strict application of the SLA is employed, the KPIs will cover the key elements of the service being delivered. For instance, this could include:

- delivery times
- completeness
- error rates
- response times
- meeting benchmarks.

Some examples of KPIs include:

- **Process-related**:
  - number of settlement failures occurring over a given time; number of times funding deadlines are missed in a given time
  - number of reconciliation differences between front office and operations department over a given period of time
  - value of interest claims incurred over a given time period
  - volume or number of transactions per member of staff in a department.
- **Non-process-related staff turnover**:
  - amount of overtime
  - percentage of staff with an agreed training plan
  - period of time to review departmental plans
  - percentage of temporary staff to permanent staff.

4.4   SLA Enforcement

Learning Objective

9.8   Describe the additional actions that have to be considered where non-performance arises

There are times when the non-performance of a service provider becomes a significant issue. This might occur because of:

- financial loss incurred by the customer
- regulatory breaches incurred by the customer
- negative impact on the customer's performance.

It is possible that the SLA provides for either:

- a basis for termination of arrangement
- financial compensation.

This may subsequently lead to more serious legal situations, so the timetable for the resolution of issues and invoking of clauses within the SLA must be agreed between the two parties.

Note: as shown in in Section 4.2, there may be disputes that concern the use of other/ third parties where the service provider maintains that the customer or another party is at fault and is the cause of the problem and is, therefore, outside the scope of the SLA. These situations should be clarified and procedures agreed within the SLA at the outset.

5. The Regulatory Impact on Outsourcing-Offshoring

Learning Objective

9.9 Understand how the global regulatory environment impacts on the process of outsourcing-offshoring and in particular how the UK regulatory environment dictates processes for a regulated UK firm

Many of the world's regulators and regulatory organisation have issued guidelines on how firms should conduct themselves when entering into, or contemplating, an outsourcing route.

Most of the regulators will point out seven main areas where firms should concentrate their efforts. These are listed below namely;

1. Due diligence in selecting the service provider and in monitoring the service provider's subsequent performance (written SLAs)
2. The contract with a service provider to provide clarity of what is being provided
3. Business continuity at the outsourcing provider
4. Security and confidentiality of Information
5. Termination procedures
6. Regulator's and market's access to books and records, including rights of inspection
7. Management oversight of the outsourced functions and associated risks.

5.1 UK Regulation

The FCA and the PRA have issued the SYSC sourcebook which sets out rules on outsourcing. Rule 8 of the SYSC sourcebook requires firms to take reasonable steps to avoid undue operational risk when outsourcing critical or important functions.

For some time, critical or important functions have generally been considered to include data storage and the day-to-day management, maintenance and support of information and communications technology. A number of regulators across Europe are now also taking the view that existing outsourcing rules apply to all functions performed through a cloud, whether those functions be the delivery of software, databases, platforms or infrastructure as a service.

The FCA rules and guidance make it clear that above all, a UK regulated firm should be clear that it retains full accountability for discharging all of its regulatory responsibilities. It cannot delegate any part of its responsibility to a third party.

5.2   European Regulation

For firms subject to MiFID or the CRD, SYSC Rule 8 applies as a rule, meaning that compliance is mandatory and non-compliance could result in sanctions.

5.3   US Regulation

The Office of the Controller of the Currency (OCC) and the Federal Reserve Board (FRB) have issued guidance on how financial institutions should manage third-party risks. The guidance issued by each agency has particular relevance to outsourcing transactions and provides companies with a roadmap of the key areas of concern to regulators. Institutions also should expect that regulators will ask them to compare their policies and procedures against the new OCC and FRB guidance.

Financial institutions can therefore use the guidance to support and bolster their position when negotiating these provisions with vendors.

Some material that appears in this chapter may have been sourced from other areas – see Appendix 4 for details of the relevant organisations.

End of Chapter Questions

1. Explain the difference between outsourcing and offshoring.
   Answer reference: *Section 1*

2. In what areas of financial services are SLAs used?
   Answer reference: *Section 4.2*

3. What principles underlie the creation of an SLA?
   Answer reference: *Section 4.2*

4. How is an SLA monitored?
   Answer reference: *Section 4.3*

5. What issues does a rigid application of the SLA raise for a relationship with the third party?
   Answer reference: *Section 4.3*

6. What is the implication for a client if a third party has SLA issues with a service provider?
   Answer reference: *Section 4.4*

7. What issues arise for managers and supervisors?
   Answer reference: *Whole chapter*

9

Chapter Ten
Data Management

This chapter has the title 'Data Management', but because the subject matter could be construed to have a very technical connotation attached to the phrase, it is very important for candidates to be clear as to the meaning of the phrase 'data management' when used in the context of this workbook.

This chapter does not attempt to address in any detail any technical aspects of data management that might normally be connected to the phrase when used in a much broader technical context. This includes things such as data governance, data architecture, analysis and design, data maintenance, database administration, meta data management, reference and master data management and business intelligence management, document record and content management, contact data management.

Within this chapter, we do refer to data security management, data quality management and data warehousing.

1.   What is Data?

Learning Objective

10.1   Describe what data is and how it can be defined

The Latin meaning of data is something given. It is the plural of datum.

There is often a misinterpretation as to what data is. Data is often transposed and/or interchanged with the word information and it is very important to understand the difference.

Data, information, knowledge and wisdom are all closely related concepts, but each has its own role in relation to the other. Data is collected and analysed to create information suitable for making decisions, while knowledge is derived from extensive amounts of experience dealing with information on a subject.

There is a very simple way to understand the difference between data and information.

When we understand the primary function of the item we are looking at (data), we see what the distinction is between the two.

Here is a simple way to tell one from the other:

- Computers need data, whereas humans need information.
- Data is the building material (building blocks) that allows information to have context and meaning.

Data is raw. It has not been shaped, processed or interpreted. It is a series of ones and zeros that humans would not be able to make use of. It is disorganised and unfriendly.

Once data has been processed and turned into information, it becomes acceptable to the human readers. It takes on context and structure. It becomes useful for businesses to make decisions and it forms the basis of human knowledge and progress.

While the bigger picture is slightly more complex, this gets us some way towards understanding what data means.

2. Who Provides Data?

Learning Objective

10.2 In the financial services industry and especially in global securities operations, information is provided by many different entities. Identify who these main providers will be and what information is provided.

In the previous learning objective, we explained the technical difference between data and information. Notwithstanding this, it is important to recognise that when working in our industry, more often than not we use the word data to mean information. So being pragmatic we are acknowledging this fact in the following descriptions.

- **Client data** – the client is likely to be asked to prove their identity, supported by passport or driving licence. Full name, address, date of birth, telephone numbers, email addresses, bank details, residency, NI number, payroll number, income, tax number, financial targets, mandates, standing instructions/orders, direct debits details, company name, company type and company number are other data that may be required.
- **Securities data** – information about listed companies will be provided by the local stock exchanges and the companies themselves, such as stock identifier numbers SEDOL, CUSIP, etc, shares/stock in issue, capital structure, share/stock prices, interest payments, dividend payments, corporate action details, yields, balance sheet, profit and loss, brokers analysis. Similar data will be available from unlisted companies if it is required.
- **Market infrastructure data** – is provided by regulators, tax authorities, CCPs, CSDs, clearing houses, central banks, data providers, government bodies, local stock exchange will provide analytic data such as indices like FTSE, DAX, CAC, DOW, etc. Governmental agencies will provide data about GDP, currency, geopolitical, population, industries, religion, ethnicity of country. Organisations such as the ISO will issue information such as currency codes. Industry organisations such as SWIFT will issue standardised data about institutional members.
- **Counterparty data** – credit rating agencies providing information about countries, companies, banks, financial institutions and stocks.
- **Standard settlement data** – institutional counterparties will exchange details with each other. These will be details about where and with whom transactions in assets should be settled and will include details such as custodian name, account numbers, account type, country location, BIC numbers, currency codes and CSD details.

All the foregoing are examples of structured data. Unstructured data is data that can be found in, for example, social media, such as Twitter and Facebook. It is also data that is randomly collected for any amount of reasons by any amount of organisations. This is being collectively referred to as big data. Big data is about combining unstructured data from varied sources to produce information that was previously impossible or hard to attain. Where this will lead is currently unknown but it is important to know that this type of data will probably become increasingly important in our industry.

3.   How is Data Collected and Stored?

Learning Objective

10.3   Explain how the data used in global operations is collected

As can be seen from Section 2, the amount of information being provided to and used by any global operations teams is vast. It is very important to understand how this data is collected by firms. To collect this data, with which we create information, is an extremely important task. Some of the information will have to be collected manually especially when dealing with retail clients. This could be done by simply getting clients to complete and sign written forms. However to collect all of this data or information manually is uneconomic for most firms. Therefore, electronic means have to be employed. This essentially means that files of data will be sent by one organisation to another by way of direct electronic links between them (leased lines) or via the internet.

This is formally known as electronic data interchange (EDI). By adhering to the same standard, two companies or organisations, even if in different countries can transmit data or information. EDI can be formally defined as the transfer of structured data, by agreed message standards, from one computer system to another without human intervention.

Whatever method of collection is used, verification of the receipt, authenticity and completeness of the data will be required to be achieved by the receiving firm.

4.   How is Data Protected?

Learning Objective

10.4   Explain how, once collected, the data is stored and protected in the UK

The safe storage of data is one of the most important jobs. Whichever way the data is held, either manually or in an electronic format, it has to be held securely.

It should also be remembered that the data firms collect will not only be about external factors, but will also include internal factors such as personal details about their employees. This data or information may include very personal details about the employee's health and medical conditions.

In the UK, firms are bound by the Data Protection Act 1988 which controls how personal information is stored, used and kept by organisations, businesses and the government.

The UK government's website says that: *'Everyone responsible for using data has to follow strict rules called data protection principles'*. They must make sure the information is:

- used fairly and lawfully
- used for limited, specifically stated purposes
- used in a way that is adequate, relevant and not excessive
- accurate
- kept for no longer than is absolutely necessary
- handled according to people's data protection rights
- kept safe and secure
- not transferred outside the EEA without adequate protection.

There is stronger legal protection for more sensitive information, such as:

- ethnic background
- political opinions
- religious beliefs
- health
- sexual health
- criminal records.

These guidelines are particularly important as they lead directly to how the data is stored and how access to data can be permitted and controlled.

The Information Commissioners Office (ICO) is the UK's independent authority set up to uphold information rights in the public interest in order to promote openness by public bodies and data privacy for individuals. This authority has issued a guide for those who have responsibility for the day-to-day protection of data. This guide amongst, other things, sets out eight principles with regards to data.

Principle 7 gives firms a guide which offers an overview of what the Data Protection Act (DPA) requires in terms of security and aims to help firms decide how to manage the security of the personal data that they hold. The ICO does not provide a complete guide to all aspects of security in all circumstances and for all organisations but it tries to identify the main points.

The Data Protection Act states: *'Appropriate technical and organisational measures shall be taken against unauthorised or unlawful processing of personal data and against accidental loss or destruction of, or damage to, personal data'*.

The ICO gives the advice that firms will need to:

- design and organise their security to fit the nature of the personal data held and the harm that may result from a security breach
- be clear about who in the firm's organisation is responsible for ensuring information security
- make sure it has the right physical and technical security, backed up by robust policies and procedures and reliable, well-trained staff
- be ready to respond to any breach of security swiftly and effectively.

As candidates will be aware this subject is extremely large and it is not practicable therefore to reiterate everything within the ICO guide. So for the sake of brevity we are only reproducing the high level recommendations.

In general terms, the security measures that are appropriate will depend on the firm's circumstances but there are several areas that the firm should focus on. Physical and technological security is likely to be essential but is unlikely to be sufficient by itself. Management and organisational security measures are likely to be equally important in protecting personal data. These will include the following.

Management and Organisational Measures

Carrying out an information risk assessment is an example of an organisational security measure but the firm will probably need other management and organisational measures as well. The firm should aim to build a culture of security and awareness.

It is good practice to identify a person or department in the firm with day-to-day responsibility for security measures. They should have the necessary authority and resources to fulfil this responsibility effectively.

Staff

It is vital that staff understand the importance of protecting personal data; that they are familiar with the firm's security policy; and that they put its security procedures into practice. Firms must provide appropriate initial and refresher training which should cover:

- the firm's duties under the Data Protection Act and restrictions on the use of personal data
- the responsibilities of individual staff members for protecting personal data, including the possibility that they may commit criminal offences if they deliberately try to access, or to disclose, information without authority
- the proper procedures to use to identify callers
- the dangers of people trying to obtain personal data by deception (for example, by pretending to be the person whom the information is about or by making phishing attacks) or by persuading you to alter information when you should not do so
- any restrictions the firm places on the personal use of its computers by staff (to avoid, for example, virus infection or spam).

Physical Security

Technical security measures to protect computerised information are of obvious importance. However, many security incidents relate to the theft or loss of equipment or to old computers or hard-copy records being abandoned. Physical security includes things like the quality of doors and locks and whether premises are protected by alarms, security lighting or CCTV. However, it also includes how you control access to premises, supervise visitors, dispose of paper waste and keep portable equipment secure.

Computer Security

Computer security is constantly evolving, and is a complex technical area. Depending on how sophisticated the firm's systems are and the technical expertise of their staff, the firm may need specialist information-security advice that goes beyond the scope of this workbook. The firm should consider the following guiding principles when deciding the more technical side of information security:

- The firm's computer security needs to be appropriate to the size and use of the organisation's systems.
- As noted above, the firm should take into account technological developments but is entitled to consider costs when deciding what security measures to take.
- The firm's security measures must be appropriate to their business practices. For example, if the firm has staff working from home, it should put measures in place to ensure that this does not compromise security.
- The measures the firm takes must be appropriate to the nature of the personal data it holds and to the harm that could result from a security breach.

Most global financial institutions will these days have things like password protection, data encryption and various layers of computer security at the forefront of their data protection armoury to be used against hacking and misuse of data.

ISO 27001

ISO, together with the International Electrotechnical Commission (IEC), have issued the ISO/IEC 27001:2013 standard. This specifies the requirements for establishing, implementing, maintaining and continually improving an information security management system within the context of the organisation. It also includes requirements for the assessment and treatment of information security risks tailored to the needs of the organisation. The requirements set out in ISO/IEC 27001:2013 are generic and are intended to be applicable to all organisations, regardless of type, size or nature.

It is becoming increasingly urgent for firms to guard against cybersecurity. In the US, the SEC has issued guidelines to its members. Essentially, the guidance urges firms to conduct a periodic assessment of:

1. the nature, sensitivity and location of information that the firm collects, processes and/or stores, and the technology systems it uses
2. internal and external cybersecurity threats to and vulnerabilities of the firm's information and technology systems
3. security controls and processes currently in place
4. the impact should the information or technology systems become compromised
5. the effectiveness of the governance structure for the management of cybersecurity risk. An effective assessment will assist in identifying potential cybersecurity threats and vulnerabilities so as to better prioritise and mitigate risk.

The advice goes on to say that firms should create a strategy that is designed to prevent, detect and respond to cybersecurity threats. Such a strategy could include:

1. controlling access to various systems and data via management of user credentials, authentication and authorisation methods, firewalls and/or perimeter defences, tiered access to sensitive information and network resources, network segregation, and system hardening
2. data encryption
3. protecting against the loss or exfiltration of sensitive data by restricting the use of removable storage media and deploying software that monitors technology systems for unauthorised intrusions, the loss or exfiltration of sensitive data or other unusual events

4. data backup and retrieval
5. the development of an incident response plan. Routine testing of strategies can also enhance the effectiveness of any strategy.

Finally firms should implement the strategy through written policies and procedures and training that provide guidance to officers and employees concerning applicable threats and measures to prevent, detect and respond to such threats and that monitor compliance with cybersecurity policies and procedures. Firms may also wish to educate investors and clients about how to reduce their exposure to cybersecurity threats concerning their accounts.

Internal Measures

To complement these measures many international and UK firms will have a clean desk policy (CDP) probably overseen by their compliance department. The main reasons for the CDP are likely to be as follows:

- A clean desk can produce a positive image when customers visit the company.
- It reduces the threat of a security incident and potential identity theft as confidential information will be locked away when unattended.
- Sensitive documents left in the open can be stolen by a malicious entity leading to possible fraudulent action.

All staff, employees and entities working on behalf of the firm will be subject to this policy.

The CDP is likely to cover when employees are away from their desks for extended periods. For example, during a lunch break, sensitive working papers will be expected to be placed in locked drawers. At the end of the working day employees will be expected to tidy their desk and to put away all office papers. Firms should be aware of the need to provide locking desks and filing cabinets for this purpose. The CDP will likely give employees some guidance, such as:

- allocate time in the day to clear away paperwork
- always clear a workspace before leaving for longer periods of time
- if in doubt, throw it out. If unsure of whether a duplicate piece of sensitive documentation should be kept, it is probably better to place it in the shred bin
- consider scanning paper items and then filing them electronically
- use the recycling bins for sensitive documents when they are no longer needed.
- lock desks and filing cabinets at the end of the day
- lock away portable computing devices, such as laptops and PDA devices
- treat mass storage devices such as CDs, DVDs or USB drives as sensitive and secure them in a locked drawer
- laptops and other portable media devices used in connection with business should be password protected.

Within the CDP there is likely to be an enforcement clause which should point out that any employee found to have violated this policy may be subject to disciplinary action, up to and including termination of employment.

Disaster Recovery

Firms are required to provide certainty of their business continuity, should any major event outside of their control occur. These plans should include the routine backing up of their computer systems and the data files that their systems contain. This will almost certainly include the offsite storage of backed up data files. This might be on the firm's own servers or it might be the use of cloud facilities.

5. The Use of Data within Global Securities Operations

Learning Objective

10.5 Understand how and when data is used and the interaction with the global securities operations environment

Conducting tasks or processes within the current global securities operations environment nowadays relies so much on STP in many aspects that it has de-skilled the industry. The fact that things happen due to the standing data that is held within the systems environment is often lost on those performing the tasks or processes. It is important therefore that supervisors and managers appreciate the interaction between data and the tasks being performed so that they may give guidance or resolve anomalies when they appear.

Within this workbook it is impracticable to analyse each data element and how it fits into every process and so we will not attempt to do that. What can be done however is to give some examples of the interaction between data.

Example 1

A very simple example is to examine a task whereby somebody in the corporate actions section of a firm runs a daily programme to produce a report from the firm's operating system of each day's dividend entitlements. Probably all that the operator needs to do is to schedule a programme to run but even that might be automated. The programme will be designed to look at all companies held within the operating system's security master file data and present to the operator any companies that have been marked as ex-div yesterday and together with any holders of that security on the prescribed date and their holdings. Previously, we have outlined the type of data contained in these feeds. This data is stored and refreshed on a daily or sometimes intraday basis.

This task relies on the system holding several pieces of complementary data:

- Today's date.
- A company name (coded identifier, eg, SEDOL CUSIP).
- An ex-div date of yesterday.
- An ex-div marker on the company record populated.
- A client name.
- An amount of shares.

The following is a very simplistic depiction of the interaction between an operations request and data that is held within the systems environment. It is not supposed to represent anything other than that.

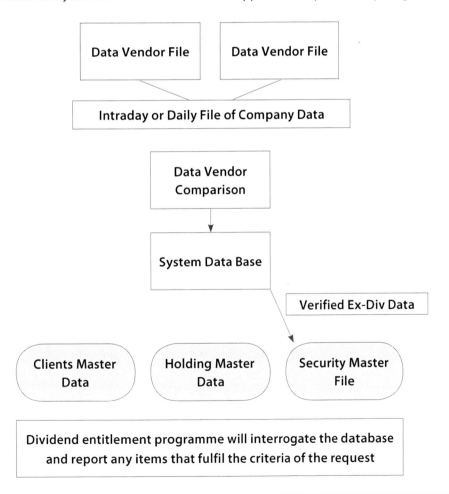

The diagram shows multiple feeds of data/information coming from an external source. Data vendors supply masses of information to the industry. The diagram shows two feeds to illustrate that there needs to be a process of verification of the data. This is often called data scrubbing or data cleansing. What this means is one source is checked against the other for verification or integrity reasons. The user firm will normally use only one source as their primary source. It is up to the firm how they or whether they verify the data. Some data vendors will advertise that they perform this cleansing before issuing their feeds. Depending upon the systems architecture the data will be stored somewhere within the firm's architecture. We have chosen to call the storage bin a security master file. So any data coming from a data vendor to do with a security on the system will be stored there. This data file is then interrogated by a myriad of different programmes every minute of every day to supply intelligible information to the user. Our example is just one of those programmes.

A more complicated example of the interaction between operations and standing data is what happens when either a sale or purchase transaction is entered into the system. Here there are several interaction points. Again this is a simplistic view for illustration purposes only.

We will attempt to depict this example differently from the diagram above because there is so much going on.

For our example we will look at a purchase. To keep it simple, we will start at the point that a purchase has been executed, verified and confirmed as good. The trade is 10,000 ABC shares purchased @ £1.00.

Example 2

Accounting Data	Exception Data	Settlement Enrichment Standing Data

Accounting Data	Exception Data	Settlement Enrichment Standing Data
• Stock identifier • Shares traded • Date traded • Time traded • Settlement date • Share price • Accrued interest • Number of days accrued • Maturity date • Yield • Commission paid • Additional charges/ fees • Calculate value of new holding in stock • Calculate new base book cost • Calculate new local book cost • FX rate used for books (system/actual) • Broker used for trade • Update commission paid to broker (day/ week/month/year) • Calculate portfolio weighting • Calculate indices weighting • Calculate risk weighting	• Trade date/settlement date convention OK • ISIN OK (already set up) • Trade date acceptable format • Settlement date acceptable format • Country holiday convention OK • Calculation price/ times shares OK • Settlement calculation OK • Place of settlement OK • Broker recognised OK (set up) • Client account OK (set up) • Client account number OK • FX required • Stock on loan OK • Stock availability checks OK • Share price vs market price OK	• Buying broker code • Selling broker code • Instructing party code • CCP code • Settlement location code • BIC • Account number at location • Account name at location • Account type at location (15% 30%, 0%)

10

As can be seen from the above, the data held in a single transaction has to be able to affect a client's portfolio account in many ways, such as fund accounting purposes, to create data for NAV calculations and for portfolio calculations that the fund managers will have to report on. Eventually, this data will be used to analyse and create portfolio performance calculations. All of this data must be stored for use at a later date.

When a custodial organisation is involved, the same data has to pass through an exception processing database that the custodian must maintain and update when necessary. This exception database will alert the custodian to any anomalies and allow quick resolution. Finally the trade must pick up enrichment data before it is sent for settlement.

Diagram 2 is shows how a purchase transaction will hold many pieces of data. We are trying to depict that this data is being fed into a system which could be within a fund management firm and/or a custodian firm and/or a sub-custodian firm. Again we have chosen to label certain data storage areas for illustration purposes only. Depending upon the systems' architecture the data will be stored somewhere within the firm's architecture.

As in diagram 1, there will be daily or intraday feeds of data coming from the data vendors. This data will be used in conjunction with the data received via the new purchases. The diagram simplistically shows/infers that the trade data goes into an accounting database that will perform the functions described in that file. In our example there is then an exception database that the transaction will interrogate or pass through to ensure that certain details are correct. It could easily be that this function makes up part of the fund manager's system architecture as well as the custodian's and sub-custodian's system architecture. Again, just for simplicity's sake, if this is a first-time purchase of this stock and the stock is not set up within the system, the trade will not be recognised. Therefore, somebody will have to do something to allow the trade to proceed. Finally, before going out for settlement, certain other data fields have to be populated via the enrichment database.

6. How Long is Data Kept and When and How is it Destroyed?

Learning Objective

10.6 Data retention is an area in which managers in global operations should be versed. Explain for how long the data used in global operations should be retained

10.7 Describe the processes of destruction of redundant data

6.1 Archiving of Data

The retention of data is a subject to which much thought must be given by firms when their data retention policies are formulated. With regards to how long data should be retained there cannot be just one answer. There will be many answers depending upon:

- the type of data that is stored, eg, reference, personal, accounting, client's income, personal correspondence and letters of complaint
- to whom the data is relevant internally or externally, eg, will external auditors need to see or access the data now or in the future, will a local tax authority need to see the data within their statute of limitations, will a regulator need to see the data now or in the future?
- who might need to examine the data. For example, the data may be required in a civil legal case or for a police criminal investigation, such as fraud
- local jurisdictions regarding statute of limitations most governments around the world will have a statute of limitations. These are laws passed by a legislative body to set the maximum time after an event when legal proceedings may be initiated.

The IT departments of most firms will have the responsibility for the archiving of data that is held electronically. How this is accomplished is important due to the details discussed above.

It is also important that operations managers and supervisors know what the data retention policy of their firm is and ensure that these policies are adhered to. Although over the years many firms have talked about having a paperless office in reality in most operations environments it is very difficult to achieve this. Therefore old-fashioned filing may still be employed. Archiving of data therefore becomes an issue for many firms and the managers of those firms. Archiving timescales and the facilities used for archiving paper-based data need to be agreed and formulated.

In the UK, the FCA states in CASS 6.6.7R: *'Unless otherwise stated, a firm must ensure that any record made under the custody rules is retained for a period of five years'*.

As stated above, it is very important that global firms understand their local statute of limitation laws.

Most UK firms are likely to ensure that they are able to provide access to historic data in excess of these periods.

6.2   Redundant Data

Data/information will be held either in an electronic format or in a paper-based format. Some of the paper that is produced will of course have been created from the electronically held data. The firm will have created its data retention policy on both paper-based and electronic-based data which will include their email systems.

Decisions about redundant data are often made by an individual. For instance having made the decision that they no longer need an email, they will hit the delete key and the email is gone! The same applies to a document held on their desktop environment: once in their view it is no longer of any use, it can be deleted. Sometimes there is an automated delete process within the firm's email system to automatically free up capacity.

But has it gone for ever? Electronically held data is actually quite difficult to erase. Although the user and anybody else corruptly using the user's workstation cannot see it, it is very possible that the data could still be retrieved.

This is why firms should have a robust view and policy on both data archiving and data erasure when data is no longer required.

There is of course a lot of paper-based data/information that naturally goes out of date. This will tend to be printed advertising material that may be useful for reference for a while. It may also be internal memos about things that were needed for a time or paper correspondence or printed emails about situations that were resolved successfully and were kept.

In the event that the firm has not made a concise and unambiguous retention policy on this type of data, the individual has to make a personal decision. The firm will almost certainly require their employees to use security bins for most paper-based data.

7.   The Regulatory Impact on Data Management

Learning Objective

10.8   Understand how the global regulatory environment impacts on data management and in particular how the UK regulatory environment dictates processes for a regulated UK firm

The topic of data management has become a very emotive subject and there have been some very high profile and news-making events concerning data over the last few years. Laptops being left on trains, computer hacking scandals, press taking photos of very sensitive documents in the hands of unwary government ministers or criminal phone hacking: it seems that nothing is safe.

Hence global regulators are urging the firms whom they regulate to become stringent about the protection of the data they become privy to, especially when that data pertains to private individuals.

Regulators are requiring their member firms to be absolutely clear about their responsibilities to their customers and to do everything they can to protect the data belonging to their customers. In many cases they are also prescribing the length of time that the client data can be held. Many government bodies also prescribe the length of time data must be held in statutes of limitations.

In some cases, there will be sanctions such as censure or fines imposed on firms should they be deemed to be lacking in their care and attention to data privacy.

The following are examples of what the global regulators for data protection are doing.

Australia

Data privacy/protection in Australia is currently made up of a mix of federal and state/territory legislation. The Federal Privacy Act 1988 (Privacy Act) and its Australian privacy principles (APPs) apply to private sector entities with an annual turnover of at least A$3 million and all Commonwealth Government and Australian Capital Territory Government agencies.

The Australian Government has indicated that the Office of the Privacy Commissioner will become a separate regulator solely charged with enforcing the Privacy Act. The Privacy Commissioner is the national data protection regulator responsible for overseeing compliance with the Privacy Act.

The Privacy Act was last amended by the Privacy Amendment (Enhancing Privacy Protection) Act 2012, which came in to force on 12 March 2014. The amendments significantly strengthened the powers of the Privacy Commissioner to conduct investigations (including own motion investigations), ensure compliance with the amended Privacy Act and, for the first time, introduced fines for a serious breach or repeated breaches of the APPs.

Following investigation, the Privacy Commissioner can either dismiss the complaint or, if the complaint is substantiated, either:

- inform the respondent they should not repeat or continue the conduct
- make a determination that includes (for example) a declaration that the complainant is entitled to a specified amount by way of compensation
- apply to the federal court or federal circuit court for an order that the organisation has breached a civil penalty provision. In such cases, a fine of up to A$340,000 for individuals or A$1.7 million for corporations can be imposed for a serious breach or repeated breaches of the APPs.

Canada

In Canada there are 28 federal, provincial and territorial privacy statutes (excluding statutory torts, privacy requirements under other legislation including federal anti-spam legislation and an identity theft/criminal code) that govern the protection of personal information in the private, public and health sectors. Although each statute varies in scope, substantive requirements, remedies and enforcement provisions, they all set out a comprehensive regime for the collection, use and disclosure of personal information. Canada's private sector privacy statutes are:

- Personal Information Protection and Electronic Documents Act (PIPEDA).
- Personal Information Protection Act (PIPA Alberta).
- Personal Information Protection Act (PIPA BC).

- Personal Information Protection and Identity Theft Prevention Act (PIPITPA).
- Act Respecting the Protection of Personal Information in the Private Sector (Quebec Privacy Act), (collectively, Canadian Privacy Statutes).

There are four primary national data protection authorities:

1. Office of the Privacy Commissioner of Canada (PIPEDA).
2. Office of the Information and Privacy Commissioner of Alberta (PIPA Alberta).
3. Office of the Information and Privacy Commissioner for British Columbia (PIPA BC).
4. Commission d'accès à l'information du Québec (Quebec Privacy Act)

PIPEDA, PIPA Alberta, PIPA BC and PIPITPA (when enacted) expressly require organisations to appoint an individual responsible for compliance with the obligations under the respective statutes. All of these regulators have the power to enforce fines. Depending upon the authority these fines can be anything up to C$100,000.

Europe

In Europe EU data protection legislation is facing huge changes. Privacy issues arising from the growing popularity of Internet services have pushed the EU to entirely rethink its data protection legislation.

In 2012, the European Commission published a draft regulation the General Data Protection Regulation, (GDPR), which will impose new obligations relevant to almost all businesses. Almost four years later, a political agreement on the GDPR was reached in December 2015. The final text was formally adopted by the European Parliament and Council in April 2016 and becomes applicable in 2018.

The current EU Data Protection Directive (95/46/EC) was adopted in 1995. It has been implemented differently by EU member states into their respective national jurisdictions, resulting in the fragmentation of national legislations within the EU. The GDPR will replace the Data Protection Directive and will be directly applicable in every EU member state, thereby eliminating the current fragmentation of national data protection laws.

At present, personal data processed in the EU is governed by the 1995 European Directive (95/46/EC) on the protection of individuals with regard to the processing of personal data and on the free movement of such data. The directive establishes a number of key legal principles:

- Fair and lawful processing.
- Purpose limitation and specification.
- Minimal storage term.
- Transparency.
- Data quality.
- Security.
- Special categories of data.
- Data minimisation.

These principles have been implemented in each of the 28 EU member states through national data protection law.

UK

In the UK the ICO is responsible for the enforcement of the Data Protection Act. The ICO warns firms that it is essential for organisations involved in the processing of personal data to be able to determine whether they are acting as a data controller or as a data processor in respect of the processing. This is particularly important in situations such as a data breach where it will be necessary to determine which organisation has data protection responsibility.

The data controller must exercise overall control over the purpose for which, and the manner in which, personal data are processed. If the ICO becomes aware that a data controller is in breach of the Act, they can serve an enforcement notice requiring the data controller to rectify the position. Failure to comply with an enforcement notice is a criminal offence and can be punished with fines of up to £5,000 in the Magistrates' Court or with unlimited fines in the Crown Court.

To serve a monetary penalty notice for a breach of the DPA, the commissioner must be satisfied that there has been a serious contravention of Section 4(4) of the DPA by the data controller, the contravention was of a kind likely to cause substantial damage or substantial distress, and the contravention was either deliberate or the data controller knew, or ought to have known, that there was a risk that the contravention would occur, and that such a contravention would be of a kind likely to cause substantial damage or substantial distress but failed to take reasonable steps to prevent the contravention.

Financial services firms regulated by the FCA may find that a breach of the Act may also give rise to enforcement action by the FCA in respect of a breach of the FCA Principles for Business. The FCA enforcement powers are extensive and can include unlimited fines.

As can be seen from the foregoing, it is imperative that all firms in our industry pay special attention to the data protection and privacy laws of their own particular global jurisdiction, in order to ensure that the details and the privacy of the individual are secured in a fashion that adheres to their regulatory requirements. Doing this brings with it the necessity to create an appropriate internal infrastructure and all that that entails.

End of Chapter Questions

1. What is data?
   Answer reference: *Section 1*

2. Where does data come from in the industry?
   Answer reference: *Section 2*

3. What organisation oversees data privacy in the UK?
   Answer reference: *Section 4*

4. What is data scrubbing?
   Answer reference: *Section 5*

Glossary

17f-5 Regulation

Legal requirements for worldwide correspondent banks which serve US mutual funds, pension funds and other regulated financial groups.

Agent Bank

A commercial bank that provides services as per a client's instructions.

Agent

One who executes orders for, or otherwise acts on behalf of, another (the principal) and is subject to its control and authority. The agent takes no financial risk and may receive a fee or commission.

Agreement Among (By) Underwriters

A legal document forming underwriting banks into a syndicate for a new issue and giving the lead manager the authority to act on behalf of the group. In the 'among' form, a direct legal relationship links each underwriter to every other underwriter. In the 'by' form, the legal relationship is established between the managers and the individual underwriter. However, the agreement also serves to define relationships between underwriters.

Allotment

The amount of new issues (ie, the number of bonds/shares) given to a syndicate member by the lead manager. Also the amount of an issue allotted to a subscribing investor.

Alternative Investment Market (AIM)

Second tier of market, run by the London Stock Exchange, where smaller, growing companies are listed without meeting the criteria needed for a listing on the main market.

American Depositary Receipt (ADR)

A depositary receipt issued by a US bank to promote trading in a foreign stock or share in the US. The bank holds the underlying securities and an ADR is issued against them. The receipt entitles the holder to all dividends and capital gains in US dollars. ADRs allow investors to purchase foreign stock without having to involve themselves in foreign settlements and currency conversion.

American Stock Exchange (AMEX)

Also an abbreviation for the American Express financial services company.

Announcement

In a new bond issue, the day on which a release is sent to prospective syndicate members describing the offering and inviting underwriters and selling group members to join the syndicate.

Annual Charge

A fee, normally between 0.5–2.5% pa, charged by an investment fund to cover the cost of investment management and administration.

Asset Allocation

The use of a range of investments by a fund manager to immediately gain or reduce exposure to different markets.

Asset-Backed Security (ABS)

A range of specific investments including debt obligations that pay principal and interest, principal only or interest only, deferred interest and negative interest using a combination of factors and rate multipliers. The issues are serviced by multiple vendors that supply the necessary data to make the corresponding payments.

Asset Swap

An interest rate swap or currency swap used to change the interest rate exposure and/or the currency exposure of an investment. Also used to describe the package of the swap plus the investment itself.

Assets

Everything of value that is owned or is due: they can be fixed assets (cash, buildings and machinery) or intangible assets (patents and goodwill).

Assignment

The process by which the holder of a short option position is matched against the holder of a similar long option position who has exercised his right.

Authorised Corporate Director (ACD)

Organisation which undertakes the role of managing the funds in an OEIC.

Authorised Unit Trust (AUT)

Unit trust which meets the requirements of the FCA to allow it to be freely marketable.

Ballot

A random selection of applicants for a new issue of shares.

Bank – Commercial

Organisation that takes deposits and makes loans.

Bank – Merchant

Organisation that specialises in advising on takeovers and corporate finance activities. These are more commonly known as investment banks.

Bank of England (BoE)

The UK's central bank, which undertakes policy decided by the Treasury and determines interest rates.

Bank for International Settlements (BIS)

Set up in the 1920s to administer debt repayments among European countries, it now has an important role as the focal point in organising discussion on international finance.

Base Currency

Currency chosen for reporting purposes.

Bombay Stock Exchange Online Trading (BOLT)

The trading system of the Bombay Stock Exchange.

Bond

A certificate of debt, generally long-term, under the terms of which an issuer contracts, inter alia, to pay the holder a fixed principal amount on a stated future date and, usually, a series of interest payments during its life.

Bonus Issue

A free issue of shares to a company's existing shareholders. No money changes hands and the share price falls pro rata. It is a cosmetic exercise to make the shares more marketable. Also known as a capitalisation or scrip issue.

Book Entry Transfer

System of recording ownership of securities by computer where the owners do not receive a certificate. Records are kept (and altered) centrally in the book.

Broker

An agent, often a member of a stock exchange firm or an exchange member itself, which acts as intermediary between buyer and seller. A commission is charged for this service.

Broker/Dealer

A firm that operates in dual capacity in the securities marketplace: as principal trading for its own account and as broker representing clients on the market.

Broking

The activity of representing a client as agent and charging commission for doing so.

Callable Bond

A bond that the issuer has the right to redeem prior to maturity by paying some specified call price.

Capital Adequacy

Requirement for firms conducting investment business to have sufficient funds.

Capital Gain (or Loss)

Profit (or loss) from the sale of a capital asset. Capital gains may be short-term (one year or less) or long-term (more than one year). Capital losses are used to offset capital gains to establish a net position for tax purposes.

Capital Adequacy Rules

Regulations specifying minimum capital requirements for investment businesses and banks.

Capital Gains Tax (CGT)

Tax payable by individuals on profit made on the disposal of assets.

Capitalisation

See *Bonus Issue*.

Capital Markets

A term used to describe the means by which large amounts of money (capital) are raised by companies, governments and other organisations for long-term use and the subsequent trading of the instruments issued in recognition of such capital.

Cash Market

Traditionally, this term has been used to denote the market in which commodities were traded for immediate delivery against cash. Since the inception of futures markets for treasury bills and other debt securities, a distinction has been made between the cash markets in which these securities trade for immediate delivery and the futures markets in which they trade for future delivery.

Cash Settlement

In the money market, a transaction is said to be made for cash settlement if the securities purchased are delivered against payment on the same day the trade is made.

CBOE

Chicago Board Options Exchange.

CBOT

Chicago Board of Trade.

CDSL

Central Depository Services (India) ltd.

Central Bank

Influential institution at the core of a country's monetary and financial system, such as the Bank of England, the Federal Reserve in the US or the European Central Bank. Its main aim is to ensure price stability in the economy, through control of inflation, and safeguarding the financial industry.

Central Clearing CounterParty (CCP)

An organisation/institution that interposes itself between the counterparties to trades, to ensure that both counterparties have matching obligations and acting as the buyer to every seller and the seller to every buyer, thus taking on the financial risk attached to the trade.

Central Depository System

Central securities depository for the Malaysian market.

Central Securities Depository (CSD)

An organisation that holds securities in either immobilised or dematerialised form, thereby enabling transactions to be processed by book entry transfer. Also provides securities administration services.

Certificate

Paper form of shares (or bonds) representing ownership of a company (or its debt).

Certificate of Deposit (CD)

A money market instrument in bearer form issued by a bank certifying a deposit made at the bank.

Chapter 11

Area of the US Bankruptcy Reform Act 1978 that protects companies from creditors.

Clearing

The centralised process of determining accountability for the exchange of money and securities between counterparties to a trade. Clearance creates statements of obligation for securities and/or funds due.

Clearing Agent

An institution that settles transactions for a large number of counterparties.

Clearing Broker

A broker who handles the settlement of securities-related transactions for himself or another broker. Sometimes small brokerage firms may not clear for themselves and, therefore, employ the services of an outside clearing broker.

Clearing Corporation (The)

Previously known as the Board of Trade Clearing Corporation, it is now owned by 17 shareholders and is an independent clearing house.

Clearing Fee

Fee charged by a clearing house or clearing broker, usually per trade or contract/lot.

Clearing House

Company that acts as central clearing counterparty (CCP) for the settlement of stock exchange transactions.

Clearing House Automated Payment System (CHAPS)

Clearing system for sterling and euro payments between banks in the UK.

Clearing House Funds

Also known as 'next-day funds', where the proceeds of a trade are available on the day following the actual settlement date.

Clearing Organisation

Acts as the guarantor of the performance and settlement of contracts that are traded on an exchange.

Clearing Process System (CPS)

Clearing system used by LIFFE (now ICE NYSE Group).

Clearing System

System established to clear transactions.

Clearnet

The clearing house for Euronext (LCH.Clearnet from 2004).

Clearstream

ICSD/CSD and clearing house based in Luxembourg and Frankfurt and owned by Deutsche Börse.

Client – Professional

A client who is assumed to understand the workings of the investment world and therefore receives little protection from the FCA's Conduct of Business Rules.

Client – Retail

A client who is assumed to be financially unsophisticated and therefore receives maximum protection from the FCA's Conduct of Business Rules.

Closed-Ended

Organisations such as companies that are a certain size as determined by their share capital.

Closed-End Fund

A fund with a fixed number of shares or units where the total number of participants in the fund remains static.

Collateral

An acceptable asset used to cover a specific requirement, eg, margin requirement.

Collateralised Mortgage Obligations

Bonds backed by a pool of mortgages owned by the issuer. They usually reimburse capital at each coupon payment as per reimbursement of the underlying mortgages.

Commission

Charge levied by a firm for agency broking.

Committee on Uniform Securities Identification Procedures (CUSIP)

The body which established a consistent securities numbering system in the US.

Commodity Futures Modernisation Act (CFMA)

Introduced in the US in 2000 to change the regulatory environment in the derivatives markets to permit the trading of single stock futures.

Commodities and Futures Commission (CFTC)

The regulator of US futures and options markets.

Common Clearing Link

The linking of the clearing of the CME and CBOT transactions under one clearing house (that of the CME).

Common Stock (US and Canada)

Securities that represent ownership in a corporation. The two most important common stockholder rights are the voting right and dividend right. Common stockholders' claims on corporate assets are subordinate to those of bondholders, preferred stockholders and general creditors. In the UK, the equivalent term is ordinary shares.

Confirm(ation)

An agreement for each individual over-the-counter transaction that has specific terms.

Consideration

The value of a transaction calculated as the price per share multiplied by the quantity being transferred. The amount paid for an asset or security net of commission and taxes.

Continuous Net Settlement

Extends multilateral netting to handle failed trades brought forward.

Contract

The standard unit of trading for futures and options. It is also commonly referred to as a 'lot'.

Contract for Difference (CFD)

Contract designed to make a profit or avoid a loss by reference to movements in the price of an item. The underlying item cannot change hands and any difference is, in effect, cash settlement.

Contract Note

Legal documentation sent by a securities house to clients providing details of a transaction completed on their behalf.

Contract Specification

A derivatives exchange designs its own products and publishes a contract specification setting out the details of the derivatives contract. This will include the size or unit of trading and the underlying, maturity months, quotation and minimum price movement and value, together with trading times, methods and delivery conditions.

Contractual Settlement Date

Date on which seller and buyer are contractually obligated to settle a securities transaction.

Corporate Action

One of many possible capital restructuring changes or similar actions taken by the company which may have an impact on the market price of its securities, and which may require the shareholders to make certain decisions.

Counterparty

Usually one party to a trade refers to its trading partners as counterparties. A trade can take place between two or more counterparties.

Coupon

Generally, the nominal annual rate of interest expressed as a percentage of the principal value. The interest is paid to the holder of a fixed income security by the borrower. The coupon is generally paid annually, semi-annually or, in some cases, quarterly, depending on the type of security.

Credit Default Swap

A swap where one side is a default event that results in the payment of the related loss and the other is the payment of a premium to secure the protection. If no event occurs, the seller of the protection keeps the premium. A type of credit derivative.

Credit Derivatives

Credit derivatives have some kind of credit default as the underlying asset. As with all derivatives, credit derivatives are designed to enable the risk related to a credit issue, such as non-payment of an interest coupon on a corporate or sovereign bond, or the non-repayment of a loan, to be transferred.

CREST Member

A participant within CREST who holds stock in stock accounts in CREST and whose name appears on the share register. A member is their own user.

CREST Sponsored Member

A participant within CREST who holds stock in stock accounts in CREST and whose name appears on the share register. Unlike a member, a sponsored member is not their own user. The link to CREST is provided by another user who sponsors the sponsored member.

CREST User

A participant within CREST who has an electronic link to CREST.

Cross-Border Trading

Trading which takes place between persons or entities from different countries.

Cum-Dividend

A term that relates to a security that is traded with (cum) the current dividend right included.

Cum Rights

A term applied to a stock trading in the marketplace with subscription rights attached which is reflected in the price of that security.

Cumulative Dividend

Dividend that is due but not yet paid on cumulative preferred shares. These must be paid before any ordinary dividends are paid.

Cumulative Preference Share

A class of preferred shares in which, if the company fails to pay a preference dividend, the entitlement to the dividend accumulates. The arrears of the preference dividend must be paid before any ordinary dividend.

Currency Exposure

Currency exposure exists if assets are held, or income earned, in one currency, while liabilities are denominated in another currency. The position is exposed to changes in the relative values of the two currencies such that the cost of the liabilities may be increased or the value of the assets or earning decreased.

CUSIP Number

Unique nine-digit number that identifies securities, US or non-US, that trade and settle in the US.

Custodian

Institution holding securities in safekeeping for a client. A custodian also offers different services to its clients (settlement, portfolio services).

DK

'Don't know', a status which applies to a securities transaction pending settlement where fundamental data is missing which prevents the receiving party from accepting delivery.

Daily Cash Sweep

The action of investing a client's cash balance that would otherwise lie idle overnight, in an interest-bearing deposit or investment vehicle. Generally performed on an overnight basis.

Dematerialised

A security that is issued and recorded solely in an electronic format.

Depository Trust Company (DTC)

The CSD for shares in the US.

Depository Trust & Clearing Corporation (DTCC)

Clearing house and depository in the US.

Derivative Instrument

Financial instrument is based on varying types of underlying securities or assets. The put examples are futures, options and swaps. Derivative securities do not create wealth; rather they provide for the transfer of risk from hedgers to speculators.

Distributions

Income paid out from a unit trust.

Dividend

Distribution of profits made by a company to its shareholders if it chooses to do so.

Dividend Cover

Dividends are paid out of a company's profits and dividend cover is the excess profits after the dividend has been calculated.

Dividend Per Share

The amount of dividend shareholders have or will receive in a year. Total dividend amount paid divided by the number of shares in issue.

Dividend Yield

The dividend expressed as a percentage of the share price.

Diversification

Investment strategy of spreading risk by investing the total available in a range of investments.

Domestic Bond

Bond issued in the country of the issuer, in its own currency and according to the regulations of that country.

Domicile

Where an individual or a business is legally deemed to be registered, based or living.

Double Taxation Treaty

An agreement between two countries intended to avoid or limit the effect of the double taxation of income. Under the terms of the treaty, an investor with tax liabilities in both countries can either apply for a reduction of taxed imposed by one country or can credit taxes paid in that country against tax liabilities in the other.

Due Diligence

The carrying out of duties with care and perseverance. Due diligence is generally referred to in connection with the investigations of a company, carried out by accountants' to ascertain the value of that company. The concept also applies from a regulatory point of view that firms and key personnel should carry out their duties with due diligence to the regulatory environment.

ECB

European Central Bank.

ECSDA

European Central Securities Depository Association.

EMEA

Europe, the MIddle East and Asia.

EUREX

German-Swiss derivatives exchange created by the merger of the German (DTB) and Swiss (SOFFEX) exchanges. Owned by Deutsche Börse.

Euronext

A pan-European securities and derivatives exchange listing Dutch, French, Portuguese and Belgian securities and derivatives, plus the derivative products traded on LIFFE. Owned by the New York Stock Exchange.

Effective Date

The date on which the interest period to which a forward rate agreement or swap relates is to start.

Eligible Counterparty

A category of client as used by the FCA.

Employee Retirement Income Security Act (ERISA)

Established to protect participants and beneficiaries in employee benefit/retirement plans in the US.

Equity

A common term to describe stocks or shares.

Escrow

A bank account specifically designed to hold money (or other assets) during a dispute between two or more parties to prevent access to those funds until the dispute is finalised.

Euro

The single European currency.

Euro Interbank Offered Rate (EURIBOR)

A measure of the average cost of funds over the whole euro area based on a panel of 57 major banks.

Eurobond

An interest-bearing security issued across national borders, usually in a currency other than that of the issuer's home country. Because there is no regulatory protection, only governments and top-rated multinational corporations can issue eurobonds that the market will accept.

Euro Commercial Paper

Unsecured corporate debt with a short maturity structured to appeal to large financial institutions active in the euro market.

Euroclear

An ICSD. A book-entry clearing facility for most euro and foreign securities. It owns the CSDs of Belgium, France, the Netherlands and the UK.

Euroclear UK & Ireland ltd

The CSD organisation in the UK that holds UK and Irish company shares in dematerialised form and clears and settles trades in UK and Irish company shares. Owned by Euroclear since 2002, it adopted its new name in July 2007, changing its name from CRESTCo. It still operates the CREST system.

European Bank for Reconstruction & Development (EBRD)

An institution established to provide financial assistance to eastern Europe.

European Investment Bank (EIB)

Set up by the European union and funded by member states to provide aid in areas of unemployment and poverty, both within and outside the EU; also assists with industrial projects.

European Monetary System (EMS)

Agreement between most members of the Common Market on how to organise their currencies prior to the introduction of the euro in 1999.

Exception-Based Processing

A benefit of straight-through processing. Transaction processing where straightforward items are processed automatically, allowing staff to concentrate on the items which are incorrect or not straightforward.

Execute and Eliminate Order

Type of order input into SETS. The amount that can be traded immediately against displayed orders is completed, with the remainder being rejected.

Exit Charges

Instead of making an initial charge, some investment funds make a charge if cashed in within, say, five years.

Expenses

The broker's costs incurred in buying and selling shares. Also costs associated with sales, marketing, client services, legal expertise, etc.

Ex-Warrants

Trading a security so that the buyer will not be entitled to warrants that will be distributed to holders.

Face Value

The value of a bond, note, mortgage or other security that appears on the face of the issue, unless the value is otherwise specified by the issuing company. Face value is ordinarily the amount the issuing company promises to pay at maturity. Face value is also referred to as 'par value' or 'nominal value'.

Failed Transaction

A securities transaction that does not settle on time, ie, the securities and/or cash are not exchanged as agreed on the settlement date.

Fair Value

For futures, this is the true price not the market price, allowing for the cost of carry. For options, it is the true price, not the market price, as calculated using an option pricing model.

Federal Reserve Book-Entry System

CSD for US government securities.

Final Settlement

The completion of a transaction when the delivery of all components of a trade is performed.

Financial Services and Markets Act 2000 (FSMA 2000)

The legislation that created the single UK regulator, the Financial Services Authority.

Financial Conduct Authority (FCA)

The independent watchdog set up by the UK government under the Financial Services and Markets Act 2012 to regulate financial conduct in the UK, and protect the rights of retail customers.

Fiscal Year

It runs from 6 April to 5 April in the UK and is the period of assessment for both income tax and capital gains tax.

Fit and Proper

Under the Financial Services Act 1986, everyone conducting investment business must be a 'fit and proper person'. The Act does not define the term; that function is left to the regulators.

Fixed Income (Fixed Interest)

A term used to describe securities where the interest is calculated as a constant specified percentage of the principal amount and paid at the end of specified interest periods, usually annually or semi-annually, until maturity.

Fixed Interest Securities

Another term for bonds.

Floating-Rate

A borrowing or investment where the interest, or coupon, pays changes at specified intervals throughout the arrangement in line with some reference rate such as LIBOR.

Free of Payment

Refers to the buying and selling of securities where there is no associated countervalue or it is not dependent on the simultaneous payment of the cash countervalue during the movement of assets.

FT Index

The Financial Times Ordinary Share Index consists of 30 large companies across a broad field and gives an indication of share price trends. The larger index, the FTSE 100 (Footsie), provides a wider indication of approximately 100 leading companies on the stock market. All stock markets have an index, eg, the Dow Jones in the US, DAX in Germany and the Nikkei in Japan.

FTSE 100 Index

Main UK share index based on the 100 leading shares according to their market capitalisation.

FTSE 250

UK share index based on the 250 shares immediately below the top 100, according to their market capitalisation. It represents the mid-capitalised companies, approximately 15% of UK market capitalisation.

Fund Manager

Individuals or specialist companies responsible for investing the assets of a fund in such a way as to maximise its value. They do this by following a strategy to buy and sell equities and other financial instruments.

Funds

General term for cash or near cash. It also refers to investment portfolios such as unit trusts and open-ended investment companies (OEICs).

Futures Contracts

A type of exchange-traded derivative. An agreement to buy or sell a specific asset at a certain time in the future for a certain price.

General Principles

Eleven fundamental principles of behaviour written by the FCA which apply to all investment businesses.

Gilt

Domestic sterling-denominated long-term bond, backed by the full faith and credit of the UK and issued by the Treasury. Short for gilt-edged security.

Gilt-Edged Market Maker (GEMM)

A firm that is a market maker in gilts. Also known as a 'primary dealer'.

Global Clearing

The channelling of the settlement of all futures and options trades through a single counterparty or through a number of counterparties geographically located.

Global Custodian

Institution that safekeeps, settles and performs the processing of income collection, tax reclaim, multicurrency reporting, cash management, foreign exchange, corporate action and proxy monitoring, for clients' securities in all required marketplaces.

Global Depositary Receipt (GDR)

A security representing shares held in custody in the country of issue.

Global System of Tax

A tax system whereby the residents of a country are taxed on their worldwide income.

Government Securities Clearing Corporation (GSCC)

Clearing organisation for US Treasury securities.

Grey Market

Generally, the market for a new issue before the securities have been distributed to subscribers.

Group of 30 (G30)

Private international organisation aiming to deepen understanding of international economic and financial issues. Established in 1978, it is a private, non-profit international body composed of very senior representatives of the private and public sectors and academia.

Hedge Fund

A fund that invests in a wide variety of instruments and strategies, often designed to generate exceptionally high returns but with higher risk of loss. Marketing and sales limited to high net worth individuals and other funds.

Hedging

A trading method using derivatives which is designed to reduce or mitigate market risk. It may include taking a position in, for example, a futures instrument to offset the price movement of a cash asset. A broader definition of hedging includes using futures as a temporary substitute for the cash position. Many other forms of derivative may be used for hedging purposes, including swaps and options.

Her Majesty's Revenue & Customs (HMRC)

The government department responsible for the administration and collection of tax in the UK. Formerly known as the Inland Revenue.

Holder

A person who has bought an open contract, for example a bond or a derivative.

Holder of Record

The party whose name appears on a company's stockholder register at the close of business on record date. That party will receive a dividend or other distribution from the company in the near future.

Home State Regulation

Under MiFID, an investment business is authorised in the place of its head office and registered office. This home state authorisation entitles it to conduct business in any EU member state via a 'passport'.

Immobilisation

The storage of securities certificates in a vault in order to eliminate physical movement of the documents in transfer of ownership.

Income Tax

An annual tax on the income of an individual.

Initial Charge

A charge – typically 5% – that is paid to cover a manager's expenses, such as commission, advertising, administration and dealing costs.

Initial Margin or Deposit

The deposit that the clearing house calls as protection against a default of a contract. It is returnable to the clearing member once the position is closed. The level is subject to changes in line with market conditions.

Interim Dividend

Dividend paid part-way through a year in advance of the final dividend.

International Capital Markets Association (ICMA)

The International Capital Markets Association, formed by the mergers of ICMA and ISMA.

International Central Securities Depository (ICSD)

Clears and settles international securities and cross-border transactions through local CSDs. There are two ICSDs – Euroclear bank and Clearstream.

International Financial Centre

A territory with very low tax rates which also offers international banking, investment and other financial services.

International Securities Identification (ISIN)

A coding system developed by the ISO for identifying securities. ISINs are designated to create one unique worldwide number for any security. It is a 12-digit alpha/numeric code.

International Standards Organisation (ISO)

An international federation of organisations of various industries which seeks to set common international standards in a variety of fields.

Investment Funds

Open-ended investment companies and their equivalents in other countries.

Investment Trust Company

Company whose sole business consists of buying, selling and holding shares in other companies. The difference from unit trusts is that investors in unit trusts do not receive a part of the profits of the company managing the trust.

Investment Business

Dealing, advising or managing investments. They must be authorised.

Investments

Items defined in the FSMA 2000 to be regulated by it. Includes shares, bonds, options, futures, life assurance and pensions.

Investment Grade

A grading level that is used by certain types of funds for determining assets that are suitable for investment by the fund. This refers to the quality of an entity's credit or demonstrated by its issued securities. To qualify, the rating must be BBB or higher according to the principal ratings agencies such as Standard & Poor's.

Invoice Amount

The amount calculated under the formula specified by a futures exchange, which will be paid in settlement of the final physical delivery of the underlying asset.

IOSCO

International Organisation of Securities Commissions.

ISDA

International Swaps and derivatives Association, previously known as the International Swap dealers Association. Many market participants use ISDA documentation.

ISSA

The International Securities Services Association.

Japan Association of Securities Dealer Automated Quotation (JASDAQ)

Jasdaq Securities Exchange Inc is a Japanese securities exchange operating an over-the-counter securities registration and trading system with an automated quotation system. It specialises in venture and growing companies.

Know Your Customer (KYC)

The Conduct of Business Rules requiring investment advisers to take steps, before giving investment advice, to determine, inter alia, the financial position and investment objectives of the client.

LCH/LCH.Clearnet

The entity created in 2003 by the merger between the London Clearing House and Clearnet.

Liquidity

A liquid asset is one that can be converted easily and rapidly into cash without a substantial loss of value. In the money market, a security is said to be liquid if the spread between bid and ask price is narrow and a reasonable size can be traded at those quotes.

Listed Company

Company which has been admitted to listing on a stock exchange and whose shares can then be dealt on that exchange.

Listed Securities

Securities listed on a stock exchange are tradeable on this exchange.

Listing

Status applied for by companies whose securities are then listed on a stock exchange and available to be traded. In the UK the listing rules are controlled by the FCA.

Listing Particulars

Detailed information that must be published by a company applying to be listed.

London Inter-Bank Offered Rate (LIBOR)

A benchmark rate which is set daily by the British Bankers Association for major currencies at which banks lend to each other.

London International Financial Futures & Options Exchange (LIFFE)

A derivatives exchange for trading in a wide variety of bonds, commodities, currencies, short-term interest rates, stock indices, stock futures and stock options. Part of NYSE Euronext.

London Stock Exchange (LSE)

Market for trading in securities.

Long

A bought position in a derivative or security that is held as an open position.

Long Position

Refers to an investor's account in which they have more shares of a specific security than they need to meet their settlement obligations.

Managed Fund

A unit-linked policy where the managers decide on the allocation of premiums to different unitised funds.

Manager's Report

Available every six months, this details the exact position of the fund, eg, its investments, the manager's investment commentary, the performance of the portfolio, etc.

Mandatory Event

A corporate action which affects securities without normally giving any choice to the security holder, though sometimes options are given.

Market

Description of any organisation or facility through which items are traded. All exchanges are markets.

Markets in Financial Instruments Directive (MiFID)

An EU directive which came into effect in November 2007.

Multilateral Netting

Trades between several counterparties in the same security are netted such that each counterparty makes only one transfer of cash or securities to a central clearing system. Handles only transactions due for settlement on the same day.

Multilateral Trading Facility (MTF)

An electronic trading platform.

Mutual Fund (US)

Fund operated by an investment company that raises pooled money from shareholders and invests it in stocks, bonds or other instruments. The equivalent UK term is 'collective investment scheme'.

National Association of Securities Dealers Automated Quotation System (NASDAQ)

A US stock exchange.

National Association of Pension Funds (NAPF) (UK)

Trade association of pension funds through which they can voice their opinions collectively.

National Insurance (NI)

Tax levied on income. The level depends on the amount earned, subject to a ceiling and payable in the UK by employer and employee.

National Securities Clearing Corporation (NSCC)

Clearing organisation and central counterparty for US shares.

National Securities Clearing Corporation ltd (NSCCL)

Clearing house in India.

National Securities Depository ltd (NSDC)

Depository for the National Stock Exchange in India.

Net Asset Value (NAV)

In mutual funds, the market value of the fund share. It is common practice for an investment trust to compute its assets daily, or even twice a day, by totalling the closing market value of all securities and assets (ie, cash) owned. All liabilities are deducted, and the balance is divided by the number of shares outstanding. The resulting figure is the NAV per share.

Netting

Trading partners offset their positions, thereby reducing the number of positions for settlement. Netting can be either bilateral, multilateral or continuous net settlement. For example, on trade date, broker X sold 100, 300 and 500 ABC securities and purchased 50 and 200 units of the same issue. The clearing system will net the transactions and debit X with 650 units (−900 + 250 = 650) against the total cash amount. This enables the reduction of the number of movements and thus the costs.

New Issues

Companies raise additional capital by issuing new securities. New issue is the name given to the bonds or stocks offered to investors for the first time.

Nil Paid Rights Price

Ex-rights price, less the subscription price.

Nominal Amount

Value stated on the face of a security (principal value, par value). In securities processing, the number of securities to deliver/receive.

Nominal Value of a Bond

The value at which the capital, or principal, of a bond will be redeemed by the issuer. Also called 'par value'.

Nominal Value of a Share

The minimum price at which a share can be issued. Also called 'par value'.

Nominee

An organisation that acts as the legally named owner of securities on behalf of a different beneficial owner who remains anonymous to the company.

Normal Market Size (NMS)

Minimum size in which market makers must quote on the LSE.

Nostro

A bank's nostro account is its currency account held with a foreign bank.

Nostro Reconciliation

Checking the entries shown on the bank's nostro account statement with the bank's internal records (the accounting ledgers) to ensure that they correspond exactly.

OASYS

Trade confirmation system for US brokers operated by Thomson Reuters.

Offer for Sale

Historically, the most popular form of new issue in the UK for companies bringing their securities to the stockmarket for the first time. The company offers its shares to the general public.

Offshore

Relates to locations outside the control of domestic monetary, exchange and legislative authorities. Offshore may not necessarily be outside the national boundaries of a country. In some countries, certain banks or other institutions may be granted offshore status and, thus, be exempt from all or specific controls or legislation.

Offshore Financial Centre

Another name for an international financial centre.

Omgeo

Omgeo is a financial services global joint venture wholly owned by the Depository Trust & Clearing Corporation (DTCC).

Omnibus Account

Account containing the holdings of more than one client.

Open-Ended

Type of investment such as unit trusts or OEICs which can expand without limit.

Open-Ended Investment Company (OEIC)

A form of collective investment vehicle. The FCA refers to these as Investment Companies with Variable Capital. A style of investment fund similar to unit trusts and common in the UK and other European countries. An OEIC issues shares rather than units.

Open Position

The number of contracts or shares which have not been offset. The resultant position will be held in the clearing organisation or custodian records at the close of business.

Operational Risk

The risk of loss resulting from inadequate or failed internal process, people or systems or from external events.

Option

A type of derivative. An option is, in the case of the buyer, the right, but not the obligation, to take (call) or make (put) delivery of the underlying product and, in the case of the seller, the obligation to make or take delivery of the underlying product.

Order-Driven Market

A stock market where brokers, acting on behalf of clients, match trades with each other either on the trading floor of the exchange or through a central computer system.

Ordinary Shares

Known as 'common stock' in the US and equities in the UK. Shareholders are the owners of a company and are protected so the maximum loss is the value of their shares and not the full debt of the company.

Oversubscribed

Circumstances where people have applied for more shares than are available in a new issue.

Out-of-Pocket Expenses

Market charges which are charged to the client without taking any profit.

Out-Trade

A trade which has been incorrectly matched or has failed to be matched on the floor of an exchange.

Over-The-Counter (OTC)

Normally with reference to derivatives. A one-to-one agreement between two counterparties where the specifications of the product are completely flexible and non-standardised. Hence an OTC termination or the OTC market.

Overdraft

Withdrawal of more money than is in a bank account at a given time.

Overnight Money

Money placed on the money market for repayment for the next day.

Oversold

Where a rush of selling shares has depressed the market for no justifiable reason. Can also be a term used to describe a dealing error, ie, sold 100 instead of 10.

Panel on Takeovers and Mergers (PTM) (UK)

A non-statutory body which regulates takeover activities.

Pari Passu

Without partiality. Securities that rank pari passu, rank equally with each other.

Payer

The payer in a swap is the counterparty that pays the fixed rate and receives the floating rate.

Paying Agent

A bank which handles payment of interest and dividends on behalf of the issuer of a security.

Payment Date

Date on which a dividend or an interest payment is scheduled to be paid.

Pension Fund

Fund set up by a corporation, labour union, governmental entity or other organisation to pay the pension benefits of retired workers. Pension funds invest billions of dollars annually in the securities markets and are, therefore, major market players.

Placement

Procedure used for new issues where a securities house contacts its own clients to offer them stock. It is almost always used for new issues of eurobonds and for equities on the London Stock Exchange – more so since January 1996 when restrictions on their use were removed.

Portfolio

List of investments held by an individual or company, or list of loans made by a bank or financial institution.

Power of Attorney

The legal authority for one party to sign for, and act on behalf of, another party.

Pre-Emption Rights

The right of existing shareholders (ahead of non-shareholders or rights) to purchase shares in a new or rights issue to maintain their percentage holding.

Preference Shares

Shares that have preferential rights to dividends, usually a fixed sum, before dividends are paid out to ordinary shareholders. They usually carry no voting rights. The rights of preference shareholders are established in a company's Articles of Association and may differ between companies in a variety of ways. In the event that a company is wound up, the preference shareholder receives dividends ahead of the ordinary shareholder.

Premium

An option premium is the amount paid up-front by the purchaser of the option to the writer.

Present Value

The amount of money which needs to be invested (or borrowed) now at a given interest rate in order to achieve exactly a given cash flow in the future, assuming compound re-investment (or re-funding) of any interest payments received (or paid) before the end date.

Pre-Settlement

Checks and procedures undertaken immediately after execution of a trade prior to settlement.

Principal Trading

When a stockbroker buys stock from, or sells stock to, a counterparty as part of its own dealing book, as opposed to an agency trade where a client passes an order via a broker to an exchange for commission.

Private Placement

Issue of securities that is offered to a limited number of investors.

Professional Client

A client who is assumed to understand the workings of the investment world and therefore receives little protection from the FCA's Conduct of Business Rules.

Proprietary Trader

A trader who deals for an organisation (such as an investment bank) rather than for clients, to generate profit, taking advantage of short-term price movements as well as taking long-term views on whether the market will move up or down.

Proxy

Appointee of a shareholder who votes on his behalf at company meetings.

Proxy Statement

Material information to be given to a corporation's stockholders prior to solicitation of votes.

Public Offering

Offer of securities to the general public.

Public Placement

An issue of securities that is offered through a securities house to institutional and individual clients.

Real-Time Gross Settlement (RTGS)

Gross settlement system where trades are settled continuously through the processing day.

Recognised Clearing House (RCH)

Examples are LCH.Clearnet and Euroclear UK & Ireland Limited.

Recognised Investment Exchange (RIE)

Status given by the FCA to an approved exchange based in the UK.

Record Date (Books Closed Date)

Last date for the registration of shares or bonds for the payment of the next dividend/coupon.

Registered Bond

A bond whose owner is registered with the issuer or its registrar.

Registered Title

Form of ownership of securities where the owner's name appears on a register maintained by the company.

Registrar

An institution which maintains records of the issue and holders of securities and maintains an issuing company's share register.

Registrar of Companies

Government department responsible for keeping records of all companies.

Repurchase Agreement (Repo)

A contract to sell and subsequently repurchase a security on a specified date at an agreed price in the future. They are used to raise finance for other purposes.

Reputational Risk

The risk that an organisation's reputation will be damaged.

Retail Client

A client who is assumed to be financially, unsophisticated and therefore receives maximum protection from the FCA's Conduct of Business Rules.

Rights Issue

Offer of shares made to existing shareholders.

Right of Offset

Where positions and cash held by the clearing organisation in different accounts for a member are allowed to be netted or between separate counterparties in OTC transactions.

Risk

The hazard or chance of adverse consequences or loss occurring.

Risk Warning

Information included within a customer agreement that must be despatched and signed by retail customers before they invest or deal, particularly in traded derivatives.

Rolling Settlement

System used in most countries including the UK. Bargains are settled a set number of days after being transacted, eg, T+1 and T+3.

Safekeeping

Holding of securities on behalf of clients. They are free to sell at any time.

Sale of Rights Nil Paid

The sale of the entitlement to take up a rights issue.

Same Day Funds

Refers to the availability of funds on the same day as they are deposited or paid.

Scrip Dividends

Scrip dividend options provide shareholders with the choice of receiving dividend entitlements in the form of cash, shares or a combination of both. The amount of stock to be distributed under a scrip option is calculated by dividing the cash dividend amount by the average market price over a recent period of time.

Secondary Market

Marketplace for trading in existing securities. The price at which they are trading has no direct effect on the company's fortunes but is a reflection of investors' perceptions of the company.

Sectors

Investment funds are divided into a variety of categories to keep together funds of a similar type, for example cash, North American, European.

Secured

A debt issued by a company that is charged against an asset or a private transaction like a mortgage, where the property is charged against the loan to purchase it.

Securitisation

The use of securities and other assets to guarantee the repayment of a debt. An example is using the rent from a property to guarantee a bond that is issued to raise capital to purchase more property.

Securities

Can mean any instrument in the market, but generally refers to bonds and equities.

Securities and Exchange Board of India (SEBI)

The Indian securities regulator.

Securities House

General term covering any type of organisation involved in securities, although usually reserved for larger firms.

Securities Lending

Loan of securities by an investor to another (usually a broker-dealer), usually to cover a short sale.

Securities and Exchange Commission (SEC)

The investment regulatory body in the US for the securities markets.

Segregated Account

Account in which there are only the holdings of one client.

Segregation of Funds

Where client assets are held separately from those assets belonging to the member firm.

Serious Fraud Office

Specialist unit established to tackle senior or complex fraud.

SETS

London Stock Exchange Trading System, the principal trading platform.

SETSqx

SETS 'quotes and crosses' is the trading platform of the London Stock Exchange for securities less liquid than those traded on SETS.

Settlement

The fulfilment of the contractual commitments of transacted business.

Settlement Date

The date on which a trade is cleared by delivery of securities against funds (actual settlement date, contractual settlement date).

Short

A sold position in a derivative or security that is held as an open position.

Short Sale

The sale of securities not owned by the seller in the expectation that the price of these securities will fall or as part of an arbitrage.

Short Selling

Selling stock that you do not own.

Society for Worldwide Interbank Financial Telecommunications (SWIFT)

Secure electronic communications network between banks and securities trading companies.

Sponsored Member

Type of CREST member whose name appears on the register but has no computer link with CREST.

Stamp Duty

Tax on the purchase of property and certificated shares in the UK or globally.

Stamp Duty Reserve Tax (SDRT)

Tax payable on the purchase of UK equities in dematerialised form (ie, those held within CREST).

Standard & Poor's

An index and ratings agency. US indices on which futures and options contracts are based. The CME introduced S&P 500 index futures as the first index-based derivative.

Standard Settlement Instructions

Instructions for settlement with a particular counterparty which are always followed for a particular kind of deal and, once in place, are, therefore, not re-instructed at the time of each transaction.

Standing Instruction

Default instruction, eg, provided to an agent processing payments or clearing securities trades; provided by shareholder on how to vote shares (for example, vote for all management-recommended candidates).

Stock

In some countries (eg, the US) the term applies to ordinary share capital of a company. In other countries (eg, the UK), stock may mean share capital that is issued in variable amounts instead of in fixed specified amounts, or it can describe government loans, eg, gilt-edged stocks.

Stock Dividend

Dividends paid by a company in stock instead of cash.

Stock Exchange Automated Quotation System (SEAQ) (UK)

Electronic screen display system through which market makers in equities display prices at which they are willing to deal.

Stock Exchange Daily Official List (SEDOL)

A securities numbering system assigned by the London Stock Exchange.

Stock Exchange Electronic Trading System (SETS)

Electronic dealing platform for most stocks on the London Stock Exchange.

Stock Market Index

Shows how a specified portfolio of share prices are moving in order to give an indication of market trades. Each world stock market is represented by at least one index. The FTSE 100 Index, for example, reflects the movements of the share prices of the UK's largest 100 quoted companies.

Stock Market

Term used to describe where securities are/have been traded, eg, 'today on the stock market, shares closed higher'.

Straight-Through Processing (STP)

Computer transmission of the details of a trade, without manual intervention, from their original input by the trader to all other relevant areas – position keeping, risk control, accounts, settlement, reconciliation.

Trans-European Automated Real-Time Gross Settlement Express Transfer (TARGET)

The system linking the real-time gross settlements for euros in the EU countries.

Tax Reclaim

The process that a global custodian and/or a holder of securities performs, in accordance with local government filing requirements, in order to recapture an allowable percentage of tax withheld.

Trade Date

The date on which a trade is made.

Transfer

Change of ownership of securities.

Transfer Agent

Agent appointed by a corporation to maintain records of stock and bond owners, to cancel and issue certificates and to resolve problems arising from lost, destroyed or stolen certificates. Also applies to a similar function for some funds.

Transfer Form

Document which owners of registered documents must sign when they sell the security. Not required where a book entry transfer system is in use.

TRAX

Trade confirmation system for the euro markets operated by ICMA.

Treasury

Arm of government responsible for all financial decisions and regulation of the financial services sector. Also a division within a firm dealing with funding, capital liquidity and cash flow management.

Treasury Bill

Money market instrument issued with a life of less than one year issued by the US and UK governments.

Treasury Bonds (US)

US government bond issued with a 20–30 year maturity.

Treasury Note

A government obligation with maturities of one to ten years, carrying a fixed rate of interest.

Treasury Note (US)

US government bond issued with two-, three-, five- and seven-year maturity.

Tri-party Repo

Repo which utilises an intermediary custodian to oversee the exchange of securities and cash.

Triple A Rating

The highest credit rating for a bond or company – indicates that the risk of default (or non-payment) is negligible.

Trustee

Appointed to oversee the management of certain funds. They are responsible for ensuring that the funds are managed correctly, that the interests of the investor are protected and that all relevant regulations and laws are complied with.

Underlying Asset/Underlying

Asset or product from which a future's or option's price is derived and which may be deliverable. Another term used is 'reference entity'.

Undertaking for Collective Investments in Transferable Securities (UCITS)

A European union term for a fund which can be marketed in all EU countries.

Underwrite

Accept financial responsibility for a commercial project or sign and issue an insurance policy, thus accepting liability.

Underwriter

As part of a syndicate, a dealer who purchases new issues from the issuer and distributes them to investors.

Underwriters

Institutions which agree to take up shares in a new issue if it is undersubscribed. They will charge an underwriting fee.

Unit Investment Trust (UIT)

In the US, a closed-ended fund used by small investors to spread investment risk. It is created for a specific period of time.

Unit -Linked Policy

An endowment or whole of life policy which invests in a unitised fund; the value of the policy is the value of the units purchased.

Unit Trust

A fund whereby money from a number of investors is pooled together and invested collectively on their behalf. The fund is divided into units, the value of which depends on the value of the assets owned by the trust.

Value Added Tax (VAT)

A type of sales tax.

Value at Risk (VaR)

The maximum amount which a bank expects to lose, with a given confidence level, over a given time period.

Vostro

A vostro account is another bank's account held at our bank in our currency. Literally 'your account with us'.

Warrant

A securities option which can be listed on an exchange, with a lifetime of generally more than one year.

Warrant Agent

A bank appointed by the issuer as an intermediary between the issuing company and the (physical) warrant holders, interacting when the latter want to exercise the warrants.

Withholding Tax

In the securities industry, a tax imposed by a government's tax authorities on dividends and interest paid.

Yield

Internal rate of return of a security or asset expressed as a percentage. There are various types and measures of yield.

Yield Curve

For securities that expose the investor to the same credit risk, a graph showing the relationship at a given point in the time between yield and current maturity. Yield curves are typically drawn using yields on government bonds of various maturities.

Yield to Maturity

The rate of return yielded by a debt security held to maturity when both interest payments and the investor's capital gain or loss on the security is taken into account.

Zero Coupon Bond

A bond issued with no coupon and at a price substantially below par so that only capital is accrued over the life of the loan and yield is comparable to coupon-bearing instruments. Such bonds redeem at par.

Appendices

Appendix 1

Global Clearing and Settlement – The G30 Twenty Recommendations
Creating a Strengthened Interoperable Global Network

1. Eliminate paper and automate communication, data capture and enrichment.
2. Harmonise messaging standards and communication protocols.
3. Develop and implement reference data standards.
4. Synchronise timing between different clearing and settlement systems and associated payment and foreign exchange systems.
5. Automate and standardise institutional trade matching.
6. Expand the use of central counterparties.
7. Permit securities lending and borrowing to expedite settlement.
8. Automate and standardise asset servicing processes, including corporate actions, tax relief arrangements and restrictions on foreign ownerships.

Mitigating Risk

9. Ensure the financial integrity of providers of clearing and settlement services.
10. Reinforce the risk management practices of users of clearing and settlement service providers.
11. Ensure final, simultaneous transfer and availability of assets.
12. Ensure effective business continuity and disaster-recovery planning.
13. Address the possibility of failure of a systemically important institution.
14. Strengthen assessment of enforceability of contracts.
15. Advance legal certainty over rights to securities, cash and collateral.
16. Recognise and support improved valuation and close-out netting arrangements.

Improving Governance

17. Ensure appointment of appropriately experienced and senior board members.
18. Promote fair access to securities clearing and settlement networks.
19. Ensure equitable and effective attention to stakeholders' interests.
20. Encourage consistent regulation and oversight of securities clearing and settlement service providers.

The full document can be obtained from www.group30.org.

Appendix 2

CLS Bank

CLS bank provides, amongst other things, elimination of settlement risk and multilateral netting of FX transactions for its members and third-party participants. The development timetable for CLS bank was:

- 1995: G20 formed.
- 1996: Allsopp Report published.
- 1997: CLS Services created by G20 banks. 1998: IBM appointed to develop IT system. 1999: Fed approves creation of CLS bank. 2002: CLS bank went live in September.

Today, CLS membership includes a significant and ever-growing number of central banks and provides a processing timeline covering the three time zones. Additional benefits include:

- real-time information
- consistent legal standards in multiple jurisdictions
- compliance and best practice
- operational efficiencies through STP: reduced expenses; minimal errors; fewer corrections; fewer settlement fails.

A key benefit of CLS bank is the removal of the risk of one leg of an FX trade settling and the other not, as was the case with Herstatt bank when, following the receipt of deutschmarks from an FX trade counterparty, the bank went bust before the payment system in the US and the US dollar leg could be paid. The figure below shows the timeline for processing via CLS bank.

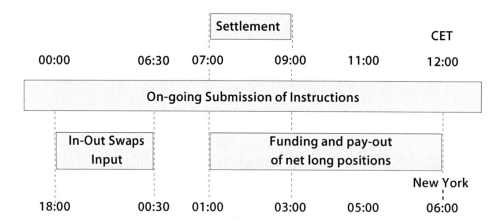

Source: CLS Bank (www.clsbank.com)

CLS bank is constantly seeking to develop new initiatives, including adding currencies catered for, multiple settlement cycles and further STP initiatives.

292

Appendix 3

DTCC/NSCC Stock Borrowing Programme

Overview

The stock borrowing programme allows participants to lend the National Securities Clearing Corporation (NSCC) available stocks and fixed income securities from their accounts at the depository Trust Company (DTC), to cover temporary shortfalls in the NSCC's continuous net settlement (CNS) System. NSCC credits members' money settlement accounts with the full market value of securities borrowed and members can earn overnight interest on that value by investing the funds. In addition, members can enhance securities inventory management in a safe, controlled environment through the programme.

Who Can use the Service

All NSCC settling members can participate in the stock borrowing programme. Stocks and fixed income securities are eligible for it.

Benefits

The stock borrowing programme enables participants to earn interest on the full current market value of their excess DTC positions borrowed by the NSCC, while lending securities in the safety of a controlled environment.

- Participants' NSCC money settlement accounts are credited on the day of the loan with the full market value of any securities borrowed by the NSCC. This allows members to invest the funds to earn interest overnight on the value received from the loans.
- Securities on loan to the NSCC are recorded as long positions in a special CNS account set up specifically for the participant's stock borrowing activity. This enables the member to benefit from lending securities within the safe, controlled CNS processing environment.

How the Service Works

By early evening on each business day, participants forward a list of securities that are available for borrowing to the NSCC. The list can be transmitted via CPU-to-CPU link or PCWeb direct. Early in the morning on the following business day. The NSCC determines the securities obligations that remain open after the CNS clearance processing. The NSCC then attempts to satisfy these obligations by borrowing from participants in the stock borrowing programme.

Selecting Lenders

If two or more participants are willing to lend the same security, the NSCC selects the order of borrowing based on an algorithm that takes into account a random number and the participant's average loans and clearing fees. This procedure permits borrowing to be spread amongst many potential lenders of a security. The NSCC uses the full quantity that the participant makes available in each issue before proceeding to the next participant in the sequence.

Crediting Participants' Accounts

After the NSCC borrows securities in the early morning, the transactions are recorded as long positions in the participant's stock borrowing (C) sub-account, a special account in the CNS system. The total current market value of the borrowed securities is credited to the participant's CNS account. These funds are available to the participant overnight. This process is reversed when NSCC returns the borrowed securities. No rebates are charged and the entire transaction occurs in the controlled CNS processing environment.

Reporting on Stock Borrowing Activity

The NSCC distributes reports to participants each morning, reflecting stock borrowing activity. In reviewing the report, participants sometimes discover that the securities lent to the NSCC are needed for customer securities segregation requirements.

In such cases, at the request of the participant, the long position in the stock borrowing account is moved into a long position in the fully-paid-for (E) account. This results in the member not being credited the current market value of the securities position. The SEC treats this 'E' position as a good control location for customer securities under Commission rule 15c3-3.

The stock borrowing programme is a service offering of the NSCC, the US's leading provider of centralised clearance, settlement and information services to more than 2,500 brokers, dealers, banks, mutual funds, insurance carriers and other organisations.

The NSCC develops standardised, automated solutions that promote connectivity, efficiency and lower risk in the financial services marketplace. The NSCC is a subsidiary of The Depository Trust & Clearing Corporation (DTCC).

Appendix 4

Organisations

The following are organisations from which some material that appears in this workbook may have been sourced:

Bank of England
www.bankofengland.co.uk

Bank for International Settlements
www.bis.org

Bureau of the Public Debt
www.publicdebt.treas.gov

Business Line (part of the Hindu Group of publications)
www.thehindubusinessline.com

CREST
www.euroclear.com

The Derivatives and Securities Consultancy Ltd
www.dscportfolio.com

The Depository Trust and Clearing Corporation (DTCC)
www.dtcc.com

European Securities and Market Authority (ESMA)
www.esma.europa.eu

Financial Conduct Authority (FCA)
www.fca.org.uk

Fixed Income Clearing Corporation
www.ficc.com

G30 (Group of 30)
www.group30.org

HM Revenue & Customs
www.hmrc.gov.uk

India Infoline
www.indiainfoline.com

International Securities Services Association (ISSA)
www.issanet.org

International Organisation of Securities Commissions (IOSCO)
www.iosco.org

Investopedia
www.investopedia.com

London Stock Exchange
www.londonstockexchange.com

The Securities Exchange Commission
www.sec.gov

SWIFT
www.swift.com

Guidance for Candidates

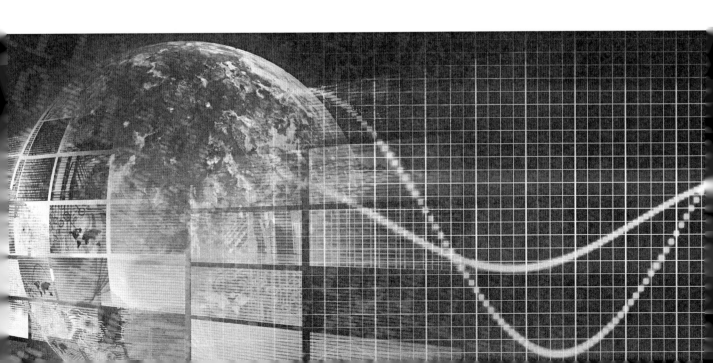

The Examination Scheme

Advanced Global Securities Operations is the first post-benchmark examination specifically for staff working in custody and settlement. Building on the Global Securities Operations (GSO) technical unit of the Investment Operations Certificate, the advanced paper has been developed to prepare staff for more demanding roles which require them to apply their understanding of the subject to practical situations in the context of their firm's environment.

Candidates are expected to have at least two years' industry experience and to be seeking to develop their managerial, professional and technical skills as operations specialists within the financial services industry. Candidates who have not taken the GSO unit in the IOC are strongly advised to read the workbook before starting their studies for the advanced level examination.

Assessment

The Advanced Global Securities Operations examination is a three-hour narrative paper comprising a mix of questions as follows:

- Section A: 10 x 3 mark questions, all questions compulsory.
- Section B: 3 x 10 mark questions, all questions compulsory.
- Section C: 1 x 20 mark case studies, 1 from 2 questions to be chosen.
- Section D: 1 x 20 mark case studies, 1 from 2 questions to be chosen.

Preparing for the Examination

Candidates are advised to allocate a minimum of 100 study hours to their preparation for the examination. This can be through private study or a combination of private study and attendance at an accredited training partner (ATP) course.

Candidates should actively engage with their study material. Simply reading and re-reading the workbook is not enough. Good revision practice includes condensing, memorising and restructuring study notes and planning outlines and answers to exemplar questions.

In addition to studying from the workbook, candidates should take note of any news coverage in the national press or trade publications that relates to their subject area, as this will help relate the theory of the subject matter to practical developments.

Most candidates will have passed the GSO unit of the IOC and it is important that candidates adapt to the change in assessment approach. While the IOC tests candidates on individual learning outcomes stated in the syllabus, the Advanced Certificate papers require candidates to draw on their knowledge from across their studies and often apply this to practical situations. It is important that candidates understand how the material in one chapter of the workbook builds on its predecessor and how it relates to the material covered in other chapters.

Candidates attending an ATP course are strongly advised to study the workbook prior to joining the course, as this provides an opportunity to talk to tutors about any items that prove particularly difficult to understand.

Candidates must ensure they have undertaken adequate revision which covers the full breadth of the syllabus before sitting the exam. Candidates attempting to predict examination questions and tailoring their study to these topics will find they are unable to answer a sufficiently wide range of the syllabus topics to be successful.

The Examination

Time management is an integral part of good examination technique. Suggested timing for the examination sections according to the marks allocation are as follows:

Section	Number of questions	Total marks for this section	Time you should allocate to this section*	
A	10 questions of 3 marks each	30 marks	50 minutes: 5 minutes for each question	
B	3 questions of 10 marks each	30 marks	54 minutes: 18 minutes for each question	= 100 marks in 3 hours
C	1 question (from 2) of 20 marks	20 marks	38 minutes	
D	1 question (from 2) of 20 marks	20 marks	38 minutes	

* This accounts for the full three hours allocated to the examination. Candidates are advised to allow less time than this for each section so they have time to review their answers at the end of the examination.

Advice from the Examination Panel

The Examination Panel brings together a number of experienced practitioners. They will be looking for evidence that a candidate has a strong understanding of the subject matter and can directly relate this to the questions posed. Advice from the panel includes:

- **Read the question and focus on it** – candidates who stray from the question will waste time and lose marks. In short – answer the question as set by the examiner, not your own preferred version!
- **Answer in an appropriate format and style, and justify your answers** – candidates should answer in a clear, concise and legible format. (Any unreadable answer scripts will be marked as incorrect by the examination panel.) Candidates should not assume knowledge on the part of the marker. The purpose of the examination is to test your knowledge, so make sure your answer is complete and does not make assumptions about the reader's grasp of the subject.
- **Distinguish between relevant and irrelevant evidence and facts** – this is a key skill and is specifically assessed in the examination.
- **Reveal your understanding of the theory as it relates to the questions** – do not recite memorised theory at length without relating it directly to the question.
- **Do not give formulaic answers** – formula answers (answers so general that they could be used for any case study or question) are easily spotted and are penalised. Answers must relate specifically and directly to the information given in the question.
- **Manage your time** – the mark allocation is very specific and should guide how much time you spend on each section of the paper. Please remember there are two case study questions. Candidates who spend too long focusing on the first case study can find they do not have the time to do themselves justice in the other.
- **Manage the length of your answers** – be guided at all times by the question requirements and marking allocation. Lengthy essay-style answers are not appropriate for every question. If using bullet points, please ensure they are complete and clear in meaning. Do not include general or vague comments which could be interpreted in various ways. Ambiguity does not score marks!
- **Review your answers** – check for obvious mistakes and omissions, which may result in lost marks.

The following are examples of the style of question, with specimen answers, that candidates can expect to receive in the Advanced Global Securities Operations examination.

Example Questions and Answers

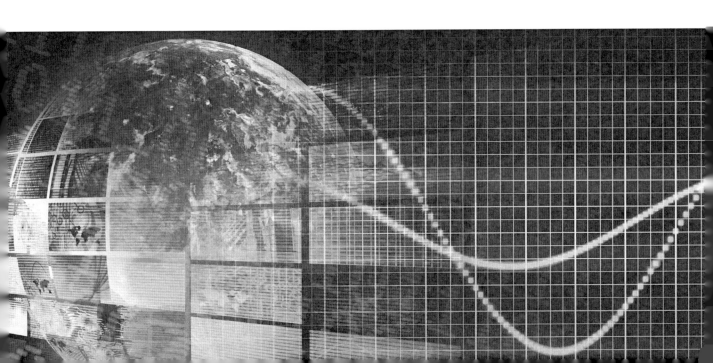

The following are examples of the style of question, with specimen answers, that candidates can expect to receive in the Advanced Global Securities Operations examination.

Section A

1. Briefly outline the effects of the underwriting process, and briefly explain the benefits to participants.

    (3 marks)

    - Underwriting is the process where, in exchange for a fixed fee, an institution or group of institutions will agree to purchase, at issue price, any securities not subscribed for by the public.
    - The underwriters must be paid regardless of whether they are called on to buy shares or not.
    - For the company issuing the shares, underwriting removes the possibility that all the shares will not be sold and so guarantees the amount of money raised from the share issue.

2. Explain what the acronym SWIFT stands for and briefly explain the main areas of activity for the SWIFT network:

    (3 marks)

    - The initials SWIFT stand for the Society for Worldwide Interbank Financial Telecommunication.
    - SWIFT provides the network infrastructure for payment systems to support bank instructions, customer instructions, advice, statements, clearing and settlement in several countries.
    - SWIFT provides securities messaging communication to support trade confirmation, clearing and settlement and custodial operations.
    - SWIFT provides systems to support confirmation messages, matching, bilateral and multilateral netting and reporting of Treasury and foreign exchange trades.

3. List three examples of a third-party relationship a firm might have and briefly describe how the relationship can be actively managed.

    (3 marks)

    - Price source, corporate action data, stock borrowing counterparty, systems supplier, custodian, broker, fund manager, trustees, transfer agents, fund administrators.
    - Can be managed via: effective service level agreements; effective management information; effective performance measurement procedures; problem resolution via relationship managers; contingency plans to switch counterparty/supplier; effective communication channels.

4. Identify the eight categories that securities messages can be classified as:

    (3 marks)

    - Trade instruction and confirmation.
    - Settlement instruction and confirmation.
    - Corporate actions and event notices.
    - Capital and income advice.
    - Statements.
    - Securities lending and borrowing.
    - Inter-depository clearing systems.
    - General.

Section B

1. In March 2004, CREST published a paper describing the operational issues that complicate automating the unit trust and OEIC settlement process. This paper suggested that adopting a central settlement system would overcome many of these operational difficulties.

   List the three main areas that would benefit from such a system, and provide details of the problems these areas suffer in relation to unit trust and OEIC trades.

   (10 marks)

   Three areas – settlement, reconciliation and registration:

Settlement

- Difficulties arise here due to timing and the lack of settlement issues.
- The only regulated standard for the settlement of unit trusts or OEICs is between the trustee and the fund manager (T+4). The product provider is under no obligation to settle with any other counterparty within a specified timeframe.
- Usually, the counterparty only knows the trade has settled when they receive the cash or the statement of holdings.
- This lack of certainty and the manual processes involved are labour-intensive and therefore expensive.
- Lack of DvP means that there is low quality of settlement and leads to added risk.
- Unit/shareholder has control over neither the securities nor the proceeds from the trade for a period of time.

Reconciliation

- Reconciliation of funds is a completely manual process. The data may not be available in an electronic format and so complicates the process.
- Process is expensive and also prone to error.
- Some firms have such difficulty receiving timely and accurate data that they have sought temporary regulatory dispensation from reconciling funds.

Registration

- There are no common standards for registration. Information used by the product provider to identify clients on the register can be completely different from that used by an intermediary. This makes it difficult to reconcile even the most basic of data.

2. The Group of 30 (G30) recommended that securities lending should be encouraged.

   a. Briefly explain why a market participant will lend and borrow securities.

   (2 marks)

   b. What are the advantages and disadvantages of using cash as collateral in stock lending agreements?

   (3 marks)

   c. Your company decides to enter into a stock lending agreement with another counterparty. Outline five areas that should be covered by the agreement and what these areas should contain.

   (5 marks)

   a. Market participants lend securities to earn fee income and, therefore, enhance the investment performance of the portfolio. Also, the lending entity may benefit from reduced safekeeping charges because it may be able to persuade the custodian that lending reduces the size of the portfolio.

   Market participants borrow securities to cover short positions, support derivatives activities and cover settlement fails.

   b. Advantages:
   - Allows securities to move on a DvP basis, thereby eliminating the risk that the exchange of cash and securities is not simultaneous.
   - Cash is often regarded as the safest form of collateral in some domestic markets.

   Disadvantages:
   - Many institutional lenders will not, or are unable to, undertake the additional administrative burden of re-investing the cash.
   - Tax laws in some countries make use of cash as collateral impractical.
   - There are added problems of foreign currencies which require several days' notice prior to placing funds.
   - There is additional mark-to-market exposure due to exchange rates when using foreign currencies.

c. Answer should include five of the topics and related comments shown in the table below.

Agreement Topic	Comments
Interpretation	Definitions of the terms used in the agreement.
Rights and title	Include reference to the protection of lender's entitlements.
Collateral	Loans should be secured with collateral. Agreement on the forms of collateral.
Equivalent securities	Securities and collateral should be returned in an equivalent form to the original deliveries.
Lender's and borrower's warranties	Statement that both parties are permitted to undertake the lending/borrowing activities.
Default	Remedies available in the event that one or other party defaults on its obligations.
Arbitration and jurisdiction	How and where disputes will be submitted for resolution and under which governing law.
Terms of lending	• Basis of how fees will be calculated. • How a client's assets will be allocated for loan on a fair and equitable basis with other clients in the lending pool. • Is the lending third party or primary? • Recall limitations.
Conditions of lending	• What happens if FM sells assets that are on loan? • Dividend and withholding tax issues.

Section C

1. Your firm has been the victim of several instances of buy-in proceedings being instigated against it.

    a. Describe how a buy-in might be initiated.

    (7 marks)

    b. Describe the consequences that could occur from buy-in proceedings being instigated against the firm.

    (3 marks)

    c. Describe the action that you would take to try to eradicate the problem of continual buy-in proceedings being instigated against the firm.

    (10 marks)

a. A buy-in is the practice whereby the purchasing counterparty of a failing trade seeks to purchase the shares on the market from another seller. The cost of the buy-in and any penalty fees are passed to the original defaulting seller.

In some countries, a buy-in is initiated after a set period of time by the local stock exchange or regulatory body. This is a compulsory buy-in and is generated automatically.

Alternatively, in markets such as the US, where a buy-in is not compulsory, it is possible for the process to be initiated by the purchaser in the event of delayed settlement. In the event of a non-compulsory buy-in, the purchaser will approach their market maker or broker and request that they seek to purchase the shares in the market from the local stock exchange or the regulatory authority on their behalf.

In India the trade would be closed-out, the original trade reduced by the number of shares that the counterparty can deliver and a cost applied for the period the trade was failing between 10–15% above the price of the stock. This cost will be incurred by the defaulting counterparty.

b. The consequences faced by a defaulting counterparty in the event of a buy-in are both financial and reputational:

1. Financial – as well as penalty fees imposed by the markets, an interest claim to cover loss of funds, together with the dealing costs resulting from a buy-in, will be sought by the buyer from the defaulting seller.
2. Reputational – a firm could potentially lose clients as a result of continued buy-ins and counterparties may refuse to trade with them.
3. Market censures – certain markets may impose restrictions on the firm's ability to trade.

c. In the event that the firm is continually facing buy-in a number of issues will need to be addressed and remedial action taken. The whole process will need to be reviewed in a step- by-step process:

1. Analyse the markets in which the problems are occurring. For example, is it specific emerging markets where buy-in procedures and censures are high?
2. Analyse the reason why the buy-ins are being instigated against the firm. Are there liquidity problems in the market? Is it a result of poor asset servicing or does the stock-lending programme need to be reviewed?
3. Review the operational processes and procedures. Are the trades set up correctly, ie, is the correct account being populated in a segregated market? Are the staff who are managing the settlements process highlighting issues quickly enough? Are they skilled and experienced enough to resolve the problems in a timely manner? In the event that a recall of loaned stock is required, is the recall process robust?

Once the risk areas have been identified, corrective action can be taken to remedy the situation and significantly improve processing.

1. Markets – if the problem is in the Russian market, for example, where trading is not particularly prolific, and the firm continues to fail to deliver in a timely manner, then certain steps will be taken.

   If it is determined that the failure is a direct result of lack of knowledge and poor communication on the part of the Russian agent, the firm will discuss the situation and their concerns with the network manager in an attempt to resolve any communication issues.

If the cost of buy-ins is high, a decision may be made to withdraw from trading in the Russian market or at least reduce the trading levels. The increase of costs and the threat of censure in certain markets might make this the only viable option.

2. Why – if the analysis highlights that the asset service processing, stock-lending programme or failure of purchases are causing problems then these can be addressed in the following ways:

    a. Asset servicing: review of data sources, staff skills/market expertise, processes and procedures. Portfolio services are both a key operational area and one with high risk exposure. It is important to ensure that all processes and procedures are both efficient and sufficient.

    b. Stock lending: if the stock is not being recalled in a timely manner then the process is deficient. The department's procedures need to be reviewed and change implemented. Simple changes include the introduction of a pending sale report detailing all imminent market sales and increased communication between the settlements and stock lending departments so that each advises the other of changes. The pre-matching of trade with the counterparty should help reduce the possibility of a trade failing due to stock shortage. By confirming all aspects of the trade with all parties involved, the settlements team should be able to make the stock-lending team aware if the stock is not available and the settlement date is the next day.

3. Trade processing – if the analysis highlights that the issue revolves around the instruction process remedial steps need to be taken. In a manual environment, where STP does not exist, it is possible for human error to result in incorrect trade bookings. For example, it is possible for the agent to quote the incorrect securities account number from which to deliver the shares, reading a false short position.

Section D

1. You have just been appointed as the manager of the trade processing department of your firm. This includes both securities and cash. The sections trade capture (which includes trade input) and trade settlement are the most significant areas within your remit. Following an audit report, this area of the business is giving the senior management of your firm serious concerns about the efficiency and effectiveness of the department as there seem to have been several costly errors made, hence your appointment.

    Given this situation, outline the plan of action that should be followed.

    (20 marks)

    The answer should include the following points:

    *   Within the first ten days, communicate to senior management the formulation of a project plan.
    *   Share a detailed project plan with senior management within the first 30 days.
    *   Review and understand specific errors that have recently occurred.
    *   Engage current staff in review.
    *   Take steps to prevent recurrence of similar errors.
    *   Conduct one-to-one interviews with current staff. Ascertain their views on current processes and procedures.

- Ascertain whether there are motivational issues.
- Gain support and agreement from current staff for a full review of process and procedures.
- Determine skills required by the department.
- Review each individual's experience and match to skill sets required by the department.
- Review past performance reviews of each member of department. Are there any performance issues?
- Engage with internal audit and/or risk management to help conduct a full review of processes and procedures.
- Compare the volume statistics against the departmental capacity.
- Check increasing overtime, use of temporary staff, changes in staff who know the systems, changes in management.
- If there are no statistics, create them by historical review over last three/six months.
- Engage with other departmental heads, discuss your plans, enlist support for any cross-functional process-review issues or changes required.
- Issue your plans to senior management.
- Implement plans post-senior management review.
- Create effective management information statistics to measure department performance.
- Monitor ongoing progress.
- Celebrate success!
- Maintain staff morale at high levels by full engagement in the running of the department.
- Cost issues and recommendation of system/risk charges.

Marks will also be available for structure, logic and cohesion of the answer.

Syllabus Learning Map

Syllabus Unit/ Element		Chapter/ Section
Element 1	**Account Openings**	**Chapter 1**
1.1	Explain the processes to be followed when opening an investment account with a UK-regulated entity	1
1.2	Identify and distinguish between retail clients; professional clients; eligible counterparties	2
1.3	Identify the timescales for market approval upon receipt of account opening applications	3
1.4	Understand the circumstances under which a client classification should be reviewed	3
1.5	Describe the potential penalties that are in place for non-compliance when opening investment accounts and outline the impact of penalties on clients and the firm	4
1.6	Outline the fiduciary principles that apply to the holding of client assets	5
1.7	Understand the various reasons when and why segregated accounts will be required, when investing in global markets.	5.2
1.8	Understand the importance of gathering the correct data to determine the client type for the purpose of correctly apportioning the clients' tax status globally	5.2
1.9	Understand how the global regulatory environment impacts the opening of client investment accounts in the UK	6

Syllabus Unit/ Element		Chapter/ Section
Element 2	**UK Market and Stock Exchange Fees**	**Chapter 2**
2.1	Identify sources of market and exchange fees and tax when trading securities for the following: retail clients; eligible counterparties; professional clients	1
2.2	Identify the charges applicable for clients of: fund manager; custodian; advisor (eg, stockbroker, wealth manager, independent financial advisor)	2
2.3	Understand how the global regulatory environment impacts on market and stock exchange fees applicable to clients. In particular, how the UK regulatory environment dictates processes for a regulated UK firm when applying these fees and charges	3

Syllabus Unit/ Element		Chapter/ Section
Element 3	**Clearing and Settlement**	**Chapter 3**
3.1	Describe the lifecycle of a transaction, ie, the purchase or sale of securities, through to the settlement in the UK and the other global markets, including the role of the broker in custody and settlement	1
3.2	Analyse the risks that arise at each stage of the settlement process post trade including the benefits and operational risks that can arise when using brokers and the additional actions that have to be taken when migrating customers	5
3.3	Understand how to trade, clear and settle UCITs and other types of funds	8.1
3.4	Identify the additional costs arising from the settlement of unit trusts and OEICs	8.2
3.5	Describe the potential to fully automate the settlement of unit trusts and OEICs and analyse its benefits, drawbacks and implementation considerations	8.3
3.6	Describe the options for registration and the impact of options on the ability to receive benefits	7.1
3.7	Explain instances when a trade settlement instruction would need to be repaired	2.1
3.8	Identify key drivers behind changing from certificated settlement to a dematerialised status	7.2
3.9	Explain the consequences when a trade is incorrectly executed and what would need to be done to repair the situation	2.2
3.10	Describe the potential factors that can trigger late settlements and the controls for minimising late settlement	3
3.11	Describe the process when a buy-in and sell-out occurs, the potential market and counterparty penalties for buy-ins and sell-outs and identify those markets in which buy-in and sell-out is automatic	4
3.12	Describe the functional features of a: central securities depository (CSD); international central securities depository (ICSD); central clearing counterparty (CCP)	6
3.13	Understand how the global regulatory environment impacts on clearing and settlement and in particular how the UK regulatory environment dictates processes for a regulated UK firm	9

Syllabus Unit/ Element		Chapter/ Section
Element 4	**Custodians**	**Chapter 4**
4.1	Describe the due diligence process for the selection of custodians/ sub-custodians, including requests for information (RFIs)/requests for proposals (RFPs)	2
4.2	Describe the factors that influence the rates of custodian charging and which are considered in the construction of the fee tariff	3
4.3	Identify the types of third-party service supplier custodians appoint and explain the governance considerations that arise from their appointment	4
4.4	Explain how custodian performance, compliance and regulation can be monitored	5
4.5	Describe the significance of the role of the sub-custodian	6
4.6	Describe the monitoring and operational controls which should be used with local sub-custodians	6.3
4.7	Describe the information custodians are expected to pass on to their clients	7
4.8	Describe the role of the client transition teams and the reasons for their introduction	8.1
4.9	Describe the milestones of a typical transition plan developed by a client transition team	8.4
4.10	Understand how the global regulatory environment impacts on custodians and in particular how the UK regulatory environment dictates processes for a regulated UK firm	9

Element 5	Securities Lending and Securities Borrowing	Chapter 5
5.1	Describe benefits and risks to organisations that borrow/lend securities: the mechanics of the process; the methods of selection of the lender/borrower; understand the implications of perfected collateral	2
5.2	Describe the operational impact of third-party securities lending	3
5.3	Describe how lenders/custodians apportion loans	4.2
5.4	Distinguish between securities lending, repo, reverse repo and buy-sell-back	5
5.5	Illustrate the types of reporting required to support a securities lending programme	6
5.6	Understand how the global regulatory environment impacts on securities lending and borrowing and in particular how the UK regulatory environment dictates processes for a regulated UK firm	7

Syllabus Unit/ Element		Chapter/ Section
Element 6	**Cash Management**	**Chapter 6**
6.1	Describe the methods used to manage surplus cash balances	1
6.2	Describe how unauthorised overdrafts can arise on client accounts	2
6.3	Explain when and why foreign exchange transactions need to be executed to align with and in relation to a settlement of a transaction in the stock markets	3
6.4	Distinguish the key differences between the features of asset-backed and mortgage-backed securities and other fixed interest products	4.1
6.5	Explain the role of the pool factor and how it is determined	4.2
6.6	Calculate and comment on old and new positions based on a changing pool factor	4.2
6.7	Understand how the global regulatory environment impacts on cash management and in particular how the UK regulatory environment dictates processes for a regulated UK firm	5

Syllabus Unit/ Element		Chapter/ Section
Element 7	**Corporate Entitlements**	**Chapter 7**
7.1	Explain the reasons for a corporation initiating a particular corporate action: rights issue; bonus issue; dividend stock option	1
7.2	Demonstrate knowledge of the differing ratio terminology (calculations) between North America and globally	2
7.3	Demonstrate the difference between the UK's and major European markets' approaches to apportionment and trading of rights issues	3
7.4	describe the underwriting procedures within initial public offerings (IPOs), rights issues and placing	4
7.5	Explain placing/underwriting in the issue of new shares	5
7.6	Understand the processes of settlement within an IPO, underwriting and placing	6
7.7	Analyse the risks and benefits associated with underwriting	7
7.8	Demonstrate the calculation of underwriting commission	8
7.9	Analyse a typical corporate action describing the management of the process and the timetable applicable at each stage	7.9
7.10	Apply the key deadlines and decision options applicable to the companies involved, fund managers, custodian, registrar, stock settlement teams, corporate actions teams and data vendors	10
7.11	Calculate the old and new positions pre- and post-capital events	11

Syllabus Unit/ Element		Chapter/ Section
7.1.2	Define the standard trading timeframes that apply during capital events	12
7.13	Explain the impact of double taxation agreements on clients	13
7.14	Understand how the global regulatory environment impacts on the processing of corporate actions and in particular how the UK regulatory environment dictates processes for a regulated UK firm	14

Element 8	Straight-Through Processing	Chapter 8
8.1	Describe straight-through processing (STP)	1
8.2	Explain the business reasons behind the development of STP	2
8.3	Describe the key initiatives behind STP	3
8.4	Explain the advantages and disadvantages that arise with STP	4
8.5	Understand how the global regulatory environment impacts on the processing in an STP environment and in particular how the UK regulatory environment dictates STP processes for a regulated UK firm	5

Element 9	Outsourcing/Offshoring	Chapter 9
9.1	Explain the definitions of outsourcing and offshoring and why they are different	1
9.2	Discuss why a firm might want to outsource or offshore some processing functions	2
9.3	Explain what the advantages and disadvantages of outsourcing or offshoring are	3
9.4	Discuss how a firm might monitor the success of any outsourcing/ offshoring project	4
9.5	Explain where service level agreements (SLAs) are used in the industry and the parties who would typically be involved	4.2
9.6	Outline the principles underpinning service level agreements and the range and typical content of SLAs	4.2
9.7	Explain the mechanisms that can be employed for monitoring and managing the relationship including the typical key performance indicators (KPIs) used	4.3
9.8	Describe the additional actions that have to be considered where non-performance arises	4.4
9.9	Understand how the global regulatory environment impacts on the process of outsourcing/offshoring and in particular how the UK regulatory environment dictates processes for a regulated UK firm	5

Syllabus Unit/ Element		Chapter/ Section
Element 10	**Data Management**	**Chapter 10**
10.1	Describe what data is and how it can be defined	1
10.2	In the financial services industry and especially in global securities operations, information is provided by many different entities. Identify who these main providers will be and what information is provided	2
10.3	Explain how the data used in global operations is collected	3
10.4	Explain how, once collected, the data is stored and protected in the UK	4
10.5	Understand how and when data is used and the interaction with the global securities operations environment	5
10.6	Data retention is an area in which managers in global operations should be versed. Explain for how long the data used in global operations should be retained	6
10.7	Describe the processes of destruction of redundant data.	6
10.8	Understand how the global regulatory environment impacts on data management and in particular how the UK regulatory environment dictates processes for a regulated UK firm	7

Examination Specification

Aim of the Examination

- To enable firms to prepare their operations staff for more demanding roles which require a broader understanding of the technical environment in which they work.
- To equip operations staff in the financial services sector with a broader grasp of the business and the regulatory issues faced by senior management and help them develop their professionalism while further augmenting their technical and managerial skills.

Audience for the Module

This module is primarily aimed at supervisors, team leaders, assistant managers, managers and senior technical specialists working in investment operations (custody, settlements, corporate actions, treasury operations/cash management, derivatives and reconciliations).

Candidates embarking on AGSO will be expected to possess the level of knowledge required to pass the Investment Operations Certificate (IOC) and are strongly advised to be familiar with the material in the Global Securities Operations workbook.

Note: For the purposes of this syllabus, the selected markets referred to herein are defined as UK, US, Germany, India and Japan.

Assessment Structure

The module will draw from across the syllabus and be assessed through case studies and a mix of three- and ten-mark narrative questions (see the testing specification below). Candidates will be expected to demonstrate that they can apply their understanding to a range of practical scenarios.

The examination will comprise:

- 10 compulsory questions, each valued at three marks each.
- Three compulsory questions, each valued at 10 marks each.
- Two case study questions from a choice of four, each valued at 20 marks each.

CISI Chartered MCSI Membership can work for you...

Studying for a CISI qualification is hard work and we're sure you're putting in plenty of hours, but don't lose sight of your goal!

This is just the first step in your career; there is much more to achieve!

The securities and investments industry attracts ambitious and driven individuals. You're probably one yourself and that's great, but on the other hand you're almost certainly surrounded by lots of other people with similar ambitions.

So how can you stay one step ahead during these uncertain times?

Entry Criteria for Chartered MCSI Membership

As an ACSI and MCSI candidate, you can upgrade your membership status to Chartered MCSI. There are a number of ways of gaining the CISI Chartered MCSI membership.

A straightforward route requires candidates to have:
- a minimum of one year's ACSI or MCSI membership;
- passed a full Diploma; Certificate in Private Client Investment Advice & Management or Masters in Wealth Management award;
- passed the IntegrityMatters with an A grade; and
- successfully logged and certified 12 months' CPD under the CISI's CPD Scheme.

Alternatively, experienced-based candidates are required to have:
- a minimum of one year's ACSI membership;
- passed the IntegrityMatters with an A grade; and
- successfully logged and certified six years' CPD under the CISI's CPD Scheme.

Joining Fee:	Current Grade of Membership	Grade of Chartership	Upgrade Cost
	ACSI	Chartered MCSI	£75.00
	MCSI	Chartered MCSI	£30.00

By belonging to a Chartered professional body, members will benefit from enhanced status in the industry and the wider community. Members will be part of an organisation which holds the respect of government and industry, and can communicate with the public on a whole new level. There will be little doubt in consumers' minds that chartered members of the CISI are highly regarded and qualified professionals and as a consequence will be required to act as such.

The Chartered MCSI designation will provide you with full access to all member benefits, including Professional Refresher where there are currently over 60 modules available on subjects including Behavioural Finance, Cybercrime and Conduct Risk. CISI TV is also available to members, allowing you to catch up on the latest CISI events, whilst earning valuable CPD hours.

Revision Express Interactive

You've bought the workbook... now test your knowledge before your exam.

Revision Express Interactive is an engaging online study tool to be used in conjunction with CISI workbooks. It contains exercises and revision questions.

Key Features of Revision Express Interactive:
- Examination-focused – the content of Revision Express Interactive covers the key points of the syllabus
- Questions throughout to reaffirm understanding of the subject
- Special end-of-module practice exam to reflect as closely as possible the standard you will experience in your exam (please note, however, they are not the CISI exam questions themselves)
- Interactive exercises throughout
- Extensive glossary of terms
- Useful associated website links
- Allows you to study whenever you like

IMPORTANT: The questions contained in Revision Express Interactive elearning products are designed as aids to revision, and should not be seen in any way as mock exams.

Price per elearning module: £35
Price when purchased with the CISI workbook: £100 (normal price: £110)

To purchase Revision Express Interactive:

call our Customer Support Centre on:
+44 20 7645 0777

or visit CISI Online Bookshop at:
cisi.org/bookshop

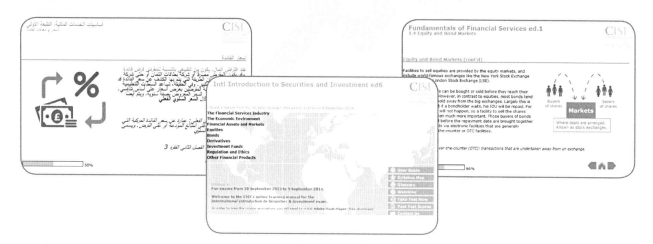

For more information on our elearning products, contact our Customer Support Centre on +44 20 7645 0777, or visit our website at cisi.org/study

Professional Refresher

Self-testing elearning modules to refresh your knowledge, meet regulatory and firm requirements, and earn CPD hours.

Professional Refresher is a training solution to help you remain up-to-date with industry developments, maintain regulatory compliance and demonstrate continuing learning.

This popular online learning tool allows self-administered refresher testing on a variety of topics, including the latest regulatory changes.

There are currently over 70 modules available which address UK and international issues. Modules are reviewed by practitioners frequently and new topics are added to the suite on a regular basis.

Benefits to firms:
- Learning and tests can form part of business T&C programme
- Learning and tests kept up-to-date and accurate by the CISI
- Relevant and useful – devised by industry practitioners
- Access to individual results available as part of management overview facility, 'Super User'
- Records of staff training can be produced for internal use and external audits
- Cost-effective – no additional charge for CISI members
- Available to non-members

Benefits to individuals:
- Comprehensive selection of topics across industry sectors
- Modules are frequently reviewed and updated by industry experts
- New topics introduced regularly
- Free for members
- Successfully passed modules are recorded in your CPD log as Active Learning
- Counts as structured learning for RDR purposes
- On completion of a module, a certificate can be printed out for your own records

The full suite of Professional Refresher modules is free to CISI members or £250 for non-members. Modules are also available individually. To view a full list of Professional Refresher modules visit:

cisi.org/refresher

If you or your firm would like to find out more contact our Client Relationship Management team:

+ 44 20 7645 0670
crm@cisi.org

For more information on our elearning products, contact our Customer Support Centre on +44 20 7645 0777, or visit our website at cisi.org/study

Professional Refresher

Top 5

SCORM COMPLIANT

Integrity & Ethics
- High Level View
- Ethical Behaviour
- An Ethical Approach
- Compliance vs Ethics

Anti-Money Laundering
- Introduction to Money Laundering
- UK Legislation and Regulation
- Money Laundering Regulations 2007
- Proceeds of Crime Act 2002
- Terrorist Financing
- Suspicious Activity Reporting
- Money Laundering Reporting Officer
- Sanctions

Financial Crime
- What Is Financial Crime?
- Insider Dealing and Market Abuse Introduction, Legislation, Offences and Rules
- Money Laundering Legislation, Regulations, Financial Sanctions and Reporting Requirements
- Money Laundering and the Role of the MLRO

Information Security and Data Protection
- Information Security: The Key Issues
- Latest Cybercrime Developments
- The Lessons From High-Profile Cases
- Key Identity Issues: Know Your Customer
- Implementing the Data Protection Act 1998
- The Next Decade: Predictions For The Future

UK Bribery Act
- Background to the Act
- The Offences
- What the Offences Cover
- When Has an Offence Been Committed?
- The Defences Against Charges of Bribery
- The Penalties

Conduct Rules
- Application and Overview
- Individual Conduct Rules – FCA & PRA
- Senior Management Conduct Rules
- Obligations on Firms

Pensions Advice
- Advice or Guidance?
- Advice During Accumulation
- Defined Contribution Pension Freedoms
- Transfers and Decumulation
- Problems with Accessing New Freedoms

Retirement Planning
- Pensions and Provisions
- Money In
- Money Out

Financial Planning (An introduction)
- Related Activities
- The Financial Plan
- Cash Flow Planning and Modelling
- Behavioural Finance and Financial Planning
- Risk
- The Regulatory Framework
- The Future Landscape

Senior Managers and Certification Regime
- Definitions
- Obligations
- Certification
- Conduct Rules
- Scope of the Rules
- Conclusion and Future Developments

Operations

Best Execution
- What Is Best Execution?
- Achieving Best Execution
- Order Execution Policies
- Information to Clients & Client Consent
- Monitoring, the Rules, and Instructions
- Best Execution for Specific Types of Firms

Approved Persons Regime
- The Basis of the Regime
- Fitness and Propriety
- The Controlled Functions
- Principles for Approved Persons
- The Code of Practice for Approved Persons

Corporate Actions
- Corporate Structure and Finance
- Life Cycle of an Event
- Mandatory Events
- Voluntary Events

Wealth

Client Assets and Client Money
- Protecting Client Assets and Client Money
- Ring-Fencing Client Assets and Client Money
- Due Diligence of Custodians
- Reconciliations
- Records and Accounts
- CASS Oversight

Investment Principles and Risk
- Diversification
- Factfind and Risk Profiling
- Investment Management
- Modern Portfolio Theory and Investing Styles
- Direct and Indirect Investments
- Socially Responsible Investment
- Collective Investments
- Investment Trusts
- Dealing in Debt Securities and Equities

Banking Standards
- Introduction and Background
- Strengthening Individual Accountability
- Reforming Corporate Governance
- Securing Better Outcomes for Consumers
- Enhancing Financial Stability

Suitability of Client Investments
- Assessing Suitability
- Risk Profiling
- Establishing Risk Appetite
- Obtaining Customer Information
- Suitable Questions and Answers
- Making Suitable Investment Selections
- Guidance, Reports and Record Keeping

International

Foreign Account Tax Compliance Act (FATCA)
- Foreign Financial Institutions
- Due Diligence Requirements
- Reporting
- Compliance

MiFID II
- The Organisations Covered by MiFID
- The Products Subject to MiFID's Guidelines
- The Origins of MiFID II
- The Products Covered by MiFID II
- Levels 1, 2, and 3 Implementation

UCITS
- The Original UCITS Directive
- UCITS III
- UCITS IV
- Non-UCITS Funds
- Future Developments

cisi.org/refresher

Feedback to the CISI

Have you found this workbook to be a valuable aid to your studies? We would like your views, so please email us at learningresources@cisi.org with any thoughts, ideas or comments.

Accredited Training Partners

Support for examination students studying for the Chartered Institute for Securities & Investment (CISI) Qualifications is provided by several Accredited Training Partners (ATPs), including Fitch Learning and BPP. The CISI's ATPs offer a range of face-to-face training courses, distance learning programmes, their own learning resources and study packs which have been accredited by the CISI. The CISI works in close collaboration with its ATPs to ensure they are kept informed of changes to CISI examinations so they can build them into their own courses and study packs.

CISI Workbook Specialists Wanted

Workbook Authors

Experienced freelance authors with finance experience, and who have published work in their area of specialism, are sought. Responsibilities include:

- Updating workbooks in line with new syllabuses and any industry developments
- Ensuring that the syllabus is fully covered

Workbook Reviewers

Individuals with a high-level knowledge of the subject area are sought. Responsibilities include:

- Highlighting any inconsistencies against the syllabus
- Assessing the author's interpretation of the workbook

Workbook Technical Reviewers

Technical reviewers provide a detailed review of the workbook and bring the review comments to the panel. Responsibilities include:

- Cross-checking the workbook against the syllabus
- Ensuring sufficient coverage of each learning objective

Workbook Proofreaders

Proofreaders are needed to proof workbooks both grammatically and also in terms of the format and layout. Responsibilities include:

- Checking for spelling and grammar mistakes
- Checking for formatting inconsistencies

If you are interested in becoming a CISI external specialist call:
+44 20 7645 0609

or email:
externalspecialists@cisi.org

For bookings, orders, membership and general enquiries please contact our Customer Support Centre on +44 20 7645 0777, or visit our website at cisi.org